continued

P9-CRP-969

BLIND INSTINCT
*Jessica Coran is plunged into one of the most unholy
murder sprees of her career . . .*

EXTREME INSTINCT
*A psycho is cleansing sinners with fire,
and now Jessica Coran is stepping into the flames . . .*

DARKEST INSTINCT
*Is the ghastly Night Crawler one killer, or two?
Jessica Coran faces double jeopardy . . .*

PURE INSTINCT
*New Orleans's Queen of Hearts Killer becomes
one of Jessica Coran's most diabolical cases . . .*

"Suspense, thrills, and psychological gamesmanship."
—*Daytona Beach News-Journal*

PRIMAL INSTINCT
*Jessica Coran must stop Hawaii's Trade Winds Killer
from turning the beaches blood red . . .*

"A bone-chilling page-turner."   —*Publishers Weekly*

FATAL INSTINCT
*Jessica Coran braves a modern-day Jack the Ripper
who has taken over the Manhattan nights . . .*

"Entertaining . . . filled with surprises [and] clever twists."
—*Daytona Beach News-Journal*

KILLER INSTINCT
*The blood-drinking Vampire Killer lures Jessica Coran
into the heartland of America . . .*

"Chilling and unflinching."

—*Fort Lauderdale Sun-Sentinel*

Final Edge

Enjoy!

ROBERT W. WALKER

Robert W. Walker

JOVE BOOKS, NEW YORK

FINAL EDGE

A Jove Book / published by arrangement with the author

PRINTING HISTORY
Jove edition / March 2004

ISBN: 0-515-13695-6

A JOVE BOOK®
Jove Books are published by The Berkley Publishing Group,
a division of Penguin Group (USA) Inc.,
375 Hudson Street, New York, New York 10014.
JOVE and the "J" design
are trademarks belonging to Penguin Group (USA) Inc.

PRINTED IN THE UNITED STATES OF AMERICA

10 9 8 7 6 5 4 3 2 1

CHAPTER 1

Lasso: captivity

At a farmhouse outside the Houston city limits

A FALL BREEZE lifted his hair and kissed his cheek as Dr. Arthur D. Belkvin raised the ax overhead, holding it over his victim's terrified eyes. The act of taking the life of this woman would engender no joy in Arthur, and he got nothing out of her terror, not like Lauralie did. Lauralie claimed to be only eighteen years old, but she gave the impression of a much older woman, her dark eyes, dark hair, and exotic skin making her irresistible to the thirty-year-old Arthur. But something in the wild, Tex-Mex-looking Lauralie Blodgett's body movements and eyes made her appear for the moment absolutely ecstatic in anticipating the fall of the ax.

Arthur felt he must say something to the soon-to-be-dead Mira Lourdes. "Don't think this was my idea. I'm not a freak," he told the woman at his feet, "but I gotta do what Lauralie tells me to do. I have no choice."

Hands tied to feet, her neck lying across a wooden post

on the earth out back of a house in the woods, Mira Lourdes struggled and choked on a gag he'd placed in her mouth. She was only half aware that Lauralie, the woman he referred to, stood nearby, watching, guiding Arthur to do the thing he was told to do. To behead Mira. "Do it, Arthur, do it!" the woman chanted.

"She's got to understand first, Lauralie. I don't want her going to her death thinking I'm one of those twisted perverts that can only feel sexually aroused at the sight of blood and carnage." He calmly continued, now addressing his victim again. "At least you gotta know that going into eternity, Mira Lourdes."

He watched her squirm, listening to her keening whine beneath the gag. He didn't want to see her suffer. "It isn't as if I'm a sociopath or a psycho or anything of that nature."

"What do you want from me?" she had begged when she had first come to, only to realize they had thrown her into the trunk of a car—that she was abducted and bound from head to toe.

"My father was a half-breed with a brain tumor, and my mother was his whore. I got issues with society! I want them to pay," said the woman.

"Them? Who are them? I don't know anything about you or them!" Mira screamed.

"But I do, and I want them—the collective *them* to pay. And they will."

"Look, my name is Mira . . . Mira Lourdes," she pleaded, "and I'm a g'damn teller in a g'damn bank! My first job since graduating college, and seven years later I'm still there. Never hurt anyone . . . And . . . and I don't have anything to do with this. You've got to . . . got to . . . to listen to me and let me go, Lauralie, Arthur, please! I won't say a word, like none of this ever happened, I swear . . . I swear!" She only wanted to go home, not to Dwayne but to her mother and father, to her childhood home. She wanted the comfort of her little pink room and canopy bed, the child's bed too small for her now, long gone in a garage sale years ago now, but she wanted it, wanted to curl up in the folds of the blanket special to her, the one her Grandma Lourdes had made for her. She wanted to see her grandma, to see her here and now, although she knew Grandma was on the other side. She wanted to be with her, to be held by her.

The small man, calling himself Arthur, shrank from harming her, almost as if he could read her desperate thoughts. She could see him literally shrinking from what Lauralie proposed. She could see him wanting to shirk it off and walk away from harming her. She read it in his body language, his eyes, his very sweat. He did not want to harm her. But the woman, calling herself Lauralie, didn't show the slightest emotion or compunction, but rather spat on Mira, before ordering Arthur to gag her. "Shut her whining up! Gag the bitch, now!"

That's when he gagged her, knowing he could not listen to her, could not get involved in who she was beyond his woman's terrible plans for Mira's body—what *she* needed her for. He didn't know Mira-the-victim from Mother Goose. Lauralie had randomly selected Mira from the phone book, after discarding several other people named Lourdes. Mira just happened to have a FOR SALE sign perched on the window of her Saab as they drove by her house. She'd bounded enthusiastically out of the house and right to them when they parked and began to examine the car on all sides, examining the relative seclusion of the house and driveway as well, thanks to the large lilac bushes all along the neighbor's property.

She really badly wanted to sell her broken-down Saab, coming down on the price as he haggled, so he had agreed to a test drive if she would come along to field questions as they arose. Shrugging, smiling, her ponytail bobbing, she quickly rushed in for the car keys, locked up the house, and joined the couple, *made to feel safe* by the presence of the woman accompanying Arthur, Lauralie, who nestled down in the rear of the Saab.

On the test drive, Arthur did all the talking—said he was a vet just setting up a practice and in need of another vehicle "to transport animals without worry to the uphol-stery, you see?"

"Oh, well, you needn't worry about spoiling the inside of this junker," she'd said, and Arthur recalled the lilting, childlike nervous laughter following her words like a bird chasing a grasshopper.

The rest of his own nervous talk centered on questions about the car, until suddenly Lauralie, from the rear seat, did what she had threatened she would. She crushed a chloroform-soaked cloth against Mira's mouth and nostrils, forcing her into unconsciousness.

The two together were so bold as to tempt fate, leaving Arthur's own car in Mira's driveway. Anyone might have come home before their return; some neighbor walking a dog might have noticed the unusual car on the street. But then Arthur and Lauralie returned, taking her groggy form from the one car and placing her into the trunk of the other before calmly driving off, all in broad daylight. Lauralie had become so excited at their accomplishment that she had almost made him wreck the getaway car into a lamppost, grabbing his face in both her hands and smothering him with her lips between cries of "We did it! We did it, Arthur!"

From the trunk, Arthur heard Mira's groans and an occasional groggy kick.

When Mira came fully conscious again, she found herself tied and gagged and inside a black world, the trunk of their car, on her way to God or Satan knows where.

She thought it amazing that they had returned her Saab and exchanged it for their own vehicle, a dark blue late-model sedan, as she recalled, a Cutlass Olds from the stamp on the dashboard, the interior clean enough to eat off, yet a strange medicinal odor permeating every fiber of the cloth seats.

Maybe Arthur was what he said he was, an animal doctor, but what did he and the woman want with her? The woman, the damned woman who had been sitting passively behind her, Mira now recalled; it had been the seemingly submissive bitch who had knocked Mira out with some sort of drug! She recalled the struggle, the cloth covering her nose and throat, filling her lungs with the same stench as she had smelled in the car, chloroform, smuggled into the backseat by that cunning cunt. The two of them had planned out every detail of Mira's abduction.

Mira tried desperately to recall everything about the car and the two people who had control of her, praying she would live through this ordeal to one day have the opportunity to point a finger at them. However, her intent to do so was becoming blurred by questions of why and how this had happened to her. She silently asked, *Why me . . . why now? What do they want with me? Did the bastards choose me randomly? No, it's got all to do with the stinking ad I placed in the* Penny Saver, *the car . . . that damn car I want to sell, the one Dwayne wouldn't lift a finger to help me with. That's what brought these two freaks to my doorstep.*

Arthur gave pause before letting the ax fall, thinking of how he had become Lauralie Blodgett's sex slave, his only wish in life to please Lauralie. She promised him pleasure and gave it to him tenfold, pleasure beyond anything he had ever experienced or imagined he could ever have found in this life without her having come to him and given herself to him, but it came with a price. Not only did she wield a wicked power over him, body and soul, but he must kill for her.

All she asked of him in return for pleasure was to kill one person for her, to take one single human life. That had been her first condition. It was soon followed by a demand that he find a suitable place and the proper tools to dissect the body of the victim. After this, she leaked bits and pieces of her plans to him as the abduction unfolded. Still, she never revealed her reasons, the underlying cause of her hatred for Mira Lourdes. That, she promised, would come in time, along with the entire story of how her life had been ruined and destroyed by others who must now pay.

"Just know that I love you, Arthur, and I need you . . . I require your help, true, but I've grown so very fond of you," she assured him. "I can hardly recall a time when we weren't together. We were meant to be together, born to be together, Arthur. No man has ever made me happier in or out of bed."

Her motives would become clear as time went by. For now, he simply must follow her and give himself over to her in blind faith; otherwise, she would leave him and find a man who could live up to her expectations and give her what she wanted. She had made the threat only once, but it was enough to make Arthur quake.

Arthur had never had a woman before, and she had treated his virginity with respect, without ridicule or laughter, but with gentleness and a genuine warmth. She cried the night of their first sexual encounter, saying she only wished that she could have come to him a virgin, untouched and unspoiled. He wiped her tears away and told her he would not change a single thing about her, ever. "I know how lucky I am that you will have me," he had said to her. "And I know that I'll never have another."

He must hold onto Lauralie at any cost. Still, what she asked of him was extremely hard.

"When I am fulfilled in my master plan to win my ultimate goal: to destroy—even if for only a time—the peace and tranquility of a man, a woman, and a major American institution, then we can have the rest of our lives together, Arthur, in peace and harmony. Trust me . . . trust me . . ."

He didn't know what she meant by this, but he promised to trust her.

As he spent more time with her, she let drop more details of her plan. Arthur thought now of how Lauralie saw it, how she talked about it, how her name would become synonymous with that of Ted Bundy, John Wayne Gacey, Lizzey Borden, Eileen Wournos, but better, she said, even more headline-fetching since she would be viewed as a distinctly *different* kind of killer, obsessed with her single-minded plan. A simple yet bold plan.

Lauralie wrapped her arms around Arthur, who remained hesitant, the ax still poised over his head. She snaked her hands inside his shirt and pants, touching, caressing, promising in his ear that he would have her forever if he would only do this small thing for her. She squeezed and rolled his penis in her hand. "Do it, Arthur . . . do it, now!"

"Okay, okay, I will."

"So let it fall and let it begin," she shouted, and Arthur hesitated no longer, letting the sharpened blade dig into Mira's white neck, exactly at the spot where he'd laid the neck across a railroad tie purchased from the local ACE Hardware to create, between ax blade and post, Lauralie's idea of a crude guillotine. Now, looking down on his results, Arthur felt a wave of revulsion as the head held, dangling by threads of tissue and bloody bone, looking like a broken doll's head, half twisted from the blow, one dazed live eye looking up at him.

Lauralie, more disappointed and angry than repulsed, shouted, "You fool, Arthur, you fucking fool!" Before he could blink, she had grabbed the ax from him and she had swung. Her blow sent Mira's head toppling off and away. It thumped to a halt and settled on its left cheek. It looked strangely up at Arthur where the underbrush below a fence rail mimicked her hair.

"Get it! Get the damn thing before some coyote or fox grabs it up and runs off with it!" Lauralie shouted.

Arthur traipsed after the head, which had come to rest in the bush at the foot of a rotting fence post. At least she's mercifully dead, Arthur told himself, her eyes are not staring at me any longer, but even as he thought it, he saw Mira's body had begun twitching as if attempting to crawl as far from her severed head as possible.

Arthur swallowed hard at this, his hands sweating in the cool evening air. Looking back at Lauralie, he saw that her eyes shone with a kind of demented delight. The bloody ax resting on her shoulder now, Lauralie calmly returned his stare now as if to ask, *What must I look like?*

"We should've thought to bring a Polaroid," she joked. "Damn but that felt good. Now we begin the fun work, right, Arthur? Just as we planned. You brought all your tools, didn't you? The bone cutter, the saws, and scalpels?"

"All my tools, yes . . . got them inside." He pointed to the old white clapboard house they had renovated for the work. He had taken hold of Mira's runaway head by the long hair, and he handed it to Lauralie's outstretched fingers.

Balling up Mira's long auburn tresses in her fist, Lauralie lifted Mira's eyes up to her own, staring into them for a long moment as blood dripped from the severed head. "Your bad luck your name is Lourdes," she said, lowering the head to her side now. Lauralie then stepped off, carrying the severed head toward the farmhouse, her jaunty, schoolgirl gait, her playful hand, and the breeze conspiring to sway the bloody dismembered thing as Arthur watched it paint Lauralie's white cotton dress and gray flannel apron as if with a repeated brush stroke. Lauiralie's hip and thigh had an increasingly large red-brown rust spot building with each step toward the house.

"God, I hope she's not planning on cooking that for dinner," he quietly said to himself.

"Come ahead, Arthur! Bring the rest of her, Arthur!" she shouted over her shoulder at him. "We'll need all of her for what we have to do."

Arthur watched a fall cardinal chase its mate into the nearby thicket.

Houston, the following evening

LIEUTENANT DETECTIVE LUCAS Stonecoat's large Cherokee hands carefully fingered the unmarked package that had arrived via courier at his apartment home. The package had been left with Jack Tebo downstairs at Tebo's Grill and Tavern, situated just below Lucas's apartment. It had been hand-delivered—no stamps or UPS or FedEx markings whatsoever. With a strange return address, that of a convent school on the north side of the city, the package simply looked out of place and unusual. The tough, seasoned cop knew no convent girls, but he had enemies both in and out of the Houston Police Department. Lucas knew he could not be too careful.

When Lucas had stopped at Tebo's, the older man had told him that he'd left a package on his doorstep, and that Lucas owed him two bucks for the tip. When Lucas had lifted the package, it had made no sound, but it felt hefty for so small a bundle, about the size of a softball; worse yet, it smelled. Not of sulfur or minerals; not even of fertilizer. Something altogether worse—something of rotting flesh—odors he'd encountered as a young man in a nameless, faraway jungle in Vietnam. Tebo's rhino-sized nostrils were so gummed up with nicotine, tar, and burger grease that he'd obviously missed the odors emanating from the package.

Lucas now carried the package inside and through his home, going for the kitchen sink. There he gingerly placed it into the basin. He toyed with the idea of calling in the bomb squad, but something nagged at him, telling him it was *not* an explosive, and that calling in the bomb squad boys would ultimately result in a big embarrassment.

He sought the tools he needed to carefully unwrap the box sent from Our Lady of Miracles Convent for Girls. Using tweezers and a paring knife, Lucas began to cut through the rough twine binding the package. As he worked, Lucas thought of the time he had come back from the dead on a battlefield strewn with bodies. He had been taken for dead, just another corpse to add to the growing pile that the Viet Cong had created of their enemies. They liked piling bodies atop one another, dousing them with gasoline, and burning the pyre of dead and dying.

In order to cope with the horror of his situation there in Nam, Lucas had gone into a coma of sorts, or what his Cherokee ancestors called a ghost walk, a weightless, bodiless existence in which the spirit leaves the body. During this time, he saw his body being lifted by two Viet Cong who struggled with his weight. They swung his lifeless form onto the hill of flesh, the bodies piled high and growing. It all came from an overhead view as if he were floating above the scene.

He focused again on his own body, lying lifeless beneath others now piled onto his own. But something within spoke to Lucas, an ancestral voice. A dead grandfather figure telepathically told him he was yet alive and that he must return to his body. Lucas found himself amid the smoke and clouds of a chasm. All around him Lucas could see the souls of others as they departed, so many wisps of smoke dissolving into the atmosphere as others from beyond reached out and took their hands to guide them.

Lucas fought to touch the ancestral hand, but the old man adamantly and stoically refused to reach out to Lucas, telling him in a telepathic way that it was not yet his time, that he must go back, that he had much yet to accomplish in this life. Then he was gone in the time it took for Lucas to take a breath of air.

Choking, he awoke amid the stench of decaying flesh. The battle had raged on for days, and many of the dead he lay above, beside, and under were decaying beneath a baking sun. Then he felt the corporeal flesh and heaviness of his own body again. Opening his eyes, he found himself crushed, hardly capable of breathing, below a mountain of dead men stacked like cordwood. For a time, his spirit had walked among the dead, but now he had fully returned to his senses and the horror of war.

Minutes later, with the odor of petroleum and decay filling his nostrils and mouth, Lucas heard the distinctive whirring sound of U.S. helicopter gunships, followed by gunfire. The U.S. Helicopter Cavalry raided the battlefield in a renewed offensive, chasing off the enemy before they could torch the bodies they intended to defile. When ground forces came near enough for Lucas to hear their talk, Lucas patiently waited for them to draw nearer. Choking on the overwhelming odors he'd been subjected to for so long now, Lucas shot a hand out from the wall of dead soldiers, grabbing hold of a live American cavalryman. The act startled the baby-faced kid and his companions where they stood, each reacting, raw-nerve fashion, weapons pointed, bodies shivering at the movement in Lucas's eyes. Finally realizing that the dead man was alive, a medic corporal barked out orders that made frozen men move. They finally dragged Stonecoat's battered body from the carnage of the death heap.

"And put out those damned cigarettes!" the medic added.

Now, here in his apartment, a world and decades away from Viet Nam, Lucas felt it all over again as he sliced away at the brown-paper wrapping of a package that annoyed his every sense—bringing back the enormous dismay and revulsion of war *through odor alone*. The Texas Cherokee detective tore open the awful "gift" sent him. And there it was ... staring back at him ... a stack of pancake-shaped decaying pieces of flesh. Human or animal, it was hard to say. A sliced section of spleen, kidney, heart tissue, sliced as he had seen done in autopsy rooms, all mixed in a soupy wash of liquid residue. The decaying organ parts swam about inside a Styrofoam-lined little wood box, looking like a miniature coffin, definitely hand-fashioned.

"Son of a bitch!" Lucas tried to picture someone going to such an extreme effort to target him and to make him ill. Which of his enemies inside or outside of the department would take such pains? Who wanted to make him turn from his Native American red to a pale green? Who had access to autopsy room debris? "Assistant·M.E. Patterson? Detective Arnold 'The Itch' Feldman and his buddies?" Lucas asked the empty room. "How big a jerk-off would it take to pull a stunt like this?

"No. Neither man would have the nerve. Then who," he wondered aloud, "and why?"

Lucas then noticed the note jammed between the wood outer box and the inner lining of Styrofoam. Using a pair of medical tweezers, he lifted the brown bile-stained note and opened it to reveal the cryptic message in a shaky hand. It read:

> *spleen on spleen,*
> *cut true and clean,*
> *kidney for kidney,*
> *bake to a pie,*
> *heart on heart,*
> *piece by piece*

I give you art,
food for thought,
and a final piece
for the feast
to grease
the way to peace

Lucas studied the tight, pinched handwriting that reeked of agitation, but even as he reread the rhyme, he could get little meaning from it, save that perhaps the author wanted him to *dine* on the awful contents of the package, using such culinary words as grease, feast, bake, pie, cut, and food for thought. Perhaps a handwriting expert could gather more from the size of the letters, the loops and swirls that deviated from the center line, and the choice of words. However, Lucas's first impulse was to know how the package was delivered and by whom. He got on the phone and called down to the bar below his apartment. Jack Tebo lifted the receiver and barked, "Tebo's!"

"It's me, Jack, Lucas."

"Wha's up, Stoney? Want a six-pack sent up? A sandwich? Special tonight is—"

"No . . . I want to know if you got a good look at the guy who left that damnable package for me? Did you pay him any attention?"

"I didn't pay her too much attention, no. Rather plain-looking young woman . . . just got a passing glance at her. Tipped her a couple of bucks, like I said."

"A woman? You saying it was a woman?"

"Had a childlike quality to her eyes, a kind of innocence in there."

"How do you mean?"

"She was kinda vacant, you know, like a kid, but man, Stoney. She was curvaceous, my friend, sexy as they come. Small, but not anorexic, you know."

"Childlike and sexy? Tebo, you could be arrested for that. How old was she?"

"My best guess, she'd have to be in her early twenties, but strange thing . . ."

"What strange thing?"

"What she was wearing."

"Which was?"

"A uniform."

"Delivery uniform? UPS? Shorts and shirt? What?"

"No, not exactly. She was in a plaid skirt with suspenders over a white blouse and little string tie."

"Sounds like a schoolgirl's uniform . . . a Catholic schoolgirl's uniform."

"Bingo, now you mention it. Skirt was just above the knees cut high. And man, did she fill out the blouse."

"A cap? Did she wear a cap?"

"She was holding a cap in her hand, yeah. Why? What's got you all fired up? What was in the package? Was the kid 'spose to sing 'Happy Birthday' or do a strip tease for you, Stoney, or what?"

"Early twenties, huh? Little old for a convent girl," muttered Lucas.

"What's got you in such a lather, amigo?"

"The return address and the contents don't exactly jive with one another."

"Yeah, Eunice was curious about that, and she didn't like the look or the smell of the package, but you know Eunice, she just raised her shoulders and told me *not* to get involved in your affairs. Frankly, I'm curious myself." He dropped his voice to a conspiratorial whisper. "Do you know this girl from the convent?"

"Convent girls aren't in their twenties, Jack, but even so, the answer is no."

"Told Eunice it was none of our business what business you had with a girl from a convent school."

"Jeeze, Tebo, I haven't one damned clue who the girl might be or why anyone from a Catholic school would be sending me disgusting shit through the mail."

"What kinda shit're we talking about, Lucas?"

"Jack, the sender is anonymous, and the contents of the package . . . well, it's highly *unusual*."

"Highly unusual?" he repeated.

"Especially for a young woman to be hauling around."

Tebo grunted. "Unusual how?"

"Come on up and see *unusual* for yourself."

"Give me a few minutes . . . be right up. Haven't seen a good *unusual* for some time, bud." Tebo imagined it must be sexy underthings.

"I need a witness to this, Jack."

"That bad, huh? Some bitch stalking you, huh?"

"I'm so glad my supposed love life affords you so many fantasies, Jack, but believe me, unless you are the pervert I suspect you are, you'll get no pleasure out of this business." Lucas breathed too deeply, catching up the odors of the package in his nostrils and throat again. His mind wafted back to Nam, but he fought the memories. Choking, he added, "So get up here, will you? I don't want to be alone with this thing any longer."

Finally a serious note came out of Tebo. "That bad, huh?"

"That bad, yes."

CHAPTER 2

Ward off evil spirits

TEBO READ THE note and stared at the contents of the package opened in Lucas's kitchen sink. A hefty, barrel-chested man in an apron with his tavern's signature-logo T-shirt blazoned and stained across his chest, Tebo sputtered, "Damn, you weren't kidding. Somebody's trying to tell you something . . . something damned serious, Stoney. This is just sick, man, too sick."

"My own personal psycho-terrorist, it would seem."

"We better not let Eunice hear about this. She gets a whiff of this, and you're outta here, amigo . . . no pun intended."

"Yeah, when Eunice learns about this, she'll have me kicked out for certain," Lucas conceded. "Look, you were a butcher for a time. Does this soup and sandwich of fleshy cuts look human or animal? If it's animal, I won't have to take this quite so seriously. I'll know for certain it's a hoax."

"Hoax?"

"Bad joke then . . . cooked up by some of the fools in the department."

Tebo examined the contents more closely, squirming, squinting, puckering his lips, retracting his nose, creasing his forehead in a mix of revulsion and thought. His beard bobbing, he said, "Sorry, pal, doesn't look like any animal I ever cut into."

"I was afraid you'd say that. I had the same initial reaction." Lucas stepped from the kitchen and fell into an easy chair. "I've seen autopsy cuts like this, when Chang wants to take a biopsy of an organ, you know. This has the stamp of a medical man behind it."

Tebo, his nose twitching with the odor rising from the sink, followed Lucas into the living room, shaking his head in disbelief, still reeling from the odor left behind in the kitchen. "You know, amigo, I didn't smell any of that stench coming off the package when it was delivered. But like I said, Eunice—she' s got a nose on her like a bassett hound—said she didn't like the smell of it. Sure gotta be some sick creep behind this! You ever give any thought to getting into another line of business? Maybe invest in that new location I'm opening on the Rivera Esplanades?"

"Yeah, I can really see you fitting in there with the cappuccino crowd. Look, I gotta call Chang, get his CSI unit over here. Hell, this is human remains. Damn sure ruined my night. They'll have to go over every inch of this thing."

"Christ!" Tebo banged an open palm into the doorway, causing some of Lucas's gun collection, hanging on the adjoining wall, to shake loose and go helter-skelter, barrels tilted, handles swaying.

"Hey, easy! My guns."

"I like having you around, Stoney. You're like *insurance* in my book, like having a pit bull around, but Eunice . . . no way I can keep a coroner's van parked outside from Eunice."

"All right, then she *knows*."

"She'll want you out, bro. And she'll bug me for every detail. Damn these times we live in . . . all kinda vipers and lunatic snipers coming out of the woodwork everywhere you turn. Can't go out to dinner anymore without packing a weapon."

"Agreed."

"What with you being a cop . . . amigo, seems doubly foolish of you to've opened that package at all. Hand-delivered, that weird return address. Suppose it was anthrax or some other infectious disease?"

"I suppose you're right, Jack."

"Tell me, Lucas, being Wolf Clan in the Cherokee Nation and all . . . you got something going with that convent chick on the side that might've, you know, pissed her or the boyfriend off maybe?"

"Hell, no. You know I prefer a mature lady."

"Then what *connection* do you have to that convent school?"

"*None,* damn it."

Tebo's frown said he wasn't buying it.

Lucas opened his palms in the universal gesture for confusion. "Look, before I gave any mind to the return address, for just a moment, I thought it might've come from some bastard on the reservation who'd gutted a deer," he confessed.

"Yeah, sure, when you got that first whiff, *whew*! First thought was reservation roadkill cookin', huh?"

It made Lucas laugh. "Thought someone was sending a buffalo burger through the mail," he said to keep the joke rolling.

Tebo laughed lightly, "Hey, don't knock the favorite tourist dish. It's on every menu now 'long with—"

"Spare me, Jack. Don't go there."

Both men had family on the Alabama & Coushatta Indian Reservation near Huntsville. Both had found a life off the reservation. Tebo's family ancestry was Coushatta Comanche, Lucas's Texas-immigrated Cherokee.

"So, you've got *no* idea who might be behind it?" asked the big man at Lucas's side as he too dropped onto the sofa.

"I suspect it's a joke. Has to be a sick prank."

"Christ, if that's true . . . Some friends you've got, amigo. You give any thought to it's maybe originating with that prick cousin of yours, Billy Hawk? Or worse yet, his boss?"

"Zachary Roundpoint's too busy with his casinos and

Indian mafia networking to play games like this with me. Besides, there's no animosity between us."

"Tell that to Billy Hawk. He still thinks you stole his wife from him."

"Bullshit. Everybody on the res knows she left him because he hooked up with Roundpoint. I had nothing to do with her leaving him. Billy brought that all on himself."

"You told me she wanted him out of the picture, so she and you could ride off into the sunset, man. I don't forget a thing like that."

"I thought I told you to forget that, Jack! I told that to you in confidence, so don't repeat it."

"Confidence? How many others've you told the same story to? Stoney, you light up on beer and peyote, and you sometimes talk, my friend, but I've kept your secret." Tebo began to pace, agitated. "You gotta at least consider that *maybe* Billy thinks you are *after* him? Maybe this is his way of striking first, sending a warning, bro. I mean, Tsali, she's not known for diplomacy or discretion, and she is living in your grandfather's house with her girls— the house you bought for the old man."

"She nursed the old man in his final days."

"We all know that, but like Eunice says, your old girl-friend's got it easy because of you, and that can't sit well with Hawk."

Lucas thought, *If it is Billy, let the bastard come,* but he said, "Come on, Jack, you're beginning to sound like the gossips on the fucking res. That shit with Billy's old water under an old bridge."

"But the woman wanted you to snuff her husband!"

"Shhhh! Can you be any louder? Damn it, Jack, when Tsali came to me with that nonsense, she'd been pushed beyond her limit. It's been a year, and I stopped seeing her, end of story."

Tebo frowned and muttered under his breath as he wiped at his two-day-old stubble. "Seems there's plenty of room between the lines for bad blood, and—"

"Not on my part!"

"—and a desire to avenge family honor, whether—"

"Bullshit!"

"—whether you've sworn off *her* or not!"

"Jack!"

"Either on Billy's part or *hers*."

Lucas pictured the beautiful, young Tsali of his child-hood, the one he'd wandered the banks of the Trinity River with, the one he had made love to before leaving for Viet Nam. The one who had rejected him when he chose to live among the whites, marrying his cousin, Billy Hawk, instead. He gave a thought to the short, stocky Billy as well, a hench-man now for the local Indian crime boss, Zachary Round-point. "What're you suggesting, Jack?" Lucas stepped back to the kitchen, pointing to the awful package stinking up his sink. "That Tsali could do something like this?"

"A scorned woman, all that, you know."

"I know her too well. Tsali wouldn't do something like this. I know her."

"How well do any of us know what others are capable of, Lucas?"

"Drop it, Jack. Tsali is doing well; I speak to her from time to time. She doesn't hate me. As for Billy, I haven't had any dealings with him whatsoever since he's taken up with Roundpoint's crowd." As much as he grudgingly admired Zach Roundpoint, Lucas's being a Houston police detective prevented any public dealings with the man.

"All right, smart guy, then who?" asked Tebo. "Who's got the cajones to send you something this bloody nasty?"

Lucas took a deep breath of air. "This's more likely the work of those bonehead idiots down at the precinct, test-ing me."

"Yeah . . . sure, that's it!" Tebo smiled wide. "When you get in tomorrow, they'll be studying your reaction. You'll see." Tebo laughed, his belly rising and falling. He decided he liked this solution.

"They will've read all the reports to see if I freaked out . . . see if I called in the bomb squad or a CSI unit, all of it, no doubt."

Both men breathed easier with this notion, and Lucas offered Tebo a beer from the fridge, and together they relaxed a moment, Lucas switching on a Houston Astros game. Tebo lifted the note with the cryptic poem on it.

To the backdrop of the announcer, Tebo mused, "Lousy at poetry, whoever the jerk—or jerks—are. So, you think they got the parts from Chang's crime lab or the morgue?"

"That'd be my guess. Sometimes waste isn't disposed of properly, you know . . . hear about it all the time. One of those bozos like itchy Arnie Feldman is in the morgue maybe . . . maybe on legitimate business when he sees this, sneaks the stuff out, wraps it up, and sends it to me."

"This's the guy everybody calls The Itch?"

"Yeah."

"Why The Itch? He got a bad case in his BVDs?"

"Well, joke goes that he's never had an itch he didn't scratch. Anyway, to add to the mystery, The Itch hires a little prostitute off the street to dress up in a Catholic school uniform to deliver the package."

"Yeah . . . yeah!" Tebo's eyes lit up. "She was maybe a hooker or a stripper dressing the part, pal," Tebo said, toasting with his beer. "She was no little kid. Kick-ass body. Had that uniform bulging. Lot of makeup, eyelashes, eyeliner, rouge, lipstick as thick as molasses."

"Gotta be Feldman scratching another itch. He spent a lot of time in vice, knows every prostitute on the street."

After a long silence, Tebo asked, "Suppose you're wrong."

Lucas silently considered this. If it weren't a stupid prank, if it had come from some enemy, it presented a real threat, a warning of some kind, or it could be someone's reaching out, pleading for the Cherokee detective to put an end to his killing again. No way to be sure. Not a clue. To Tebo he simply said, "Got to be a prank."

Lucas's red face somewhat camouflaged his scarred right cheek and neck, until the scar flinched with his consternation, as was the case now. The twinge called to mind how he had gotten the scar in a fiery shootout early in his career as a police officer in Dallas. Now a detective in Houston, he had little desire to relive that day many years before, but he could not escape it either, tattooed as it was on his countenance.

Tebo considered the worried look on his friend's face, and he thought how tall and angular Lucas was even here in his sitting position.

The phone rang, and Lucas grabbed it up as if it might be a lifeline to take his mind away from the package and what it portended.

Dr. Meredyth Sanger, the precinct psychiatrist, gasped out her words. "I need you right away, now, to come over here, Lucas. Can you come over now?"

He heard the desperation in her voice. "What's happened?"

"Something awful . . . arrived in the mail . . . can't fathom it."

Lucas thought she must mean some bad news, a death in the family perhaps. "I have something I've got to deal with right here at the moment that requires my presence here. Believe it or not, my apartment may be in need of a crime-scene unit."

"What do you mean?" she asked.

"I got a strange package in the mail," he explained, "extremely strange."

"Is it . . . in any way human body parts?" Meredyth's voice rose.

"How did you know?" Lucas nearly shouted.

"I got a package too."

"Body parts in a Styrofoam-lined box?"

"Eyes . . . a pair of eyes, Lucas, and two teeth! I freaked out."

"Take it easy. Tebo and I wanna believe it's some of the guys down at the precinct, pulling a hoax, you know, using autopsy debris."

"It's a pair of eyes, Lucas. Hardly autopsy culls. Some sick SOB has mailed me a pair of bloody eyeballs and . . . and teeth . . . with a crumpled note and a CD."

"Eyes, teeth, a note, and a CD," he repeated, "Christ."

On hearing this, Tebo switched off the TV and leaned in to listen.

Lucas added, "This is too foul even for Feldman and Patterson. Tell me, what does the note say? And have you played the CD?"

"It's fashioned in poetic lines." She read the note to him. " 'Eye for eye, tooth for tooth, I give you peace beyond the confessional booth.' Whoever sent it knows I'm Catholic."

"Sounds similar to what I have here. Whoever it is, he's targeted us both, and if it *isn't* the idiots downtown . . . if it's for real, we need to protect ourselves, Mere."

"Agreed. Sounds like a revenge motive of some twisted sort. Listen to what's on the CD."

Coming over the line were the lyrics and music of the song "(I Had) The Time of My Life" from the hit film *Dirty Dancing*. In the context of the moment, given that someone had cut out the eyes and organs of a body and sent it to the two police officials, the lyrics proved chilling.

Lucas pictured Meredyth, her tall frame shivering at the circumstances, and yet she had steeled herself enough to have played the CD while alone with the heinous package she had opened. Lucas found her beautiful and intelligent as well as courageous, as he had worked many cases with the ash-blond psychiatrist's invaluable help.

When she came back on the line, she said, "Maybe it's somebody we put away."

"No. Everyone we've put away is either dead or still behind bars."

"Someone's behind it . . . someone who hates us both. Perhaps orchestrating it from behind prison bars," she persisted. "Whoever did this must hate me a great deal, Lucas."

"We'll find out who's behind it, Mere. Trust me. Where are the eyes now?"

"Spoiling my gray carpet in the living room. I dropped them the moment I realized what I had in my hands."

"How was the package delivered, by hand or via the mail, what?"

"Left with the doorman, who brought it up for a tip."

"Any return address on the package?"

"My private office downtown. It looked harmless enough."

"I'm on my way. Go to a separate room until I get there."

"I already have. I'm calling from outside on the deck."

"I'm on my way," he reassured her.

Lucas gave Tebo the number to call Chang's crime scene unit. "Dispatch them to both locations, Jack. I'm on my way over there to Meredyth's."

Tebo waved him out the door and once alone, he realized he'd been abandoned with the *thing* in the other room. He stared through the doorway at the opened parcel in the sink, and suddenly felt a raw fear waft into the living room. He got on the phone to dial Chang. While Chang's phone rang, Jack Tebo tried to imagine the kind of mind that could conceive of such a deed, and then follow through with this insulting attack on both Stonecoat and Dr. Sanger. He himself could not harm a hair on the head of a mouse, knowing the deep empathy he would feel during such an act, even on the smallest of sentient creatures. Destroying a life would haunt his sleep. He could not imagine how anyone calling himself a human being could operate without falling apart after committing murder. Lucas had told him all about the sociopathic mind-set of murderers and serial killers in particular, but still Tebo could not fathom the kind of thinking that went into long, tedious fantasizing of rape, torture, and murder plans. He wondered now about the kind of mind that could do this to his friends.

Chang's assistant Lynn Nielsen came on the line, and Tebo explained that Detective Stonecoat needed a CSI unit at both his apartment and the condominium home of Dr. Meredyth Sanger immediately. Dr. Nielsen replied, "I cannot, sir, Mr. Tebo, authorize two CSI units to descend on locations on the say-so of a friend of a detective's."

Tebo gnashed his teeth and lied, "We got an *anthrax* letter here *and* another one at 1220 Belmont Drive, Dr. Sanger's place. Do you, or do you not, want to take responsibility, Dr. Nielsen?"

"All right . . . all right . . . I'll dispatch the teams on Detective Stonecoat's order. Have him call immediately."

"Damn it, he's in transit to Dr. Sanger's."

"All right. I'll get his dispatcher on the line. I'll speak to him directly."

Nielsen hung up and Tebo stared at the phone, and spoke to it. "Maybe it is all a gag! Maybe this Dr. Nielsen is in on it. Hell, maybe even Dr. Sanger's call is part and parcel of the prank. Gotta be it. They're all in on it."

"In on what?" Tebo's heavysct wife stood in the doorway, having come to look for him when she saw Stonecoat fleeing off in a panic. "What's that awful odor?" she asked, going for the kitchen.

Tebo stood and blocked her way, pleading, "Don't go in there. It's not something you want to see, Eunice . . . Eunice!"

She pushed past him and into the kitchen, going for the thing in the sink sitting amid the discarded wrapping paper. The stench and the sight made her gag and ask, "What the hell is it, Jack? What the hell has that man brought down on our place now?"

"You can't blame Lucas for this."

"Who else you know in this life who's going to have such a horrible thing sent to him? I want him outta here, Jack. This is the limit, the camel and the straw, believe me! Out he goes or I go! You gotta make the choice, Jack Tebo. That man is a magnet for trouble. Trouble, hell, he attracts danger and death."

DR. ARTHUR BELKUIN had a nightmare that wouldn't go away, the unremitting, repeating replay in his head of the ax coming down on Mira Lourdes's neck, and in the nightmare, her head revolved in a one-eighty-degree turn, her eyes open and staring up at him, her lips parting, asking why . . . why . . . why?

He still could not give her an answer, because he didn't himself know why Lauralie had selected her for death. He had watched how Mira Lourdes had been selected, but he didn't know why she had been chosen, but chosen she was, right out of the White Pages. Lauralie had opened the hefty Houston city directory to the Ls, saying she needed someone named Lourdes to kill.

"Lords as in *gods,* like my Lords?" Arthur had asked.

She'd spelled it out for him as her eyes scanned the directory page. "L-O-U-R-D-E-S, Lourdes."

"Why Lourdes?" he'd asked.

"Only a Lourdes will do." She then found four candidates listed in the book.

They took down each address and cased each home. One was in a faraway, upscale gated community north of the city. A second was in a pleasant neighborhood and had a high fence around it, guard dogs, and a prominently displayed ADT alarm system. A third was in a rundown section of the city that was dangerous to drive through, and Arthur's expensive car stuck out like a zebra there, she had told him. The fourth house proved perfect. At the end of a cul-de-sac, bushes all around, and a car for sale sitting out on the lawn. It was a perfect excuse to ring the doorbell and to put Mira Lourdes at ease. Lauralie claimed their finding Mira Lourdes was nothing short of fated, that she was placed before them by God.

Arthur stared up at the ceiling fan he had installed in the old farmhouse bedroom; he lay on his back, looking about the room, unable to sleep, feeling Lauralie's heat beside him. He had never known anyone to exude so much heat from her body as did Lauralie.

From outside at the pens, the sound of his two beautiful greyhounds wafted in to him, a low, guttural chorus of baying. Arthur had wanted to bring the dogs inside, knowing they were agitated at the new home, and he'd always kept them indoors at night before, but Lauralie didn't care for them so much, and she had pleaded that she wanted Arthur all to herself tonight, and as always, she got her way, and here he was, the sex over, lying awake in a fitful stew of images that refused to let him so much as doze. True slumber kept just ahead of him, just out of mental reach, denying him even a moment in the land of nod.

By comparison, she lay sound asleep; in fact, she slept nightly like a newborn innocent, a kind of pink fluff cloud seemingly hovering over her angelic chaste features. A slight nasal whine welled up from her, escaping in a contented breath, while he tossed and turned, unable to get the images of Mira's death out of his head, and unable to flee the quivering questions that swam like so many water beetles skimming over the surface of his consciousness, slowly driving him out of his mind.

Arthur watched himself once again dropping the ax on Mira Lourdes's neck without enough force to severe the head cleanly; he watched Lauralie finish the job. He saw himself against the night sky, struggling with the body, trying to get a grip on it without directly looking at the huge, bloody cavity that remained of the wounded neck, trying desperately to get no more blood on himself. All this while the greyhounds protested fiercely, the smell of blood agitating them into a competition of braying and baying.

He detested blood. "Why can't we simply poison her?" he had asked Lauralie when they had planned the killing, but Lauralie had said she wanted the death to be fast, final, and traumatic; she'd added that Mira's death was the least of her concerns, but that law-enforcement officials and the public must be outraged on learning how she'd died in a beheading with her parts scattered.

He had argued about getting Mira's blood all over, using an ax as Lauralie planned. She had countered, "Then we'll do it outdoors."

While carrying Mira's body, Arthur looked up at the stars and the three-quarter moon that looked on their deed. The body felt like an overstuffed potato bag, bulging here, sliding there, slipping here, as if the thing wanted escape from his arms, as if even in death she detested him and his touch. He struggled to get the body inside where Lauralie awaited them.

Stepping inside the little farmhouse, he heard Lauralie talking to the severed head. Lauralie stared into the dead eyes as she spoke. "They'll pay now. They'll all pay now, especially Dr. Meredyth Sanger and her lovey-dovey friend, Lieutenant Detective Lucas Stonecoat."

"Why do you hate them so much?" Arthur asked, standing in the house at that point, blood dripping from the corpse's enormous cavity. "You must tell me now . . . now that I've killed for you."

"You call what you did killing? Shit, I had to finish the job you started. And remember, I've killed before."

"You didn't really kill your own mother, did you?"

"I did. It was easy. She made it easy, too easy, in fact."

She'd told Arthur how she had used her mother's own alcoholism against her.

"Why Mira Lourdes? Why'd you need to kill someone named Lourdes? And why do you hate Sanger and her friend so much?"

"In time . . . in time, Arthur. For now it's enough for you to know that I hate them passionately." She considered the body for a moment as he placed it onto the steel table at the center of the room. The house had been converted into an operating room of sorts, Arthur having accumulated equipment and furniture from his once-thriving, now-failing veterinary practice in Houston, where he had had to lay off personnel.

Lauralie had returned her attention to the severed head again, its eyes staring wide at her from the shelf she had placed it on.

Blue and lustrous, seemingly alive yet still as stones are those eyes, Arthur had thought. He thought of how those eyes had pleaded with him for mercy and how he had had to ignore that plea. And then he thought that they still bored through him like a dual pair of drills, angry now, spiteful, furious in their blueness.

Lauralie noticed his having been frozen in place by the dead woman's eyes. She taunted him, saying, "Just imagine, Arthur, the life inside these so-called dead orbs"—she paused to touch the eyes with her fingers—"still in movement at the subatomic level, the only life left only seen through a microscopic lens. Makes you wonder, doesn't it?"

"Wonder what?" he asked.

"Wonder if on some level, Mira can still *see us* in this world." She laughed. "When I harvest those baby blues of yours, Mira, they'll make a nice gift for someone, not to mention your other lovely parts . . ."

"Why, Lauralie? Why are we doing this? I gotta know; I have to understand."

"In time you will. In time even Mira here will understand. Now, do that magic you promised me with your medical wizardry. I want two of her teeth and both her eyes from her head. From the body, I want slices of her major organs."

A failed medical student, Arthur had become a veterinarian in order to remain close to medicine. What Lauralie now proposed, carving up the body, he hadn't done since medical school, and he had never removed anyone's eyes, not even those of a cadaver, and he had never pulled a human tooth. Still, that night when Lauralie had come up to him in the bar, she had gotten him talking, and he had bragged about his abilities in animal surgery. She had easily talked her way into his bed that night, and soon he was making promises to her. He promised her that he could do any surgery necessary on any animal brought to him. It wasn't until much later that he learned the animal she was interested in slicing up was a human being. But by then, Arthur had said whatever was necessary to impress Lauralie, and now was the moment of truth.

He pulled on his surgical gloves, and using his bare hands, he dug a finger into the eye cavity and began to work the eyeballs loose from their moorings. Once he had them popped out, he used his scalpel to sever them from the optic nerve.

Lauralie was delighted beyond reason, beyond any delight she had ever displayed in Arthur's embrace.

Again the cry of his dogs stiffened Arthur's spine. He thought of getting up, giving up sleep altogether, and going out to his two babies outside in the cold. But it might wake her again. He'd better stay put.

Arthur rolled over onto his side, struggling with his

mind to leave him in peace, to turn over one hour of blank-ness on the screen of his skull to slumber, but instead the images of horror kept up a constant barrage against him. "I'm not cut out for this kind of business. I'm too weak for this. God help me," he lamented.

Lauralie rolled over and placed her arm over him, say-ing, "Jesus H. Christ, Arthur, go to sleep, will you? You're keeping me awake again."

CHAPTER 3

Rain clouds: prospective

DR. MEREDYTH SANGER'S tearful sea-green eyes widened on seeing Lucas at her door; she next threw the door open and leaped into Lucas's arms. In his arms, her body heaved, fearful and shaking in his fervent embrace. They had been close friends for a decade now, and they had tested the boundaries of that friendship to include a sexual interlude from which she'd backed off while Lucas had patiently awaited a time when they might renew their mutual passion for one another. She feared "losing herself" in him, analyzing what they had out of existence. They had argued heatedly, all that she'd needed to back further from the relationship and see to other men.

Lucas brushed her hair and held her against his chest. "It's going to be all right. It's going to be all right," he assured her, taking her face in his hands now, making her focus on his dark eyes. "I'm here now." Lucas wondered where her boyfriend, Byron Priestly, might be as she answered his thought for him.

"Byron left me alone with it . . . ran out the door."

"Are you kidding? He was with you when you opened the package, and he just ran out the door?"

"Said he could not put up with my patients and their sick claim on my time anymore, not after this. The sight of the eyes in the box scared the shit out of me, but it terrified him."

"Then I suppose he won't be back?"

"He wouldn't dare," she replied. "But Lucas, his prints're gonna be all over the wrapping."

"Why're his prints all over the packaging?"

"He *insisted* on opening it. I had put it aside . . . not wanting to deal with it tonight, in no rush, but him! No, his curiosity was burning a hole through his brain, so I gave in, chucked it to him, and told him to have a ball."

"And he got it right between the eyes, so to speak . . . two eye*balls*. How prophetic."

"More like pathetic, his *lack* of balls."

"I can understand how a package with eyes might upset a fellow who calls himself By."

"Everything fell out, including the note, the CD, and the teeth . . . all over my carpet."

"Must've shook ol' By up."

"Shook us both up! Lucas, I've wracked my brain for anyone who might be capable of this, and even my worst client is not capable of this—and to send a foul package to you as well. Lucas, who could be behind it?"

"On my way over, I wondered if one of your clients might be behind it. Perhaps one who somehow knows our history together? One who knows about our having worked cases together, and that we have been intimate with one another?" he asked.

"The first one I thought of was Herman Philip Teal, my weirdest at present, but as for knowing about the connection we have, Lucas, anyone reading the newspapers last spring, following the Walters case, would know how closely we work together." Meredyth had offered not only profiling advice on the case, but she had helped interview Samuel Irving Walters when Lucas had arrested him for the rape and mutilation murders of six teens—*all male*—all occurring in the concentrated areas of West University Place, Southside Place, and Bellaire.

Meredyth took a deep breath, nourishing her shattered nerves and calming in his presence. He had that effect on people. She focused on his reassuring power and gaze, and the soft words of encouragement and support. "You're all right now. We'll get past this together, Mere."

They still stood in the foyer, the door left to stand open, neighbors creeping from their doorways, curious but tentative. It was clear she wanted out of the apartment, to run out like her boyfriend before her; she certainly didn't want to go back into the condominium alone. But seeing the prying eyes of others, she pulled him inside and closed the door.

Lucas firmly said, "Point me in the direction of these wayward eyes, Mere."

Leaning against the door now, she simply pointed to the interior.

Across the room lay the pair of human eyeballs, still attached to the optic nerves that trailed after like the fantail of exotic jellyfishes. The sight had an unholy irreverence about it, the eyes lying askew in the thick pile of her plush gray carpet, fibers clinging to the gummy irises. The flesh was as freshly cut from a human corpse as the selection of human organ tissue sent to Lucas himself.

"What the hell's going on?" he asked aloud, expecting no answer but feeling a need to keep talking.

A step closer and the image was replaced, the eyes now looking like two smooth white Ping-Pong balls with tubular extensions, and strikingly dark, deep-blue seeds for pupils at each center. He wondered to whom the eyes had once belonged. Were they male or female? Mexican or American? Italian or Irish? Then he grotesquely heard the song lyrics *"when Irish eyes are smiling"* flit through his cop's brain. Had a roomful of cops been present, at least one or more would be humming the tune by now, putting into practice the time-honored black humor so necessary in dealing with such a horror as this pair of errant eyes presented. *Eyes that followed you across a room . . . eyes that pinned an opponent, that popped a gasket, that darted for*

*escape, that stabbed at the heart, that were windows to the
soul, and that were only for you* . . . All the cliches rushed
to mind, doing little good against the edginess of the situation.

To add to the revulsion of the scene, Lucas saw the pair
of human teeth—also scattered from the fallen box—lying
at a distance from the eyes, each having taken different
paths. He intuited the eyes making a soft landing and
remaining fairly close to where they had made contact with
the plush carpeting, but the teeth he saw bouncing wildly,
like a pair of dropped earrings, when the parcel was overturned. This would explain how far they'd traveled from
the epicenter of the large stain where the liquid residue
of the spoiling eyes had slipped from the Styrofoam-laced
box. From this, he determined precisely where Byron had
been standing when he had insisted on tearing open the
delivery and subsequently dropping it.

Lucas went into the kitchen and banged around in
search of something, the sound of silverware clattering off
silverware as he rummaged, making her call out, "What're
you looking for?"

"Tongs . . . found 'em!" he said, returning and going to
the discarded packaging, and using the white Teflon tongs,
he crouched and reached for the crumpled paper that had
been wrapped about the box to examine the handwriting.

"Do you have to use my best tongs?" she asked.

"All I could find. Look here," he said, turning the block
lettering on the package to his eyes. "It's the same block
lettering."

He replaced the packaging precisely where it had lain.
He then reached for the scripted note, another little poem
from the look of it. "I'd swear it's the same handwriting as
the package sent me. Only difference, return address is
your private office downtown."

"It's a ruse; no one from the office would do this, no one."

"What about one of your patients?"

"Perhaps. We could start there. I have handwriting on
all my patients, but it's most likely whoever did this would
disguise the hand."

"Disguised or not, there'll be patterns. We'll get a top-notch handwriting expert to find them and rule in or out anyone you might suspect from your practice. Same for the cops you've counseled at the precinct, and any criminals you've interviewed recently."

"How can you suspect any of the men at the Three-one, Lucas? They're all grateful for my help."

"Does that include Lewis Adiwa, the guy you helped IAD nail for that prostitute murder?"

"He's in jail clear 'cross the state in Shackleford State Penitentiary. Clear to Abilene, Lucas."

Lucas shrugged. "Cells and bars don't keep men from operating on the outside. Not anymore. They've got civil liberties, phone calls, opportunities like never before. You see that new reality show on prison bands? Give me a break."

"Maybe Adiwa should be examined. He did threaten my life, but I really doubt any of your colleagues at the precinct could be behind this."

"I don't think you know how nasty cops can get when they're pulling off what they consider a joke."

"A joke! This is no damned joke, Lucas."

"I suspect it may be all a prank aimed at the two of us, concocted by Itchy Arnie Feldman maybe, encouraged by others *maybe,* and given the means—the human tissues by Dr. Frank Patterson—whom I've had my run-ins with— *maybe*."

"That's a lot of maybes."

"Perhaps."

"And besides, it's . . . it's just too . . . too damed *crazy*. They'd have to be fools! They could lose their jobs for this kind of insane prank."

"Not if they come waltzing up to the door right now with a beer keg, pretzels, and claimed responsibility, and we all laugh it off."

"I'd have their badges, and they know it."

"Not if it can't be proven, and if The Itch—that is, Feldman, has someone working the inside of the lab with him, the lab guy will've known to use parts from a body long since buried or even cremated. Wouldn't take much to fudge the records and rob off pieces from a John or a Jane Doe autopsy."

"You think so? How do you do that, Lucas? Get into the heads of such sickos? It can't be easy or fun."

"A gift or a curse. I have a hell of an imagination, you might say."

She took a deep breath, considering more seriously his theory. "It almost makes me feel better, at least in one sense, to think it's all some sort of inside joke by the boys of the Thirty-first—as sick as that may be, but why pick on us, Lucas?"

"How many people you know that're jealous of a close bond, Mere? We have that. Others dislike us for it. Simple Psych 101."

"If it's true, it'll certainly narrow our search."

"I plan to watch their reactions tomorrow when I go in; you do the same."

"Damned juvenile behavior . . . typical cop crap," she muttered. "Bastards."

Lucas had offered an explanation she could handle with a great deal more ease, at least tonight. He mentally patted himself on the back for having calmed her. She was visibly more at ease, so long as she kept *her* eyes off *the* eyes. A hoax seemed far preferable to this being a horrible prelude to worse psychological attacks. It had the added virtue of an end in sight. Lucas asked if she would make coffee, sending her into the kitchen, away from the disagreeable objects littering her living room. She had taken a step toward the kitchen when a loud knock at her door sent a new shock wave through her.

"CSI Team, Houston Police Department! Open up, please!"

Lucas stepped to the door and opened it for young Ted Hoskins, a pale-faced twenty-six-year-old evidence tech with the CSI unit whose thick glasses, thin mustache, and stylishly cut hair made him look like a college boy. Behind Ted stood two others, a crime-scene photographer named Steve Perelli, and a young female intern he only knew as Lil.

With them, hanging back, was the doorman who'd led them up to the Sanger condo.

"Detective Stonecoat," began Hoskins. "Guess this must be the place, the Sanger residence? Something to do with human body parts being found?"

"This is the place," Lucas informed them, and the two men filed into the living room area, followed sheepishly by the intern, being careful as they formed a kind of circle around the obvious evidence.

The concerned doorman called in to Mcredyth, asking if she were all right. He'd been taken by surprise by the arrival of the CSI van with the city coroner's logo.

"I'm all right, Max," she said, going to the door and assuring him of the fact.

"Who died?" he asked her.

"No one, Max . . . I mean, no one that I know of. It's likely just a joke in extremely bad taste, but we have to be thorough all the same."

Meanwhile, Lucas explained to Hoskins, "Dr. Nielsen contacted me via dispatch as I drove here from across town. I received a similar package around the same time at my place. I briefed Nielsen on what to expect at both locations, and I assured her that it had nothing to do with anthrax."

"Where'd she get that notion?" asked Hoskins.

"Don't know where she got that idea."

A number of additional evidence technicians filtered in now.

"You still want that coffee, Lucas?" Meredyth asked.

"Sure . . . let's make ourselves scarce. Get outta the way here." He guided her back into the kitchen. She brewed a pot of coffee, while Lucas made a phone call to a friend on the force, Sergeant Stan Kelton. He informed Stan of what had happened, asking him if he'd heard or seen anything unusual about the station house that might cement Lucas's theory that it was all a stupid prank.

Kelton assured him, "If any such nonsense were afoot at the Three-one, Lucas, I'd've gotten wind of it. All the same, I'll sniff around, let you know."

"Let's get some air on the terrace," Meredyth suggested.

Taking their coffee with them, Lucas escorted Meredyth out onto the deck overlooking the twinkling lights of downtown Houston, the ever-changing cityscape in the near distance. They were thirty stories up.

Meredyth came from old money, and could easily have lived the quiet country club life of her friends—*like Byron Priestly*—and relatives, but she had chosen instead to become a forensic psychiatrist. Lucas admired her for the dedication and determination to achieve her goals and live up to her ideals.

She sat at the patio table, a light breeze playing whimsy fairy with her hair, rustling between the buttons of her blouse, causing a mild flap. The cool night air felt refreshing against her face and skin. Lucas stood behind her, his hands squeezing her shoulders as he surveyed the skyline. Here on the terrace, Meredyth had plants growing, and Lucas, hoping to distract her from what was going on in her living room, asked, "Whataya call these plants here? Is this one a geranium? Maybe plants is what I need at my place, you know, to brighten it up a bit."

She looked over her shoulder at him, frowning. "Other than that cactus flower in the corner, which you dug up and gave me for Christmas, Lucas, I've never put you together with plants, but you sound positively Martha Stewart tonight."

"No, I'm really interested."

"Yes, that's a geranium, no longer in full bloom, but the others at the end of the terrace, they're all hibiscus plants."

"Okay, you give them individual names, like pets?"

She laughed lightly. "I'm not one of these people who gives names to her plants, Lucas."

"I take that as a good sign."

"I love the cactus flower most, you know."

"Courtship," he said.

"What?"

"On the res, when a boy gives a girl a cactus flower, it's the beginning of their courtship."

"All this time and I never knew. Why didn't you tell me before?"

Lucas didn't reply, going to the plants at the terrace edge instead, running his fingers lightly over them. "Hibiscus . . . they're called hibiscus, huh? Sounds Greek."

"Greek or perhaps Latin, I'm sure."

"Interesting word, hibiscus. Interesting lilt to it, a single word with its own melody is rare. Hibiscus . . . think I bet on a racehorse once with that name."

"I'm sure you have."

He returned from the edge to stand again behind her where she sat sipping her now-lukewarm coffee. He placed both hands on her shoulders, saying nothing.

"Listen, Lucas, thanks for rushing over like you did."

"What else is a friend to do under the circumstances?"

"Most friends I have would do like Byron and run the other way *under the circumstances*."

"I didn't do much."

"Your being here is enough. So trust me when I say you don't have to make small talk and—"

"Small talk?"

"—and pretend an interest in my potted plants, Lucas."

"Whoa up there, Doctor. I'll remember that if and when I should make small talk and idle chitchat," he countered.

"All I'm saying is that you don't need to resort to pretense to please me or in some vain attempt to distract me from the fact someone's mailed me a set of human eyes and a pair of teeth, and that my living room's become a crime scene, and that my personal security—my home in the clouds here—has been breached and defiled."

"Easy, sweetheart."

She reached up with both hands and covered his where they continued to squeeze her shoulders. "That feels good," she told him.

They continued to hold hands while the evidence techs created a crime grid of her living room. "Do you really think the whole horrible thing is an elaborate stinking joke, Lucas, or was that just another attempt to get me to calm down?"

"If it is a hoax, the bastards've let it go too far now. The costs involved in sending out a CSI unit, the time and manpower in running all this as evidence in a crime, hell . . . can you imagine the heads that'll roll?"

"You've never liked Frank Patterson, have you? And as for Feldman, how long has that feud been going on?"

"Creeps, both of 'em, cut of the same cloth. One concern in life, self-gratification now! Couple of pricks of the first caliber."

"Sounds like you know it's them and calling it in to the crime lab was to get back at them maybe?"

"Stir their stew counterclockwise, you mean?"

"They cooked this up, and you plan to cook their gooses? You're as much a juvenile as they are, Lucas."

He came around to face her, hands extended. "No way I would be disrespectful of human organs, desecrating someone's body or bodily parts this way. You can't put me in the same *nincompoop* class as they're in."

"No, I don't . . . I mean, I didn't mean to imply that, Lucas. I have great respect for you, but be careful not to allow *them* to pull you down to their level."

He dropped into the cushioned metal chair across from her. "Not a chance. Look, so far as I know right now, Mere, what you and I received via hand-delivered mail is a felony, and it smacks of a far worse crime, *murder*. That's the way I'm playing this out *for now*." He leaned in over the table as he spoke, his body language and eyes sincere.

"So you've called the town crier—Sergeant Kelton— posited the theory of it's being a hoax in his head, so you don't even have to point a finger. Before daybreak, it'll be all over the precinct."

"I know, out in the open."

"Dr. Chang and Captain Lincoln will hear the story that human remains were stolen from the crime lab."

"And the proverbial shit hits the proverbial fan. But Mere, at this stage, it's as good a theory as any we have."

"Look, if it is a horrible hoax perpetrated by some bozos, I want the bastards to pay dearly for it. Don't get me wrong."

"Then we're on the same page."

They fell silent for a moment, in one ear the sounds of the people bagging and collecting the evidence inside, in the other ear the sounds of traffic and the city.

"You know, Lucas, I like the way you call me Mere. Have I ever told you that you're the only one I know who calls me Mere, that is, aside from my mom and dad?"

"No, you've never shared that with me, Mere."

"My dad used it kiddingly. Called me *Night*-Mere sometimes!"

Lucas laughed lightly at this. "That's a good one."

"Fits, you mean."

"Maybe that too."

From inside, the *click-click-click* of the digital photographs being taken filtered out to them. They heard Dr. Leonard Chang's distinctive voice now, ordering that the poetic note and the CD be bagged and taken into evidence as well.

"I'm going to check on Chang's progress, and let him know about Byron's prints being on the wrapper. You might best stay out here. Can I bring you a drink from the fridge?"

"Yeah, there's some iced tea in the flask."

Lucas returned to the living room, where it appeared the techs were closing down their investigation. He saw that each eye and each tooth had been placed into separate baggies, and while each tooth was dropped into a pocket within a black valise, the two eyes were dropped into a medical cooler filled with ice.

Dr. Leonard Chang slowed Hoskins up, wanting to look once more into the depth of the eyes, holding them now in his gloved hands, staring through the cellophane bags. When Lucas came alongside him, asking him what he thought, Chang erupted from his inscrutable silence. "How horrible this must have been for Meredyth. How is she holding up?"

"She's gutsy; she's holding up." He told Chang about Byron Priestly's having handled the package. "Leonard, I'd like you and maybe Dr. Nielsen to investigate your labs for missing tissues, eyes, teeth."

"My labs? What're you meaning to imply, Lucas?"

"These items and those sent to my place—autopsy

slices of human organs as far as I can tell—may've originated in-house as a sick joke against me and Meredyth."

"That would be in the worst taste imaginable."

"Yeah, tasted bad at my place too."

"What kind of package did this fiend send you?"

Lucas described the packaging as identical down to the Styrofoam-lined interior that soaked up much of the liquid residue coming off the warm contents. "The hand-printing job and the scripted poems appear the work of the same person, so I'm wondering the same thing you are right about now."

"Which is?" The slight Chinese M.E. looked piqued that Lucas should suggest that his thoughts could be read.

"Are the body parts from the same victim, and who is the victim? And could the victim have been a resident of your morgue?"

"I'll hang anyone who might have taken human tissues and organs from our labs, Lucas. There will be no mercy for such actions. No one working under my direction can take such *despicable* liberties. It can't happen, not in my morgue."

"Come on, Leonard. You know who I have in mind. Scratch the surface of the man and what've you got?"

"You want me to question Frank Patterson about this?"

"Just watch him carefully, and I'll keep my eye on Detective Feldman."

"Itch? Itch and his friend Frank. Scratch the surface, you say. Should we say it is a game of itch and scratch? You can't truly believe it, Lucas. That they could be so stupid, so irresponsible, so . . ."

"Despicable?"

"Exactly."

"Hey, only a hunch, but the two of them've become quite chummy lately, and Feldman's done worse, and he's a bad influence on Frank."

"I hope you're wrong. Meantime, analysis of the tissues will tell us something about the victim or victims—certainly whether or not all the tissues come from the same female and how long she's been dead."

"You already know she's a she?"

"Eyes are small but mature, feminine eyes, my guess."

"You're the best, Chang."

"I still must treat this as a crime, Lucas, and a possible murder, and *not* a stupid-ass practical joke. And since law-enforcement officials have been targeted, we will work around the clock until we have answers for you, Detective."

Houston, like most major American cities, had passed tough laws against people who targeted the homes and families of police and firemen, so prevalent had crimes against law-enforcement officials become, anything from stalking to attempted murder of police in their homes.

Chang was now examining the poem, holding it up to the light with a pair of tweezers. "Poor dear Meredyth," he said to Lucas. "The idea that such a *monster* as the kind we deal with gains *entry* this way . . . in her home. . . ."

"Yeah, I felt the same way at my place."

"Screwy poem, but I'm no literary critic." He ordered Hoskins to slip the poem into a glassine case, careful not to smudge prints that might show up under a blue light.

"There was a CD left with the contents as well," Lucas informed the M.E., adding, "and ahhh, Meredyth placed it in her machine and played it."

"Where is the player?"

Lucas pointed it out. Chang pressed the play button and listened to a few bars of the old but popular tune, the singer's enthusiastic melody honoring "the time of my life."

Chang ejected the CD, slipped it into a plastic bag, and placed this into his black valise. "All this reminds me of that *fan* of mine who broke into my house a year ago." Chang gripped the back of his head and rubbed it in thought, looking rather Woody Allen-ish in clothes too baggy for his slight build. "This . . . this has to be *unnerving* for both of you."

"Like I said, Leonard, my first instinct was to think it a scam, you know, put together by some of the lunatics down at the precinct. At the moment, that suggestion has soothed Dr. Sanger somewhat."

"The lesser of two evils, you think?"

"Exactly."

"Feldman, *hmmm* . . ." He rubbed his chin in thought, trying to picture Arnie Feldman behind the prank. "Suppose you are wrong about Feldman. Suppose this is the work of some lunatic after all."

"Then we've got a real nutcase on our hands, don't we, Doc?"

"Perhaps in the meantime, while I am examining the eyes, teeth, and tissues, you might start an investigation with Missing Persons."

"I can put in the necessary calls."

"The eyes are fresh but with no ice crystals, Lucas. If it were from a corpse in the morgue, and this was done recently, there would be traces of ice. Whoever the victim is, her eyes are still pliable and firm. Not dry and breaking down from exposure to the elements or exposure to freezing."

"And that spells?"

"If not a recent—very recent—cadaver tampering, as you suggest, then a very, very recent missing persons case perhaps."

"I see. The death is recent, which might point to a recent disappearance, a recent—"

"—abduction-killing," Chang finished for him.

Lucas stepped away from Chang and into the kitchen, mulling over what Chang had said. He remembered Meredyth's request for iced tea, and he found it in the fridge, grabbed a clean glass and ice, and filled it to the brim. When he returned to the living room and passed through to the terrace, he found that Dr. Chang had gone out to talk with Meredyth. Lucas stepped into the middle of their conversation, the ice in her tea signaling his arrival.

Chang stood at the terrace rail, staring out at Houston's joyful skyline as it was being gobbled up by a fog. He seemed to be studying the clear demarcation where the blankness of night met the artificial orange glow of the city lights, lights that softly pushed back at space only to create a twilight meeting ground in between. The final effect created a swelling, growing smokiness around the tall buildings of downtown Houston. The effect seemed both real and unreal at once, composed as it was of reflecting colorful lights in battle with bleakness.

Chang seemed to be taking in the strange view as he consoled the psychiatrist. "My lab will work day and night to bring this lunatic to justice, whoever he may be, Dr. Sanger, be assured, and I am so sorry that you were put through this horror."

"Thank you, Dr. Chang, Leonard."

"I can't imagine the kind of brain we are dealing with, to send the eyes ripped from a young woman to terrorize a beautiful person like yourself, Meredyth. If you wish, of course, Kim and I will make room for you at our house for the night."

Meredyth sniffled. "That's so sweet of you, Leonard. But it won't be necessary. I can use my parents' home in Clover Leaf."

"Yes, and how are they enjoying their new place, Colony in the Glade? Father getting in a lot of golf there? Mother using the gym, maybe the pool?"

"They're in Paris."

"Really?"

"Anniversary."

"Long time since we last dined together, all of us."

Lucas now leaned over her and handed Meredyth the glass of iced tea, and she quickly grabbed it up and drank heartily while Chang informed her of the gender of the eyes. "They are those of a young woman, likely out of her teens, most certainly younger than forty. The teeth appear to be consistent with this finding as well."

"How can you be so sure?" she asked, setting her glass down.

"I'll know better once we have examined them under microscopic lens, of course."

"But how do you know the eyes belong to a woman?" pressed Meredyth. "I mean, it's not as if they had eyelashes attached."

"They are fully mature orbs, but slightly smaller than those of most males, so unless we are dealing with stunted growth or a male dwarf, which is highly unlikely, I am eighty- or ninety-percent certain they are the eyes of a middle-aged or a young woman in her late teens or early twenties."

"An educated guess," commented Lucas.

"One most likely corroborated by closer analysis, blood and serum tests, and DNA typing. And I intend, at Lucas's suggestion, to see if there is a match in DNA typing to any recent *visitors* to my autopsy rooms, morgue, or labs. If there is any sort of nonsense going on behind my back, I will determine it and prosecute anyone found to be involved."

"I'll be looking into Missing Persons tomorrow morning, Meredyth," Lucas informed her. "On the off chance this isn't the work of that beer-guzzling crowd down at the squad room."

"Oh, really?" she replied.

"It is at my suggestion," Chang explained. "The eyes show no signs of decay whatsoever, and no sign they were ever frozen. If they came from my labs, it is likely they would have spent some time in a freezer unit."

"I see."

Lucas leaned against the railing now, giving her a reassuring smile. "We'll soon know who's behind this ugly business, Mere. Tomorrow I'll coordinate efforts with Jana North."

"Jana, yes, of course."

"See if Missing Persons has someone recently gone missing without a trace . . . see if maybe there's a piece of this puzzle they can help with. Once we get a fix on *who* she was, then we can get a fix on *who* she knew, what happened to her, and how parts of her came to visit us."

"Why wait till tomorrow? Why not get on it tonight?" she asked.

"It's almost two A.M, Mere, and we're both emotionally and physically spent. Besides, we need to see what Leonard's experts can tell us. Aside from that, by morning, I'll have a copy of Perelli's photographs to work with."

"You don't really hope to match severed eyes to a photograph of a missing person?" she asked.

"Doubtful, but I'd like to have the photos to help explain the situation to Detective North and, when and if the time comes, to Captain Lincoln when I nail the bastard behind all this. As for matching the teeth, that ought to be far easier and more scientific. Whether she came from Leonard's lab or is in a missing persons file someplace, she'll have dental records. Reason we have procedures, right, Leonard?"

Chang nodded reassuringly at all of Lucas's conclusions. Leonard then said, "Well, Lucas, now I go over to your place with Hoskins, Perelli, and the others. See what we have there."

"My friend and landlord is minding things there, name's Jack Tebo."

"Aren't you coming?"

"I'll meet you over there."

"Don't leave me alone here, Lucas, not tonight," pleaded Meredyth.

Lucas corrected himself. "*We* will follow you over, Leonard."

DR. LEONARD CHANG'S expert team of technicians made short work of the soup-layered, thin-sliced autopsy cuts in Lucas's kitchen sink; unlike the scene at Meredyth's place, the criminal contents were contained all in one area, except for the note left by the killer. It lay on a sofa table where Tebo had left it. Lucas pointed it out to Chang, and Tebo, who had tried to stay out of the way, now tried being helpful, about to grab the note and pass it to Chang.

"Don't touch it!" shouted Chang.

Lucas confessed, "We already have. Both of us. Sorry, but we tampered with it before realizing how serious the situation was."

"I expected as much from Dr. Sanger, but you, Detective Stonecoat, you should know better," chastised Chang.

Lucas weakly apologized again, but as with Meredyth's

reading of her note and playing the CD—handling both—
Lucas had felt *compelled* to act as he did. "A knee-jerk
reaction to being attacked in this twisted manner," Lucas
told Chang now.

"No doubt," replied the M.E.

"Like I said, at first I thought it was a sick prank."

"Prank, this?" asked Perelli as he snapped shot after
shot of what lay in Lucas's kitchen sink.

"Maybe some of the guys down at the precinct or the
morgue. You know how they can be, sick SOBs that they
are. Keep it to yourself, though, will you, Perelli?"

"You don't think I had anything to do with it, do you?"
asked Ted Hoskins, his eyes riveted on Lucas for a reaction.

"No . . . never crossed my mind, Ted. I know you'd be
no part of such as this, no."

"Well . . . it does look like precision cuts from liver,
spleen, kidney, and pancreas," Chang thoughtfully mused
as he poked a retracted scalpel at the materials inside the
box. "I can understand your thinking it came from a crime
lab. The slices are the work of a careful professional, or
someone who has studied autopsy work. Certainly someone using the right tools. Amazing what an amateur can do
with the right tools. Remember the I-10 sniper? Turned out
to be a kid with his first scoped AK-74."

"You can tell all that from just looking?" asked Tebo.

"Absolutely," replied Chang. "First impressions are usually right. Whoever cut out the eyes and removed the two
front teeth, he knew precisely what to do and how to do it.
Again, unless these tissues, organs, and teeth were already
excised for him, which is Lucas's hopeful theory, this fellow
has access to precision tools and is skilled in using them."

"Makes it the more horrible," said Meredyth, who had
gnashed her teeth and gasped on seeing what had been forwarded to Lucas. Meredyth held a handkerchief to her nostrils to fend off the foul odors of the decaying matter sent
to Lucas. "This has to be from a separate victim," she said
now. "It's older, further along in decay."

"Your eyes and nose deceive you. Unlike the soft tissue

of the eyes, left whole, these internal organs—hard tissue that has been split off from the organs—already have a strong odor about them. Like cutting into an onion, you release the odors." Everyone followed Chang's explanation. "These internal cold cuts, if you will, are actually quite fresh, like the eyes. It will be surprising if they did not come from the same source."

The out-of-place human organ materials were then quickly scooped into bags, which were sealed and removed, along with all the paper and wood and Styrofoam that had housed them. Chang said good night as his techs filed out.

Tebo took a deep breath and shook his head after the retreating CSI team. Lucas said to his friend, "Thanks for hanging on here all this time, Jack."

"No problem . . . don't mention it. Wonder why people always say don't mention it just after someone mentions it. Little late by then, right?" He laughed, trying to get the other two to laugh with him. They did not.

"Good night, Jack," Lucas said.

Tebo hesitated, something on his mind.

"What is it?" asked Lucas, certain it had to do with Eunice. She'd been here, seen the package, and she'd be spreading the word from here to the Coushatta Reservation by morning. The *moccasin grapevine* in the hands of a truly vociferous specialist was wonderful to behold.

Tebo knew Lucas's conclusion, reading it in his eye. "Never mind. We'll talk tomorrow. Good night, Dr. Sanger, Lucas."

They were alone with one another now, and Lucas asked Meredyth if she wanted anything to drink.

"I'll have some of that Mexican gin you like so much."

"Tequila? You?"

"If it'll help me sleep tonight, yes, unless you have a better suggestion."

"Well . . . matter of fact, I do have my own remedy for insomnia."

She gave him a knowing look. She knew of his drug habit, that it was linked to his accident and near-death experience of years before, that it helped him to maintain a front in his personal war against the pain that was ever with him. She knew he smoked marijuana and peyote for *medicinal* purposes, and at times he drank to excess.

She watched him go into his bedroom, and following, she saw him scrounge beneath the bed and come out with a cigar box. "This stuff won't leave you with a hangover."

"Promise?"

He pulled forth a pipe and his stash of Texas reservation peyote. "Old Indian cure-all. Come on, let's get comfortable." He led her back into the living room, tossed some pillows on the floor, and got down on the rug, crossing his legs. She sat alongside in her jeans, also cross-legged now.

"So, this is how you stay so loose," she said.

"You've known for some time, I'm sure. Poking around in my medical records. I know you've got friends in Dallas can tell you all about me." Lucas lit the pipe, took a long drag on it, and passed it to her.

Meredyth cautiously breathed in the smoke, and still she coughed, making him laugh. She tried a second puff, and succeeded without coughing this time.

"That's it, right, Mere. You're on your way to the Cherokee promised land now! I *guaran-damn-tee* you, darling," he promised. "Going where nothing bad can happen ever again."

"That's all I ask . . . at least for now."

CHAPTER 4

Headdress: ceremonial dance

THE FOLLOWING DAY, Lucas awoke in Meredyth's arms, a place he had sought on and off for as long as they had known each other, but this time it felt right. He sensed her comfort in his arms, and he reached around her, holding her closer, tighter, filling his nostrils with the smell of her hair, all the while wondering when and how they had made it to the bedroom from the living room.

Her eyes came open, and she tenderly, longingly returned his embrace, until soon they were locked in a passionate kiss.

When she broke it off, coming up for air, she said, "That peyote works wonders."

"Here I thought it was me . . ."

"I was referring to sleep."

"Then you slept restfully?"

"I did, and I dreamed."

"A pleasant dream, I hope," he replied.

"Dreamed of a world of clouds to walk on and waterfalls to stand beneath, of a warm spray of water cleansing my body, and there were hillsides of flowers and roaming deer, birds overhead, a lake, a canoe, snowcapped mountains in the sky and reflected in the lake."

"Sounds like Indian paradise. The peyote payoff, I call it," he joked.

"It was beautiful, Lucas. A million miles of far away . . ."

"Were you alone or was I there?" he asked.

"You came into the viewfinder about the time I woke up."

"Figures!" He placed a finger to her cheek, tracing a line to her lips before he again kissed her. She leaned into him, and their bodies tingled against one another. He inched downward and buried his face in her bosom, nibbling at her neck, biting at her bra, and making sounds like a wolf. Lucas became hard and firm, and Meredyth responded by sinking her teeth into his shoulder and sucking on his skin, bringing up a red welt.

"You're now officially a marked man," she joked, and seriously added, "and no one, not even your Tsali, can have you now. And no one but I can be your cactus flower. Only me."

"I'm all yours," he promised, then gently rolled further atop her and passionately found her. Together they entwined, becoming one sentient being with a single purpose.

Their lovemaking rose to a crescendo and ended in mutual exhaustion, until she revived Lucas, and their playfulness turned again into burning passions that rose anew like a flame from the ashes. The loving continued for another hour in waves, eddies of shivering passion. Finally, they lay in the aftermath of their passions, their lovemaking over, and Lucas climbed from the bed. He began putting on his pants.

"Hey! Where're you going so fast, *Injun*?" she complained.

"I'm going to rustle you up some breakfast, sweetheart," he said with an exaggerated Texas drawl.

"Don't you think we ought to . . . you know . . . at least talk about what just happened?"

"Don't analyze it, Mere. It's why we've never made it as a couple in the past."

"What do you mean?"

"Oh, God, here we go."

"What do you mean?" she repeated.

"You . . . you and your . . . *shrinking response*! I'm beginning to think it's your coping mechanism, your way of pushing me away whenever we get intimate."

"Shrinking response . . . Clever, very clever, but what's that supposed to mean? And since when did you start using words like *coping mechanism* and *intimate*? You been sneaking episodes of Phil and Oprah?"

"I don't want to get into another disagreeable confrontation with you over a perfectly natural fondness we have for one another. Just let it be, like the song says."

"Fondness? Is that what this is, a *fondness* for one another? Is that how we wound up in bed together last night? And come to think of it, how did you get me in bed last night? And you call it fondness? We make mad passionate love this morning, and it's out of a *fondness*?"

"How do I know how we wound up in bed? If you don't want to accept the fact that I genuinely care about you, then blame it on the peyote."

"Seriously, how did we wind up in bed last night?" she asked.

"I don't know." He shrugged and disappeared as a pillow came at his head.

With him gone, she lay back in the bed, smiling, secretly pleased with the direction they had gone in. Perhaps this time the bond would be stronger than the sum of all her fears, fears that had kept her at arm's length from Lucas all the years they had known one another. He had always represented a dark and perilous ocean to her, a man she thought dangerous, a man who made her lose herself entirely at the end of his fingertips. She even feared telling him this simple truth.

She got up, showered, and dressed, and in a happy frame of mind, she found him in the kitchen, the sink having been thoroughly Ajaxed. With the smell of bleach and

bacon competing, Meredyth attempted to continue the bedroom topic over breakfast. "Are we just going to call it a
drug-induced stupor—what has happened between us—or
are we going to pursue a lasting relationship, Lucas?"

"I would like to keep you, Meredyth, but not at the price
of analyzing every action I take, every g'damn word I say."

"Whatever are you talking about? God, you can be
so . . . so . . ."

"Fond of you? Like when I said the word, you felt compelled to ridicule it. I meant it in the best of all possible . . .
meanings."

"What about love? Would you say what we have
between us is *love*?"

He clenched his jaw and hesitated a moment.

"Well, Chief?" she pressed.

"Yes, damn it, I believe it is."

"Is what?"

"Is what you said."

"Is what I said? What'd I say?"

"You know . . . what you said."

"You can't even bring yourself to say it, can you?"

"Maybe because of the fact that you, Mere, have always
made it clear that . . . that guys like Byron . . . or someone
like him are more suited to you and your social standing
and the lifestyle to which you've become accustomed."

"After last night and what he did, trust me, Byron isn't
suited to me in any way, shape, or form. He's history. I
should have known him better than I did."

"Oh, really? I didn't know. Then I'm the rebound
guy . . . maybe?"

"No, Lucas, I've always . . ." Now she hesitated.

"Always what?"

"Felt great . . . *fondness* for you; it's just that I've also
always . . . well, always . . ."

"Always what?"

". . . also *feared* loving, that is, *feeling fondly* toward
you as well."

"Come on. What's to fear?"

"You'll break my heart, one way or another. Your job

for one. If I let myself love you as totally and completely as I want to, and something should happen to you . . . I'd be . . . devastated."

He stood and walked around to the table to her, and taking her in his arms, he kissed her anew. They embraced for some time, their clothing beginning to shed, when a phone call interrupted them.

"Damn, let it ring," she said.

He kissed her deeply, probing her mouth with his tongue. As he did so, he lifted the receiver and listened to the voice on the phone. He pulled back from her lips, held the phone up and away, covering the mouthpiece with his hand, and said, "It's Uncle Tebo. Curious if we know anymore about last night's goings-on." He then spoke into the phone and urged Tebo to have patience. "Not even Chang works that fast. By the way, tell no one about this. I don't want it broadcast in the *Res Report* at the Coushatta, any more than I want it in the *Houston Chronicle,* okay?" he finished, and hung up knowing he'd asked the impossible of Tebo.

"Take me home, will you, Lucas? I really have to change before going in this morning."

"Maybe you ought to take some time off, visit a relative or friend. Leastways go stay at your parents' house in Clover Leaf like Leonard said."

"Get outta Dodge, you mean? Run and hide? Nice try, and thanks for the protective thoughts, but I'll be damned if I'm going to let some nutcase chase me from my home and duties. No, I've got a full calendar both at the precinct and at my private office downtown. So, if you don't mind, sweetheart, get me there on time."

AS THEY PULLED up to Meredyth's condo, he pointed out the doorman and asked, "Is that the fellow who delivered the bundle of eyes to your door, Mere?"

"No, that's Max. You want the day man, Stu. Max comes on at ten P.M."

"So when does Stu come on duty?"

"Nine, nine-thirty in the morning, somewhere in there."

"Someone needs to grill him about who handed him the package. Maybe we can get a composite going."

"I'm sure he'll cooperate. I'll ask him to drop by the Thirty-first on my way out. Now stop worrying," she said, exiting the car. "You do *love* me, don't you?"

"I do, Mere. I've always loved you, but you know that."

"I haven't . . . not always, not when you were with Tsali."

"That was a mistake. I know that now."

She leaned in though the window and kissed him good-bye.

"Are you sure you're up to driving?" he asked.

"Worrywart. Lucas, I want my own car, and I want to walk through that door and up to my home without fear. I won't be *run out* of my apartment any more than I'll be *run out* of my life."

"Despite my misgivings, I respect your motives and wishes, so I am smiling and saying see you later, my white Anglo beauty."

Meredyth waved him off as he pulled away from the curb. In his rearview, he watched her go toward the safety of her door. Earlier, he had scanned the entire street, looking in all directions for anyone appearing suspicious or overly interested in either of them. The only one seeming to take notice of Meredyth was the night-shift doorman, who courteously opened the door for her as he chimed, "Good morning, Dr. Sanger. I do hope all is resolved and you won't have any further problems."

"Thanks, Max, and would you have Stuart ring me upstairs when he comes on? I have to speak with him."

"Sure, sure, Dr. Sanger."

"Thanks, Max, and for your concern last night and this morning."

"Don't mention it, ma'am. Only wish I coulda done more, Dr. Sanger. If you'd like, I could ride up to your place with you, have a look around before you go inside, if you'd like, I mean."

"That won't be necessary, Max. I'm the only one with a key, and it's thirty floors up. Not likely to be anyone lurking inside, but thanks for the thought all the same."

Max tipped his hat to her and nodded. "You're welcome, ma'am, Doctor."

She went for the elevator, feeling Max's eyes on her, curious or sympathetic, most likely both. She also wondered at the creeping inchworm of doubt that suggested that Max or Stu or any number of people she saw on a daily basis in the building could have had something to do with frightening the hell out of her and Byron the previous night. Foolish thought, she reasoned, but when the elevator door opened, she had to smile at four people exiting the building who smiled back, all long-term tenants save one, the newest face in the building, a petite but buxom young girl in jogging suit, her Jack Bull terrier straining at his leash as they exited the elevator.

"Morning."

"Morning."

"Morning."

"Morning."

They all sounded genuine; they all looked harmless enough. They all also had heard something about police and a coroner's van having descended on their condo homes. She could only imagine the buzz at the next owners association meeting.

How much did her neighbors know? How much had Max already revealed to the people living in the building? Who was that new girl? What'd she do for a living? Wasn't there some association rule about dogs in the building when she had bought into her condo? What had happened with that?

The elevator doors closed on Meredyth, and she found herself alone with all the dizzying bombardment of questions and the whirring vibration of the cab ascending to her floor. "Who's wanting to make me fear my own neighbors?" she asked aloud.

She arrived at her floor, glad to exit the confining cab and briskly walked to her door. But she was stopped on seeing a note tucked beneath the knocker. It made her pause.

"Likely just a concerned neighbor," she told herself. She stepped up to the door and snatched the note open.

It was from Byron. A note of apology. Said he'd been back to look in on her. Felt panicked at being unable to reach her by phone. Tried her parents' house in Clover Leaf. When that failed, tried driving out to Lake Madera to the ranch house getaway, but car threw a gasket. Repair took hours. Returned here by cab, knocked knuckles raw. Gave up. Again sorry for rude behavior in having abandoned her when she most needed him. Signed By.

"Fuck you, Byron," she replied, pushed the door open, and stepped into her home.

The message light on the phone blinked so rapidly it seemed to be screaming at her. Byron, no doubt.

As she changed, she thought of how best to break it off with him. What she really wanted to break off, however, would get her jail time.

ONCE AT HIS Precinct 31 basement office, Lucas Stonecoat found his wide oak desk as cluttered as ever with pending caseload work—Houston criminal cases gone unsolved for generations, known as cold cases. Cold casework had become Lucas's expertise, as he had spearheaded tracking the backlog for a decade now. When he had first come on as a Cold Case detective, he'd found the basement offices here a cluttered library filled with dust-laden files and boxes bulging with the murder books on people whose often violent and mysterious deaths had gone unanswered and untangled. Confronted by whole walls from floor to ceiling filled with files Lucas had transferred to computer disks. The old files themselves were in the process of being destroyed, most already at the city dump incinerators, but one murder file had intrigued Lucas, had in effect called out to him, and so he had set it aside, saving it from destruction. Its uploaded counterpart on the computer screen didn't have the same aura of spirit surrounding the hard file and the actual crime-scene photos, only three of which could be transferred to the database, that number having been agreed upon by those in charge in order to save on memory.

Lucas had stockpiled hundreds of murder-scene photos dating as far back as the 1890's with the intention of creating a publishable book with comments on each photo from a forensic photographer—Perelli, a forensic shrink—Meredyth, and a murder cop—himself. But the project had bogged down as all of them were kept so busy in their respective fields, and while Lucas himself dealt with overseeing the enormous task of transferring hard files to disk. While he had a crack team of men and women under his direction who worked independently and well without a lot of supervision, the Cold Room created its own steady stream of work-related headaches.

Lucas had been assigned the Cold Room files from the moment he had walked into Precinct 31, and he had made the task his own, coordinating with every precinct in the city to create a database of Cold Cases for use across the city, the state, and the nation. While the COMIT program had limitations, he had had the files cross-referenced with Detective Jana North's Missing Persons division. She had unsolved cases dating back to the 1920's. She'd admired what he had done with the Cold Case murder books, and now she was coordinating MP files in other jurisdictions with her own, modeling the COMIT in her area of expertise. Other cities, across the state and the nation, had begun to fashion similar programs after the Houston model, and as a result, Lucas had often been called away to assist in developing those programs. Even the FBI had taken an interest in COMIT, giving Lucas an opportunity to visit Washington, D.C., and to meet such luminaries as the Director of the FBI and forensic guru Dr. Jessica Coran.

Even more impressive, Dallas, his former home and police department, with which he had parted on very bad terms, had put in a request for his help after all these years. Dallas PD had refused to pay him compensation for the injuries he'd sustained when he and Wallace Lafayette Jackson—both off duty at the time—had given chase after a young Hispanic-black hellion who had been terrorizing the city with a robbery spree growing increasingly violent. They'd expected the robbery spree to escalate to murder at any time. Jackson had been driving, and when they cornered Elzono, Jackson's car careened into the suspect's car, the impact setting Jackson's car ablaze. Jackson was shot and slumped over at the wheel as Lucas leaped from the fiery vehicle, returning fire under a hail of bullets from Elzono. Lucas killed the young man, later made into a saint of the neighborhood, Hector "Malcolm X" Elzono, who, after seeing the movie and reading the book, had proclaimed himself, "The reincarnation of Malcolm, returned from Hell, ready to set this world on fire, man!"

All bullshit, as Elzono's interpretation of X and his Muslim teachings was as perverted as the teachings of Al Quaeda.

Jackson, hit in the chest, was enveloped in smoke and flame and burned alive while Lucas fought to pull him free of the inferno, Elzono still shooting and laughing at the sight. Finally, Lucas's aim sent Elzono to his grave, and with Elzono shot dead, Lucas tried even more desperately to pull the trapped Jackson from the flames. Lucas burned his hands, arms, cheek, and neck in the failed attempt. He had also been hit by bullets, and had suffered head and internal injuries in the crash. Lucas would spend almost a year in rehabilitation while fighting for compensation from the Dallas department.

Dallas's Internal Affairs jumped on the alcohol content in Lucas's system, and that in the seared body of Jackson as well. Following policy, the department denied benefits to either man, and Lucas wound up suing for both himself and for Jackson's family. He won his case only after years of struggle and condemnation on both sides. Lucas had had to start over in Houston, but not as a detective. He'd had to prove himself over again, starting from the bottom rung as a new recruit, and even after beating these odds and overcoming his physical problems, still Houston PD, remembering Dallas, placed him on desk duty here in the Cold Room. However, Lucas had not let the desk ride him. He pursued cold cases with the vengeance and tenacity of any competent detective pursuing a muder, disregarding the negatives, and as a result, he spent as much time on the streets, tracking criminals, as any detective on the force. His aggressiveness had earned him the respect of others, commendations, and a gold shield—reinstatement as a murder cop, a detective. He had made the best of it, and now he ran the place, having solved more cold cases than anyone in the history of the room, surpassing even the fabled Detective Maurice Remo, who had run the CC room for thirty years, retiring as Lucas had come on.

Given his bad history with Dallas, he understood why HPD brass had placed him on unsolved cases. They wanted to keep him off the streets, and they fully expected little of him beyond keeping the records tidy. The idiots had no idea how Maurice Remo and other good CC cops operated. After the grueling hours on the phone, running down people who were often in geriatric care or even dead, a Cold Case cop had to commit to a theory like a Jack Bull terrier sinks his teeth into it, and this meant hitting the pavement, ringing doorbells, interviewing, cinching a lead, following up, locking on, arrest, and interrogation—the entire gamut of the hunt.

The brass hadn't expected the Indian Cold Case worker to know anything about computers either, but again they were wrong. COMIT was a program he instituted with the help of able others. Even the FBI were now modeling their unsolved backlog storage program on the COMIT model.

Lucas thumbed open the old dusty file that had caught his attention: a skimpy murder book on a young girl named Yolanda Sims, just turned nine years of age, the picture of an angel in 1956—the year of her death. She had been found with a scarf tied tightly around her neck, and the assumption of death by manual strangulation after being tortured, beaten, and raped by some fiend had been dismissed by the pathology report made out by a Dr. Wisniewski, who signed off as Wiz. The strangulation with the scarf came after death by internal hemorrhaging from the beatings about the head and abdomen. The odds of her killer being found alive today were slim at best, but the girl remained unavenged, and the eyes in her photo struck Lucas to the core, asking, "If the monster is alive, he has enjoyed fifty years of life that should have been mine. So what're you going to do about it?"

The odd features of the crime itself posited few clues. She had sawdust in her natty hair and over her nude body. Aside from a closed adult fist, a carpet layer's nail-filled wood stripping had been used in beating her. She had cigar-sized, round burns on her legs and arms from a large soldering iron—said Wiz. She had been brutalized with what the coroner thought a screwdriver, and finally she had bled to death of internal wounds. The girl's body was left on a doorstep of a home in the southwest corner of the Jacinto City area, at the exact house number as hers but one block over from her house. The geography, the buildings, the neighborhood must be all entirely different now, and most certainly relatives, friends, neighbors—all different, older, moved on, and moved out. Nearly fifty years had come and gone. What hope of ever solving this little girl's murder now?

Still, something about the deep pools that were the black girl's eyes, the cut of her dimples, her pigtails, the simple cloth dress, the smile in the life photo comparing so starkly with the empty eyes and down-turned lips of the death photo. It all spoke to Lucas, pleading with him to take the next step. "What is the next step?" he asked himself. Talk to her parents? Was either alive? Talk to her brother, her sister, her uncles and aunts? Some of them were younger than she was when the crime was committed; they'd be in their forties and fifties now. What could they possibly know that might help? Would any family member care to go there with Lucas as guide? Besides, hadn't the original investigative team asked all the pertinent questions of all the pertinent family members? Perhaps not. Lucas's reputation for uncovering blunders piled upon blunders in earlier cold cases had earned him recognition and kudos from most, but it never endeared him to the cops his investigating had revealed as bungling. In other cases, it wasn't so much the errors of investigators as the *era* of ignorance of such scientific breakthroughs as criminal profiling, technological advances, and DNA fingerprinting.

Law enforcement had learned a great deal about child abduction and murder since '56, such as the fact that only 20 percent of child abductions fell under the umbrella of stranger abductions, that the other 80 percent were abductions by someone known to have had at least some passing acquaintance with the victim. The Ward Weavers of the world came to mind, those who wooed their victims with promises and gifts and a place to stay the night, a place to light up on weed, a place to hide from their own threatening home life.

The 1956 police reports proved sketchy as Lucas's eyes scanned over the aged paper and the old script. There was a record of the detectives having talked to the parents, but a reading between the lines spoke of a bigoted—or at least jaded—police force that had written them off as shiftless *niggers* whose lifestyle had brought the tragedy down around young Yolanda's head. Unofficially, the dead child's parents were at very least negligent, having allowed a live-in uncle to send the nine-year-old out after dark for cigarettes and coffee. She made it back with the grocery bag, and was allowed to play out back of the house as a reward. The child then disappeared from their backyard, skirted by an alleyway, and she was returned later, dumped on the doorstep of a home a block over. The numbers on the two homes corresponding as they did—1214 Denton—*Yolanda's home*—to 1214 Denby Street—*home of startled neighbors who'd discovered Yolanda's body and called police*—nagged at Lucas, tugging like a fish on a line. He pictured the startled neighbors trying to explain to a desk sergeant over the phone what lay on their front steps, this *before the days of 911 emergency dialing.*

One of the original detectives felt the killer had confused the two addresses on his return. If this were true, then the killer couldn't have been a long-time resident of the neighborhood, like the girl's uncle, who had a record of burglaries, or the neighborhood dirty old man, or the pair of teens brought in for questioning. In fact, Yolanda's killer might be a total stranger to the area, and so not likely known in the area. Somebody would notice a stranger in a close-knit community, or someone new to the block, but how close-knit was this area in 1956? Was there a welcome wagon lady in the area who might know of anyone recently moved in, and if so, was she still alive for questioning? Not likely on both counts.

Lucas wondered about the possibility of a recently released sex offender taking up residence at a time when news of such releases was not divulged to the public. He thought of pursuing such a record, lost to time. What prison would he begin with, Huntsville? It was the nearest, but hardly the only one in the state.

An aged black man had been hauled in for questioning, a man who lived a few doors down. Sixty-two-year-old Jacob Perry, a man with a record for attempted molestation of a minor, was known for hanging about the schools and parks of Jacinto, always with an eye on the local children, but the detectives could not shake his alibi. He'd gone into the hospital that weekend for a hip replacement. Besides, reasoned Lucas from the standpoint of fifty years of police growth and hindsight, since the "dirty old man" was well versed in the terrain, he would have known the child's address and *not* confused it with a corresponding number a block away.

"Unless he was suffering from Alzheimer's," Lucas told himself now.

A pair of young thugs from the neighborhood were also questioned, Donnell Knight and Rory Billings, both of whom knew the neighborhood intimately. The detectives on the case reasoned the boys might have *deliberately* dumped the girl's sexually molested, tortured, and brutally beaten body on the wrong doorstep to throw suspicion away from themselves, but by the same token, police interrogators deemed the young men stupid and sloppy, seemingly contradicting their own findings. And it had been Lucas's experience that, despite popular novels and films glorifying the evil genius of killers such as Hannibal Lecter, ninety-nine percent of murderers were far too stupid to know how to divert attention away from themselves, and in practice, when they tried, it created a net thrown over themselves. In this case, the two boys' families alibied for them and they too were released.

Lucas read on. A year passed without any breaks in the case, and the thin little emaciated murder book traveled from upstairs to here, the dungeon of dead case files, and here it had remained all these years for Lucas to regard as one of thousands that deserved special heed. He didn't know why it deserved his care now, but it did. Maurice Remo had jumped in on it, when it arrived on his desk, the same desk Lucas sat at now, and the great Remo had not been able to crack the case either. In fact, Remo appeared to have given it short shrift, but he did write some marginal notes indicating that he, like Lucas, ruled out the girl's uncle, the old man, Perry, and the two boys as the killer based on the known evidence. Remo's signature on a routing sheet hinted at more information, perhaps a second volume to the investigation, but Lucas could find no additional tombstone in the paper cemetery he called home.

Maurice Remo was likely in a Florida retirement community by now, if not passed away. Lucas pushed the file to a corner of his desk, as if the gesture would put an end to its nagging him; he firmly told himself that pursuing it would only be a waste of time.

In an effort to escape Yolanda Sims, he got on the phone and called upstairs to Chang's lab, anxious now to learn anything new about the godawful packages forwarded to Meredyth and him. When he located Leonard in his morgue, he asked, "Anything you can tell me about last night's findings at my and Meredyth's place?"

"Blood and serum tests show it's all from same body as I suspected. DNA typing is ongoing. Will take more time. Pretty sure now we have a young female, somewhere between seventeen and twenty-nine or thirty . . . healthy tissues, all of it."

"Then it's either from a murder victim or materials stolen from some medical facility, likely a morgue."

"So far as I can tell you, we here can account for *all* human tissues and organs, nothing missing or stolen."

"So far?"

"I have Dr. Lynn Nielsen doing the work, investigating two weeks of intake and output, paperwork to burial, and what's remaining in our freezer units. Of course, most of the bodies we process go either to one of the potter's fields or into the hands of family, and in turn into the care of a local mortician who preps 'em for funeral and burial services. Along that route, any number of people might have absconded off with body parts, especially if it's a close-lid affair."

"With missing eyes, I should hope so."

"News out of Florida has been full of unscrupulous morticians, but I don't know of *any* who's packaged up body parts and forwarded them to police personnel, do you?"

"No . . . no, that's a new wrinkle, Leonard."

"So far, Dr. Nielsen has found *no* discrepancies to indicate anyone stole anything from us," Chang reiterated. "They don't call me *No Waste* for nothing, Lucas."

"I always thought that referred to your slim *waist,* Doc."

"Both, I'm told. Of course, you know, Lucas, the parts *could* have come from another lab, morgue, or medical school."

"And you found no indication of cause of death, no toxins, no disease?" Lucas asked.

"No, nothing points to cause of death. Eyes show none of the microscopic hemorrhaging, no telltale signs of strangulation in the tissue. Nor do any of the tissue cuts show any sign of toxins or disease."

"A perfectly healthy woman without a name or a face." Lucas leaned back in his chair, his weight making it squeal. "What's our next step, Leonard?"

"Well, on the chance the human materials were stolen from someone's care, I took the liberty and contacted every hospital in the state with its own morgue where autopsies can be legally performed by trained pathologists. The number is considerably smaller than you might think. Only a few counties still allow hospital morgues to perform autopsies, and even these must be affiliated with a medical school or with the city or state Medical Examiner's Office."

"That's a good thing, isn't it?"

"Better reporting of suspicious and unknown cause of death, yes."

"I guess the number of funeral parlors in and around greater Houston is too astronomical to begin to contemplate. And I doubt anyone's going to phone in to tell us they've lost a pair of eyes, teeth, and four slices from a cadaver's abdominal organs."

As usual, Leonard did not always follow Lucas's sarcasm. He flatly replied, "Not all morgues have responded yet, but so far, none admit to having lost any human tissue whatsoever on the scale we are talking about here."

Lucas momentarily wondered if Chang meant to imply that there was an *acceptable* scale of medical waste and tissue loss in most hospitals, that this was chalked up to the cost of doing business. "Any way to get help from the teeth?" he asked.

"Absolutely, yes. DNA from the marrow is being matched to DNA from the organ parts. And if we find someone to match teeth to, then they will be of great benefit."

"My money's on it all coming from the same body . . . same person."

"I told Dr. Sanger this is my suspicion too."

"She called you?"

"Stopped by."

"Then she's in her office?"

"I suspect so by now, yes."

"Thanks, Leonard. I'm going to interface with Missing Persons. See if anything pops there."

"Pops?"

"Matches, makes any connection."

"Ahh, I see . . . yes. But first you may want to speak with Dr. Purvis, our expert forensic ophthalmologist. She knows a lot more about eyes than I do, so I left the eyes with her."

"Purvis, sure. I'll do that."

"Oh, and by the way, Lucas, Kim and the kids keep asking me to have you over again. You were a big hit with my girls."

"Yeah, I'd like that sometime soon, Leonard. Say hello to the kids and your beautiful wife for me."

Lucas hung up and called Dr. Catrina Purvis. She could only add in a painfully strident voice that the eyes were in need of correcting, that the owner would have worn a serious prescription with more than one prism. "She could not have worn contacts. Somewhere there's a pair of relatively thick, certainly expensive glasses gone missing. She would have worn them everywhere."

"You can tell that from dead eyes?"

"With today's technology, yes."

"Thanks, that helps, Doctor."

Lucas then telephoned Sergeant Stan Kelton at the front desk, asking if Meredyth Sanger's day doorman, Stu, had either called or come into the precinct. Kelton had not heard from the man. Lucas suggested he call Meredyth, get the number, and strongly urge Stu to come down to help with a composite on the delivery person. Kelton, who knew only what was the buzz about the case, agreed to take care of the matter. "And call Jack Tebo to come in and do the same. He spoke to the delivery person who showed up at my place." Lucas gave him Tebo's number.

Lucas hung up and then opened his computer, logging on and going to the MP files. He scanned for *recent* missing females—recent disappearances, females between the ages of seventeen and thirty, according to Change's estimates of age, gender, and the freshness of the stolen human tissues.

Just then Meredyth came through his door. The Cold Room was open to any and all detectives and personnel who might have a vested interest in a Cold Case, and consequently, the door was opening and closing all the time. Lucas's focus was on his computer, and he assumed whoever had entered would sign for anything they'd come for, be it a hard copy file or a floppy disk. Lucas kept working.

Meredyth reached her hands out to him, taking his shoulders in her grasp, causing him to flinch in surprise. "Hey, Wolf Clan man, it's only me," she said, soothing him, referring to his clan name. "God, you're as tense as I am over this thing, aren't you?" Then seeing the array of photos of young women on his screen, she half-joked, "What're you delving into here, a lonely-hearts-dot-com singles match website?"

"Missing Persons files, Mere. They're on-line now, and I'm trying to match what we know of the body parts to anyone on this list," he said, pointing to the screen. "Look at them, all sizes, shapes, ages—the missing souls of a nation." He typed in Texas, narrowing the field. Houston and vicinity narrowed it. Finally, he called for a fifty-mile radius from downtown Houston. With each new request, the numbers of the missing dwindled, allowing more focus. When he narrowed his search by age, the files and corresponding photos came up fast and furiously. There were nine people missing. He then limited search parameters to only those missing in the last seventy-two hours.

Seven files and photos remained. Lucas had to click on the photo to go into each file.

Lucas began the process, taking each in alphabetical order, unsure what he was looking for beyond those beautiful sea-blue pupils he'd seen on Meredyth's carpet. "We can rule out all but the blue-eyed missing," he said, asking the computer to comply, and this narrowed the number to four. He then narrowed them to girls wearing corrective lenses. "Catrina Purvis tells me whoever belongs to the eyes, she had a serious prescription with prisms."

"Really? She's good."

"Jane Doe was a four-eyes. Wore them everywhere."

This latest entry narrowed his search to three remaining young women. Meredyth looked on with interest. The youngest MP was nineteen, a Helga Muncie, the oldest at twenty-eight, a woman named Mira Lourdes, and the third a girl of twenty-one named Irma Nance. "Any one of them might have once carried those eyes and teeth in her head," said Lucas. "Or else none of them have any *connection* to the wayward eyes."

"Oh, the wayward eye is a restless eye," sang out Dave Casey as he passed by. "Everybody's heard, Lucas, about your encounter last night."

"That thrills me, Dave. How's the Conroe case going?"

"Plodding along."

Lucas returned his gaze to the screen, staring at the photos of the three remaining possible victims, all of whom had disappeared without a trace. He tried to will himself to recognize the eyes. Helga's looked close, Mira's looked closer, and Irma's looked closest. Then, on a second go-round, they all looked closest. "No way to tell from the photos. For one, the glasses they wear obscure the eyes."

"Stare long enough and all you see are the eyes," Meredyth muttered, still holding his shoulders.

He clicked on the photo of Helga Muncie, opening the first of the three files. "This'll take some time."

She looked at her watch. "I've got a group session upstairs I've got to be at, and then I've got to get uptown." She looked around, saw no one else at the other desks in the room was watching, and pressed a kiss to the back of his neck. "Let me hear from you if anything should click."

"Will do, but it may take some fieldwork. Only so far a computer screen will take you."

"Keep me apprised, will you?"

"Sure thing." He patted her hand on his shoulder, but his eyes remained on the screen as he began reading the first file.

Lucas didn't recall seeing Meredyth leave, and he took each of the MP files in turn, studying them in order with an eye to eliminating his search further, but instead, he had to hold Helga's file in abeyance. Perhaps it had been Helga's eyes.

One by one, he read through the details of each story, the information supplied by family members, friends, coworkers about the missing person, nothing but shining accolades. No one in any of the three cases had the slightest notion how their loved one or friend could simply vanish, but in each case they had.

When he looked up again from the computer files, it was nearing two in the afternoon, and he hadn't eaten. His research had focused in on how much trouble each girl had with her eyes. Unfortunately, all three had serious sight problems and eyewear. Still, he felt good that he'd been able to narrow his search from hundreds to only these three.

Lucas again called Chang. "I've narrowed my search from reported missing persons cases that might match the unusual circumstances of our case down to three, Leonard."

"Fantastic."

"From these three, I'm going to obtain dental records on each, and we'll get your pal Davies to see if any of them are a match with the teeth found at Meredyth's." Dr. Thomas Phillip Davies, the forensic orthodontist Lucas referred to, had already extracted DNA from the teeth for Chang.

"Wonderful idea. Good work. I've already provided the teeth for Dr. Davies, so when time comes, let us know."

"Thanks again." Lucas hung up and then he called upstairs to Meredyth's office, hoping to catch her and update her on his progress, but he was informed that she'd left for her private practice and could be reached there in an hour. He decided to get a bite to eat and call her afterward.

He ran a hard copy of the three files he thought could be a match to the eyes and teeth. He'd spend the afternoon obtaining the dental records he required, knowing it would be tough to get these, as all three files indicated dental records had *not* been forwarded for *any* of them. He wondered how common an oversight this was in Missing Persons, and made a mental note to ask Jana North about this.

Now, unfortunately, it was left to him to locate first permission and then the actual dental records for each young woman. He must make the request via the next of kin, and had to impress upon them how urgent his need was. Such a request would trigger fears in family members, and since they didn't know him, they would be doubly wary, slowing him with questions, getting their hopes up, as well as arousing misgivings, old doubts, regrets, and fears. Dental records usually meant a match with a corpse if a match were to be made at all.

He knew at this stage he must involve Detective Jana North, Missing Persons. She had done most of the work of logging on all the MP files in the COMIT system. He knew her well and trusted her. She'd be an asset in going after the dental records of each of the girls Lucas proposed investigating. Certainly, she had far greater experience in dealing with anxiety-ridden, bereaved loved ones than most of the cops at the precinct put together. He rang her number.

"Have you had lunch yet?" he asked Detective North.

"Matter of fact I haven't, why?" replied Jana. "What'd you have in mind?"

"I haven't eaten either, and I have some cases to go over with you. Meet me at Crazy Calories in ten minutes?"

"I've been seeing your turkey track on the COMIT-MP interface. Something cooking?"

"You found me out."

"Has it to do with rumors I've been hearing about you and Dr. Sanger being targeted by a mad mailer sending packets of body parts?"

"You're well informed. Try to keep a secret around here."

"Make it fifteen minutes and you're on. See you at Crazy's."

Lucas strapped on his gun and put his Wellington overcoat on, going for the door. He called out to other detectives who manned Cold Case desks in the room that he was out for the day, "Tracking leads," he announced.

"Lucky SOB!" Casey shouted in response.

Lucas had looked in on Itchy Arnie Feldman that morning for any sign of foul play on his part, but if Arnie was involved, his poker face gave nothing away. Not the slightest twitch or snicker. Lucas had also dropped in on the M.E., Frank Patterson, and dropped a few hints about what had occurred at his and Sanger's apartments, but didn't find Patterson the least bit edgy or revealing anything in his body language. The cruel incident looked, as time had passed and the day wore on, to have no hoaxsters behind it after all.

Lucas walked the short way to the bistro, his insides screaming for a roast beef sandwich and a drink. In the back of his mind, he knew that the missing persons avenue, while a logical and methodical step to take, might net nothing. Still, he had no other lead at the moment.

He stepped off a curb and a car screeched to a halt inches from his legs. Lucas stared at the driver, his jaw clenched as the man in the car laid on his horn and cursed. The irate driver then leaped from the car, rage on his face as he came toward Lucas with a tire iron.

Lucas snatched out his badge in one hand, his Glock 9mm in the other, extending both to the charging bull's eyes. The beefy red-faced Texan stopped cold, gestured for clemency, backed to his door, climbed into his pickup truck, and roared off, leaving Lucas standing in the street.

"What the hell's the matter with people?" he asked no one in particular as he holstered his weapon.

In a moment, he carried on toward the restaurant, hoping Jana wouldn't keep him waiting long.

CHAPTER 5

Crossing paths

AT THE CRAZY Calories Bistro on a one-block, one-way street in downtown Houston, two blocks from the precinct house, Lucas laid out the situation to Detective Jana North, starting with details of what some sick animal had forwarded to Meredyth and to him the night before.

"So you think the parts might be related to one of our more recent MPs, huh?"

"That's the prints I'm tracking, yeah."

"Damned ugly business, and if I can help you get this guy and clear a case, Lucas, just tell me where and when."

"Today, now. You can help me with the families, to ease the process of getting dental records for each of these young women." He pushed the hard copies run from the computer files across the table to her.

"I heard there were teeth in the mixed bag of goodies sent to you. You're saying none of these three have dental records on file?" she asked while thumbing through the paper files, caught by the photos. "Nice work, narrowing the subjects to three."

"I had help," Lucas said, explaining how he had gotten key search items from forensics, and how Purvis had revealed the victim had a serious vision problem.

"Still, I'm impressed."

"Computer did the rest."

"Thanks to our interfacing program, Lucas."

"And to your cooperation and all the hard work of months of loading all that information, Jana."

She nodded, smiled, and toasted. "To COMIT-MP, may it bring us some resolutions."

"Then you'll ride shotgun for me this afternoon, get these dental records I need?"

She frowned. "Drop everything and race to your aid? Hmmm . . . all right, as a favor to you and Meredyth."

"Thanks, I need this expedited. Any delay could cost us dearly."

She nodded. "Understood. I'll do what I can however I can."

"All I can ask."

They ate and spoke of lighter things, the weather, the lottery, the home teams, the "up" economy. Using her cell phone, Jana called ahead to the families, telling them to expect her visit. After leaving the restaurant, they would go to the first address where they had to obtain proper release signatures to gain access to the needed medical records.

They walked back to the precinct together, and from there took Lucas's unmarked radio car. As he drove, Jana North studied the files of the missing in more depth. "I remember this one case, Lourdes. Odd as hell how she disappeared."

"Tell me about it."

"Only what I know."

She began the story, and Lucas looked across at her from time to time as he drove. Jana North was an auburn-haired, beautiful woman with sparkling blue eyes.

The story of Mira Lourdes's disappearance, while sketchy, involved a so-called eyewitness. Lucas always took this news with more than a grain of salt, knowing that most eyewitness testimony proved false if not downright misleading.

Before Jana could finish her story, they arrived at the home of seventeen-year-old Helga Muncie, a habitual runaway. Runaways more often than not were penniless and relied on hitchhiking to make their way across the country to high-profile places from Aspen, Colorado, to Hollywood, or such destinations as Panama City or Daytona Beach, Florida—magnet communities for teens on the run. Teens on the street proved easy marks for rapists and killers who might encounter them along the thousands of miles of Interstate they traveled to their various false Meccas.

Lucas pulled into the driveway of the Muncie home, left the motor running, and they climbed from the car under the gaze of someone peeking out from behind a curtain. As they approached the house, Jana took note of the yellow ribbons strung about the porch. Lucas rang the bell, and when a middle-aged woman answered the door, Jana took the initiative, flashing her badge and saying, "I'm Detective North with Missing Persons, and Detective Stonecoat here is with the HPD's Cold Cases Division. Show Mrs. Muncie your badge, Lucas."

Lucas did as told, but the lady paid no mind to him, asking Jana through the screen door, "You have news of my Helga? Thomas! Come listen! They have news of Helga!"

"Not exactly, but we're here about Helga, yes, ma'am," replied Lucas.

"We'd like to get those dental records my office requested when you first filed the missing persons report on your daughter, Mrs. Muncie," said Jana.

The father, Thomas Muncie, had come to the door, a gray ghost behind the screen, shouting, "Then you've found her! Haven't you? Dead, dead?"

The woman went weak, collapsing into her husband's arms, as Jana North waved her arms and said, "No, no, no! We're only here to complete her file, Mrs. Muncie. We simply want the dental records in her file."

"Then you've found someone—a body—fitting her

description?" pressed the husband. "You want to compare her dental records with a corpse."

"No, not exactly," replied Jana.

"What then?"

"We're investigating a possible homicide, Mr. Muncie," began Lucas, careful not to stir anywhere near the truth—*a mutilation murder.*

"We want to rule your daughter and two other young women out by process of elimination, sir, ma'am," added Jana. "We need you to sign the release form for the records." Jana held out both the form and a pen. "Just sign on the bottom. I'll fill out the rest. It'll expedite matters . . . for your daughter's good."

"Lies . . . lies," replied the man. "Examining the dental records means you've got a corpse."

"All right . . . Thomas!" shouted the wife. "We do what they tell us. We got no choice. We got to cooperate." She cracked the screen door enough to take form and pen inside, where after a moment's examination, she signed.

"If we thought we had your daughter, sir," said Jana through the screen, "we'd simply have you travel downtown with us to identify her remains."

Mrs. Muncie had regained her composure, and Thomas simply walked off. Mrs. Muncie apologized for her husband in a whisper, and then she said, "Her dentist is Dr. Sullivan, 1240 North Belmont. I'll call ahead, so she will know you're coming." Finished, she pushed the form and the pen back through the cracked screen door and into Jana's waiting hands. Through the screen mesh, she added, "I want you people to let me know when Helga has been ruled out like you say, all right?"

"Absolutely, Mrs. Muncie," Jana assured her.

"Absolutely, really? You young people nowadays use that word to mean *nothing*—bahhh, *absolutely!* Everybody at that police station tells me they will absolutely get back to me, but it has been a week and not a word until you two show up on my doorstep asking for dental records. Two people I don't know. Where is Detective Ambrose? Where is Detective Sculley?"

Lucas wanted to point out that it hadn't yet been a week, only seventy-seven hours, but he curbed his tongue. Jana handed the woman her card. "You can call me tomorrow afternoon, and any time. Detectives Ambrose and Sculley work for me, Mrs. Muncie."

The woman stared at Jana as if seeing her anew.

Lucas thanked Mrs. Muncie for the name and address of the dentist, and they stepped off her porch. "Moments like this make me feel ill," said Jana. "It's so difficult dealing with the loved ones."

"Empty feeling inside, I know. Makes me feel like a scavenging crow." Lucas stepped up the pace to his waiting car.

Leaning in over the top of the car, Jana said, "We *try* to get the relatives to forward us all medical and dental records when the case becomes official. Short of that, we *try* to get them to sign a release, so we can obtain records on our own, but a lot of people at that early stage simply have a psychological block about getting it done, you know?"

"Can't say as I blame them. Can't imagine the pain of losing a child to oblivion, the not knowing, or losing a child to a vicious murderer and knowing, for that matter."

"Not sure which is worse."

They got in the car. Inside, Jana said, "Short of a DNA sample, orthodontia ID is still the most reliable method. Sometimes the teeth are all that survive by the time we uncover the decayed body of a missing person stuffed in a trunk, behind a wall, in a pipe, or anchored below some watering hole, river, or lake."

Lucas backed down the driveway, nodding at her discourse.

She continued, asking, "You hear about that case where we found three bodies within close proximity of one another down on the Brazos?"

"Down around Rosharon?"

"Three prostitutes all murdered by strangulation."

Lucas pointed the car in the right direction and drove for North Belmont. "Yeah, yeah, I recall . . . all clumped together only twenty or thirty yards apart, killed over a period of weeks."

"Dogs sniffed out the bodies from aboard a flatboat."

"Aboard a boat?" Lucas glanced at her. "I heard they were found in the brush on shore."

"No, no! They were weighted down with dumbbells lashed to them with wire fencing."

"Dogs sniffed them out?"

"Amazing noses those dogs, how they just lean out over the side of the boat and strike on the odor of a decaying body some fourteen, fifteen feet below the surface of running water. Some noses on those babies."

"If memory serves, wasn't one of the victims so badly decomposed you had to call in a forensic anthropologist to reconstruct the facial features over the skull to get a likeness for the papers and TV?"

"Another case, Lucas."

"Shit, after a while, after so many, they begin to blend together. Sad commentary on American life."

"State's talking about renting property from private farms and ranches to build more potter's fields to bury all the Jane and John Does," she said.

"Nahhh . . . heard they're thinking now of buying up lands around the penitentiary at Huntsville for new fields and putting the inmates to work as grave diggers."

"That'll never happen. Violation of their civil liberties. Can't turn the prison force into a state work force."

"Legislature's sitting now, and they could change that. This is Texas, after all." Lucas swiped the hair from his eyes. "Yeah, I recall the case now," said Lucas of her original question as they turned onto North Belmont Avenue. "Guy doing the killing out at the Brazos park, wasn't he the—"

"Ran the rowboat concession at the lake."

"Right . . . right sick too."

"Fucker was fat like Gacey, and he gave out free rides to the girls."

"Pelhan, yeah . . . now sitting on death row, appealing his conviction, right. Tapping into his civil liberties."

Jana confided, "I had the chance to shoot the bastard

down like a dog when we busted in on him. He raised a gun to me. I should have let him have it."

"Don't worry. He's bound for the execution chamber—eventually."

"Yeah, but it's the eventually that pisses me off. Ten fucking years eventually, if not more, while the victims' families have to relive their grief and anguish over and over again. Man, I hate the creep's lawyer almost as much as I hate him."

"Understood," said Lucas, squeezing her hand.

"Got to tell you, this is my first case where all we have are eyeballs and teeth to go on."

"Don't forget the salami slices sent to me."

"Strangest nutcase you ever chased, I'll bet, hey, Lucas?"

"Watch for the address, will you? Don't want to miss it."

"By the time we get to the third address on your list, it'll be after hours for dentists."

"Then we'll just have to continue this tomorrow morning, if you're free, that is."

"After Dr. Sullivan's, I'd suggest Mira Lourdes's address."

"Right, it's closer than the Nance place."

The stop at Dr. Sullivan's for Helga Muncie's dental records went quickly, and they pushed on. They found Mira Lourdes's live-in boyfriend at the address in the file, disappointed on learning he was not her husband and so could not grant them access to medical records.

Dwayne Ira Stokes told his own tentative version of how Mira had simply disappeared without a trace. Their last conversation had been about a car that sat glumly neglected out in the driveway, a car she was trying to sell.

Stokes repeated himself a lot, Lucas observed. "My last conversation with her was like over the g'damn phone, and it like centered around that damned cursed car of hers."

"What about the car? Why do you say it was cursed?" asked Lucas.

"Because it was! Like everything that could go wrong with it, like did, man. So finally, I like convinced her to like sell it, you know, put a sign on the damn thing, place an ad in the *Penny Saver,* see."

"And she was showing the car when she disappeared?" asked Jana.

"A neighbor saw her talking to a couple of people, yeah, and like she looked away to wipe a dish or something, and she looked back out to where Mira and these people were, and they were gone, but they left *their* car behind, so she— the neighbor—she like didn't think anything of it, you know. Why leave your car behind if you're going to abduct somebody, you know? That's like how Mrs. Paulis was thinking, she said. Me, I was at work at the time. I work retail, odd hours, always being called in even on what's 'spose to be my day off, which it was that night."

"Mrs. Paulis is the eyewitness I told you about," Jana told Lucas.

"They all three took off in the cursed car," added Stokes.

"And supposedly the abductors left their car behind?" Lucas asked, his tone incredulous.

"That's right."

"But the car she was selling is sitting in your driveway right now," began Lucas, pointing at the unfortunate, sad-looking Saab, its body littered with rust and dents. The FOR SALE sign was still in the rearview window.

"Right, that's it. Damn car has a curse on it. Like a bad penny, it keeps coming back, but not Mira, she didn't come back. She took off with this couple and like never came back! I mean, at first, I thought maybe she just ran off; like we haven't been getting along too good lately, like sniping and backbiting, no biggy, but like annoying twenty-four-seven all-the-time stuff, you know."

Lucas thought if he heard the words *like* or *you know* come once more out of Dwayne's mouth, he would strangle the kid. Dwayne appeared much younger than Mira's twenty-eight years. Lucas guessed him at "like twenty-two or three."

"Maybe we should talk to this neighbor of yours, Dwayne," suggested Jana. "Get more details from her. You say it was a couple. Do you mean a man and a woman or two men?"

"A man and a woman. That's what was so bizarre about it, why like Mrs. Paulis didn't think much of it, you know."

"There's no record of any of this in the Missing Persons file, Dwayne," Lucas pointed out.

"That's 'cause Mrs. Paulis's on vacation. The only one here having fun—in the Caribbean Sea someplace they say. Missing Persons people talked to me. Told the same story, but they said they needed to hear it from the party of the first part, some shit like that, but Mrs. P, she was booked on a cruise, and now she's in Jamaica, I think." He laughed lightly, displaying a missing tooth. "Where I'd like to be," he added, "Yeah, baby, Jamaica. . . ."

"You don't remember me, Dwayne?" asked Jana. "I was with the two detectives who questioned you that night."

"Oh, yeah, wait on a minute . . . sure, now I recall. You kinda stood back, and you checked out the car."

Lucas exchanged a side glance with Detective North, his accusing eye stern on hearing that Missing Persons officers had already gone over this ground and it seemed nothing had come of it. Jana ignored the accusatory glint in Lucas's eye and said to Dwayne, "Do you have a copy of the ad Mira placed in the newspaper?"

"I got a copy on the porch, yeah." He went to fetch it. Returning with the thin local *Penny Saver,* he pointed out the ad. Jana began reading for any clues that might help them. It merely gave the year, model, and make of the car, condition, mileage, and contact number. Call Mira or Dwayne at 555-1220.

Lucas had stepped away from Dwayne and Meredyth, stepping down from the steps of the brownstone home and going toward the small car on the lawn with the FOR SALE sign on it, staring at the Saab, wondering if anything in the interior or the trunk might tell a tale of violence. "Do you know it's against the law to park a car on your lawn, Mr. Stokes?"

"It is?" he said from the steps. "Didn't know that, but look-it, it's not on the lawn. It's in the driveway."

"We'll have to impound the car, Dwayne. Any objections?" Lucas asked, his own instincts leaning toward Dwayne's having made Mira disappear. "Any objections to us hauling off the car, Mr. Stokes?" he shouted.

Dwayne stood shaking his head, saying, "Oh, hell, no. Haul it off anytime. I got nothing stashed in that ol' thing."

Lucas ciphered it out. Mira had placed an ad in the local *Penny Saver,* had had a few interested calls, and she felt certain she was on the way to unloading the Saab, according to Stokes, when she simply vanished after a male/female team interviewed her, not for the car but for Mira. It seemed a bit far-fetched and fortunate for Dwayne that the only so-called witness to the abduction was gone to Jamaica. The story seemed a well-orchestrated fiction, the clever twist in it being that a *couple and not an individual* had abducted Mira.

"Are you sure Mira isn't simply hiding from you, Dwayne?" Jana asked.

Her question was dripping with sarcasm, but it went well over Dwayne's head, and he excitedly answered. "No way. Like I checked with every member of the family—hers and mine—and like every single friend, close and like not so close even. I tell you, I'm worried shitless about Mira. She's a good woman, certainly my better half."

Lucas had studied Dwayne's body language and speech, his hands and eyes. His concern *appeared* genuine; he was shaken and certain something awful had happened to Mira. His act, if it were an act, was well rehearsed and performed; either that or the weed Dwayne had been smoking was good stuff.

Jana reminded Lucas of the reason they had come, and she suggested they not bother with the car at the moment.

Overhearing, Dwayne said, "I told her mom to forward the medical records card thing you guys left with me when I filed the report."

"Well, Mrs. Lourdes has failed to carry through," Jana assured him.

"The woman thinks Mira wanted to get shed of me, and that Mira ran off and doesn't wanna be found. She's sitting around waiting for a phone call from her," Stokes confided about the mother.

He gave them a phone number and an address, and as they walked away from Stokes, he added, "Crazy mother of hers thinks maybe I did something to Mira! Don't listen to none of her bullshit. It's a lie!"

They left for the mother's house, and along the way, Lucas got on the phone to the CSI unit downtown, getting Nielsen on the phone. "I've got a Saab story for you, Dr. Nielsen."

"Oh?"

He explained that he wanted Mira Lourdes's Saab impounded and detailed for possible clues in her abduction, whether she was a match to his case or not. He gave her the address. "The boyfriend has okayed our taking the car, but you best get a warrant anyway, to cover our behinds."

"Will do."

"And please contact me should you get there and find the vehicle mysteriously gone."

"I will call you in such an eventuality, Detective."

Once at the home of Mira Lourdes's parents, they went through a similar tirade as with Dwayne, except here both parents had nothing but vile words and suspicions surrounding Dwayne. They had a hatful of stories illustrating Dwayne's mistreatment of Mira that included physical and emotional abuse. Finally, the parents allowed Jana to get what they had come for, the release signature and the name and address of the dentist they must see.

Lucas and Jana arrived next at Irma Nance's home, as it was closer than Mira Lourdes's dentist. The seventeen-year-old's parents were a pair of drunks who talked over one another, trying to top each other for stories of how Irma was no good, but that she always came home with money from her job. When asked about the type of work she did, neither parent knew anything of how she earned "enough to keep them in booze." This was followed by a gaggle of laughter. The Missing Persons report had been filed by an aunt and uncle, while the mother and father "expected Irma to walk through the door at any time." They hadn't filed a dental release form because they didn't *think* she was truly missing, claiming that Irma was in the habit of disappearing for days at a time.

"Probably at a friend's house. She sleeps over a lot." Mother took another sip on her beer bottle.

"You guys like a beer?" asked Father.

"Do you know her friend's address or phone number?" asked Jana.

Lucas looked on stoically holding onto his calm. The father, scratching beneath his T-shirt and ogling Jana, replied, "She don't tell us who her friends are. How're we supposed to know who they are, much less have a number on 'em. Could we interest you two in a cold one?" he repeated.

"No, just please sign the medical release for her records, sir, and we'll be on our way," Jana said, her skin crawling.

Lucas escorted her off as soon as Mr. Nance released the pen and returned the signed card. When they got out of earshot, Jana whispered, "Missing Persons runs the entire gamut of human experience, Lucas, trust me. We see all kinds."

"Sad part is that they're parents. Ought to have a DMV-type office where people have to register before having kids."

Now they raced to a Dr. Patel's office for Irma's records, getting there just at closing. The Pakistani doctor didn't want to be bothered, something about his kid's soccer game, but Lucas urged the doctor into cooperating, pointing out that he could be liable in a lawsuit if someone's child died because he was too busy to cooperate with police. They got the records.

Calling ahead to Mira's dentist, Dr. Edward Palmer, they got the answering machine. Too late for office hours, but in case of emergency dial Dr. Palmer at 555-9293.

Lucas made the emergency call, and got Palmer on a cell phone in his sports car, Lucas listening to the rev of the powerful engine in the background. Palmer, in sharp contrast to Patel, was instantly curious and interested in helping in any way that he could, promising to meet Lucas and Jana at his office.

"I'm turning around right now," he said. "Mira's a lovely, wonderful person, beautiful bicuspids."

They met Palmer outside, and he eagerly opened his office to them without question, hardly glancing at their badges. "I got a call earlier from her mother, but when you guys didn't show, I guessed you'd get around to it tomorrow. Any rate, here are her records. I had them pulled earlier." He lifted the file filled with Mira's charts from his desk and handed it to Lucas. "God, I hope she's all right. She's a great soul, that one. Full of life, always with a bright smile and kind word for everyone, you know? Wonderfully cared-for teeth."

Not any more if she's our girl, Lucas painfully thought.

"Thanks for your cooperation, Dr. Palmer," said Jana, who caught the doctor eyeballing her straight, bright teeth as if he wanted to get a closer look at them.

Outside, Jana congratulated Lucas on achieving the impossible, gathering up three dental records in one afternoon.

"I owe it all to your help," he countered. "Couldn't have done it without you. Fact is, if you hadn't *like* been with me to *like* deal with Dwayne Stokes, I might have *like* shot him."

She laughed at this. "I'm thirsty. Let's stop for a drink somewhere, shall we?"

"First things first. Next step, get all the data into Dr. Davies's hands and hope for a match."

"All work and no play, Lucas. You haven't changed."

Lucas drove Jana back to the precinct and thanked her for her help. It had grown late, and Jana decided to call it a night, so they parted on the street in front of the station house. "I hope you find the bastard who set you and Meredyth up, Lucas. And if there's anything else we can do over at Missing Persons, don't hesitate. Fact is, should there be a match with one of our girls, you'll have to include us."

"Will do."

"Good luck and good night."

"Thanks again, Jana."

"Nothing succeeds like results, Lucas, and you get results. It's why people respect you. You're no ordinary detective on the force, you *are* a force."

Lucas caught a light in her eye and a curl to her lips, a subtle invitation to call her at any time. She waved as she stepped away, again saying good night, adding, "It's been fun."

Overhead, in a precinct window, other detectives stared down on the scene, and Lucas could almost hear their cat-calls and whistles behind the windowpane. He saw several of his colleagues raise hands and wave in the universal gesture that all men recognized as "go get 'em." Lucas knew instantly that rumors would be flying about Jana and him.

Lucas entered the precinct and went for the crime lab. He found the place empty save for a few medical personnel working at microscopes and a handful of others working on an autopsy. Chang was at the center of the postmortem, which looked as if it would go on for some time. Lucas looked around for anyone who might help him.

Dr. Lynn Nielsen stepped through a door and stood face-to-face with Lucas. The tall Scandinavian and the tall American Indian stared into one another's eyes. They had had few dealings with one another, she having only recently come on staff at the crime lab.

"Detective Stonecoat," she said, "we've found nothing but healthy tissue on the specimens found in your possession."

"Careful how you word that. I wouldn't want Internal Affairs thinking I had anything to do with excising those organ portions from someone's abdominal cavity."

"I'm certainly not proposing such a thing," she countered, as if angry he should suggest anything of the sort.

"Sorry," he heard himself saying. "Translation problem," he suggested now. "At any rate, I have here three separate sets of dental records on possible matches, and the records need to go to Dr. Thomas Davies's team as soon as possible and put on priority."

"Oh, yes, Dr. Chang told me of your plans."

"Is Dr. Davies in?"

"He's promised to return after dinner and get right on it if we can have the records and the victim's teeth all in one place."

"Then you'll call him back, and he'll begin his analysis tonight?"

"You can be sure, Detective."

She took the three dental files from Lucas. "You work quickly," she commented.

"Is there any other way?" he asked, smiling. "Besides, if we can identify the victim, then we have a chance—"

"I know, we may be that much closer to the killer."

"Exactly."

"More so if the killer knew her."

"Precisely." Lucas thought of Dwayne Stokes. If the teeth belonged to Mira Lourdes, he would be elevated to suspect number one, but then why send her brutalized parts to him and to Dr. Sanger? What did Stokes have to gain by such a bizarre action? To throw them off his scent? Lucas could not fathom Stokes ever having that much cunning.

"Is everything all right, Detective?" she asked, seeing his troubled face.

"Yeah, fine. Just a passing thought. Okay, then you'll have Dr. Davies call me when he has results?"

She nodded, holding the dental records against her ample bosom with one hand and extending the other. As she shook his hand and said good night, she added, "I hope we have a long and fruitful working relationship, Detective." It sounded like a rehearsed line she had likely repeated often since coming on board.

"Yes, of course," he replied.

She then stiffly turned and went for her desk to make any necessary calls and arrangements. Her back to him felt like a dismissal.

LUCAS, TIRED AND hungry, left the crime lab and returned to his desk in the bowels of the precinct house, a building that had been built before the turn of the 19th century, in 1898, as a schoolhouse. The Spanish architecture and stone exterior gave it an Alamo appearance, despite all the modern improvements. Here in the closed-in Cold Room office in the dungeonlike basement, its stone walls dripped with condensation. The conditions under which the old files had been housed since the early twenties had prompted the move to place them all on computer before they were entirely consumed by time, mold, and mites. In fact, some of the oldest of the lot had crumbled to dust and could not be saved.

Lucas stood over his desk and punched the memo pad on his computer for any messages. He had it rigged to play the familiar Indian warpath tune to alert on any messages. There were the usual number of reminders of investment opportunities for city employees, 401K information briefings, AA meetings, town hall discussions on union issues, weekend fish fries and ball games, but nothing from Meredyth. He yawned and dropped into his chair, his arm batting the yellowed Yolanda Sims file, accidentally sending it over the side. Cursing, he bent to pick up the scattered reports and photos, finding Yolanda's image—a close-up of her looking like a death mask, staring back at him in what felt like an accusatory fashion, as if to say, "What've you done for me today?" Gnashing his teeth, Lucas gathered up the aged material, realizing that anyone else would have let it go long before.

"Nineteen fifty-six, Lucas?" asked Detective Harrelson, another cop who worked cold cases. "God, I thought we did away with all the hard copy stuff. Mind?" He lifted it from Lucas's grasp, examining it. "Hell, hardly enough here to call it a murder book. Real bottom-drawer, Lucas. How much time and energy you puttin' in on it?"

"None, not really. Like you said, found in a bottom drawer upstairs and dropped on my desk," he lied.

"You're kidding. Sloppy, huh?"

"Too right."

"Well, calling it a night myself. Catch you in the A.M."

"Night." Lucas found a large brown envelope and

dropped the thin murder file into it, not wanting anyone else to third-degree him on it. Harrelson was right. Hardly enough to call it a murder book, he told himself. No one in his right mind would waste valuable time on it; only a fool would pursue it. Lucas called out to Lorna Mendez, the in-charge night person here, telling her he was gone for the evening, and going for the door, he stopped, fingered the file in the envelope, and snatched it up, taking it with him.

Outside in the cool evening air, he searched the sky, unable to find a star or a moon, the firmament shut out by a ceiling of artificial daylight, the reflective mirror of an entire city under a blanket of the orange glow of sodium-vapor lights. It made Lucas feel trapped, earthbound. He thought of what city dwellers gave up in the name of safety, wondering if Yolanda Sims might have lived that warm night in 1956 had her neighborhood been lit up then as it was now. No way to determine, no more so than deciding on rain, wind, lightning, hailstorm, an early frost, clear skies on the cusp of an Indian summer. No way to know—given the limited view from here on the precinct steps. On the reservation or in the hills, where his grandfa-ther had taught him to read the desert signs both on the earth and in the sky, things were simpler, easier to read. In the cityscape, with its constant electrical pulse beating in the ears, a tracker like Lucas must travel down concrete canyons that cast deep shadows, and dig in the subter-ranean recesses for the scum-sucking trolls, the stone-hearted gargoyles, and the urban predators that flourished on this plain. For Lucas, the reward was in putting away such animals, a far cry from frightening off coyotes from the sheep herds with a .22-caliber smooth-bore.

Lucas made his way down the steps to the city's electrical pulse—stepping to the dull music—a reverberating echo ris-ing out of a stone gorge, unrelentingly steady, distant yet near, hollow yet thunderous, the tempo taken up a notch each time a siren joined in the melody of what was Hous-ton's symphony. The daily Houston metropolitan symphony, he thought as squad cars came and went from the parking lot, uniformed officers bantering with one another, putting each other on, laughing, coaxing a boxing match here and there. Across the street a firehouse bustled with men returning from a fire call, and somewhere another siren sounded as a city bus belched and roared in its effort to accelerate, a kind of urban pachyderm putting everyone on notice, charging ahead. Lucas's nostrils pinched with the odors of the city, his throat clogged with the spent emissions, as his ears took in the sound of the city. How long, he wondered, before a man became absorbed by it all to no longer be apart from it?

Walking toward the lot, he caught the scintilla of a fresh coppery odor flit by—ozone. So there was electricity in the air overhead, promising rain to a parched city, teasingly so. Beyond this, Lucas smelled discarded and molding foodstuff and the trail of rats scurrying about the sewers underfoot. He thought of how just below the surface of calm lived the degenerates, the sociopaths, the kind of man who could slice up a woman and send parts of her to him and to Meredyth, and the kind of man who could take the life of a small child in 1956 and get away with it all these years, the kind of man who had no compunction about his crimes then or now.

"Lucas, that you?" asked a beefy uniformed cop passing him in the lot. "It's me, Pete."

"Pete Blackhorn! Been a while. I thought you were in the Two-five now." Blackhorn was one of the few other Native Americans on the force. He was an Alabama mixed Sioux, who went by Pete Black in the white world.

"Just transferred over. Heard about that nasty package you and Dr. Sanger got. Weird shit, man. What's up with that?"

Lucas and Blackhorn had been in the academy together, and while they occasionally bumped into one another on the job, they had not seen each other socially since those days at the academy.

"How'd you hear about it, Pete?"

Blackhorn blew out air. "You kidding? It's all over the precinct and the res. I've had calls from the family. Word out at the Coushatta is you and Billy Hawk have bad blood going again. That true?"

"Fuckin' gossips're going to make it true if they repeat it enough. Shit, aside from everything else, I'm going to have to look over my shoulder for that damned fool cousin of mine?"

"What is it the cowboys say, amigo? You can pick your friends, but you can't pick your kin?"

"You get a chance, set the record straight. There's no feud going on between Billy and me, understood?"

"Then you don't think he sent you and your white friend those Care packages?"

"No, I don't. Eunice Tebo and her cronies are at it again, stirring up ancient history they can't let go of. They got no fucking life of their own, do they?"

"Not to speak of . . . not so's you'd notice, no. But it's you too, Lucas."

"Whataya mean, me?"

"It's 'cause you're you, Stonecoat, Houston's most decorated Native American cop. You kidding? On the res, you're like Jimmy Smits or Lou Diamond Phillips, man. Get used to it."

"Indian tabloid press headlines, I know, and I'm sick of it."

"Can't bury a story like this. It's got everything. Red hero, white blond heroine, old love in the background, and Billy Hawk playing the heavy."

"Blackhorn, it's most likely some nutcase who's seen me on TV or read about Meredyth in the papers and is going for his fifteen minutes of fame by targeting us."

"Yeah, that sounds more logical, agreed."

"Some lunatic demanding his place in the media spotlight beside the 'luminaries' of murder history."

"So you want me to put it on the grapevine like that for you?" Blackhorn had extensive family ties on the reservation, whereas Lucas's had dwindled to a handful of distant relatives.

"I'd appreciate it, yeah," he said to Blackhorn.

"You know, it's also all over the station house too, Lucas, and speculation's pointing a finger at that guy they call Itchy and some of his crowd."

"I'm aware," Lucas replied, his shoulders heaving in a gesture of defeat. "I had hoped for some time to work the case before it became gossip fodder. Next it'll be headline news."

"Wouldn't be the Three-one or Houston if it were otherwise, amigo."

Lucas failed to say that he had himself started the ball rolling downhill on Arnie Feldman and his pals, but as for the *Houston Chronicle* and papers like the *Star Gazette* getting hold of it this soon in the investigation, he hoped not. Still, given the sheer number of people involved in the crime-scene work, Pete was right. The newshounds would soon be all over the story. He wondered how best to protect his and Meredyth's identities when the story of this bizarre *attack* on a detective and a forensic psychiatrist broke. He'd have to rely on the discretion of an army of so-called professionals, some of whom did not particularly care about his comfort or discomfort.

"Let's get a beer sometime, Lucas," Pete suggested. "I'd like to see that gun collection of yours."

"Right, we really ought to do that. Give me a call."

"Night."

They parted just as Meredyth Sanger drove into the lot. She would normally be parking in her reserved spot in the small underground lot, but she had spotted Lucas in his Aussie-looking Wellington leather coat out here with Blackhorn, so she drove in waving to him. "There you are," she said to him as she climbed from her car. "Where've you been?"

"I've spent the last several hours gathering dental records on those three missing persons we ID'd this morning."

"Great, anything shake out?"

"Too early to tell for sure. Tried reaching you around two, but you'd bugged out."

"I see, and next you'll be saying that you missed me."

"I did actually."

"I'm sure that Detective *North* took your mind off such bothersome thoughts as me."

"Hey, whoa up there, cowgirl. Where's this coming from?" He wondered how she'd learned of his having spent the better part of the day with Jana North. "Jana smoothed the way for the family introductions and the permissions. She was a great asset. No way I could've gotten through it in such a short time without her help, believe me."

"I'll bet she was just that, a big *asset*."

"Are you deliberately picking a fight, or are you merely jealous?" he asked.

"Not in the least." She didn't sound convincing.

"Not in the least to which? Fight for fighting's sake, honey-be-mine, or jealousy for jealousy's sake? 'Cause while the jealousy thing is flattering, the fighting just looks like the old arm's length excuses of the past, Mere. So, which is it?"

"Damn it . . . I just thought you'd call."

"Mere, I did call, but I missed you. You were busy, remember, in meetings? Then I got super-busy. You know how that goes. What're you doing back here anyway?" he asked.

"I want to get a file I left in my office."

"Sure you didn't race over here to catch me with Jana, only to find me with Pete?"

"I came back for the file, Lucas."

"Come here." He hugged her close.

"So what did you two find on the missing persons front?" she asked, changing the subject. "You must've learned something?"

"Very little, but let me take you to dinner, and I'll fill you in."

"I want to change, freshen up. My place at around eight?" Meredyth suggested.

Lucas reached out an open palm to brush aside her falling hair from her eyes, but Meredyth shied off, saying, "I'd really like to keep our personal life to ourselves, Lucas, so if you don't mind, the precinct house parking lot isn't the place to display our affections."

Did she get a call from some exaggeration-monger telling her that he and Detective North had had a rendezvous here only moments before? Had she rushed over to catch a glimpse of Lucas in Jana's company to determine if she had something to worry about or not? He wanted to reassure her that nothing untoward was going on between him and Jana, but he realized that if he began down such a road, it would simply sound like a cover-up or even a lie, despite the truth.

"Trust me," Meredyth continued, reading his silence as a disagreement. "Romance in the workplace always wreaks havoc of one sort or another, so let's try to keep what we have a private matter."

"Sure it isn't your professional reputation that you're worried about?"

"I don't mind saying that that's part of it, yes."

"You ashamed of what we have, Mere?"

"I didn't say that! Never. It's just that the leeches and termites in the house will find ways to make it uncomfortable for both of us."

He nodded. "Of course, you're right, but you aren't having second thoughts about us . . . about this morning, are you?"

"Aren't you?"

"Then you are . . . having misgivings."

"Don't try to tell me you're not," she countered. "I mean, it all happened so fast, and we were both emotionally distraught, our nerves stretched to the sea and . . . and . . ." She stopped, seeing the accusatory look in his eye.

They both stood in silent scrutiny of one another, weighing up, trying to determine the depth of hurt their words and actions had already caused. Meredyth had backed away from him in the past, usually with a great deal more speed than presently. Finally, Lucas said, "I have no regrets, Mere. None whatsoever."

She gauged his sincerity, reading his body language and the deep brown eyes. "We'll have to keep talking about it. Later tonight then."

"See you later then."

She took the steps for the precinct, going inside to retrieve that file she'd forgotten, Lucas imagined. He climbed into his unmarked car and drove for home, wondering why she was afraid to love him unequivocally and unconditionally.

CHAPTER 6

Gila monster: desert signs

ONCE INSIDE HER inner office, Dr. Meredyth Sanger made a series of phone calls to the crime lab, asking about any new developments in her and Lucas's case. She was put through to Dr. Lynn Nielsen, who civilly and curtly brought her up to date on the progress being made. And while Nielsen was overtly courteous, she finally told Meredyth in a firm, controlled, and accented voice, "If we were left alone to do our jobs, then the information you and Detective Stonecoat want would be that much more forthcoming sooner."

Mereydth felt satisfied that Lucas had indeed spent the day as he had said, and that he had kept her abreast of each step he'd taken in the investigation. *Checking up on a man?* She chastised herself for going to such extremes. She had never done such a thing before. Maybe Lucas was right. Perhaps she was looking for any little excuse to cut off the legs of their newfound intimacy before it could walk off with her heart entirely. They had been friends for years, always testing one another, teasing, and had in fact been intimate at one time, but Tsali had destroyed that earlier attempt at a life together, and Meredyth wasn't about to go down that heart-wrenching road again. She just knew that he would never get over Tsali, that he had built up a romantic fantasy about life with her and her two girls that he'd always wonder about.

Dr. Nielsen came back on the line. "Detective Stonecoat left us with three sets of dental records, which we then left for Dr. Davies's perusal against the teeth. Dr. Davies has them now."

"Would you please have Dr. Davies contact me with the results as soon as possible, please."

"I'll do that, and Dr. Sanger, I am sorry that someone has victimized you in this *appalling* manner."

"Thank you for your concern, Dr. Nielsen."

"It is a horrible thing; I can only imagine how horrible."

The ice woman almost thaweth, Meredyth thought, but said simply, "Again, thank you, Doctor."

Sergeant Stan Kelton knocked on Meredyth's door and peeked into her office. "Heard you had come in, Dr. Sanger."

"Stan, do you sleep here at the precinct too? You seem to be here day and night."

"Pulling double shifts lately. Two men out with the flu. Hope to hell it isn't a West Nile virus thing."

"God, hope not."

"Anyway, two items for you." He held up an artist sketch in one hand and a hefty parcel wrapped in brown paper in the other. "Sketch is too damned generic to be of much help. Looks like any number of Bill Gates lookalikes. Makes you want to believe your doorman, Stu Long, took the package from a guy who was simply paid to deliver it."

Meredyth only half-heard him as her full attention was on the compact little box he'd placed on the corner of her desk. For a moment, she pictured kindly Stan in cahoots with others trying to drive her insane.

Stan hadn't skipped a beat. "Still, if we could find the delivery guy. . . . Any case, this package arrived for you. Been at central desk all day, except for the time spent in X ray with the bomb squad."

"X ray? Bomb squad?"

"Given what's up, regarding the incidents with you and Detective Stonecoat, I thought we'd best be cautious. The X ray cleared it, found it to be what it purports, office supplies from Staples."

She took the hefty package from Kelton and thanked him for his thoroughness, recalling making the order through her secretary.

"Sad day when we have to tiptoe around our own mail," he said as he closed the door behind himself.

Meredyth took a moment to examine the artist's sketch of the man Stuart Long, her doorman, had described. Kelton wasn't kidding. It was so generic, it could be mistaken for the Wal-Mart happy face, or any fourth person she might encounter on the street with a pudgy face and spectacles. The glasses perched on the nose didn't help to make the picture distinctive.

Alone with the unopened package, Meredyth now stared at it, realizing that until this madman was caught, she'd have to question every item of mail coming to her at home, here at the precinct, and at her private practice.

She grabbed up a letter opener and ripped open the small box forwarded from the office supply shop down the street. True, it was unmarked save for the shop's logo, and true, it could have been hiding something sinister beneath its brown wrap, explaining Kelton's caution over it, but why did she have to live like this? It recalled the anthrax-letter scare of the fall of 2001.

She then noticed an unopened manila envelope in her in box. It could be from another department in the precinct, it could be from another precinct, or it could be from *him*, the maniac that had taken a deviant interest in her and in Lucas.

Using the letter opener, Meredyth carefully unfastened the metal clip on the file-sized envelope. It proved to be routine papers on several uniformed cops, two plainclothes detectives, and a captain, all of whom needed her expertise in dealing with street shootings and work-related stress, and for routine psychological checkups. Every cop who fired his weapon, justified or not, underwent psychiatric review to determine how he or she was coping with the results of his or her actions. A cop who was having serious marital problems that had or could escalate to physical abuse, and some engaged in verbal and emotional abuse situations, looked to her for help. The yearly diagnosis, tests, and checkups were departmental policy.

Lately, there had been a rash of police-involved shootings. These things went in waves, it seemed to her, almost as if one police shooting begot another, as if news of *one* infected a squad. Perhaps it did. Someone ought to do a study, she thought, but good luck to the shrink who tried. As a group, cops proved the most uncooperative of clients she had ever treated.

She shut off her light and stood up, about to leave, when she heard someone in the outer office. Had Kelton returned? She called out, "Stan? Is that you?"

No answer.

She opened the door between her office and her secretary's office. No one there, but the door leading to the hallway stood ajar.

She rushed to the door and stared down the hallway. Empty of life, but she heard a door close and footsteps on the stairwell. She reached into her purse for the hefty little .38 Smith & Wesson that Lucas had taught her to fire. She inched toward the stairwell door and peeked through the crack to find the stairwell empty, but the unmistakable sound of heavy footsteps rose from below, someone in a desperate rush. Known for his laid-back attitude and general laziness, Kelton was not one for rushing anywhere, and would surely have taken the elevator.

Meredyth pushed through the door marked STAIRS, and she rushed after the sound of the footfalls.

Whoever it was, he or she had gone to the basement, heading for the small police garage. Most of the units were parked in an open-air lot, but anyone servicing the building and willing to fight for a space in the underground lot, other than the spots reserved for police brass, might park there. There was no gate or toll booth to bother with in this first-come, first-served garage.

Pushing through the door to the underground lot, she saw a dark blue sleek Mercedes or BMW sedan rushing up the ramp, disappearing too quickly to scan the license plate. She neither saw nor heard another sound in the lot, the garage as silent as a tomb, a ghostly grayness filling the space all around Meredyth.

Then she saw it. A small package on the floor of the garage, just sitting there as in a dream, as in a Dali painting, out of place here, staring back at her. All her horror of the night before over opening the parcel containing the eyes and teeth came rushing back at her. She recalled the CD and the chilling lyrics, *I had the time of my life. . . .*

She got on her cell phone and called Kelton upstairs, telling him she'd followed a man who'd entered her outer office and fled to the basement, where she now stood staring at yet another brown-paper-wrapped box the shadow man had left behind.

"Geeze, Doc, I just left you," Kelton lamented.

"Stan, he must've been right on your heels. I thought he was you!"

He remained dismayed. "We were just talking in your office!"

"Just please send a couple of broad-shouldered uniforms down here to take control of this . . . this box and this . . . possible crime scene, will you, Stan?"

"On it, Doctor."

"And get some of Chang's people down here."

"Soon as the bomb squad clears the package of explosives, Dr. Sanger. They're on alert and on the way with an X-ray device. They'll get a clear picture of what's inside the thing."

"Just get me some muscle down here for now."

She heard Kelton shout at two officers to rush to her aid. "Someone will be right there, Dr. Sanger," he said. "Stay calm."

"Trying to . . . trying to, Stan." She inched closer to the package. It was slightly larger than the one she'd gotten at home, but the familiar block lettering in her name and in the address of the 31st Precinct appeared to be by the same hand. Whoever had torn out of the lot had left it for her, knowing she was following.

She quickly dialed Lucas's cell phone.

LUCAS WAS HALFWAY home to his apartment, picturing the henpecked Jack Tebo—urged on by Eunice—rehearsing how he would tell Lucas to take his things and get out of the flat by end of week. He wondered where he would go, and groaned at the thought of finding another place to live, dreading the idea of a move. He had put a lot of holes in Tebo's walls, hanging them with traditional blankets and his gun collection. Where else in the city would he be free to do that without hassle? He'd also miss the proximity of draft beer and hot meals. If Eunice was good for anything other than gossip, it was her fine Native American cooking. No one could beat her homemade cornbread and biscuits, her venison stew or Southwestern veal omelet.

With these thoughts sifting through his head, he almost missed the sound of his cell phone. Snatching it off his belt, he said, "Stonecoat."

"Lucas! It's me!"

"Mere? What's up?"

"My blood pressure, I need you again."

"What is it?" He recognized the fright in her voice.

She shakily informed him what had occurred. When she was still in mid-story, he made a U-turn, stopping traffic and garnering curses, horns, and gestures from the motorists around him. "I'm on my way back! Sirens and lights!" He placed the strobe light atop his car and switched on the siren. "Ten minutes tops! Be there. Hold on."

By the time Lucas had returned, he found the police parking garage crawling with cops and crime-unit technicians, and among them, a bomb squad official and a bio-threat cop in protective wear sharing a light for their cigarettes, having already determined that the box contained nothing of interest to either of them. Lucas also saw

Dr. Lynn Nielsen, and beside her, Dr. Leonard Chang carefully, painstakingly opening a wooden box with a Styrofoam lining, a mite larger than those they had seen the night before, but the packaging distinctively the same.

"Where's Meredyth?" Lucas asked, scanning the area for her when Stan Kelton rushed to him, telling him she was in the squad lounge upstairs with a pair of policewomen and a cup of coffee, calming down.

Lucas was held in check when he saw what Leonard Chang's gloved hands now plucked from the white interior of the little coffin left for Meredyth. It was a human hand, a petite, feminine human hand, severed at the wrist in as neat and clean a cut as Lucas had ever seen. No jagged edges, nothing dangling, not so much as a thread of artery. The neatness of the cut gave it an unreal, mannequin appearance until Chang turned it over.

There was writing on the palm in black marker—a short laundry list of items. Everyone craned to see it more clearly. "What is it?" asked Ted Hoskins of Chang while Steve Perelli flashed shot after shot.

"What's the writing on the hand say?" asked Lucas at the same time.

"Reminders. Things she wanted to get on her next visit to Wal-Mart, I suspect," said Dr. Nielsen, her tall frame towering over Chang but not Lucas. "She was out of TP, hairspray, nail polish, and onions."

"She was left-handed," commented Chang, "to write this on her right hand."

Lucas recalled that Mira Lourdes was reportedly left-handed. He wondered if it could be her right hand he now stared at.

"At least we've got fingerprints now," said Dr. Nielsen, sighing.

Chang shook his head. "Look closer. No fingerprints." Chang put a magnifying glass over the fingertips, demonstrating how they had been burnt off with some sort of chemical. "The epidermal layers of skin have been altered."

"Acid bath?" asked Nielsen.

"Carefully applied. Likely over-the-counter item. Muriatic acid would be my guess."

"Kind you get at any pool store," muttered Lucas. "What the hell does this motherfucker want from Meredyth?"

"If we knew that, we might know better who he is," said Meredyth. She had materialized from the tunnel leading to the garage, two uniformed female cops with her. "We must have really pissed him off sometime . . . someplace."

Lucas wanted to go to her, hold her to him, and she read this clearly in his eyes, but they had made the pact to keep their renewed romance a secret for now. "We need to sit down, go over every case we ever worked together, and find this psycho before he decides to attack with more than these sick offerings," he said.

"I couldn't agree with you more," she replied.

The unspoken questions on everyone's mind were where the rest of the victim's body was, what would be forwarded next, and what kind of connection existed between the killer, Dr. Sanger, and Detective Stonecoat.

Lucas turned back to Chang. "What can you tell us about the victim from what this lunatic bastard has left us, Leonard?"

"Not much beyond her general size and weight. She was small-boned, not large, healthy by all reckoning. Freckled. The hand came from a fresh kill, like the eyes and organ slices. I'd need equipment and tests to tell you any more than that."

"Are you guessing it to be from the same victim?"

"One might suppose so, yes."

"Bastard is poaching off pieces of his victim to taunt us. It's sick."

Captain Gordon Lincoln, having heard of the latest incident in this growing cancer, drove into the lot, climbed from his car with some difficulty, and stood in a disarrayed overcoat thrown over his casual civilian clothes, a golf shirt and pants. His size and weight made him a force to be reckoned with, and he chewed on an unlit cigar. It was past nine P.M. and Lincoln's eyes burned with curiosity, confusion, and concern. "What in hell's going on, Stonecoat? Did I hear right? Another goody bag left for Dr. Sanger? After you gave chase to some phantom who breached the security of my precinct? Are you all right, Dr. Sanger?"

"Yes, I'm fine," she replied at the same time Lucas said, "You heard right, Captain. Some creep lured her here and saw to it she was alone with this sick *gift* he left behind. A human hand, female."

"We suspect it's from the same body as gave up the eyes and teeth, but we'll have to run tests to be certain, Captain," added Chang.

Lincoln exchanged a quick smile with Dr. Nielsen, nodded, and bent at his hefty waist for a closer examination of the severed hand. Nielsen leaned in and spoke in his ear, explaining both the lettering and the raw fingertips.

Lincoln mouthed the words written across the palm of the severed hand. "Sad business . . . terribly sad," he muttered.

"Handwriting on hand . . . printing actually, doesn't appear the same as on package," Chang said.

"I suspect the victim was in the habit of writing messages to herself on her hand. Lot of people do it," said Meredyth, who now had a chance to examine the awful contents of the third ugly parcel.

Lincoln straightened up with a mild groan. He ordered everyone's silence on the incident, knowing it would be the precinct buzz before midnight and leaked to the press before dawn. "Chang, I know this is already first priority in your lab," continued Captain Lincoln, pacing, "but anything . . . anything more you can do to speed up our evidence-gathering and knowledge of this SOB will be appreciated."

"We're doing all we can to expedite matters, Captain, I can assure you," replied Chang.

"I'm sure you are. Keep me posted." Lincoln took Lucas aside, escorting him to his car, out of earshot of the others. "Do you have *any* inkling as to who might be behind this, Lucas? Are any of your loony street connections or snitches telling you anything? Any word from anyone fresh off the reservation? Didn't you have some enemies on the res? Wasn't there a thing between you and a woman there that got messy?"

"That was my cousin's wife, Tsali, and it hasn't a thing to do with this, no."

"Any connection possibly to Zachary Roundpoint?"

"Sir, I can assure you there is none whatsoever."

"Then you do admit to knowing Roundpoint well enough to know he has nothing to do with this shit?"

"IAD's cleared me of all those charges, Captain. You got the report. I do not have any personal relationship with Roundpoint or anyone in his organization."

"But FBI approached you and suggested you help them to infiltrate Roundpoint's operation, to wear a wire."

"I turned 'em down. I got no juice with Roundpoint."

"All right . . . all right, don't get testy. I'm just throwing out ideas here, brainstorming. When you brainstorm a case, no idea is too radical for consideration. Nothing personal, and when and if the Feds start up anything with you, Detective, remember, you're under my command, and I stand by men under my command. *Kee-mo-sabe?*"

Lucas could feel his jaw tighten. He had a good idea where Lincoln would be standing if and when a federal grand jury were convened and Lucas were called to point a finger at Zach Roundpoint, one lone lieutenant of Native American descent against the power of the U.S. Government. An old story, Lucas told himself.

Lucas told his captain, "Meredyth and I suspect that whoever's behind these foul mailings will be someone we have a history with."

"Both of you?"

"Yes, both of us. It'll be someone we may've put away, or a relative of someone we put away. Remember the vengeance Jimmy Lee Purdy took out on Judge DeCampe after his death? Through the twisted thinking of his deranged father?"

Lincoln breathed deeply of the stale parking lot air and fumes, considering the horror of the case that had brought Lucas Stonecoat so much federal attention, the case of an abducted and cruelly tortured appellate court judge and personal friend of Lincoln's. Maureen DeCampe had been abducted in a municipal underground parking lot, not unlike this one, forced into a coffin, and transported across the country to a deserted farmhouse. The sentence against her was carried out by a maniacal old man thinking himself a prophet of God or some such nonsense. Isaiah Purdy, hearing his executed son's voice in his head, believing his son to be God or God's angel, had followed Jimmy Lee's orders to fulfill his last request. Isaiah lashed her to his son's decayed body, holding her hostage to a slow death for a week before Lucas and Meredyth had helped to discover her and put an end to her misery. The old man's plan was to kill her via rotting her flesh as it came into contact with the rotting flesh of his dead son. The poor woman still had lingering psychological scars. Cooperating with the FBI, Lucas and Meredyth had helped save the judge's life. However, Lucas had come under suspicion by the Feds himself when they targeted Roundpoint for a series of killings in North Dakota, all related to a hate crime involving a young Native American. Someone had seen to it that the boy's killers met their end when federal prosecutors announced they hadn't enough evidence on anyone to bring charges.

"Canvas the old cases you've worked together," said Lincoln now. "Beyond that, shake loose the talk on the street. Somebody somewhere has to know something."

"Currently, we're working up a victim profile, awaiting more information from our dental forensics man, Davies."

"Yeah, the teeth . . . good idea . . . good work."

"Narrowed down three recently reported cases of missing persons who fit Chang's assessment of the age range, size, and weight estimates."

Lincoln climbed back into his car, waved Lucas off, and drove up the ramp and out of the garage. Lucas's eyes followed his car until it was out of sight. He and Lincoln hadn't always been in agreement; they had had their battles. Still, the captain was genuinely concerned about the awful thing happening to him and to Meredyth.

Lucas returned to Meredyth, and he saw that Chang was through with the evidence-gathering and photo-taking at the secondary crime scene. In the back of everyone's mind was the question of the primary crime scene or scenes, where the killer had first abducted his victim, and where he had chopped her into multiple pieces.

"Come with me," Chang told Nielsen, "and we'll get a closer look at that."

"At what?" asked Lucas.

"Dr. Nielsen asks a good question. She wonders how the hand can look so fresh if the victim is the same. It has been twenty-four hours difference and still not a single spot of decay."

"What does that suggest?"

"I suspect under the electron microscope, we will find ice crystals beneath the skin."

"So he's keeping the body in a freezer now?" asked Lucas.

"That would be my guess."

"We found a cloth fiber and hair inside the box too," said Nielsen.

"The fiber and hair are likely the victim's, but we could get lucky . . . they may belong to our killer," Chang added.

Lucas thanked the two M.E.'s for their extra effort on the case, and then he took Meredyth aside. "I'm taking you home now, Meredyth. No arguments."

"I'd like that. Thank you, Lucas."

Lucas escorted her to his car and opened her door, but she stopped, looked into his eyes, and began relating the story of exactly what had happened to her.

"Save it for the ride, Mere. Let's get out of this place." She climbed in and he closed the door, came around the car, entered, and pulled out.

"Whoever this creep is, he came up from the garage to my office," she said. "He wanted to leave the package in my office. He was sneaking around up there when I heard a noise, and I stepped out to the outer office to investigate. From there, he beat it back down to the garage. Not seeing my car in the garage, he'd thought I wasn't in, so he'd brought the package up the elevator or stairwell with him to leave on my desk."

"But he panicked."

"I think so, yes."

Lucas darted in and out of the traffic of the bustling city, listening attentively for the details while the lights, horns, sirens, and shouting of people bounced off the rolled-up windows. It had become darker still, a faintly chilly nip in the air, and the promise of rain had gone unrealized. "Nice night for a desert drive. You want to get out of the city for a while, find the stars?" he asked.

"Damn it, Lucas, you're not hearing me. This guy has been watching my every move. He knows my habits. I wasn't supposed to be in the office this late."

"All right, I hear you. We've got some sort of wacko stalker on our hands. But you need to get some respite from it. I'm not leaving you alone again until this bastard's caught, so where to? Your place or mine? I gotta warn you, though, that—"

"What were you saying about the desert stars?"

"I know a place where we can spread a blanket."

"You got a blanket?"

"In the trunk, sure."

"Stars . . . maybe some moonlight? Sounds good, yeah."

"Great choice." Lucas took the Interstate west, exiting onto a small highway, finding a still-smaller two-lane on which they found a family-run restaurant where the proprietors and their children—Mexicans—all knew Lucas and welcomed him like an old friend, while Meredyth stood back observing, smiling, nodding as Lucas chatted in Spanish with them.

In a matter of minutes, the father held out a fully packed picnic basket with cold cuts, bread, cheese, and wine, and Meredyth took it while Lucas pushed money into the man's hands.

A few miles down the road, Lucas turned onto a deserted desert road, tall cactus looking on like silent sentries while Lucas's car sent up a flume of particles and sand. A dirt cloud followed them like a dervish as they raced for the lavender-hued rocks beneath the moon and stars in the distance.

The moonlit night painted the hills and corresponding gulches with a variety of colors, deep and abiding, yet changing from moment to moment, like the breeze itself. Meredyth was caught up in the sights, the peace, and the feel of this hideaway he wished to share with her. "I come here alone a lot," he said. "When I have more time, I go out farther, all the way to the Diablo Spinata—Devil's Spine. Now there's a mystical place, filled with ghosts and spirits of the past."

"Take me there sometime," she replied.

"I will."

"Promise?"

"Promise."

From the trunk of his car, Lucas produced an Indian blanket, beautifully woven, and with the basket of food and drink in hand, he escorted her to a favorite spot, spread the blanket, and welcomed her to partake. Together they lay for a time beneath the twinkling lights of the firmament.

Pointing back in the direction of Houston, she asked, "What's that strange light in the distance?"

"That'd be Houston."

"Houston, really?"

"Lights of the city."

"I thought it was a kid's ball field all lit up."

"Nope . . . trust me, it's the dome of light over Houston." He then pointed to the crisp, clear sky directly overhead. "No show like *this* in Houston," he said, falling back on his elbows and going into a deep silence.

After a long moment of listening to the desert sounds, she said, "Thanks, Lucas, for bringing me here."

"You must be hungry. Let's eat."

She reached over and grabbed hold of his shoulders, pulling him down over her, kissing him passionately. For the moment, the food was forgotten.

"Ever spend the whole of a night in the desert?" he asked.

"Well . . . no . . . not till now."

DR. ARTHUR BELKVIN couldn't stop shaking. He was almost caught *inside* a police station with a box containing the severed right hand of Mira Lourdes. It had been the second package he had delivered to Dr. Meredyth Sanger, while Lauralie had delivered a second package to Detective Lucas Stonecoat. And still she had not explained why they were doing this.

He thought of his practice, his livelihood, his clients, and the multitude of animal patients he helped each day, and he thought of how it would play in the newspapers if it should ever come out that he, Dr. Arthur Belkvin, Professor of Animal Surgery at the Dean King School of Veterinary Medicine, had been arrested for misusing his surgical skills to pick apart a dead woman's corpse for sexual favors from a woman half his age, one of his students. Being a murder accomplice somehow did not bother him so much as the humiliation he'd brought down on his profession, a profession that had its own Hippocratic Oath— to do no harm.

He shivered at the thought of being found out. Of being called out. Of being labeled a man who had once been a fine upstanding practitioner in the art of saving life, but who now dealt in death. *But I've killed no one,* he told himself. *She's done the killing. I couldn't even swing the ax hard enough. Anyone can see that I'm not the monster here. No,* he told himself now, *I'm not a monster . . . just an Igor to her twisted Frankenstein.*

As Arthur drove home, anxiously checking his rearview for the flashing lights in pursuit, certain that at any moment they would come, he wondered at his own hold on reality. Common sense told him that most certainly someone had taken down his license plate, but another voice kept saying he could—if caught—end it all here and now! Flag down a cop and put the blame where the blame belonged, square on Lauralie, whose very presence turned him into a spineless lapdog. God, someone had to know why he did what he had done.

How certain he felt that someone had recognized the make and model of the car. He pulled down the street on which he lived, for the first time calming as he saw his apartment come into view. He could see his two grey-hounds in the window grown big with excitement on see-ing his approach. Smart boys, they knew his car from sight. Lauralie was somewhere inside the apartment as well, likely watching reruns of *Buffy the Vampire Slayer*, which he hated.

Lauralie awaited him inside, but he hesitated going any further toward the steps. "Am I crazy? This isn't me! I don't behave like this. I'm not a psychopathic maniac, but what I'm doing . . . that's psychopathic, man! What the hell else do you call going about the city delivering parcels stuffed with the remains of a dead woman! Maybe I am mad. And to what purpose? And to whom do I owe this deviant behavior if it's not to please Lauralie? And what is her purpose in all this?"

A neighbor, walking a dog, having watched him talking to himself in such animation, embarrassed at now being seen, waved and called out, "Howya doin', Dr. Belkvin? Nice night, huh? Not too many good ones left before that old East Texas cold's going to set in."

"Doing fine, thanks." Lauralie's shadow was doing a sen-sual dance behind the blinds, music blaring. The neighbor watched her form gliding about for a moment before saying, "Well . . . got to walk dinner off. Later, Dr. Belkvin."

"Later, Harvey."

Harvey would have something to talk about when he got home, Arthur thought.

Lauralie now peeked elflike from behind the drapes, having put the dogs into the back bedroom. So lithe and beautiful a prize Lauralie represented, a symbol of an ideal of sorts, something of a joie de vivre that raced around in his brain—a Tinkerbell, always fragile, always just out of reach even when you had her in hand, Arthur thought. Joy, yes, but she was also an annoying ethereal scratch across Arthur's soul, because Arthur knew that he denied the truth that lay in wait, that Lauralie would never be possessed by anyone, and could never truly be his. She was like the lover who sang in the song, *We'll sing in the sunshine, we'll laugh every day-yay . . . and then I'll be on my way.* That folk-song character promised a year before she had to leave, and Arthur knew that he'd have even less time before Lauralie flew away, despite her protestations and promises and declarations of love.

She gestured for him to hurry up, her large lips puckering into a teasing kiss against the glass. No doubt she was anxious for his report on tonight's *success.* She'd want to know all about it, every detail of how he had infiltrated Sanger's world. He'd have to make it good; he must keep her happy, but what about his own happiness? He was far from happy, he told himself as he made his way to the front door.

He jammed the key in the lock. "Well, God damn it, it's time *I* got some details," he shouted to the empty night.

"I couldn't agree with you more," she said, pulling open the door, revealing herself as nude, and tugging him inside.

Arthur fell into her warm arms, his determination to get to the bottom of her obsession with Dr. Sanger put on hold. Lauralie's young body, radiating a passionate heat, her eyes aglow in the soft light of the apartment, her arms tightening around him, her thighs wrapping about him, inviting him into her, to become one with her, all conspired to melt away his fears, doubts, questions, and agitation.

Arthur couldn't resist. He embraced her, and she kicked the door closed, passionately pawing at his clothing and alternately kissing him and pleading for the details just as he'd expected. "How did it go? Did you place the package on her desk like I told you to?"

She was turned on, her body heat permeating through his clothing. She swallowed his mouth in hers, sucking in his tongue. Gasping for breath, he pulled away only to hear more words spilling from her. "Tell me . . . damn it, out with the details!" she insisted as her hands roamed over his clothing, tearing away at his buttons and his belt.

He replied with lies between panting breaths and kisses, "Yes, yes . . . just as planned. Went smooth as silk."

"Tell me everything . . . while we make love. Tell me what her office looked like." She went to her knees, ripping his pants and undershorts away to get at the prize she wanted, and he hoped that with her mouth around him, she would be stopped from asking any more questions.

"Like . . . any . . . office, but big, large."

"What kind of pictures did she have on her desk? You see a photo of her parents? I've got to learn more about them." She somehow talked with him inside her mouth.

The alternating of talk-suck, talk-suck, talk-suck only heightened Arthur's delight, making him gasp out answers he snatched from his imagination while at the same time seeing lights exploding in his head.

She had him on the floor now, and he was in her and pumping with eager anticipation over her, driving into her, glad she had finally shut up with the questions, when she asked, "W-what . . . k-kinda pic-tures a-and paint-ings . . . she h-have on . . . her walls?"

"Pictures?"

"Paintings, photographs, prints, what?" She choked him with both hands. "Tell me! Fuck me and tell me!"

"I . . . didn't really . . . pay . . . much . . ." He gasped. "Heed!"

Arthur came inside her and fell atop her.

"Think!" she demanded, pushing him off and onto the rug where they had remained in the foyer. "What *graced* her walls? And what little knickknacks did she have on her shelves and on her desk? A paperweight with a photo inside, a Waterford crystal ball, a letter opener, a calendar, blotter? Any trinkets or mementos? Personalized pen set?"

"Jesus, I was only there a second or two when someone came waltzing by and I had to rush out, Lauralie."

She pushed away from him, getting to her knees over him. "You've got to remember something!"

"All right . . . all right . . . she had a Van Gogh print on one wall."

"Which one?"

"Which wall?"

"No, damn it, which Van Gogh?"

"Ahhh . . . the one with all the stars."

"Sure . . . yeah . . . *Starry, Starry Night*. That figures. She's one of those eternal optimists, I bet. The bitch. So what did she have on her shelves?"

"Books, lots of books, and one of those plastic models of the brain, and . . . and a photo of that guy, Stonecoat, and a lot of papers, stacks of papers," he continued to lie.

"The bitch has a full life, doesn't she. An excellent job, good money, the lover she wants. All of it is coming to an end . . . and soon, soon."

Arthur wondered why the very paintings on the other woman's walls were so important to Lauralie, and he wondered if she would ever learn of his lies. He wondered if at some time this Sanger woman had taken a lover away from Lauralie, if maybe it was this guy Stonecoat or that other guy Lauralie had mentioned, Byron Priestly.

Arthur wondered how Lauralie would react if she ever learned that he had no idea what was on Sanger's walls and shelves and desk. That he had not gotten past the shrink's outer office to have one damn look in her actual office. He certainly couldn't tell Lauralie the truth at this point, that he'd had to leave the parcel in the garage for Dr. Sanger as she pursued him out the building. It was a secret he felt best kept in a vault inside his head.

He propped himself up on his elbow. "When are you going to tell me what this is all about and why you hate her so much?" he pressed Lauralie.

"I want to hurt her, hurt her badly."

"That's rather obvious, but why? What's it got to do with her cop lover, Stonecoat? Did the two of them once hurt you?"

"She did."

"And him, Stonecoat? Did he hurt you?"

"It's enough that she loves him. I hurt him, I hurt her. Simple as that."

"How did she hurt you?"

"Enough. I don't want to fucking talk about it." She lowered herself over him and swallowed up his penis in her mouth again to shut him up, her hair tickling his stomach and groin as she worked to make him groan and end his list of questions.

When she finished, she propped herself on her elbow and said, "I left the *big* package for Stonecoat with UPS addressed to him at the precinct. It'll arrive tomorrow. This one'll kick ass."

CHAPTER 7

Coyote track

AN UNUSUAL SILVERY spray of desert rain played lightly over their features, awakening Lucas and Meredyth where they had slept with the creatures of the rocks, here beneath the starlit night that'd become twilight morning. The first of the eastern sun rays had still not reached the boulders, and now Meredyth sat watching the light creep in, creating long dark fingers out of standing cactus plants until these shadows stretched across the desert to them. On first awakening, Meredyth had found herself in the crook of Lucas's arm, and it felt not only good but safe.

They had agreed to turn off their cell phones, and so no one had been able to disturb their evening. On waking, Lucas had pulled free, checking any messages he might have as he rummaged about in the picnic basket and said, "Hey, you hungry? Let's see what's left to drink and eat. Makeshift breakfast here."

She was checking her messages, three—all from Byron Priestly—still desperately seeking her forgiveness. *Let him beg another week,* she thought, *then cut him off at the knees.* Byron had caught her at her private practice downtown, where they had often met for dinner and the theater in the past, but this time, she had stormed off from him, leaving him standing in the garage. She'd told him not to call or to come by, but here he was, bugging her.

She joined Lucas and they finished off what was left of the wine and bread, and after watching a circling pair of screeching hawks claiming the territory, Lucas suggested they start back for the city and the other reality awaiting them.

"We didn't make love," she commented on the trip back.

"We were too busy making love to the desert," he countered, "together—of one mind. It was great."

She smiled at this. "You're more the romantic than you pretend, aren't you, Chief? My Wolf Clansman."

Lucas and Meredyth arrived back in the city and at Meredyth's place a few minutes past nine A.M. in a steady rain, and the day doorman, Stuart Long, greeted them with an envelope from Byron and complaints. "Lost time on the job over this thing . . . long and frustrating hours spent with that sketch artist. So I took over Max's shift last night, and so here I am, bloodshot eyes, dog's at home alone, nobody to feed 'im, putting in *long* hours here—get it, *Long* hours. *Hi and hello,*" he added, taking Lucas's hand, shaking it. "I'm Stuart Long."

"Detective Stonecoat, Lucas." Lucas then asked, "So, you got a sketch done at the station house?"

"Talk about long hours . . . going downtown to give a statement and a description of the guy who left that damnable parcel with me. I told 'em what little I know, Dr. Sanger, but it wasn't much. The guy was an *everyman* type, you know, nothing whatever to distinguish him. The guy was like medium *everything,* medium height, medium weight, medium shoe size, medium brown hair, glasses, kinda geekish-looking, wore a buttoned-up Ralph Lauren polo shirt knockoff over ordinary slacks. Nothing about his features stuck out. Clean shaven. I think the composite they did may's well be a blank slate."

Meredyth had torn open Byron's envelope, glanced at

the communique, and angrily stuffed it into her purse when she could find no nearby trash container. In her purse, she came across the folded copy of the sketch Kelton had given her the night before. She snatched it out, offering it to Lucas.

He frowned and stared at the depiction—mostly blank space—and said, "*Hmmm* . . . I see what you mean, Mr. Long. This . . . this is extremely"—*useless,* he thought but didn't wish to insult—"extremely *helpful.*"

"BS, Detective. It's all *medium* . . . everything about the guy was *medium,* even his nose. When they showed me those books of collected ears, noses, eyes, chins, shit . . . all I kept picking out was the medium ones," Stu continued nonstop as if on speed, his shoulders rising and lowering as if on automatic. "I'm for damn sure going to be more observant in the future."

"Not at all, Stu," replied Meredyth, waving him down. "Thanks for taking the time going in and giving the artist what you could."

"Did you notice any odors clinging to the man?" asked Lucas out of the blue.

"Odors . . . hmmm . . . That's interesting you should ask." Long bit his lower lip, contemplating this. "On account-a-there was something . . . something odd like . . . like . . . can't place it now."

"Detective Stonecoat is a great believer in the power of the olfactory nerves to bring back visual memories, Stu. Being a psychiatrist, I'd have to agree."

"It is, after all, the first sense used in tracking an animal," Lucas commented.

"I tell you, there *was* something odd clinging to this guy . . ."

"Go on," urged Lucas, "an odor like the inside of a really raunchy pair of old sneakers perhaps?"

"No . . . not exactly."

"Or the back room of a moldy tenement?"

"Yeah . . . mold, only . . . only a little different than that . . . something like . . . like mildew, only added to a faintly nauseating chemical odor."

"Chemical odor?"

"You know, like you smell in a hospital."

"Excellent," said Meredyth. "You do remember some-thing, Mr. Long, and it's more than a *medium* memory."

"Oh, and there's something else I remember that was unusual about the guy now," replied Long. "He had this mole right here on his left cheek." Long pointed to the spot. "Like . . . like that kid character in the Waltons, John Boy? Only . . . only there was a nasty hair growing out of this mole. Damn, I didn't tell that to the sketch artist."

"Anything else?" pressed Lucas.

"Keep recalling that odor on his clothes, on his skin," added Meredyth. They both knew that recalled odors brought back more recall in the visual imagery centers of the cortex.

Long announced, "His eyebrows were black."

"And so how is that important?" urged Meredyth.

"Well, his hair was blond . . . maybe dyed. Maybe that was the smell coming off him? I told the artist he had blond hair, but now I think about it, the roots were dark, and def-initely the eyebrows were dark brown or black. Didn't get that detail into the sketch either."

Lucas asked, "You sure it wasn't a wig?"

"Could've been . . . I suppose."

"Did the sketch artist give you his card?"

"Yeah, *she* did. I'll give her a call. In the meantime, Dr. Sanger, you'll want to see the early edition of the *Chronicle*." He held the newspaper in his hands up to her. "I swear I had nothing to do with this. I like my job too much."

Meredyth took in the front page headline: "***SHRINK-ING IN HORROR**—Killer Sends Victim's Eyes, Teeth to Police Shrink*."

"Damn," she moaned, shaking the paper. "They've got the story already."

With Stu Long helping passing residents at the door, Lucas read over Meredyth's shoulder. The details remained sketchy, and the reporters had used no names, but she and Lucas knew they'd soon be reading follow-up, *in-depth* pieces, and that radio and TV news would soon be airing the story as well—with all the gusto and details their crack reporters could muster.

"Who the hell're these unnamed sources?" she wondered aloud.

"Probably *Bye-bye* Byron?" His suggestion fell flat.

"No . . . not Byron."

"Why not? His fifteen minutes of fame?"

"He wouldn't, that's all."

"Like you know him well enough to know?"

She went to her mailbox, opened it, and snatched out several bills and junk mail.

"Mere, you didn't expect him to run outta the condo and leave you holding the bag either, but he did."

"Lucas, he's not going to be allowed back into my bed, all right? Satisfied?"

"Then why're you hanging onto his letter?"

"It's trash and I don't *litter*. I'll burn it upstairs if you like, but I won't be convinced that he's talking to the press."

"Even if he isn't talking to the press, they're likely tailing him right to you."

"Drop it, Lucas!"

"Whoever the *unnamed sources* may be, it won't be long before the hounds sniff out news of the severed hand," he replied. "And once it becomes public . . . about where this *connected* incident occurred, *anyone* might surmise the central characters in the story are you and me, Mere."

"I'm so glad my parents are out of the country."

"It's likely just what this certifiable creep is looking for, his fifteen minutes of fame," he suggested, dropping the newspaper back onto the information desk.

Lucas turned to find her gone. He had to dash to keep pace. Meredyth had stiffly stalked off, rushing through the posh lounge area, pushing through an inner door, and now she leaned into the elevator call button. He caught up with her there, still talking. "It's the new American way, Mere— do *anything,* go *anywhere* for a fleeting moment before the new idol in the desert."

"What the hell're you onto now, Lucas? Have you been into your stash this morning already?"

"The golden calf's now the golden camera, and you *Anglos* have created your own nightmare," he said, ignoring her question.

"What's that supposed to mean, Lucas?" she fired back, reminding him of how fragile their relationship really was.

"In a culture that can award an Emmy nomination to the Osbornes for best TV reality programming," Lucas began as she boarded the elevator and he stepped in behind, "a culture that rewards a sniper killer with literally millions of minutes of air time and creates an event out of the most wanted man in America, a cowardly murderer, it should come as no surprise that some nutcase thinks he can make *prime time* by turning a murder into a game show for a perverse idol—*himself.*"

Moments before the elevator doors closed, an elderly woman with a schnauzer came aboard, the little dog yipping at Lucas as he continued lecturing Meredyth. "Look at our case, Mere. The media attention is already in full swing. What body part will next appear? Ears, toes, arms, what? Odds-makers in Vegas and on the Internet will be making book on it, believe me, and *Real TV*'ll have their cameras rolling."

The dog continued barking, and the white-haired lady hugged the dog protectively in the folds of her coat, cooing his name, soothing him. "*Pudgy-woo, pudgy-coo . . .* it's all right, baby." She gave a disapproving look in Meredyth's direction. "Really, Dr. Sanger, there's been so much disruption in our building of late."

"I'm sure everything's going to calm down now, Mrs. Chandler. You and little Pudge don't have to worry."

"I've had inquiries, you know, from all sorts of people, but as I tell them, I know nothing of what's happened in the building."

The elevator doors opened on her floor, and Mrs. Chandler and Pudge alighted from the cab.

Lucas and Meredyth rode up the rest of the way in silence, each contemplating what lay between them and ahead for them, dividing their thoughts between a lunatic who had targeted them and their struggling relationship.

As they now approached Meredyth's door, they saw there was no eerie little package left in her doorway. "This is crazy . . . like walking through a minefield just to get home," she complained.

Lucas thought the analogy apt, that the killer had put them through an emotional minefield.

Opening her door, stepping inside, they found stains still on the carpet. "I have a cleaning service coming in tomorrow. They couldn't fit me in any sooner," she told him when she noticed Lucas staring at the marks on the plush gray pile. He watched her eyes roam the room to be certain nothing had been left inside by any well-meaning doorman.

"We made it," he declared for her.

She tossed her purse and keys on a table and said, "I gotta get a shower, wash away the stress. Want to join me?" she called out over her shoulder. Not waiting for an answer, Meredyth instantly went for her bedroom and shower, telling Lucas, "If you're not coming in, at least make yourself a sandwich. Make yourself at home."

"I need to make a call, okay?"

She was gone. He heard the spray of the shower like the dull cascade of a waterfall wafting down the corridor from her open bedroom door. Lucas called into the precinct, telling Kelton he and Dr. Sanger would be late arriving this morning, that she'd needed time to recuperate. "And I'm not leaving her alone here, understood? Anyone desperately seeking either of us, we can be reached at her home number."

"Good idea. She's been through hell. You've gotta get this creep, Lucas, and fast."

"My sentiments exactly. Workin' on it."

"You see the *Chronicle?*"

"Saw it."

"Can't keep a story like that under wraps, Lieutenant. May as well try to keep a wolverine in a birdcage."

Lucas grunted and asked, "Put me through to the crime lab, Dr. Davies if he's available."

Lucas waited to be patched through. "Yes, this is Tom Davies."

"Detective Stonecoat, Doctor."

"Oh, good . . . glad you called. Saves me calling round for you and Dr. Sanger."

"Then you have news one way or the other regarding the dental records and the teeth?"

"I do. We have a winner, a hit."

Lucas's fist clenched in the gesture of victory. "Great! Excellent."

"Want to take a stab at which of the three matched?" Davies offered.

Lucas recalled the M.E.'s determination that the hand found with the writing on it indicated a left-handed victim. "Mira Lourdes," he guessed.

"Uncanny," replied Davies. "Someone told me you were psychic."

"I had a lot of help on this one, Doc."

Davies went on. "The victim's teeth, an upper and lower, one bicuspid, the other a front tooth, matched perfectly with Lourdes's dental chart."

"No doubts or margin of error here, Dr. Davies?"

"I've made nineteen comparison points on one tooth, fourteen on the other. Enough to hold up in any courtroom in the land."

"That's good news, Doctor. You must have worked all night. Don't let anything happen to the evidence."

"Not to worry. After hearing about what occurred in the garage last night, I felt it best to make short work of it, Detective."

"Thanks again."

"My pleasure. Hope we can end this nightmare for the two of you."

"Mira Lourdes was a woman with a boyfriend who claims she disappeared when trying to sell her car. Claims she was abducted from her own driveway."

"It has happened before," Davies replied.

"Something screwy about the guy."

"If you say so, Detective. You seem to have terrific instincts. Look, I'll have a copy of my full report on your desk by mid-morning. The original will go to Dr. Chang to

accompany the mounting evidence against our man, whoever he is."

"Yeah, now all we need is to answer the question of
who would want Mira Lourdes dead and why."

"And why the game with the body parts?"

"Someone who can tell us all about what only he and
we know."

"Chang says the hand was severed with a powerful
rotary saw, exactly the sort used in an autopsy," added
Davies. "Very odd game he is playing with you and
Dr. Sanger, odd indeed. Well, I'm exhausted and am going
home now."

"Yeah, kind of tired myself. Think I'll go take a shower."

"Good luck on tracking down this fiend, Detective."

"Thanks, I'm doing my damnedest."

Lucas hung up, deciding he could use that shower and
some foreplay with Meredyth, and perhaps convince her
that they should take the day off. He went toward the bedroom, stripping away his shirt and pants, going for the
shower. Inside the bathroom, a steam cloud filled the space,
billowing out at him and the adjacent bedroom. He
stripped down completely now, dropping all his clothing
and stepping into Meredyth's cloud, recalling her peyote
dream of the other night.

When he opened the shower door and stepped through
the cloud and into the cascading spray, he took her in his
arms and kissed her, his long mane of hair blending with
hers.

"Just what the hell're you doing?" she said in mock
alarm.

"I've come to fulfill your dream."

"We're not the least conceited now, are we, Lucas
Stonecoat?"

"No, I mean, I am stepping into your cloud . . . like in
your dream? Coming into your dream cloud." He held his
arms out to indicate the steam cloud around them.

She laughed. "Oh, yeah . . . I get it, stepping into my
cloud."

"You see me now, don't you? That I belong in your cloud with you?"

"Perhaps clearly for the first time," she replied, wrapping her glistening, soap-covered arms around him. She kissed Lucas, and he returned the kiss. She ran her fingers through his long hair, saying, "Let me wash that long mane of yours, my Indian lover."

Lucas turned his back to her and allowed her to do exactly that.

BY MID-MORNING THEY were driving to downtown Houston and the precinct. On the trip, Lucas brought Meredyth up to date on Dr. Davies's findings, that they had an identity for the Jane Doe whose body parts some geeky-looking wacked-out maniac was sending to them piece by piece.

When Lucas told her the name of the victim, Meredyth repeated it, "Mira Lourdes . . . Mira Lourdes . . . means nothing to me. What possible connection is there between us, Lucas? What do we know about her?"

Lucas told her all that they had learned of Mira Lourdes, and how she had supposedly disappeared. "I suspect her abduction was random, that it had to do with her placing the ad, and inadvertently letting her guard down, placing herself in a vulnerable position by going with this couple seen by the neighbor, *unless* the boyfriend's story is a complete fabrication. I'm sure we'll be talking a great deal more to him if he doesn't lawyer up."

They fell silent as the car whizzed past gas stations, fast-food restaurants, newsstands, parking garages, bus stops, churches, mosques, all reflecting off the windshield. "Wonder what that chemical odor was that Stu smelled on the guy who delivered the package," she said, breaking the silence.

"Anything from disinfectant to formaldehyde, I suppose," replied Lucas. "Points again to a medical type of some sort."

"Do you really think we're dealing with some kind of medical Jack the Ripper?"

"The way the organs were sliced . . . the precision . . . the way her hand was severed so cleanly with a surgical saw. Not to mention the removal of the teeth, and the eyes intact. Yeah, I'd bet on it; our guy is a medical man."

"Or a butcher, or a carpenter, or a barber. Hell, he could be anyone, Lucas! A lousy failed gynecologist or Navy chef, any moke with the right tools for plucking out eyes and pulling teeth and cleaving off a hand."

"Whoever did this also opened up the chest cavity and removed internal organs, Mere. It requires some precision to make the cuts he left for me. Even Chang was impressed."

"Impressed? Nothing this monster can do to us can ever impress me, Lucas."

"Perhaps impressed is a poor choice of words." They had arrived at the precinct when Lucas's cell rang out. He lifted it and immediately acknowledged Jana North's voice, unaware that this made Meredyth stiffen alongside him. When he got off the phone, he told Meredyth, "Jana's waiting for us in your office. Wants to discuss the case with us. Seems she's talked to Dr. Davies and has informed the family that Mira Lourdes is being chopped into little pieces and put into boxes and forwarded to you and me."

"Jesus, Lucas, this thing's blowing up fast now, and we haven't a clue as to who is behind it. This is going to make us look like . . . like . . ."

"A couple of incompetents, I know. Shit! I can't believe Jana's done this."

"Why not? From a Missing Persons departmental point of view, she's solved *her* case. Mira Lourdes has been located, so to speak."

"Determined dead maybe, but Jana's got no corpus delecti."

"Only bits and pieces of the corpse."

"She damn sure could've waited on it, and given us more time."

"So, you still think Byron's the *unnamed source* we need to worry about? Just tell me this, Lucas Stonecoat . . ."

He gnashed his teeth, readying for her attack. "What?"

"Are you going to take Detective North to task?"

"Damn straight."

She inwardly smiled. "I want to see this."

DETECTIVE JANA NORTH was awaiting them both in Meredyth's office. She and Meredyth exchanged perfunctory hellos, knowing one another professionally. "I've informed the parents and Mira's live-in, Dwayne Stokes, that we *know* Mira is dead and that *parts* of her are being sent to law-enforcement officials in a sick game of cat-and-mouse initiated by the killer."

"Jeeze, Jana, that information's gone out to the family and that idiot Stokes? It's going to be all over the six o'clock news."

"This is a Missing Persons case, Lucas. We have to keep the family informed. It's the way we work."

"No Jana, it's a murder case, a homicide. That takes precedence over your jurisdiction, and you know that. You also know we don't work homicide that way."

"Ease off, Lucas," Meredyth said. She addressed Jana. "God, it must've been extremely difficult breaking such news to the parents." Meredyth felt a genuine guilt now, seeing that Jana was hurt by Lucas's words.

"They had to know, Lucas," said Jana. "Soon as I learned about the match made by Davies, I tried to find you. When I couldn't, I went over there to talk to the parents. I swore them to keep it confidential for now."

"Can't imagine the shock of it for the parents," Meredyth sympathetically added.

"But you didn't stop with the parents. You told Stokes what we have. Just wish you'd have held off, Jana." The annoyance in Lucas's voice hung in the air. "I would've liked to have seen Stokes's reaction."

"All right, maybe I should've held off."

"How'd Dwayne react to the news?"

"Devastated, as far as I could see."

"He's hiding something."

"He lost his legs and his breakfast. As far as the parents go, better they should get the news through us than hearing it on MSNBC or reading it in the *Chronicle,* and the way information's leaking from your precinct, Lucas, I think I did the right thing."

"Regardless of Stokes's theatrics, Jana, I think we need to get him in here and grill his ass for all he's worth," said Lucas. "I think he knows more than he's telling."

"I'm on top of it, Lucas."

"How, Jana, are you on top of it?"

"He's in interrogation now, and has stuck *tenaciously* to his story. That she was abducted by a *couple* to whom she was showing the Saab."

Meredyth piped in, saying, "Whoa, it was *my* understanding that he never actually saw the couple, that he only *heard* about them."

"Right."

"Then how is he sticking to the story?"

Jana looked firmly in Meredyth's green eyes. "Doctor, I meant he is sticking to *his* alibi—that he was at work at the taco stand in the mall where he is the night manager, and his multiple alibis are being checked. In the meantime, he's cooperated in helping us to get the neighbor to take a deposition as a witness through official contacts we've made in Jamaica. So both of you, ease off Jana, okay?"

Lucas and Meredyth exchanged a look and each apologized to Jana. Lucas then asked, "What about the impounded Saab? Anything found there?"

Jana made herself comfortable, taking one of two chairs facing Meredyth's desk. Meredyth sat behind her desk, and Lucas took the seat beside Jana.

"A CSI team is going over the Saab. So far, they've found a stain on the front passenger side, the cloth seat. Nielsen says it's chloroform."

"Chloroform, really?"

"Which explains how she was subdued," said Meredyth.

"The abductor likely took her from behind while *inside* the car, from the *rear* seat," explained Jana.

Lucas, nodding, added, "Which suggest two perps at work here, one driving, one attacking."

"All of which verifies Dwayne's story—or rather Mrs. Paulis's story."

"Really? Then Stokes is off the hook?"

"Perhaps. Waiting for a call from Jamaica."

"Still, good ol' Dwayne may've hired the couple that abducted and killed her."

"Possibly," she agreed, "but as much as he hated the car, don't you think he would've paid them to take it as well?" asked Jana, smirking.

Lucas smiled wryly and nodded.

"Any case, he's agreed to a lie detector test. That's being arranged as we speak."

"Any other news?"

"Well, you asked about the car. CSI did find strands of Mira's hair, and fibers from the cloth seat in the trunk, not unusual since it's her car, *but* it could indicate she spent some time locked away there."

"Imagine the gall," said Meredyth, picturing it as Lucas had described the circumstances surrounding Mira Lourdes's disappearance, "leaving his own car at the scene of the abduction . . . taking Lourdes back to her own driveway . . . switching cars and switching Mira from the Saab to the car he arrived in . . . and finally driving off with her."

"We need the woman in Jamaica to give a description of the guy's car," said Lucas. "Get what you can from her on it."

"The bastard did it all with the passive assistance of the girlfriend or the wife, whoever she was—likely in great fear of him," Meredyth added. "So she assists in abducting a *surrogate*."

"Surrogate?" asked Jana North.

"A stand-in for herself."

"Stand-in for what?"

"A punching bag, a sex slave, a torture chamber victim, you name it. The wife or girlfriend tires of being these things that pleasure him, so together they strike up a plan to abduct someone to fill the role, so the wife-girlfriend can step out of that role of victim. Both partners are happy with the new arrangement. He gets a new sex partner to bully and torture, and she gets shed of his bullying and torturing."

"Then her role in abducting and premeditated torture isn't so passive after all, is it?" asked Jana.

"No, not always, not entirely. If she sat in back while he drove, for instance, she attacked Mira and sent her into a defenseless unconsciousness."

Lucas added, "I've seen such domination of women myself. Meredyth could be right."

The three sat for a moment in silence, contemplating the new developments.

Then Jana asked, "Does the name Mira Lourdes mean *anything* at all to you, Dr. Sanger?"

"Nothing. A total blank."

"We haven't found any connection between us and Lourdes," Lucas assured Detective North.

"So where does that leave us?"

"The connection is to the killer," concluded Meredyth. "Mira Lourdes is somehow connected to her killer, not us, not Lucas and me."

"But this abduction seems random. According to her family and the boyfriend, she had no enemies." Jana shook her head. "What does that mean, Dr. Sanger?" she challenged.

"There may be no connection in *our* reality, Jana, that is, the real world, but maybe there is a connection in *his* reality, his warped mind."

"I see, a warped fantastical notion that Mira Lourdes belongs to him is all the connection he needs. But that could just as well apply to his attraction to you since, obviously, Mira Lourdes did not *work out*."

Meredyth stared at Detective North and swallowed hard. Lucas contemplated the ramifications of what Jana had just said.

"If that is the case," said Meredyth, "then some nut-ball is stalking me for a surrogate slave, and his woman is helping him in this fantasy turned on me. But such a theory doesn't take into account his taunting Lucas."

Meredyth paced to the window and stared out to the busy street below. "As far as *connecting* with me or Lucas . . . well, the creep could well've seen us on the tube, you know, during the Walters case, or even the Castle trials, or being interviewed when we broke that Internet murder ring ten years ago for all we know."

"Yes, well, that's true. You two have made news. You both come with the badge of notoriety as a result."

Meredyth returned to her seat and dropped into it, looking defeated. "Maybe it's time to change professions."

Lucas leaned across the desk and said to her, "Mere, I know it has occurred to you that the killer is simply interested in the *notoriety* that *he* can achieve or . . . or create for himself."

"Big bucks these days in *murderabilia*," she replied.

"Murderabilia?" asked Jana.

"You know, the peddling of murder paraphernalia, serial-killer collectables and trading cards. . . ."

This set Lucas's teeth on edge, and he further explained. "Buying and selling of anything connected with sociopaths and psychos, from John Wayne Gacy's clown suit, his circus clown paintings, to Danny Rollings's nose clippers and the radio knob offa Ted Bundy's Volkswagen, or the car itself, all going for auction on eBay."

"Christ, perhaps that's all he wants, to be ranked among the big boys of criminal history," suggested Jana, her forehead creasing with the implications of such a notion.

"In which case he may *believe* he knows us, but we don't have any idea who he is or any connection whatsoever to him in *our* reality, only in *his,* as I said," Meredyth added. "His *relationship* with Mira Lourdes may well've been another twist in the same path. Say he saw her at her place of work, interacted with her, and she became a luminary *star* for him."

"That's scary," replied Jana. "Reminds me of an obsessive

boy who tagged me as his special angel when I was only sixteen."

"When was that, last year?" asked Meredyth, smiling.

"Thanks for the compliment."

"So we're talking stalking behaviors, stalker-think, that all too familiar brand of magical thinking affecting too damn many American males nowadays," said Lucas.

"If we're dealing with a guy with a psychosis, perhaps he's a patient or former patient of yours, Dr. Sanger," Jana suggested, moving about the room now, thinking on her feet. "I'm sure you've considered that possibility."

"We're going to spend the day going over recent and old cases and patients," Lucas assured Jana.

"I mean, it could just be a guy with a grudge," cautioned Jana. "A screwy revenge motive connection that has nothing to do with the media spotlight?"

"Quite possible," conceded Meredyth.

"Either way, I guess the killer has selected you two for his purposes, and he *thinks* you have a personal relationship, twisted as that may be," said Jana. "I suggest you need a third partner in this, someone with a bit more objectivity, and since the victim is one of my missing persons cases, I'd like to be that person."

"I have no objection," Meredyth replied. "Given Captain Lincoln's order to catch this freak before things get any further out of hand, we welcome your help, Jana."

"Lucas? What do you say?"

They shook on it and together they went downstairs to interrogation to see what progress, if any, had come of the Dwayne Stokes polygraph test. Lucas joked with Jana along the way, asking, "Will the questions like be couched in phrases beginning with like, dude?"

Jana laughed. Meredyth kept her eyes on Lucas, and she hoped her plan, to keep her rival for his affections—the enemy—close, might work.

Jana's best interrogation team had Dwayne hooked up and sweating out every answer to questions. He was hooked up to two machines simultaneously, a typical lie detector/polygraph, all looking normal, and a state-of-the-art, computer interface polygraph with a computer screen for a readout and electrodes that attached to a skullcap placed on the head, looking like something out of a modern-day Frankenstein tale—a modern-day, extremely intimidating lie detector that purported to read lies via brain-wave activity.

For the first time, Lucas felt some compassion for young Dwayne. The fellow looked like a frightened guinea pig, fearful his brain would either be fried or transferred to the polygraph operator. The sight gave Lucas pause, and he related a method he had used on occasion to extract a confession. He told Jana and Meredyth about a time when he and other detectives routinely fooled suspects into believing an ordinary Xerox copier was capable of reading thoughts, that it was a sophisticated brain-wave lie detector. He had personally gotten six confessions using the old Xerox machine.

When Jana stopped laughing, she opened the intercom link and asked the polygraph examiner, a young man who looked fresh out of high school, to step outside for a moment. He did so, and she introduced Meredyth and Lucas to Police Force Cadet Peter Markson.

"Peter here is our resident expert on the new brain reader in there," she explained.

"It's a BPR hooked to an IBM imaging computer that prints faster than you can blink," said Markson.

"BPR?" Lucas asked.

"BrainPrint 2232, deluxe model."

The second polygraph inspector joined them, leaving Stokes alone inside, nervously snatching cables from his body and brain. The second operator handled the older polygraph using galvanic skin responses. He introduced himself to Lucas as Earl Harmond and he pumped Lucas's arm, his eyes wide with admiration. "Mr. Stonecoat . . . Detective . . . you're a hero and local legend. I-I'm so proud, sir, to be acting as HPD civilian support personnel on one of your cases. I've been a fan since I was a kid."

"Your help is appreciated. What do your machines say about Dwayne Stokes?"

"Rules him out. He's telling the truth."

"No way he could be faking it," added Markson. "The BPR never lies."

"You implying my machine does?" argued Earl.

"I'm saying, Earl, our machines agree, and so can we." Markson led Lucas closer to the one-way mirror and pointed in to where Stokes was taking off the final electrodes.

"See the electrode attachment cap for his head? This technology measures brain-wave patterns as well as galvanic skin response—a perfect blending of old and new technologies. We've got all the bases covered. Unless this guy is Houdini, he gets a pass."

"Then we work on the assumption the abduction took place as he pieced it together from the neighbor," said Lucas, seeing that Earl had reentered the interrogation room, telling Stokes that he had passed with flying colors.

Meredyth said, "We need to get the neighbor back to Houston. Get her to our sketch artist, hypnotize her, whatever it takes to get more details from her."

Jana looked at her watch to punctuate her words. "I'm working on that now, but it's sometimes hard to get citizens to cooperate in an investigation. Too many have seen what happens to witnesses on *The Sopranos* and *Law and Order*. Look, I gotta go." She dashed off.

"If the Jamaica connection calls, let us know!" Lucas shouted after Jana. Meredyth dug a heel into his boot.

"Hey, what's that for?" he asked.

"You don't have to be so chummy with Detective North, Lucas."

"Hey, Mere, what the devil're you talking about?"

"Men really are from Mars."

"Why don't we get started on those old case files of yours."

"I told you before, Lucas, confidentiality laws prohibit me from sharing patient information with cops. Haven't I always kept your confidences even though on occasion it meant breaking the law? How'd you like it if I shared what

I know about you with, say, IAD? It'd put you behind bars, Lucas. See now why these rules of conduct and ethics need to be in place?"

"All right . . . you and your intern can go over the *shrinkology* files, but there's nothing says I can't explore old cases brought to trial by you, me, or the both of us."

"Fine, let's divvy the workload up that way, but I expect to find you up to your elbows in paperwork, not up to your ass in Jana North."

She stormed back toward her office, a handkerchief dabbing at her eyes. He started after her, but stopped and shouted instead. "That's uncalled for, Mere!"

Markson came around a corner with a cup of coffee paused at his lips. "Something wrong?"

Lucas, ignoring the cadet wiz kid, shouted down the corridor at the fleeing Meredyth. "You're doing it again! Push me away! Go ahead! Create excuses out of thin air."

She turned and with her teeth set in a firm jaw, began to speak, but only stammered.

"It's all smoke and mirrors, your little magic show," Lucas shouted, "so you don't have to really deal with *us,* with what's happened between us over the last two days, Mere!"

But she slipped into the elevator, disappearing from his sight. Lucas was left standing all alone, people around him politely pretending they'd heard nothing, going about their business. Lucas went for the stairwell, deciding the only safe place might be the Cold Room and his desk.

CHAPTER 8

Deer tracks: ample game

LAURALIE BLODGETT BREATHED deeply, taking in the crisp cool morning air, leisurely strolling the woods around the farmhouse, a quaint little white clapboard home. She had convinced Arthur to rent the house and property for their purposes. Although it had a useless fallen-in barn and shed, there was a fenced-in dog run that appealed to Dr. Belkvin's dog-loving nature.

"Hell, out here, you could let your dogs run free," she had told him. "Arthur, it's perfect!"

Arthur said it could be a sign that she wanted some stability in their relationship, indeed, in her life, that she had never enjoyed before, being an orphaned child without security. She hadn't dispelled Arthur's cockeyed notions, but rather allowed them to build in his lightly dusted sandy-haired head.

There were aspects of Arthur's little homey dreams that did appeal to Lauralie, but she had far too many unrealized plans to settle just yet into a life with anyone, much less a four-eyed Dr. Doolittle with a hairy mole on his right cheek.

She shook off any further thought of it, wishing to enjoy the moment amid the freshly watered earth and grasses, the leaves dripping still with last night's cleansing rain. Nature taking a shower, replenishing herself, she thought. It'd been *forever* since Lauralie had replenished herself, or simply taken some time for herself. Having learned the whereabouts of the woman who had taken her from her mother, Lauralie had spent untold hours researching, following leads, examining clues, exploring evidence, learning, and stalking her prey, planning and deciding how best to destroy her. She didn't want Dr. Meredyth Sanger to die quickly, but rather to suffer a long and torturous harassment, to be made to feel responsible for the deaths of others, and to lose her hold on her sanity, a fittingly ironic end for a professional sanity peddler. After all that, then it *might* be Dr. Sanger who would spend eighteen years under the control of an institution, told when to get up, when to eat, bathe, take her pills, sleep, get up again, and relentlessly repeat the process without deviation or question. To die inside slowly over years, knowing she was the cause of Lauralie's pain and the death of everyone Meredyth loved.

Birds chased one another among the juniper trees just ahead of Lauralie, catching her fascination, and the morning sun glistened on the still-wet dew. A faraway hawk cried out to its mate, no doubt spotting its prey on the ground. As she high-stepped through the tall grass, a soft murmur of insect activity surrounded Lauralie, creating a cloud of fairylike creatures captured in the morning sunbeams.

The stream that ran along one end of the property trickled in her ear as she examined the leaves on the variety of trees here, every sort of hardwood. It was a bountiful, beautiful location, an oasis of green amid miles of brown and red earth on all sides, and she wondered what had happened to the family that had once farmed here. She imagined the children all grown up, that they had abandoned the life here, going off to the big city, taking jobs in factories and mills, leaving the land. No doubt their grandparents and parents had each in turn died in the old house.

Lauralie fancied that she could feel their spirits in the clapboard farmhouse; she sensed their shock and amazement over her shoulder each time she wrapped and addressed a parcel filled with parts of the Lourdes woman. To anyone else, the old house stood empty and abandoned, but Lauralie knew better. While it had been abandoned by its previous tenants, it had never been *completely* abandoned by them. Fortunately, the ghosts of the house had no method of contacting the authorities about the use to which Lauralie had put the old place.

She could see the house through the trees, the kitchen screen door and the large freezer unit that Arthur had purchased for her, one of his earliest tests. She gave thought to Arthur, and how *malleable* he was in her hands as she found that kind spot in his heart, the one all balled up with his sex drive. Yes, Arthur was so kind to her, giving in to her every whim.

She strolled further from the house, deeper into the thicket, until she came on a neat little circle of grass surrounded by bush, an Alice in Wonderland clearing. An area blanketed with pine needles, a cushion placed here for her to sit against a tree and let the sunshine play across her face and body, warming her through her clothing, a simple cotton dress.

She thought that in another life she could easily have been happy simply being a farmer's wife. *Perhaps she still could be,* said a voice inside a niche inside a cubbyhole corner of her mind. After this was all over, perhaps she could convince Arthur to set up house here, to remain here for the rest of their lives. Arthur would do it too. *He'd do anything for me,* she thought, *anything I want. Arthur is a dear.*

Of course she knew better, that she had no future. She began to feel an overwhelming need for sleep. She hadn't been getting much rest lately, her appearance telling the story, and so in closing her eyes, she felt the peaceful voice of slumber whisper in her ear, gently calling her name as in a chant, the lord of sleep, Morpheus, a motherly matron in Lauralie's estimation, luring Lauralie into her soft arms.

Now that Lauralie's birth mother had crossed over, Lauralie felt certain the woman had come to a new realization of the error of her ways; Mother had learned her lesson, and she too beckoned with a soft voice inside Lauralie's head, asking to curl up alongside her daughter now. *Sleep, sleep,* with sunshine warming the eyelids.

As she dozed, her mind took her back to her upbringing at the convent for orphaned girls. She had been put up for adoption at birth, and only recently had she learned who her mother was, and more importantly, where the woman had been all these years. The horrible truth was that her mother hadn't been a world away, not thousands or even hundreds of miles off as Lauralie had always imagined, but worse, here in Houston all these eighteen years.

She recalled in her dream how she had shown up at her mother's doorstep unannounced, surprising the woman, who looked strangely like herself. "Are you Katherine Anne Croombs Blodgett?"

Her mother didn't have to answer, but the woman's parched lips parted, and she mouthed the word *yes* as if expecting this day to come all her life. From the first glance, and given the nature of the question, and the way in which Lauralie had put it to her, the woman calling herself Katherine Croombs nowadays knew the young woman on her doorstep was her daughter. The daughter she had abandoned stood before her, and after an awkward silence, Katherine invited young Lauralie into her ramshackle home on Groilier Street in a run-down neighborhood in the shadow of the Interstate overpass. As Lauralie entered the house, she heard the noise and felt the vibration from traffic overhead on the Interstate. Cars exceeding the fifty-mile-an-hour limit, whistling by at sixty-five and seventy, literally shook the little two-flat tenement rental home.

After their initial meeting, Lauralie took her time getting to know Mother Katherine Croombs and her lifestyle. She worked hard and patiently to win the older woman's trust. Lauralie provided her with money and stockpiled her with what seemed most important to Katherine—*alcohol.*

Later, when Katherine died, no one questioned the woman's death by alcoholic poisoning, certainly not the authorities. No one ever knew or guessed the truth, that on the night of her death, Katherine Croombs Blodgett had learned the full extent of Lauralie's wrath.

Lauralie had tied her down to the bedposts, and she had force-fed whiskey into Katherine until it was coming out her pores. Officially, she drank herself to death. Unofficially, Lauralie had seen to it.

Lauralie had fulfilled her desire to kill her mother, but not before weeks of working her mother around to explain it all, to tell Lauralie how she could possibly have given away her own flesh and blood daughter. "Me, me, Lauralie, Mother. How could you give me away like I wasn't worth your time?"

After Lauralie's visits had become somewhat routine, Katherine, having had enough drink to loosen her tongue, finally tried to explain her actions, prefacing her words with, "Now . . . this isn't any excuse. I-I-I can't offer no excuse," she stuttered, "but-but-but it kinda explains where I-I was at at the time, where my head was at . . . how bad it got. You see . . . sweetheart . . . I . . . I . . . I had a mental disorder, and a drug habit on top of that."

"You coulda gotten help!"

"Damn it, honey, I pleaded for help! I wanted help. I-I-I *sought* help, but they took you away from me because . . . because . . . I don't know the reason why, because I was so out of it, I-I-I couldn't follow what was going on, and so I-I put my trust in a woman working for the child welfare people."

"You were unwed too, and you didn't know who the father was, did you? You still can't tell me who my father is, can you?"

"He died a few years ago of a brain tumor."

"You lived together? As man and wife?"

"John and me, we ran into one 'nother on the street seven or eight years after I gave you up. He was limping badly, crippled from a construction accident. He was in bad shape, and I-I felt sorry for him and took him in. We lived together for the last ten years, helping one 'nother out. I guess you could say we loved one 'nother."

"John what? What was his name?" she pressed, even though she already knew the answer.

"Blodgett, I gave you his name, Blodgett."

"Tell me about Daddy."

"He was three-quarter Indian, Native American, part Mexican."

"What was *his* excuse for never coming for me? All the days and nights of my life, believing that one day one or both of you would come and take me home!"

Katherine turned her gaze away and walked off. She wrung her hands and shook her head, unable to find words.

"He never knew? You never told John Blodgett, did you, ever?" Lauralie asked. "You gave me his name on my birth certificate, but you never told him, did you?"

"No . . . no, I never told him. Not even on his deathbed."

"But why?" Lauralie pleaded. "Were you ashamed of me, your half-breed daughter? Was that another nail in my coffin, another reason to keep me your dirty little secret?"

"No, it was never like that. I-I-I was ashamed of *myself,* of what I'd become and for . . . for having to give you up, and too afraid of John's reaction by then, that he might leave me. He could have a violent temper at times too."

"I want a picture of dear old Dad then."

Katherine found a wallet-sized photo of a dashing, young man with a roguish smile below a full mustache. He had dark skin and black eyes, and the eyes looked mischievous and bold. Lauralie put the picture into her purse.

"I want to know more about this woman with Child and Family Services, the one who helped you out so much when you *needed* it. The one who took me away from you."

"But why do you want to dwell on that awful time, Lauralie? We have the here and now to make up for all those years."

"I want to know all about her, Katherine, Mother, please." Lauralie kept her drinking.

"She was a young woman, younger than me, but very smart about the law and legal aid, all that. In fact, she was a young medical intern, I think."

"Medical intern? Studying to be a doctor?"

"A psychologist, I think."

"Her name, Mother. In case I want to look her up, you know, thank her for all she did for you when you were completely alone."

"It's been so many years, dear. She most likely doesn't even live in Houston anymore."

"Her name, Mother, her name!"

"Mary or Merl or something; I can't recall the last name. Anyway, she led me into court, and next thing I know, you were being put in an orphanage, and me . . . I-I-I got so down on myself after that, well, I-I-I thought you'd be better off once you were *adopted,* once they found a good home and a loving family for you."

"I understand all that. I know you put your *trust* in this woman."

"I put my trust in the court, Harris County, the system, all these *people* telling me what I should be doing next. It was their job to . . . to find you a *good* home, something I couldn't've given you in a hundred years, baby."

"But you never checked to find out whatever became of me, did you, Mom? If you did, you'd've known I was *never* adopted. I've spent my entire life in that *prison* you condemned me to, that convent school."

"I'm sorry . . . so, so sorry."

"Tell me more about the woman who took me away from you! I want to know *everything,* every word she said to you."

"She came to the house, picked me up in a nice car, brought me down to the county courthouse, and she spoke up for me. She made out like she would see to it I got off drugs, away from the booze, that I'd get me a job, you know, and get better, *rehabbed,* and that someday . . . someday I could get *you* back . . . someday, but that day just never came, honey."

"How old was I then, Katherine . . . Mommie? How old?"

"Six months."

"Six months into the year of my birth." Lauralie calculated the month in 1984 of her mother's court appearance, and since Katherine hadn't changed cities in all these years, Lauralie knew where the court records would be housed for her case.

After killing her biological mother that night and sleeping alongside her for the first time in her life, Lauralie, the following morning, went searching for this Mary or Merl who had taken her away from the life she *should have enjoyed* with Mother. The chief cause of all Lauralie's grief, her lifelong agony, the woman who had lied to her mother. The woman who'd stolen Lauralie's childhood.

Going out the door, waving to Mother's corpse that morning, Lauralie had felt a great sense of accomplishment. She had amassed a lot of information in a short amount of time without setting off the powder keg of emotions that might easily have led to an explosion between her mother and herself, which would have accomplished nothing. This way, Lauralie had gleaned all she needed to know; she had garnered useful stuff, ranging from her father's having died of a brain tumor and her mother's bipolar disorder—explaining much of Lauralie to herself—to Mother's drug problem, and how a separation in Lauralie's sixth month of life had been pushed through the courts by a court-appointed welfare worker with connections to the convent and the Houston medical community. An intern working her way up the ladder whom Lauralie meant to find and destroy.

The people at the shelter where her mother had gone for help had called in assistance from the Child and Family Services, and they'd sent someone to assist Katherine and her newborn, a child Katherine had only called Baby, a child Katherine hadn't even given a name to six months after Lauralie's birth. The sisters at the convent orphanage held a contest to name Baby Blodgett, and the winner was Mother Orleans with *Lauralie*.

Katherine had not acted alone in her decision to give up Baby for adoption. Somebody with a name and a life of her own had strongly influenced and encouraged Katherine. Mother could not be held *completely* responsible for her *misguided* actions, so that someone else must also pay. Lauralie meant to lash out at society as well as the individual responsible for the *theft of a child's life*. It was the system as a whole at fault, to allow such things to go on unchecked. A system that dealt in infant children as if they were unfeeling plastic dolls with glass eyes and empty insides, as if she were a mannequin.

After killing Mother, she had walked down to the corner and boarded the Houston Metro for downtown and the Harris County courthouse, where she eventually uncovered and examined some extremely important eighteen-year-old documents, records that revealed the full name of that meddling Mary or *Merl Someone* her mother had confided in and trusted, a someone who'd promised Katherine—and by extension Lauralie—a reunion that never came, a someone now in need of a lesson about tampering with other people's lives—a *Meredyth* Sanger.

Lauralie startled awake, brushing at her hair, having felt something crawly scuttle across her brow and into her bangs. She leapt to her feet, pine needles clinging to her cotton print dress. She shivered at the tingling in her skin, realizing she'd slept for several hours, the sun now on the other side of the clearing. She'd been baked somewhat, but had been saved by the shade of the tree. She got her bearings by locating the house.

She knew Arthur was due back from his school duties soon. He'd complained of having missed too much class time, that he'd be missed, possibly called into the Dean's office and reprimanded. She had told him to go, that she could use some alone time.

He'd be hungry when he got back, she imagined. She walked back to the house, trying to decide on opening a can of Chef Boyardee ravioli for him or a can of tuna for sandwiches.

The greyhounds in the run barked at her as she neared the house. She threw rocks at them, shouting for them to shut up. Pushing through the door and entering the kitchen, she had to wiggle around the large freezer filling the room. "Just enough wiggle room," she said as she went about preparing a stack of tuna fish sandwiches for Arthur.

She caught a glimpse of her reflection in the dirty window over the sink. "The little homemaker, yeah . . . that's me."

LUCAS THREW HIS leather Stetson boots atop his desk, and leaning far back in his chair, scanning the Sims file again, he wondered if he'd missed a crucial piece of information. His phone rang. It was the front desk, Sergeant Stan Kelton, telling him that a large parcel had just arrived via UPS, addressed to Stonecoat care of the department. "Looking suspicious, no return address," Stan said, "so I called for the X-ray machine and—"

"You didn't nab the delivery man?"

"The delivery came through UPS, all legit, Lucas. We had no cause to hold him. I've got people looking into where the parcel originated from, both at the UPS address and the return address. Best we can do."

"Jerk likely used cash with UPS. Credit card and we'd have 'im. So what's the return address?"

"Lucas, we've got the X ray on it now."

"The return address, Stan?"

The numbers meant nothing to Lucas, an address down near the shipping channel on Lowe.

"You'll want to come upstairs now and take a look at this for yourself, Lieutenant."

"How bad is it, Stan?"

"Bad? All I can say is that your creep's been playing footsie up till now. This one's *godawful bad*, my friend."

"I'll be up there as soon as I alert Dr. Sanger and Detective North, Stan."

"I've got people already alerting them, Lucas. You're all to come down to the conference room off Captain Lincoln's office. See you there."

"Lincoln already knows about the package then?"

"Lucas, he insisted I keep him informed of anything else suspicious coming into the squad room. After what occurred with Dr. Sanger, he wants to be kept informed. His orders."

"Gotcha . . . understand."

Lucas arrived at the conference center moments ahead of Meredyth and Jana, the two of them chatting as they entered the darkened room, going silent on seeing what awaited them. On the wall screen, they saw the fuzzy video of the interior of the box addressed to Lucas. Staring back at them were a pair of blank, horrific eye sockets that dominated the terrible image of a young woman's head. The X-ray photo was black and white, like an old Bogart movie still.

"Some still life, hey, people?" asked Lincoln, stepping out of shadow and into the picture, blocking the screen.

No one laughed at the dark joke. Meredyth, Lucas, and Jana could make out the woman's thick, dark hair and features. It was unquestionably Mira Lourdes's head. In the black-and-white, grainy X-ray photo, the empty eye sockets gave the still-fleshy severed head the look and feel of a skull.

"It's her all right." Meredyth tore her eyes away from the image and dropped into a chair, holding back tears.

"That'd be my guess," Lucas said, agreeing about the identity of the eyeless woman's cranium.

Kelton stood by like a silent sentinel.

"Chilling." Jana fell, disheartened, into a chair.

"Crazy how even though we *know* Mira's body is out there someplace," began Meredyth, "that her body's in the asshole's freezer, chopped up to fit into boxes . . . and knowing the likelihood . . . the probabilities . . . that is, expectations being what they are . . . why then does this horrible puzzle piece have so devastating an impact as it has?" She wiped at tears with a handkerchief.

"Such a callous game he's playing," added Jana.

"A crude inhumane monster," agreed Lincoln, "desecrating her body like this."

"Don't you see, it's the killer's *body language*," said Lucas.

"What the hell're you talking about, Detective?" asked Lincoln.

"The bastard's speaking volumes to us."

"Lucas is right," said Meredyth. "He's showing us scorn, hatred, disdain. By deriding our societal beliefs, mores."

"Can you speak in English, Dr. Sanger?"

"For instance, our cultural and spiritual need to bury our dead, the concept of the sacrosanct body as temple of the soul, our core belief in the sanctity of familial ties, and on and on. He's pissing on all of it, and that's the message. Mira's body is merely the medium for his message."

Everyone fell silent, contemplating this.

"The medium is the message," said Lucas. "A severed eye, a severed tooth, a severed organ, a severed hand, and now the head. A pox on you and yours. A curse. He's cursing us."

"Whatever the hell he's doing, cursing or scorning, damn it, people, I want an end to this post-office-happy fiend," shouted Lincoln. Calming, he added, "People, we have to end this madness and end it quickly. This can't go on; it can't drag on!"

"We're on it, Captain," Jana said, trying to assure him. "We know something about this maniac. We know he's interested in trying to shake us up in a spectacular fashion."

"Is that a fact?" Lincoln's sarcasm spewed forth thick and biting. "What we know is that this creep is creeping us all out, but he's particularly interested in you two, Dr. Sanger, Lucas. He's got a bug up his ass for you! Why? He's got something personal going with you two and . . . and g'damn it, I want to know what the fuck it is."

"We *think* that he *thinks* that by choosing us as targets that he can grab off the front-page headlines, a most-wanted wanna-be," said Lucas.

"Key-rice . . . please, not another one. Will the Lord of *Joe-has-a-fit* deliver us."

"This monster is scratching to get into the Serial Killer Hall of Fame," Meredyth added. "Simple as that."

Captain Lincoln walked around to stand over Meredyth, placing a hand on her shoulder, seeing how distraught she had become and how she fought to keep her eyes off the image on the wall or the still-closed box sitting at the center of the table. Captain Lincoln calmly asked, "You mean he wants John Walsh or the FBI to come after him?"

"It's a theory."

"A theory? I need more than a theory, Dr. Sanger."

"What do you want from me, Gordon?"

"You're the expert on psychotic behavior, the demented mind, the maladjusted, discontented, rage-filled disenfranchised aberrant soul out there on every street corner, so you tell me, Doctor, are you *convinced* this is the maniac's motive or not?"

"I'm not completely convinced, no."

"And why is that?" pressed Lincoln.

"Because . . . because I keep feeling like there's a bell tolling in my ear, and it's ringing specifically for me and Lucas, that he's more interested in destroying our peace of mind than he is in acquiring a legendary reputation as a blackguard of negative fame. But on the other hand, perhaps he wants *both*."

Lincoln paced back around the conference table. He contemplatively muttered, "For whom the bell tolls, huh? It tolls for thee."

"All I'm saying is I feel we're being stalked for reasons other than his wanting media attention," Meredyth added.

Lincoln continued to pace the room. "I want everyone who has been involved on the case in any way, shape, or form to come down and have a look at what this motherfucker's shoved in our faces in our own house. Call in Chang, his CSI team, Purvis, Davies, anyone in your department who's been helping out, Detective North, Dr. Sanger, and get them all down here pronto! We begin to end this terrorism here and now. Call it an ad hoc task force, but get them here. We'll open your UPS box, Lucas, with Chang's people in attendance. All right, everyone, go out, make the necessary calls, get your heads together, and get back here ASAP."

* * *

IN A MATTER of twenty minutes, everyone who had had
any hand whatsoever in the strange case of what was being
called the Post-it Ripper stepped through the doors of the
darkened conference room to stand and stare at the ugly
image on the wall. Dr. Tom Davies was the last to enter,
finding a seat near Chang and Nielsen. At one end of the
table sat Jana North and the two men who had interrogated
and polygraphed Dwayne Stokes. In addition, Jana had
called in the two men who'd gone over Mira Lourdes's
Saab. Stan Kelton, Lucas, and Meredyth sat at the other
end. Between and among them sat various evidence technicians who had handled segments of the evidence gathering
and/or specimen analysis from the crime scenes at either
Meredyth's place, Lucas's apartment, or the police garage.
Among them were photographer Steve Perelli and evidence tech Ted Hoskins. Alongside them, Dr. Catrina
Purvis sat tapping a pencil nervously atop a notepad.

Finally, Anna Tewes, the sketch artist, was moving
about the room, averting her eyes from the screen, busy
handing out the updated description of the suspect. The
new sketch, a blending of actor Richard Thomas's features
with those of Microsoft's Bill Gates and director Ron
Howard, included the hairy mole, black eyebrows, blond
head, larger ears, and thicker glasses. The additions, courtesy of Stu the doorman, had transformed the bland "happy
face" original.

With all assembled, Captain Lincoln pointed to the eyeless image of the severed head on the wall, and informed
them, "Our crack team of detectives here, armed with a
photo of a missing person, has told me this box you see at
the center of the table contains the severed head of a young
woman named Mira Lourdes, ladies and gentlemen."

A photo of Mira Lourdes was thrown up on the wall
beside the X-ray image of the head in the box, and
Leonard Chang maneuvered the photo image to overlay
the X-ray image. It formed a perfect match, down to the
high cheekbones.

"Now you know who you've been gazing at since your arrival. A young murder victim, and the bastard that killed her, this Post-*hole* guy the press is chewing up our asses to know more about, has the temerity to dump this on *my* doorstep, here at the Thirty-first—our house, folks." Lincoln moved around the room, pausing to let this sink in. "Mira Lourdes's severed head."

"This is the fourth parcel this creep has forwarded to us, all addressed to either Dr. Sanger or myself," said Lucas.

Lincoln continued, saying, "We are now going to open the second little present addressed to Lieutenant Stonecoat care of the department via UPS. Lights up, please."

Someone near the switch gratefully brought up the lights. "Dr. Chang, I bow to you," Lincoln said, dropping into a chair in a near genuflection. "Open the damned box, and we'll all have a firsthand look at what this madman has seen fit to send us."

"In the flesh, so to speak," commented Hoskins in a lame attempt to lighten the moment if only by a hair.

Chang and Nielsen had laid out a white sheet on the table and placed the parcel atop it. "The sheet will catch any fibers or hairs that might go airborne on opening the box," Chang explained.

"Steve, get photos of this from beginning to end, please," said Lincoln.

Steve Perelli instantly found his feet and moved about the table, obviously glad to be working instead of staring. Using a compact film camera, he quickly began creating a photo history.

His hands gloved and steady, Leonard Chang next carefully cut away the plain brown wrapping from the box to reveal a liquor box beneath, the words Jim Beam prominently displayed. Chang then proceeded to cut away the tape holding the box closed. He next carefully pulled back the flaps, Perelli continuing to record it all with his camera.

Chang's face twitched slightly as he stared down into the box, and Perelli focused over his shoulder, both men privy to the still-vibrant color of auburn that was Mira's hair. Chang reached into the box and lifted out the dismembered head to the combined gasps of the men and women present, while Perelli somehow continued to roll film.

Chang held the head by a fistful of the wilted auburn hair, and he gently turned the eyeless face, examining all sides of the cranium for fractures or abrasions, but he found none. "Hair is damp, possibly indicating it was washed by killer, or simply wet from thawing out."

Liquid gruel dripped from the open gullet held over the white sheet. Chang reached a gloved hand up and into the gullet, stating, "The semicircle of the hyoid bone is shattered so horribly, it is unlikely she was strangled to death. Likely shattered by an ax."

No one said a word. The only sound was the quiet hum of Perelli's camera. Finally, Lucas asked, "How do you know it was done with an ax?"

"Two blows," replied Chang. "First blow not so neat as second strike of the ax, Lucas. My best guessestimate with naked eye."

Chang continued. "The lack of coloration around the wounded eyes indicate she was mercifully dead when the eyes were removed."

"Thank God for that much," muttered Dr. Purvis, holding a handkerchief over her mouth and nostrils, fending off the ever-growing odor of the contents of the box. She contemplated the eyeballs that she'd declared those of a young woman.

"However, coloration at the neck wounds—at least two wounds from what I can see," continued Chang, his eyes so close to the severed neck that his nose might be touching her hair, "gives me suspicion that she was alive when her head was chopped off."

"What kind of weapon do you suspect?" asked Jana North.

"A guillotine of some sort?" asked one of the polygraph men.

"A blunt blade, not a surgical tool, likely an ax, a dull one. Notice the jagged edges, the puckering and pigmentation of the skin around the wound, and the scarring at two separate angles."

Everyone remained silent, picturing such an attack.

The young sketch artist, Anna Tewes, suddenly and noisily knocked over her chair as she stood and pushed away from the table, rushing for the door, holding back her morning's breakfast. She had brought a cup of coffee into the room with her, and its contents had spilled over the white sheet, creamy brown rivulets creating competing little serpent trails moving toward the severed head that Chang had plunked there. Lynn Nielsen threw a cloth over the coffee while others in the room stared at Tewes's exit, thinking they'd like to make an escape as well, but everyone remained seated, calm save for Dr. Purvis's coughing jag into her handkerchief.

No one could miss the jagged edges, dirt, and particles adhering to the gullet; all of it spoke of a messy, blunt ax job. "Lizzy Borden took an ax and gave her mother forty whacks," commented Ted Hoskins. The comment didn't lighten the mood around the table.

Dr. Lynn Nielsen leaned in toward Chang for a closer look at the assaulted neck. "Dr. Chang is correct. There is nothing of the care we saw taken with the removal of the hand." Nielsen's Scandinavian voice echoed in the silent room, deep and rumbling. "That bit of butchery we determined to be accomplished with a rotary *medical* saw of the sort we use in autopsies."

"Those things are loud as hell, aren't they?" asked Lincoln.

"Only when going through bone or the skull," Nielsen countered.

"So whoever this creep is, either people are used to his noise, or it's perfectly normal given the circumstances, as in a butcher's shop," suggested Stan Kelton, who'd remained stoically silent until now.

"Yes, Stan, or an autopsy room," added Chang.

"Or he's in an area where the noise can't be heard," suggested Lucas.

Chang, expanding on these comments, added, "None of the previous parts of our Jane Doe—now Mira Lourdes—

indicated cause of death, but now we know how she died. Here is our answer, a ruthless and clumsy beheading."

"But who is behind this circus of death, and why?" asked Lincoln. "Why all the care and preparation and surgical neatness and tidiness with each part after you've clumsily put an ax through someone's neck? Explain that one!"

"He's deemed it time to show us exactly how Mira died," said Lucas, "rubbing it in our faces."

"I fear it's more than that," added Meredyth. "It's almost as if the killer is playing some sort of endgame, the rules, boundaries, bonuses, and goals known only to him. He means to shock us, to make us play against our will, to force it on us. Behind it, I believe there's a cry . . . a cry for help."

Dr. Davies, gnashing his teeth, suddenly exploded. "A cry for help, Dr. Sanger? You call what this freak is doing a cry for help? I suppose you think he needs coddling as well? Foul murdering heathen." Davies stood and added, "Between pulling the woman's eyes and teeth out and now this, I've seen enough to agree with the governor about the future of the electric chair in Texas, thank you." Dr. Davies paced to the opposite end of the room, as far from the severed head as he could get.

After a silence, Chang continued. "Once Mira was dead, the killer began the autopsy cuts from the abdominal cavity, the removal of the eyes, the teeth, the hand most of us have seen."

Meredyth replied, "Apparently the SOB was disappointed by our lack of response to his earlier parcels, likely dissatisfied with the lack of *play* he's gotten in the press as well."

"Exactly," agreed Jana North. "Apparently he means to shock us more deeply into a greater response and achieve more media attention in the process."

Lincoln asked Meredyth and Lucas to share their belief that the killer might simply be seeking serial-killer status and fame in all his efforts. The others listened to the theory, nodding, contemplating its validity and any weakness it might have. Davies returned to his seat, jaw clenched, listening to the conversation.

Anna Tewes quietly and shyly reentered the room, going to her seat, which Lucas had righted and replaced at the table. She made no eye contact with anyone in the room, looking like a deer going for her nesting ground.

"Put it away, Dr. Chang," said Gordon Lincoln of the severed head, echoing everyone's sentiments. "I think we've seen enough of this horror."

Chang, with Nielsen's assistance, placed the head into a red and white ice-filled medical cooler, and Nielsen tagged it with a case number. The odors emanating from the head and the Styrofoam-lined cardboard box had begun to make people in the room choke and squirm in their seats.

"So, let me see if I understand correctly, Dr. Sanger," said Dr. Davies, staring at Meredyth. "You believe that this homicidal nutcase is sending us a wake-up call of sorts, that in escalating the size and awfulness of the body parts he's forwarded, that he's saying play my game and give me more media attention or else?"

"Quite possibly, yes."

Catrina Purvis asked, "Or else what? That if we fail to share what we know with the six o'clock news, that he'll send larger sections of his victim, and possibly parts of another victim and another until he gets what he needs from us?"

"He's always sent a written note before now, Dr. Chang," said Lucas. "You'll want to look closely inside the box."

Meredyth, seeing confusion written across many of the faces in the room, explained. "In each of the earlier *treats,* the Ripper was considerate enough to forward a handwritten note, and in one case a CD."

"Is there anything else in that bloody box, Leonard?" Lincoln asked.

While Leonard tipped the box, searching for anything in addition, young Anna Tewes, a handkerchief over her mouth, her curiosity greater than her embarrassment, found her voice. "What kind of CD was it?"

"Music from the film *Dirty Dancing.*"

" 'Time of My Life' ?" Tewes asked.

Lucas nodded to a collective groan.

Leonard Chang announced, "There's something at the bottom of the box, a note, swimming amid the fluid left by the decaying head."

"I am detecting the odor of formaldehyde below the odor of decay," said Nielsen.

"Yes, quite," said Purvis. "The head spent some time in a formaldehyde solution."

"Folded paper," added Chang as he fished for it and plucked it from the soup in the Styrofoam-lined box. As Leonard Chang held it up to the light, everyone stared at the spoiled, folded note that dripped of foul and runny liquid. Chang dropped the messy note onto the white sheet beside the medical cooler, which Nielsen removed to a chair beside her, giving everyone a clear view of the opening of the folded note.

Using his gloved hands and tweezers, Chang carefully plucked open the sticky folds of the note and plastered it down. Lucas came close, Meredyth inching alongside, both looking over Chang's shoulder. Perelli squeezed in as well, rolling film.

"What the hell does it say?" roared Lincoln.

Lucas read the note aloud, " ' Works of magic oft do require cool heads of logic and fathomless eyes of fire. . . . ' It is written in poetic lines."

"What the hell does that mean?" asked a frustrated Captain Lincoln.

"Like his motives, the killer's little rhymes may only have meaning for himself, a kind of mirror only he is reflected in, you see," suggested Meredyth.

"Come again?" asked Hoskins.

"He's obviously psychotic, so it becomes necessary to appease only himself. Classic symptoms if we read between the lines."

Jana North said, "Or his written messages and the music may be just another way to taunt you and Lucas, to piss you off, Meredyth."

"The son of a bitch is doing a good job of that,"

Meredyth agreed, feeling a smile flash over her, allowing a diminutive laugh to escape. But she didn't feel as brave as she wanted others in the room to think, as her eyes scanned the blurred words on the blood- and bile-stained note:

> *Works of magic*
> *oft do require*
> *cool heads*
> *of logic*
> *and fathomless*
> *eyes of fire. . . .*

CHAPTER 9

Eagle feathers: chief

CAPTAIN GORDON LINCOLN had given everyone a fifteen-minute break, "Time enough to call home, let your significant other know you're going to be running late, grab a snack, make for the johns, whatever cranks your shaft."

That fifteen minutes had gone by in the blink of an eye, it seemed, and now they had reassembled at the conference table.

"All right, people, quiet now . . . listen up," began Lincoln. "I want cooperation among you all, and I want this case cleared *post*haste, pun intended. If there's any upside to this Postmortem Ripper guy, it's that we have only *one* victim to our knowledge, but the *downside* is this continued butchering of her body. Dr. Sanger informs me this may well have a powerful symbolic meaning for the killer, that he is killing her over and over with each severing.

"Which likely means he's nurtured a long-standing hatred for this Mira Lourdes," concluded Lincoln. "Are we on her acquaintances, former boyfriends, relatives?"

"We've cleared her live-in," said Jana, "and there's no

one else who fits the bill, according to her parents. No one was stalking her, no one disliked her. She went from work to home and back again in a steady routine in which nothing untoward should ever have happened to her."

"But it did," said Lincoln. "Canvas the neighborhood for perverts living in the area, anyone recently moved in, any recent sex offenders released from Huntsville. Talk to her friends at work too."

"My team's all over that," Jana assured him.

"The fact he's sending parts of a single victim over and over could signify his belief that life has screwed him over again and again, that it has cut him up slowly in pieces over the years," suggested Lincoln, playing at shrink himself now.

Meredyth cut him off, saying, "The killer may also be sending pieces of his victim to us again and again to direct our attention to his powerful scorn and disdain for us, for law enforcement, and societal sanctions. A complete psych profile is being worked up. I'll get a copy to each of you by day's end."

Lincoln thanked her for the input. "Whatever it takes, manpower, currency, overtime, you people are it for the time being—the front line in this twisted little war we have had thrust upon us. Time is our enemy along with this monster out there. So I want brainstorming and answers before this bastard forwards so much as another fingernail, understood? Damn it, I don't want any more pieces of her sent off like a Christmas package to Lucas or to Dr. Sanger. And I want it cleared before the press eats us alive on it, understood? And I don't want any more leaks coming out of the Three-one, clear?"

"Captain, we had an obligation to inform the Lourdes family and her boyfriend, who made the initial missing persons report," said Jana.

"Yes, I heard all about that, Jana." Lincoln looked in Lucas's direction. "It's done. Let's just not give any more guns to the Indians . . . ahhh . . ." Lucas had shot him a grim look, "I-I mean, ammo to the press, okay?"

"You're going to have to deal with the press sometime, Captain," said Lucas. "They need to be *handled*."

"Yes, but *most* of the Lourdes woman's remains . . . well, *remain* missing, Lucas, and until we can say we have *all* one hundred percent of her in our safekeeping, well . . . I suspect we'd best keep this in-house. Is that understood?"

Lucas lunged in, adding, "It's already out there, Captain. They're coming for us on all sides. Some sort of press conference or at least a release needs to be put together to stave 'em off."

Lincoln sighed heavily, heaving his gut; he ground his teeth so hard it hurt others in the room to hear it. "Why the hell can't we keep a lid on our own fucking cases?"

"We already brain-graphed and polygraphed Lourdes's boyfriend and he sailed through the tests," Lucas replied, "so now he's out there on the street with what he knows and what he suspects."

Jana added, "And if an idiot like Stokes can read the papers, he can put two and two together. . . ."

"He's likely selling his story to the *National Inquirer* right now," Lucas said.

Meredyth added, "Any number of uniformed cops at my place, at Lucas's, in the garage the other night, not to mention civilian personnel. They're all talking about the choice of delivery system—the variety of method, and what's going on between this creep and us, Lucas and me. Sorry, Captain, but there's no lid big enough to put atop this thing, not anymore."

Lincoln looked as if he wanted to roar, but he calmly said, "All right, so I guess we should expect a barrage of embarrassing publicity."

"Which, if Dr. Sanger is correct, will feed the killer's appetite and hopefully appease him," added Jana, "but I rather doubt that any amount of publicity for his crimes will ever be enough, not once he gets a taste for it. Like a wild animal that acquires a taste for human blood, he'll be back for more."

"We have to be smart and use the media to our advantage," Lucas suggested. "See if we can get at him through a judicious use of the press. Give him an E-mail address where he can contact us, chat with us. Start by releasing some choice photos of the packages from Steve's collection along with Anna's new and improved sketch of the suspect." Lucas gave a thought to Jack Tebo's having failed to come downtown to work with Anna Tewes on a sketch of the girl who'd delivered Lucas's first parcel.

Lincoln gave in, outvoted. "I'll get our best PR people on it. Play up the fact we're closing in on the creep, banter the catchphrase Postmortem Ripper, is it? Put out the fact we've got a face to go with the victim within forty-eight hours of receiving the first package, all that."

"Post-it Ripper," corrected Nielsen. "*Postmortem* is what I do."

"Oh, yes, sorry." Lincoln's eye lingered a moment too long on the lanky coroner. "Okay, well, then . . . what was I saying? Oh, yes. Then that means you people in this room are going to have to show some progress beyond learning the name and address of the victim."

Meredyth addressed the others from where she sat, her voice firm, the occasional crack in her tone contradicting her outward resolve. "We have already discovered a great deal about our man in the short time we've had to work this case. He's got a *hard-on* for Lucas and me, but there may or may not be a connection there; it may be he has seen us on TV in the past and simply zeroed in on us, but we will be going over clients I've counseled as well as perverts we've encountered in the line of duty, ruling them out as we go in a process of elimination. Fact is, that process is already under way."

"Still, it's going to require considerable man hours and manpower, given how long we've both been in the business of putting perverts away," added Lucas. "As we come up with possible leads and suspects, we may call upon any one of you to follow up, whatever that entails, from getting a search warrant to using your special talents."

With that said, Lincoln declared, "Thank you all for

being here and withstanding the assault on your sensibilities that Dr. Chang, Dr. Nielsen, and I orchestrated, but I wanted you all as committed to this as Dr. Sanger and Detective Stonecoat, so I wasn't sparing anyone's ahhh . . . ahhh . . . what's the word?"

"Emotions?"

"Senses?"

"Yeah, those things."

The wrapping paper and the note were bagged, destined for the documents experts already poring over the previous handwriting. The cooler containing the head was carried off by Nielsen, destined for the freezer in Chang's lab. This time the foul contents *purported* to have originated at an address in the 2700 block of Lowe Boulevard, a grimy business district off Clinton Drive, near the ship channel, a stretch of urban real estate devoid of apartments or homes. Lucas had earlier jotted down the address.

"It's most likely a phony address to throw us off, like the convent school," he told Kelton, handing the note to him and asking Stan to check it out and report back to him on what he learned.

"Should not take long. I sent a cruiser over to the address to eyeball it. Probably got round to it by now."

"If not, goose 'em for me, will you, Stan?"

"Sure thing."

Leonard Chang doled out assignments to the remaining CSI members with respect to the newly acquired evidence. Meanwhile, Tom Davies wondered aloud to Meredyth and Lucas why he needed to have been in on this meeting, feeling he had already done all that he could to further the investigation along, "Unless," he confided in her, "you can bring me some of the *killer's* teeth to work with."

Lucas replied, "I'd like nothing better than to kick this mother's teeth out of his sick head, believe me."

Dr. Davies nodded, smiling, and quickly followed Catrina Purvis and Anna Tewes out the door. Meredyth now looked long and hard into Lucas's eyes. "Do you think this maniac is sending us all these parts because he thinks we can put Mira back together again?"

"All the king's horses and all the king's men, you mean? Hadn't occurred to me, but who knows . . . maybe . . . maybe he's that damned batty."

"What's he going to send us next, Lucas? Her heart? Her torso? He is attempting to shock us more and more by escalating the vileness of his gifts to us, and I gotta say, it's working."

"I'm going to the convent this afternoon, poke around there, ask a few questions of the people in charge. You want to join me?" he asked.

"Convent? What *convent?* I heard you mention something to Stan about a convent." Her squint told him clearly that she was confused.

"Our Lady of Miracles, a church and girls convent—an orphanage for girls. Not too far from my place."

"But why?"

"It was the return address on the first package I received, remember?"

"No, I *don't* remember."

"And the delivery was made by someone sporting a Catholic schoolgirl's uniform, according to Tebo."

"You never told me any of this."

"But you were there, at my place, when Chang and I were talking about it."

"No, I wasn't *all* there. I was extremely upset that night, and I didn't pay close attention, not after what I'd been through, not that night. Tebo saw a Catholic schoolgirl deliver the package?"

"I'm not sure she was a girl. He seemed to think she was heavily made up, older than a schoolgirl, but she wore a Catholic school uniform."

Meredyth considered this, picturing the killer luring some young woman to do his godless bidding for him.

"I'm fairly sure it's just a ruse to send us on a wild-goose chase, so I haven't given it top priority. But at the moment, I'm at a loss for what our next step should be, so . . ."

"So, let's go see the nuns. Ask them if they've noticed any unusual person hanging around the school."

On their way out of the precinct house, going past the

front desk, Lucas was stopped when Stan Kelton called out to them. Stan gestured for them to come near.

"What's up, Stan?" he asked the big Irish sergeant.

Kelton had come around his front desk and whispered conspiratorially, "That address on Lowe . . ."

"Yeah? You got it pinned down?"

"Morte de Arthur's."

"A restaurant with medieval cuisine?" guessed Lucas.

"No, it's a mortician place, funeral home—a *chain* mortuary."

"What's a chain mortuary, Stan?"

"A chain of mortuaries. Supposed to be cheaper way to send off your loved one. They're listed with penny stocks. Have their own website where, if you like, you can bury your dead on-line. Don't ask me how that works. The lady said she'd happily send over brochures."

"I'm sure she did. A chain-store undertaker's you can buy into? A franchise?" asked Lucas, amazed. "What'll they think of next?"

Meredyth, listening in, tried to put the fact of the mortician and convent as return addresses together with the return address on her two packages—both indicating her downtown office. She tried to put it all together with the various poems and the CD. "Creep is just yanking our chains, Lucas, having a gay ol' time."

"Then I guess we follow where the yanking chain takes us."

"Play his game out to the end? That could be dangerous."

"What choice have we at this point? He's holding all the cards damned close to his chest, so come along, Mere."

"All right."

"If there's time enough, we'll visit Morte de Arthur's after we visit the house of miracles and nuns."

Kelton waved them off, saying, "Good luck, you two!"

AS THEY MADE their way to Our Lady of Miracles—a shimmering fall sun slapping *on-off, on-off,* on the windshield as the car darted beneath rows of trees—Meredyth asked, "Lucas, do you know who Our Lady of Miracles refers to?"

"I'm not sure I follow you," he replied, confused.

The sunlight first dimmed and then disappeared altogether from the windshield, Lucas commenting on the sudden cloud cover.

"The Lady of Miracles, do you know *who* she was in life, in the history of the Church?"

"I assume the Virgin Mary? Right? I mean doesn't she represent everything to the Catholic believer?"

"Yes, and Our Lady of Miracles is Our Lady of Lourdes—*Lourdes*. Get it?"

"Whataya mean, as in our victim, Lourdes?"

"A French village, city now . . . Lourdes, France, Our Lady of Lourdes . . . the movie they made of it, *Song of Bernadette?* About the village girl to whom the Virgin Mary appeared, thus Our Lady of Lourdes. She is said to have appeared on several occasions."

"I've heard of it, of course. Bernadette had visions when she was a child. An angel told her where water would spontaneously appear out of the earth, right?"

"At the mouth of a grotto, yes."

"A cave."

"Yeah, like a cavern mouth, and to this day, a spring created by the Angel of Lourdes wells up in the town, and it has been made a shrine to which people the world over make pilgrimages in hopes of a miracle cure for various illnesses."

"Lourdes, sure. Didn't they make the little girl a saint?"

"Not before she was put through hell. Religious *celebrities* are put through the ringer by the Vatican."

"Tell that to Joan of Arc."

"Eventually, after years of examinations and investigations, Bernadette was made a saint, but by then, she could not live comfortably in Lourdes. She joined a convent and spent her adult life in the service of Christ."

"So now you're thinking there's a definite link between Our Lady of Miracles convent and our victim, Mira Lourdes, that it's too much coincidence to be just a twist of fate or happenstance?"

"The killer's hand is all over this chance fluke. He *gave* us the convent as a return address, and he gave us enough of Mira to identify her—her teeth and next her head. And how many times have you told me that you don't believe in coincidences in a murder investigation?"

"Touché. So our killer is a *saint killer?*"

"Perhaps contemptuous of Catholic icons—pictures, symbols, idols, and saints."

"So we're chasing someone who might have a history of destroying or disfiguring . . . say . . . a statue of Saint Francis of Assisi?"

"Or even a crucifixion cross, or a painting of mother and child—the Pieta—an altar, or an image of the baby Jesus."

Lucas drove with one hand and used his radio with the other, calling into headquarters and speaking to Kelton. "Get the word out, Stan, that we're interested in any reports of religious vandalism in Catholic churches, schools, grave-yards, anywhere in the city, understood?"

Kelton replied, "We get calls like that all the time, Lucas."

"Anything recent, say in the past week?"

"Usually turns out to be corner-hugging teens so bored out of their skulls they don't give one damn thought to the consequences of their actions," Kelton replied.

"Any unsolved, recent vandalisms of religious icons, gravestones, statues, or paintings, Stan?"

"Fact is, we got an outstanding on a grave site at Green-haven Meadows off Berwyn."

"Whose grave, Stan?"

"Some guy named Blood . . . John Blood, as I recall. I can look up the report. Came in from the caretaker. Said the dirt around the grave was disturbed, and the stone was cracked from what had to be a sledgehammer."

"Anything else? Anything to do with a church?"

"No, nothing."

"Keep an eye out for such things, Stan."

"I'm on it." Kelton was gone.

They drove on in silence under the increasingly over-cast sky, each taking silent counsel, she with her training in human nature, he with his grandfather's words in his head, and both weaving what little they knew of the killer with the puzzling scraps they had collected thus far, and now this new notion involving the Catholic Church. Meredyth's profession didn't like coincidences of this size any more than did Lucas's Native instincts. This matter of Our Lady of Miracles being Our Lady of Lourdes, and their victim being a Lourdes. Had the poor young woman paid the ultimate price because she bore the name of the convent?

Meredyth broke the stillness, saying, "There's too much here to be called *mere* coincidence, Lucas, and . . . and there's something else I have to tell you."

He looked at her, her tone signaling a confession of some sort. "What is it, Mere?"

"Almost twenty years ago, when I was a psychiatric intern doing social work for my degree, I had some dealings with the orphanage at Our Lady of Miracles."

"Another strange harmony?"

"What astrophysicists call a *concurrence,* I think. Ongoing occurrences on a collision course."

"Too close for comfort," he agreed.

"But Lucas, it's the first real clue that the killer may have targeted me for some specific reason other than my notoriety as a forensic psychiatrist."

"And what reason is that, Mere?"

"I . . . I didn't recognize the name of the convent orphanage right off, but since you mentioned it, I've been sitting here struggling, dredging up a twenty-year-old memory."

"Connected to the convent?"

"It's our first real *connection* to the killer. My history with this place we're going to. The killer intentionally pointed us in this direction."

"And what is the history, Mere? Were you once thinking of joining the convent? Did you go there as a child?"

"No, no! I had very little relationship with the convent really, and it was all so long ago."

He turned sharply into a small street, causing a pedestrian a bit of distress, the man shouting an obscenity at Lucas.

Lucas merely waved and kept going. "Go on," he told Meredyth.

"I was a teenager, my first year of college, and I knew I wanted med school. I was a student trying to get brownie points by getting my sociology requirement out of the way early on, you know, to impress my academic counselor. I kinda had a crush on him."

"That's the extent of your association with the convent? You did your sociology internship there? What, one quarter term? Seems pretty weak as connections go."

"No, not even that. I did my internship with Child and Family Services with the county, and I helped place a handful of children with the convent orphanage. I spent all my time at the courthouse downtown. I never saw the orphanage itself. Never set foot in it actually."

"That's it, huh?" He took another turn. They passed storefronts, taverns, eateries.

"I haven't been associated with them since those days in my first year of college. I represented indigent single mothers in cases involving newborns, to give them a home."

"Damn lot of responsibility for a kid."

"I was aggressive, and the caseworker I was helping out, she was swamped. I mean, case files to the ceiling. She was glad to have my help, and no one questioned it. Hell, it was 1984 and it was benevolent work."

"So you worked in finding foster homes and making adoptions possible?" he asked. "Benevolent work."

"My responsibilities ended at the courthouse door. I merely counseled and helped out the mothers who turned their children over to the orphanage for adoption. The county, the court, the nuns, under the mother superior, they saw to the actual adoptions. I just facilitated the paperwork and acted as advocate for the mother, and by extension, the child."

"Then your job was to . . . to . . .?"

"Expedite the transition for the mother; help her with her decision after weighing all options. Basically, all *I* signed off on was the mothers' understanding and state of mind . . . you know, sound mind, clear understanding of adoption. Had to make sure Mom knew what rights she was signing off on. It was just interview work."

"I see, and you never actually handled the children involved?"

She shrugged. "Occasionally, one of the infants was thrust into my arms when the mother needed to locate a proof of address or needed both her arms to sign papers."

The drive had taken them onto the Interstate, and after passing several exits, Lucas found Crockett Avenue, where he exited onto the surface street. The grim and growing cloud bank had engulfed the city, thrusting them into a daytime night. The car now moved through a crowded little neighborhood of narrow streets and boxy houses.

Meredyth continued speaking in a level voice. "Frankly, almost all of the women that I helped in my year of internship with the legal system didn't really have any options, hooked as they were on drugs."

"You spent a year at this social work requirement?"

"Well, two college terms, eight credit hours, a fall and a spring."

"And how long ago was this?"

"It was like two freaking decades ago, 1983 . . . '84 may be."

"Given the fact the killer has pointed us to the convent, we need to look over the records of your cases that year."

"The case files should be on record with the courthouse downtown. I have no idea what sort of records we'll find at the orphanage or what condition they will be in, but my name isn't likely to be on anything there."

"And you spent no time at the convent school?"

"Like I said, my job ended at the courthouse steps. The children were taken by the nuns from the judges' chambers."

Lucas wondered aloud, "How many kids are we talking about, Mere?"

"A handful . . . a dozen at most that I handled, certainly no more."

He pulled the car over and parked outside a Starbucks. "How about a cup of coffee and a grain of truth?" he asked.

"All right, I'll tell you about it."

* * *

LUCAS AND MEREDYTH sat at a table inside the coffee shop and watched the drizzling rain against the windows. Tentatively sipping at her steaming coffee, Meredyth began her story.

"A terrible situation had evolved in the seventies and into the eighties, when I started this internship—against the wishes of my parents, I might add. I was more surprised than *anyone* when I found myself making life-and-death decisions for drug abusers and their children."

"Were they all drug abusers?"

"To a woman, yes. Heroin, cocaine . . . hard-liners, most of them, their arms full of tracks, their noses pink red. I despised them, Lucas, for what they did to their babies. I was unable to have children, am unable to have children, Lucas. Something you have a right to know."

He reached across and took her hands in his. "Go on."

"And here these women were, slaves to addiction, giving no thought to how they were harming their children's health, *poisoning* their unborn children. I took it all quite personally, and it wasn't long before I knew I couldn't do this kind of work objectively."

"You were just a kid, Mere."

"It was a time of rampant drug use among pregnant teens. This created so many thousands of crack mothers having crack babies. These typically single-parent mothers were unable to fend for themselves, much less take care of a sick child's multiple needs." Meredyth paused to drink her cooling coffee.

Lucas picked at a giant cinnamon bun he'd placed between them to share. He said nothing, but she felt a disapproving coolness had come over him, something in his eyes, a judgment.

"Look, Lucas, organizations and high-minded institutions—"

"Like the Harris County court, the government, the Catholic Church?" he finished for her, interrupting.

"Yeah, like the Church . . . they took an interest in

helping the children, many of whom were born with mental and emotional problems, some with serious, irreversible damage and retardation. Few doors were open to them, and there weren't a lot of people or resources to throw at the problem."

He sipped at his coffee to the sound of FM music piped in, a Gordon Lightfoot tune . . . *don't you come creepin' round my back stair* . . . and angry words rising from another booth in the cafe. Lucas glanced at the couple arguing. Something deep within him wanted to go over and yank the man to his feet and plant a fist in his face. Instead, when Meredyth squeezed his hands, he returned his attention to her. "Go on. I'm listening."

"The orphanages were filling up with many thousands of such children, and Our Lady and other such homes opened their doors wide. They were constructing more housing! We took advantage. Here was hope, a chance to find decent homes for them."

"Or a lifetime in orphan care."

"I always believed it the lesser of two evils as did the lady I worked for, as did the system."

"Your ever think of adopting one of them yourself?"

"There was one, yes. She had no name, Lucas. Her mother hadn't given her a name. I thought that so sad."

"That is sad."

"I assume because the mother didn't want to get attached, knowing she was giving the little girl up. She'd made that decision before I even got involved. But I was a kid in college myself, my plans laid out, my days and nights filled. Her mother pleaded with me to find her a good home. I did what I could and went on to fulfill my dream to become a forensic psychiatrist. I just wanted to earn my degree, go on to help people."

"Like these destitute, addicted women who had no chance of ever getting their children back, right?"

"There were programs in place, rehab programs, but for most"—she grimaced and shook her head—"the program was an impossibility until they broke the cycle of loss of identity, loss of self-esteem, loss of direction, values, faith."

He remained stone-faced, his Indian features impossible to read.

"Whatever you're thinking, Lucas, don't condemn me for what we did for those children back then. We did what we had to do. Nobody wanted to deal with the problem."

"Anyone think to keep records on these children? To see how they did one, two, three years later?"

She shook her head. "We're talking about sick children. The fact we found orphan homes willing to take them was reason for celebration."

"And no one kept trace of the crack mothers, right?"

"Correct." Her long face dropped. The noise level at the other booth had continued to rise. Lucas glared at the couple, realizing now that the woman had an infant in a little plastic carry on the seat beside her. *Take it to the* Maury Povich Show, he wanted to shout, but kept his calm.

Lucas thought of the thousands of Native American children who, in the early part of the 20th century, had been ripped from their parents by state welfare systems across the West—placed in "good" white homes by well-meaning white officials anxious to Christianize and Anglicize these *heathen* children. It was nowadays considered one of many disgraceful episodes in U.S.-Indian relations sanctioned by the U.S. Bureau of Indian Affairs; it had been a part of the "war" to end once and for all the aboriginal problem of the Native American races, to homogenize, tame, incorporate and blend them into the white race and make farmers of them all. The policy of assimilation of the races had begun as early as the 1820s, with successful results in the peace-loving Five "Civilized" Tribes led by the Cherokee Nation and including the Creek, Chickasaw, Choctaw, and Seminole.

In 1861, when war broke out between the states, the Cherokee Nation had more English-speaking schools and post offices flying the American flag than did neighboring whites in the state of Arkansas, and American Indians formed regiments in both the Federal and the Confederate armies. The Five Tribes fought at Pea Ridge, Arkansas, up and down the Oklahoma Indian Territory, along the Texas corridor, and struggled for control over the Indian Capitol of Tallaqua. Federalist Indian regiment soldiers lost—alongside their Confederate brothers—more casualties *per capita* in the Indian State than did any other state in the Union or the Confederacy, yet it never appeared in a U.S. history book. No Hollywood film or Ken Burns documentary had ever been made of their heroism, either in the war or as leaders in following the *White Path* of peace over the *Red Path* of war against the people who had forced them on to the Long Walk of the Trail of Tears. Only a handful of dust-laden studies and historical treatises on these lost facts dealt with the Indian regiments of the Confederacy and the Union.

After the Civil War, and after the loss of Lincoln as their president, *all* the *civilized* Indians of the Territory were punished for the actions of those who sided with the Confederacy. Five Tribes simultaneously stripped of all the dignity and freedom they had earned as U.S. citizens in their once-proud U.S. Protectorate, not to mention their land and businesses. The president of the Cherokee Nation, John Ross, lost his dream along with his steamboat company, but the tribes had lost the entirety of their treaty lands, seeing them given away to white settlers flooding into the Cherokee Strip to create the state of Oklahoma. Strip was the right word for it. Government-sanctioned, the rape of the Indian Territory was overseen by armed military forces. Then came the sweeping missionary influx and the welfare brigades. And in far too many instances, Native American children were forced to renounce their heritage and very DNA and take on the manner and characteristics, the language and religion of the majority race without any protest allowed beyond the tears shed when they were taken from their loving parents. The biography of such men as Jim Thorpe told the story. In too many cases, these children were taken out of perfectly fine family environments and placed with foster homes, causing the children as adults to be alienated in a white world. Jim Thorpe had beaten the white world at its own game, only to be stripped of his Olympic medals, left in the end depressed and beaten, left to drink himself to death.

"Where did you go, Lucas Stonecoat?" Meredyth asked. She'd quietly studied his strong features and iron eyes, a beautiful brown with specks of green and incredible depths she could easily lose herself in. "Where were you just now?" she repeated when he did not answer.

"Bad times."

"Tell me about these bad times."

He shared his thoughts on the history of lost Native American children who had grown up a generation of lost adults. "My father had been one of them," he confessed, "and he died the ignoble death of a drunken Indian, drowning in a mud puddle on the Coushatta Reservation, thousands of miles from the lost ancestral home where his fathers were born, lived, died, and joined the netherworld."

"I'm sorry, Lucas, very sorry for your pain, but . . . but you can't compare what the Bureau of Indian Affairs did from the nineteenth century through nineteen-thirties and nineteen-forties to what we tried to do in the nineteen-eighties. Our intentions were good and honorable."

"So were those of the missionaries. The road to hell is paved with good intentions. Isn't that what Anglos say?"

"I'll see you at the car," she said to this, standing and starting away.

He grabbed her wrist, saying, "I'm not saying it's the same thing, but it brings back bad memories, that's all."

She pulled away. "I need a moment alone."

Lucas sighed heavily, finished his coffee, and tossed down a tip for the hardworking busboy. He glanced out the window to where Meredyth sat in the car, pensively waiting for him.

He noticed the quiet that had come over the cafe, the music gone, replaced by an ad man touting a debt-free existence, the arguing couple with the infant now cuddling one another, the young man having come around to her side of the booth, the infant between them. They now presented a picture of peace and tranquility.

Lucas wanted an excuse to punch something, but nothing presented itself as the target he needed. Instead, he found his cell phone and called Mother Elizabeth Portsmith, the lady in charge at Our Lady of Miracles, to inform her of his and Meredyth's delay, but promising to be there within ten minutes. A cheery feminine response told him they anxiously awaited his arrival.

As he went for the exit, Lucas's boots made a slapping noise against the tiles that made the couple look up from a kiss to stare after him.

Lucas hoped the clue of the convent school, the connection to Lourdes, and the connection to Meredyth would lead them quickly to the maniac behind the abduction-murder case they worked.

He stopped short, looked up into the falling rain, allowing it to cool his face, and wondering if his getting intimately involved again with Meredyth Sanger was not a fool's errand. How much had her change of heart toward him had to do with this case, her running scared, her confused vortex of swirling emotions . . . her temporary desperation? Once the case was solved, he wondered if she'd throw up real roadblocks to their being together, go running back to her previous lifestyle that included such as Byron Priestly, men who asked little of her, the way she liked it.

He climbed into the car beside her, forced a smile, and asked if she was okay.

"Fine . . . drive. Let's get this over with."

CHAPTER 10

Ceremonial dance area

A CONTINUING LIGHT drizzle dampened Lucas's windshield under the gunmetal-gray sky that had encircled the city since he'd exited the Starbucks cafe. The convent orphan home emerged from the smudged-gray overcast distance, prompting Lucas to point and say, "Damn, there it is. Man, this place looks bleak."

She agreed, staring ahead. "Dour, like something out of a Dickens novel."

Our Lady of Miracles stood in stark contrast to the other structures in the residential and commercial area, as if it silently claimed special historical status, attested to by its cornerstone, dated 1914. Its light gray stone walls had been planted here before Houston's urban sprawl had engulfed it, as if the urban blight had mushroomed around its ivy-covered walls.

On all sides of Our Lady's gated grounds, the noisy, busy streets crisscrossed one another while seeming to divert around the convent church. East, west, north, south, all the streets were filled with traffic and low-rent, high-rise apartments, duplexes, brownstones, and gray-stones in need of upgrading and repair. Trash, bottles, cans, fast-food bags, crushed containers, scattered cups, careworn, bruised automobiles with flat tires and broken windows, all littered the area as one cancerous blight.

The convent itself appeared neat, orderly, and clean, but its gates had captured a lot of the debris, clinging to the black wrought-iron stays that separated Our Lady of Miracles from the community.

The convent was also encircled by billboards and an array of mind-numbing signs touting establishments ranging from McDonald's to strip clubs. The old convent church looked besieged, surrounded as it was by storefront establishments—a pizza parlor, a Blockbuster, a beer hall, a coffee shop, an insurance firm, and a carpet-and-tile outlet. Sitting squarely in the middle of all the hubbub of the teeming city, Our Lady's ancient stones and spiraling pinnacles, the solid, gray shape of its bell tower some three stories high, stood behind its locked iron gate. Attached to the church itself stood a long, meandering orphanage, a building for housing, boarding, feeding, and schooling the young women who called this place home.

Lucas next saw a short, heaveyset nun in a black habit struggling to keep an umbrella over the head of a taller woman in a white habit, the mother superior, Sister Elizabeth Portsmith, no doubt. Portsmith raised a single hand to acknowledge the car at the gate, her features half masked by the black umbrella. She seemed to be directing traffic, telling the shorter, stouter, and younger woman what to do. The younger nun struggled to keep her mother superior dry with one hand while getting the gate open with a jammed handheld electronic device. Finally, the gates opened inward on a small square of fieldstones that made up a parking lot and driveway.

Meredyth traced the enormous pinnacles of the church skyward, the gray stones streaked from the rain. The drizzle had not worsened, but the darkening sky had become nearly black by the time Lucas found a comfortable parking spot alongside a convent van. The little lot was tight and difficult to maneuver in, but finally he switched off the engine.

Climbing from the car, Lucas and Meredyth saw that the mother superior and her assistant had made their way to a doorway alongside the church parking lot, and both the assistant and Portsmith were motioning Lucas and Meredyth to enter at this cottagelike entrance where a red door stood. Mother Superior Elizabeth appeared quite aged and winded, as if the short time she had spent out at the gate had been too much for her, Lucas thought. He wondered at her age, at the number of years she'd spent here and elsewhere in service to her faith.

She appeared the obvious mainstay of her small citadel, stern, stoic, accepting that at such times as this, she must allow her bastion to be compromised, allowing a nonbeliever like Lucas inside. He guessed that if she could have her way, Mother Elizabeth would keep them out like the clutter plastered against her gate.

"She look in good health and happiness to you?" Lucas whispered in Meredyth's ear, referring to the mother superior, whose face appeared dusted with flour.

"Careful, Lucas. She could kick your red butt."

By now the shorter, sprier nun had disappeared into the church ahead of Mother Elizabeth. After introductions, Mother Elizabeth, looking even older than before, guided them through a winding, semidarkened corridor to her expansive, mahogany-lined, ornate office. Inside, the walls were lined with oak-wood shelves filled with books and religious objects. Once seated behind her massive, shimmering dark wood desk, Mother Elizabeth finally asked, "Now precisely *how* can *we* at Our Lady of Miracles *possibly* help the Houston Police Department in a *homicide* investigation, Lieutenant Stonecoat, Dr. Sanger?" Mother Superior seemed to stress every other word. She radiated gravity, solemnity, grace.

Lucas outlined all that had occurred, the story causing Portsmith to gasp more than once. He brought the horror of the Post-it Ripper back to her doorstep, explaining that the package sent to his home had Our Lady as its return address.

"Such cruelty in mankind," she muttered. "But to think anyone here could possibly have anything to do with such horrors, no. No, it *must* be a ruse," she instantly suggested, her right hand holding down her left on the desk before them. "It can't *possibly* have anything to do with our home here."

"There's another connection to here," Lucas added, "two, in fact. One, my landlord, who took the parcel, said it was delivered by a young woman dressed in a Catholic school uniform. Two, your convent school is not far from where I live."

"It's impossible," she automatically replied. "Only a handful of our girls are considered trustworthy enough to go beyond the gates of Our Lady, and none of our girls could possibly involve herself in such a soulless crime." The mother's *hackles* rose up now, the hair on her neck alert, her very skin bristling, her eyes and ears like those of a hunting dog alerting on a kill. She gritted her teeth behind a firmly set jaw and searched Lucas's face, and then Meredyth's, for some sign that they must know they were in the wrong place and wasting not only their time but hers.

"From an investigative standpoint, Mother Elizabeth," replied Lucas, "it's good news that you can narrow down the number of young ladies here who enjoy the freedom to come and go."

"It'll save us a great deal of time," agreed Meredyth.

"I'm not so sure I should simply turn my girls over to be interrogated by police. Should I call in Carver?"

"Carver?"

"The convent lawyer."

"That will only complicate things," Lucas replied.

"For you perhaps."

Meredyth waved her hands. "We only want to *speak* to the children to determine if one among them *delivered* the package, possibly for money, Mother Elizabeth. We don't think the girl in question *knew* what was in the parcel."

"I still think I should call Mr. Carver. I am not well versed in any law other than ecclesiastical law. And while his expertise is property and investments, I know his first question to me will be did you two display a warrant to question my girls, minors most of them." She lifted her phone, making Lucas groan. She glared at him. "I am a simple woman and need guidance."

Lucas looked her firmly in the eyes. "Carver will only cost you more hours, Mother Elizabeth, and isn't time your most valuable commodity, aside from your flock here, I mean? If we have to go and come back with a court order, it'll only mean more disruption of your schedule here."

Mother Elizabeth had only to punch her speed dial for Carver. She held the phone in a moment of silence, her eyes closed as if in prayer. Finally, she calmly placed the phone back on its cradle. "All right, but you realize if one or more of the girls refuse to talk to you, she has the sanctuary of these walls, and therefore the right of refusal. If you have a problem with that, then perhaps I should call Carver."

Lucas opened his palms to her. "Refusing to talk to police? We get that all the time, Mother. It's called the Fourth Amendment."

"Sanctuary predates the U.S. Constitution, Detective."

Meredyth grabbed him and huddled heads with him, whispering, "Don't try to match wits with this woman."

Meredyth then straightened in her seat and addressed the mother superior. "We accept *any* conditions necessary to speak to the girls," Meredyth added.

"All right, Dr. Sanger, Detective."

"But before you begin piling on more conditions, ma'am," Lucas said, "I want you to know what we have. Fact, a twenty-eight-year-old young woman, abducted and brutally murdered, her head severed with an ax, two"—he held up his fingers—"two whacks with a dull blade, and some fiend sent her head in a UPS box to us. If one of your girls can give us a description of the man who she acted for, then we may stop this satanic individual from harming his *next* victim, who quite possibly could be one of your girls, if she's spending time with him."

Meredyth added, "The Lourdes woman's family deserves some closure, Mother Superior. Surely, you can understand our need to act quickly before another part of this woman is mailed to someone, perhaps her mother and father."

The mother superior relaxed her gaze and relented. "Well . . . I suspect our Mr. Carver has enough on his plate. All right. I'll have the trustworthy girls we allow to inter-face with the community called up to my office, and you may speak with them, but *I* must be present during any . . . *inquisitioning*."

"In-what?" asked Lucas.

"During interrogations, Lucas," explained Meredyth.

"Your presence could make them hesitant to talk freely," Lucas pointed out.

"Those are my terms. Take them or . . . or we call in Mr. Carver, and you can deal with him."

"No, no. Your being present actually may spur the truth from your girls, I suspect," said Lucas.

"Are there any other girls who you suspect capable of finding their way off the grounds other than your trustees?" asked Meredyth.

"None. We run a very taut ship here. Now, I'll have Sis-ter Audrey call each of the girls to come out of their classes. There's a room to your left where you can question each."

"I'd also like to examine your records," added Meredyth, who had stiffened somewhat in her seat, her eyes roaming about the convent office. "I'm particularly interested in newborns turned over to your care in 1984."

"And the significance of that year has to do with your case?" she asked, her forehead creasing below the line of her habit.

"A third connection to the convent orphanage, Mother Superior," said Lucas.

"I was involved as an intern at the time with Child and Family Protective Services—it was called then, placing children in the care of various orphanages in and around Harris County and Houston, including yours." Meredyth took a deep breath. "We may be far off here, but there may be some connection between the killer's interest in your convent and my short association with your orphanage, Mother Elizabeth."

"That was some twenty years ago, and I was not here in 1984," she thoughtfully replied, "and those records will be difficult to access."

"But you have them?" asked Lucas.

"In the basement, yes. Along with anything and everything stored there since before my time here." She made a *tsk-tsk* noise with her dentures, her wrinkled face puckering. Lucas guessed her age at somewhere between sixty-nine and seven-five.

Mother Elizabeth then pressed the button on what appeared an ancient intercom system, spoke to her aide, Sister Audrey, and asked her to round up the six girls she had in mind. "Anyone else you know who may have had any dealings outside the gates in the past week, send them along as well, Sister Audrey, dear."

A voice like a clanging cowbell came back over the intercom, "But Mother Superior, that will disrupt a number of classes."

"Just arrange it, Sister."

"Right away, Mother Superior."

"Would you care for coffee and a roll while you wait?" asked Mother Elizabeth, pointing to an urn beside which lay an array of pastries, cups, saucers, and napkins. "All prepared here on the premises. I have made the school here completely self-sufficient, save for a few necessities we require. You must stay long enough to inspect our gardens in the courtyard, our dining facilities, the sleeping quarters, and the classrooms. We teach all the subjects, including the arts, music, Latin, and Greek, but we also teach self-sufficiency—self-reliance as well as a reliance on God."

"I'm not sure we have that much time this trip out," said Meredyth, "but perhaps next visit."

From somewhere in one of the buildings, the sound of stringed instruments wafted up to them, muffled with the occasional strident chord.

"Detective," said Mother Elizabeth to Lucas, "do help yourself to coffee and a pastry, and I'll have mine with cream and a cinnamon roll. Dr. Sanger?"

"Just coffee, black, Lucas, thanks."

Lucas played host for the elderly nun and Meredyth as they continued to talk. "How good is your success rate for placing children, Mother Elizabeth?" asked Meredyth.

"We pride ourselves on an eighty-five-percent rate, but that does leave fifteen percent behind, but even these girls have a better start in life than they might otherwise have had. The ones who grow up here, once they reach eighteen years of age, can decide on remaining or going out into the world."

"Finally given *choice*, hey?" muttered Lucas from the coffee urn.

"At age twenty-one, I'm afraid we *must* push them from the nest altogether. Church policy."

"Then actually they have *no choice* at twenty-one, only at eighteen," Lucas replied, serving Elizabeth's coffee and roll, and drawing a disapproving look from Meredyth, whose eyes clearly reminded him of what she had warned—*don't challenge the old girl.*

"We'd like a list of young women who've left this year, both the twenty-one-year-olds and the eighteen-year-olds who've opted out," replied Meredyth. "Is that possible?"

"I'm quite sure Sister Audrey can provide you with both lists, yes, before you leave today. I suppose one of our *graduates* could be your *courier*. Much likelier than one of the girls you'll meet today."

Meredyth and Lucas exchanged a glance as he placed her hot coffee between the two women. He sat back down with his own coffee and roll, not hungry but forcing it down out of an attempt to keep Mother Elizabeth happy. As in Cherokee custom, it felt true here that an offering of food should not be turned down. That it was an insult to do so.

Mother Elizabeth thanked Lucas and added, "You must tell us what you think of the girls' cooking. The children do all the food preparation themselves."

Lucas sampled the offerings. "Delicious," he declared.

"Has this work ethic of raising crops, food preparation, and doing other in-house jobs always been in place here?" asked Meredyth.

"I'm afraid not. I began slowly making Our Lady work as a self-sufficient entity with the children being the principal workforce when I came here in 1994. It took some doing to move the chore list out of the hands of the sisters of the convent and into the hands of the children, I can tell you, but it has paid off handsomely for the well-being of all."

"It makes good sense to me," said Lucas. "Keep them busy. Idle hands . . . devil's playground, all that."

"I'm just guessing, but did you grow up on a reservation, Lieutenant? You are Native American, aren't you?"

"Yes to both questions," he replied.

"Then you know the importance of a self-sustaining village. The Church was at one time planning to close down Our Lady altogether, but miraculously and with a lot of determination and everyone's effort, we returned it to a viable and healthy institution."

"What you mean is that the orphanage was no longer losing money. Is that right?" asked Meredyth.

"We must operate under a budget like any other institution, yes."

"You're paid so much for each child you take in each year they remain with you, correct?"

"Correct."

"Then what incentive have you to find them homes?"

Lucas wondered when Meredyth had decided to challenge the matriarch of this fortress.

"The incentive of the heart, Dr. Sanger." Mother Elizabeth's eyes penetrated through Meredyth now like ice picks. "The cost-saving measures I have implemented here do not include *sabotaging* legitimate foster care and/or adoptions. We are *still* quite aggressive in finding suitable families for our girls, and I *resent* any implication to the contrary, Doctor. I'm not so sure you're not still with Child and Family Welfare, Doctor, sent here by that terrible woman, Allison Talmadge, who has, for a year now, *attempted* to have our license to act as an orphanage and adoption agency *revoked*."

"Trust me," Meredyth quickly said. "I have no ties to

that agency any longer, and I don't know anyone named Talmadge."

"We're here strictly on a police matter," added Lucas, fearful the woman would invoke the name of her lawyer again.

"That Talmadge woman has sent *spies* here before, all of them anti-Catholic in their thinking."

"I'm sorry, Mother Superior, please," Meredyth said. "I really didn't mean to imply—"

"You asked what *incentive* we have to place our children. The incentive that has always been the very *spirit* of Our Lady of Miracles, to inspire the love of God and the trust in Him and hope in *their* young and innocent hearts. Certainly, we are not *always* successful, but I am extremely proud of our results, so your coming here like this in search of one of our children, who may have had a hand in this crime, either wittingly or unwittingly, well, it is unsettling to begin with, but I am not so old and brittle as to have no fight left in me, my dear doctor."

Lucas simply smiled and nodded to her, displaying his admiration for the elderly woman. She was a match for anyone. He couldn't help but like her.

"Please accept my apology if I've offen—"

Sister Elizabeth's phone rang, and she halted Meredyth with an upraised hand, and grabbed the phone with the other. She began to converse with someone at the other end. "*Don't* be taken in, dear. *Listen* to yourself. You know very well what to do. You're telling me, so *tell* the man! You *will not* accept pitted, wrinkled, ugly discards!"

Meredyth took this opportunity to lean into Lucas's ear and whisper, "Don't forget that the abductor had a woman working with him."

"And you think she could be a recent graduate from here?" asked Lucas.

"I don't know. Do you?"

"Ask her if she's had any recent vandalism or destruction of religious icons in the church."

Mother Elizabeth continued on the phone. "Be firm, Rachel, dear! You're in charge down there! It's *your* kitchen, and what happens if you bake with poor ingredients? Exactly." She hung up, a smile and a lilting shake of her head, and she explained, "Some neighborhood vendor trying to pawn off bad cherries and vegetables back of the kitchen. Rachel's twenty years old, and she's leaving us next year, but for now she's still in charge of our kitchen."

Lucas made a mental note, picturing the savvier girls as knowing a way off the grounds via the kitchen. If vendors came to that *back door* to barter, that door must swing both ways.

"So Rachel's one of your fifteen percent whom you could find no home for."

"Not I. She was sixteen when I arrived. You know the odds of placing a child of sixteen? Of course you do. Mother Orleans tried to place her, of course, but Rachel simply never worked out in any of the homes Orleans placed her in. I've read the poor child's history."

"She's spent her entire life here?" asked Lucas, standing now, staring out the window down on the rain-soaked courtyard.

"Not so bad really. Since age four when her parents were killed in a plane wreck, but she has learned skills and life lessons to carry her through. Still, she has a hard time saying no to people. We have little time left to work on it, but she'll get it if I have to brand it on her forehead."

Elizabeth's intercom buzzed into life. Sister Audrey's voice came over. "First of the girls is here, Mother Superior."

"Who is it, Sister?"

"Melanie Polk, Mother. Do you want me to send her in now?"

Sister Elizabeth held Sister Audrey in suspense for a moment, addressing Lucas and Meredyth instead. "I know this child is innocent, but I promised you all our *trustworthies* who go out into the community. Shall we go into my conference room?"

"Yes, let's," replied Meredyth, gathering up her coffee.

"Send the child round to the conference room hallway door, Sister Audrey. We'll speak to her there. And Sister, send for Rachel Wade too, when she can get free."

As they moved into the conference room, Lucas and Meredyth sitting beneath a painting of the Last Supper, Lucas asked, "Mother, has there been any vandalism or destruction of property done against the convent?"

"Nothing major . . . nothing we haven't been able to handle internally."

"Then there has been some?"

"The usual mischief one expects with children."

"Defaced paintings, statues?"

"Mustaches and spectacles from time to time. Nothing serious, although someone set a fire in the convent once, again before I came on here."

Lucas asked, "The convent . . . the residence rooms, sleeping quarters, all that?"

"Yes, it was a fire begun in a broom closet beside Mother Orleans's room—now my room. On damp days, I can still get a whiff of the charred walls.

"Again, I was not here during Orleans's stewardship of the convent, but they determined it was student smokers. The little darlings had found what they thought a good place to light up. Carelessness and youthful stupidity. I'm told a book of matches and some butts were found among soiled rags."

"Anyone charged or reprimanded?" asked Lucas.

"From what I understand, the mother superior handled their punishment, and it was *severe*."

"This girl Rachel . . . was she involved in the fire?" asked Meredyth.

"Yes, among others. Orleans got to the bottom of it, got hold of the ringleader."

"Rachel?"

"No, Rachel is a follower. It was her friend of the time, Lauralie."

"We'd like to talk to this Lauralie as well then," Meredyth said. "Whoever our girl is, she's got a bold streak in her."

"That would be Lauralie, but she's no longer here. Graduated in 2000 . . . January, and has been out there on her own since. She dropped by from time to time at first, but she stopped coming by."

"And why did she stop coming by?" asked Meredyth.

"She would have to tell you that, but I'm afraid I have no current address or way to get hold of Lauralie. So . . . shall we begin the *inquisition* of my young ladies now?"

Meredyth caught a glint in the old girl's eye, and she realized now that Mother Elizabeth wanted to corner their quarry as well, if and when she could be identified.

Mother Elizabeth opened the door on the first young lady, the voices of others who'd begun to gather at the bench outside wafting into the conference room. "Do curb your tongues, ladies," she called out to those in the hallway. "This isn't an amusement. Claudia, let's begin with you."

A frightened young lady demurely entered, her big eyes curious about the visitors from the outside world. Her attention to Meredyth's clothes and jewelry seemed all-consuming, like a fire burning from within, dying to get out but held in check.

Lucas put himself in the girl's shoes, faced with a detective, a psychiatrist, and a mother superior asking questions of her. Either it would terrify some truths from her, or it would cause her to shut down and provide them with nothing. Lucas had interrogated hundreds of teens with criminal records or on the way to building one, but he'd never interrogated anyone with an austere nun perched in a corner, looking on vulture-fashion. He feared they would get nothing from the girls.

THEY HAD EXHAUSTED the afternoon in interviewing nine young women, ranging in age from a plump fifteen-year-old to a series of seventeen-soon-to-be-eighteen-year-olds, and three at nineteen and twenty, two of whom sounded less than eager to leave the convent, and one who appeared downright troubled at the prospect of leaving, and was weighing the wisdom of becoming a nun herself. "Possibly in order to stay cloistered here," Mother Elizabeth said of the girl after she'd gone. "Not a good enough reason to join the order."

All the young ladies exhibited good manners and respect for Elizabeth, even love, mixed in with fear of her. They all spoke highly of Mother Elizabeth and the programs she'd instituted at Our Lady of Miracles.

Their last interview was with Rachel from the kitchen. As with all the other girls, Rachel knew nothing about delivering a parcel to Lucas's house above Tebo's tavern. "I'd *never* go near *no* tavern, Mother Superior," she repeated.

"Please, Rachel, dear, say *any* tavern, not *no* tavern," admonished Mother Elizabeth. "We do *not never* speak in *no* double negatives . . . *not* around here," she explained to the adults, making Lucas frown.

Meredyth quickly asked the girl, "Rachel, do you know how we could get in touch with your friend Lauralie who's left the home? Lauralie?"

"I dunno where she is. I swear I lost touch. We stopped being friends like way before she left."

Meredyth sensed a fear in Rachel, but a fear of what, of whom? Mother Elizabeth or Lauralie or both? Mother Elizabeth suggested, "Why not speak to the *sixteen* girls who've recently graduated and opted to leave the convent, all now living on the outside? They're all on the list Sister Audrey's preparing you. Lauralie Blodgett is only one of them."

"Is there anyone in that group, Rachel, who had a boyfriend on the outside?" Meredyth pressed the girl, ignoring Elizabeth's interruption.

Rachel again looked to her mother superior before saying, "You should try to talk to *all* of them."

"Any among them who didn't like life here at the convent or was discontented in general? Anyone who liked destroying things around here, maybe setting a fire?" asked Lucas.

Rachel looked to her mother superior again before answering. Getting a nod from Mother Elizabeth, she replied, "That'd be Lauralie."

"We keep hearing that name come up. She was something of a bully, I understand, always getting into trouble and detention," said Meredyth.

"Everyone was glad to see her go."

"But you two were friends, weren't you?"

"I broke it off with her; she started wanting to do things . . . I-I-I didn't wanna do."

"What sort of things? Like smoking? Getting into trouble?" pressed Meredyth.

"Mother Superior, I don't like to talk about this."

"It's all right, Rachel. Be forthright. Tell the doctor everything, Rachel."

Rachel wrenched her hands and stuttered. Finally she spat it out. "Sexual things. She wanted to play with me, to put things into me. Wanted to fondle me, sleep with me."

Mother Elizabeth sat without the slightest twinge, a stone statue. "It's all right, child. It's all right."

"Lauralie had a way of making you do things. I had a hard time with her. Saying no to her. I finally told Mother Orleans, and she was going to punish Lauralie, but that's when Mother Orleans had that awful accident, and after that Lauralie left me alone when you came to the home, Mother Elizabeth."

"Lauralie was always looking for someone to love her," said Elizabeth. "She somehow had gotten the fixed idea in her head that she could only be loved in a sexual manner."

"Perhaps she was abused in one of the homes she was placed in at an early age?" asked Meredyth.

"I have no record of an incident of that type." Elizabeth sighed deeply. "Sad really. Even Father William could not help Lauralie, try as he might. He called her a hopeless child once. I had to straighten him out on that, none of our charges is without redemption. Lauralie had her redeeming qualities. She was tenacious and persistent in her struggle to learn who her parents were, for instance, admirable in her determination, I'm told, even at an early age."

"She just always said . . . said we both of us needed the *experience* for when we got out into the real world," said Rachel, her voice having raised an octave, as if wanting to outdo her mother superior. "I had to fight her off every night for a time. She liked to kiss me and touch me all over."

"That's enough, Rachel!" Mother Elizabeth put an end to it, and Rachel curled back in on herself like a closing flower.

They said good-bye to Rachel, Mother Elizabeth walking her out to the hallway, conferring with her in a whisper. Meredyth and Lucas only caught snatches of each voice:

Mother: ". . . don't care—"

Rachel: "She's evil—"

Mother: "What you think—"

Rachel: ". . . name shoulda been Laura-LIE! with . . . capital let—"

Mother: "Enough."

Rachel: "You tell me . . . stand up . . . strong, but . . . won't let me."

Mother: "Get back . . . kitchen, now!"

Rachel: "And Father Wil . . . touched me again."

Mother: "No more. Later . . . talk privately."

Rachel, stomping off, shouting back: "She pushed her."

Silence . . . more silence. Then a reverberation of Rachel's voice from the end of the corridor. "She's evil . . . was always evil. She hurt the mother."

Mother Elizabeth rejoined them in the conference room, quickly reassuring her guests that "Lauralie Blodgett was not so discontent or unhappy as the picture the other girls painted. True, there was a time she was in constant trouble, but her discontent came of a genuine longing to know her roots, to know about her birth mother and father. That's quite understandable, don't you agree, Doctor?"

"Yes, quite."

"Her school record is filled with cases of theft and lying as a child, and constant bouts and arguments with both the sisters here and her classmates."

"Any bouts with statuary, icons, paintings?" asked Lucas.

"She was often caught destroying property, yes. But she was just a troubled child, not so different from Rachel, unable to fit in with foster families. Very similar histories, those two, and for a time they *were* friends, and I thought it good for Lauralie . . . she was such a loner, you see. I encouraged their . . . closeness, but I had no idea until Rachel came to me with her lurid stories of nighttime rape that . . . that what Mother Orleans had put a stop to had again flourished. For a long time, I prayed Rachel was making it up to get attention, but I caught Lauralie at her one night and that was the end of it."

"This Mother Orleans was in charge here when Lauralie first arrived as an infant?"

"My able predecessor, Mother Sara Orleans."

"The one whose room still smells of smoke?" asked Lucas.

"The one who had an accident? Is she in retirement? Can I meet with her?" asked Meredyth.

"The unfortunate accident proved fatal. It's why I was called here to take over."

"How did she die?" asked Meredyth.

"A fall down a flight of steps in the night. She apparently got up in the middle of the night and slipped on the stairs. Her skull was fractured. She was in a coma for weeks until the decision to release her came from the family. Tragic really."

"Sounds like Mother Orleans lived a dangerous life for a convent nun," said Lucas, drawing a stern look from Elizabeth Portsmith.

"Let's get back to this Lauralie," said Meredyth. "Was she ever adopted?"

"No, never adopted, but once . . . no, twice actually, she went into a foster care situation; both before my time here. However, I've read about the placements in her records, the reasons behind her being returned to Our Lady. I always read the histories on all the children I am responsible for."

"What are the reasons she didn't do well with her foster parents?"

"In both cases, she never made it past the trial period. In both cases, wonderful situations that ought to've led to adoption simply failed, largely due to Lauralie's self-destructiveness."

"Can you be more specific, Mother?" pressed Meredyth.

"Unruliness, stubbornness, a kind of underlying fear of being out there and not in here where at least she knew the rules. She was eleven the first time, thirteen the second time. But by then—"

"Patterns of behavior were set," Meredyth finished for her.

"Did she burn down a house? What?" asked Lucas.

"No, nothing so dramatic, but just as destructive in its way. She wouldn't be *guided,* would not follow the *simplest* of rules, throwing temper tantrums, balling up into the fetal position for hour upon hour, refusing to eat, starving herself to skin and bone, lashing out, acting out. She simply refused to be a part of her new family. Hurt newfound siblings. Pitiful shame really. It was quite severe when she was young, but by the time I came on the scene, she was simply withdrawn and sullen."

"Is that when she started the fire in the closet in the convent?" asked Lucas.

"By that age the children who have not been adopted, often they become, I hate to say, *toughened* to the fact that they are not adorable little creatures that people want to adopt, and so they often play the role of the exact opposite, the unadorable, unruly delinquent. It can become worse still when they leave our controlled environment. It's why I counseled Rachel and Lauralie to remain with us to at least twenty-one. Rachel chose to remain, Lauralie did not."

"In what ways did she hurt her adopted family siblings?" asked Meredyth.

"She scalded one with hot soup. Another time, she almost smothered one to death with a stuffed animal down her throat. I forget the other instances."

Rage, Meredyth thought. "And after leaving here, she cut off all communications?"

"Not at first. At first, she'd call from time to time. I lost touch after her call about her mother's death."

This got Lucas's renewed interest, and Meredyth said, "But she had just found her mother."

"That's what made it so tragic—this beautiful reunion cut tragically short, but then God works in mysterious ways."

Mother Elizabeth stood and glided back toward her office. Lucas and Meredyth followed, Lucas getting the door for them. Elizabeth continued speaking as they walked. "He certainly confuses me at times, to put so much heartache on that single forsaken child. I called her my fawn, my poor forlorn child, so lonely and abandoned."

"How exactly did her mother die?" asked Lucas.

The mother superior had returned to her desk, sitting stiffly behind it now, as if using it as a barrier between herself and the city officials before her. "Lauralie's sudden appearance after all the years obviously brought back a great deal of grief, and one night Lauralie's mother, an alcoholic, drank herself to death. I suppose in a fit of remorse and guilt over having abandoned Lauralie in her infancy.

"Imagine, she located her birth mother, living right here in Houston, and they were getting to know one another, doing famously according to Lauralie, when suddenly she *left* her again. After that, Lauralie's calls became infrequent, and soon nonexistent. She'd been living with her mother, but I tried contacting her there, only to learn she'd vanished, and I've worried about her, prayed for her since, and now you are here."

"What about her father?" asked Lucas.

"Deceased. She learned of it from her mother. Died some years before. She told me she laid flowers at his grave."

"When Lauralie was here at Our Lady, given her record of trouble and vandalism, however did she become a trustworthy?" asked Meredyth.

"She *earned* it. *Straightened* up her act, as they say, mightily. Took Mother Orleans's death very hard, she did . . . as did all the girls, but I convinced her that Mother Orleans would want her to pull out of her depression."

"And she made a miraculous recovery?" Meredyth

watched the nun's response closely. She had begun to analyze the woman, Lucas realized.

"Yes, miraculous . . . with the help of God . . . came to
her senses, began using that intellect I convinced her she
had to use to survive on the outside."

"Inventive, resourceful, and adroit, would you say?"

"Only in the best sense. She turned a corner in her
mind, began soaking up knowledge, learned to like the
programs I put into place, and excelled."

Meredyth, nodding added, "Particularly the Work for
Trust Program?"

"In everything, she began to excel, to discover her own
power, that she *owned* her intellect and her emotions and
must turn them toward the greater glory of God."

"Despite all the hardships life had meted out to her?"

"Perhaps because of them. Small miracle, I say. She
learned to control her pent-up rage and anger at the world,
and win *trust points* in the bargain."

Mother Elizabeth stared out into space as if picturing
Lauralie. "Previous to my taking charge, she would do
nothing around the convent, and although a bright girl, her
grades were deplorable." She shivered with the thought.
"She spent most of her time staring out the windows and
swinging on the gate out there. After my programs were
initiated, she was soon outside those bars looking in."

"Then as early as what, fifteen, sixteen, she was off the
grounds at times, looking for her parents?" asked Meredyth,
probing.

"Oh, no! It took time, *years*. She took to winning trust
only *after* she'd turned seventeen, and she graduated and
opted to leave at eighteen. It was in her junior year of high
school that I allowed her some *latitude* in her search for
her parents, although I warned her she might not like what
she found out there beyond the gates of Our Lady."

"Careful of what you wish . . . you may get it," commented Lucas.

"Something like that, yes."

Meredyth, a strand of hair falling over her right eye,
asked, "Did you open her records to her?"

"Not exactly. She broke into them one night and found them on her own."

"Clever girl."

"Cunning when she wished, yes. This was *before* we had our heart-to-heart. It was after that that I gave into her unquenchable desire to locate her parents, to help her in any way that I could. However, I failed her miserably."

"How so?" Meredyth tiptoed lightly. Lucas knew to keep quiet. Mother Elizabeth wiped a tear from her eye.

"Her mother was no longer at the recorded address or phone number, and I had an institution to save, and so. . . . Still, that young lady kept doggedly at it, taking it entirely upon herself to research her mother's whereabouts. Primarily, that meant she was spending more and more time away from here and on the street in her quest."

"Where are the records on Lauralie's adoption now? Can we have a look?" Meredyth asked.

"Archive files, as I said, in the basement. Not pleasant surroundings. Are you sure?"

"I'll brave the surroundings. Perhaps your assistant could show us the way?" asked Meredyth.

"I'll fetch Audrey, and we'll both show you the way. I need the walk, exercise for a bad hip and knees." Ignoring the intercom, she went next door to Sister Audrey.

Alone with Meredyth now, Lucas said, "Remember what Kelton said about the vandalized grave of a guy named Blood at Greenhaven Meadows?"

"Off Berwyn, yeah."

"Blood is not far off from Blodgett. This girl's name is Blodgett. You think Kelton may've gotten it wrong?"

"Or maybe we have a genuine coincidence?"

"Might be worth a look-see all the same. Greenhaven Meadows Cemetery's not too awfully far from here."

"If there's time, depends on the condition of these records I want a gander at, and I want to get back downtown before the courthouse closes, and you . . . you wanted to hit the mortuary, remember?"

"First things first, I know. Lauralie, you're reckoning, is one of the infants you placed, right?"

"If so Lucas . . . and if she turns out to be the courier we're seeking, God forbid but then there's a *tie* between this place, the Ripper, her mother, the murder of Mira Lourdes, and me. . . ."

CHAPTER 11

Rattlesnake jaw: strong

MOTHER ELIZABETH HAD not exaggerated the inaccessibility of their files and records. Going back as far as 1984 proved a daunting task. Meredyth wondered if she'd ever locate the files she'd come to peruse. While Mother Elizabeth apologized, saying they had not had money to place the records on computer, and that they hadn't the space for the hard files anywhere but in the basement, Meredyth and Lucas knew better. Record-keeping simply hadn't ever been a big priority here, and certainly not given the attention that it ought to have been given over the years. The orphanage was lucky to have gotten away with such poor record-keeping this long. And hadn't Mother Elizabeth said something about some woman associated with the state who wanted to shut them down? It likely began with a look at the records relegated to this damp and dismal place.

"If you don't want that Allison woman to shut you down, Mother Elizabeth, you really ought to do something about these records," Lucas warned as Meredyth stumbled over boxes.

She had had to literally climb over and past obstacles ranging from retired podiums and old furniture to ancient garden tools, box springs, and file boxes. Amid the leftovers of a lifetime in the convent, on neatly stacked crates, they finally found some promising old files labeled with black marker. They had to wipe away cobwebs and beetle debris to read the labels.

Lucas had gotten no answer from the elderly nun or Sister Audrey, and staring across the dimly lit room to where they stood in the doorway, he read a glazed dull look in the old woman's eyes, and a pained look in the younger woman's gaze. Shaking her head as if looking at a problem without solution, Mother Elizabeth chose to leave so as to not look at the problem a moment longer. Sister Audrey ducked out with her.

By this time, wheezing had evolved into sneezing for both of them, but Lucas had developed a case of nonstop asthmatic coughing. His eyes began to tear up from the particle dust and mites.

A handheld flashlight helped somewhat in the poorly lit area in which they worked.

"Here! I've found 1984," announced Meredyth.

She pulled the box from beneath another as Lucas held and replaced the one that had sat atop it. Lucas then took the box from Meredyth's grasp, and he carried it up the stone steps, into a corridor, and out into the open church where at least some air circulated. He placed the box on a pew and Meredyth rifled through it, looking for any court papers with her signature on them. She found none. "I'm trying to recall if I had any of these cases, but its all a blur. So long ago. None of these documents would have required a social worker's signature, so I have no way of tracking it from these files."

"What about this Lauralie Blodgett? You find a file on her? Wouldn't you recall a name like Blodgett?"

"No, I don't remember the name. The mother was likely unmarried . . . likely using her maiden name."

"Of course."

"All the same, I'm looking for Blodgett now." Meredyth

began digging for the Blodgett file, but it was not in alphabetical order where it should be. She rifled through, searching other possible ways it could be filed, under L for *Lauralie,* under B for *Blood.* "Nothing . . . it's not here," she finally concluded. "I'd hoped to locate a photo of her at the very least."

"Maybe it's been filed in the wrong year," he suggested.

"Or maybe Lauralie got at it a second time. Maybe she took it with her when she left this place."

"Perhaps."

"Do you think *she* sent us here? That she was the sexpot in the schoolgirl uniform Tebo took the package from?" Lucas continued to wheeze and cough. During a lull, he managed to say, "Guess I gotta return this file box to the basement. Can't leave it here."

"You don't want to get on Mother Elizabeth's bad side."

"No ma'am, *not never. . . .*"

Lucas returned the box, leaving Meredyth standing alone in the central church, staring up at the larger-than-life, yet lifelike depiction of Christ on the cross. She had been raised Catholic herself, and it had been literally years since her last confession. She had traded in her religion for her scientific bent and her profession, and she knew it. She had broken every vow, and she was now sleeping with and contemplating marrying a Cherokee Indian named Lucas Stonecoat whose beliefs were a mix of mysticism and native folklore. A man who found God in all of nature and whose own nature held a spiritual side that was loving and caring on the one hand, but quickly moved to anger and vengeance if he saw an injustice. He was a man also capable of great wrath, and the *law of blood*—vengeance for a relative—ran deep in his Cherokee genes. She had seen it over the years, his ability and willingness to track a man down and kill his prey, and walk away without remorse. It was what made him an exemplary detective, but more than once, she had seen him lose control under extreme conditions, as when he thought her life in danger. Lucas had rescued her from death on more than one occasion. He had been the one she called in any crisis.

Lucas credited his upbringing largely to his grandfather, who believed in the old ways and customs. A shaman of his people, Keeowskowee had made of Lucas a strong and determined man, yet Lucas's childhood remained as far from her upbringing as that of an Eskimo.

With these thoughts and misgivings swirling about in her head, Meredyth crossed herself and knelt before the crucifix. Then from behind, she heard someone's footfall. She wheeled, imagining it to be Sister Audrey come to check on their progress, or Mother Elizabeth, but no one materialized.

"Is there someone there?" she asked.

No answer.

The silence that had been the silence of this place only deepened. "Is there anyone here?" she asked more empahtically. This time, when she received no answer, she returned her gaze to the face of Christ. Once more, to her rear, she heard a sound, and this time, she watched a shadow, someone in a hooded cloak, a priest who stepped into the confessional booth. Had the noise she heard been the priest? Had he moved that swiftly?

Was it a sign? she wondered. She took a step toward the confessional, thinking it would do her good to go to confession, but with Lucas about to return any moment, she stopped shy of the coffinlike booth. She could hear the man inside yawning.

Then, out of the side of her eye, she saw movement again, a young woman dressed in the uniform of the convent school darting from a hiding place and out the door at the front of the church. It might have been any one of the girls she and Lucas had interviewed.

Was it perhaps Rachel? Wanting to tell Meredyth something out of Mother Elizabeth's earshot? "Wait!" Meredyth rushed for the exit, but she was stopped at the holy water fount, seeing the unusual cigar-shaped item in the water, trifling swirls of blood creating a mosaic over what appeared a human finger. Like a pale dead fish, the finger floated just below the surface, submerged yet floating above the bottom of the fount—the *source* where the holy water *originated,* at least in the *symbolism* of the Church.

Whoever had left the ugly gift in the fountainhead knew its symbolic meaning, she was sure.

"What's going on?" asked Lucas, startling her, suddenly at her side.

"Look, the holy water."

Lucas groaned at what he saw there. "Damn it, they've followed us here; they've been on our heels."

"I heard her back here, and I saw her dash out the front. It was a girl in the school uniform."

He used a handkerchief to fish out the right index finger presumably left by the girl she had seen scuttling out into the rain.

"The confessional booth, Lucas!"

He turned to look down the aisle at the booth. "What about it?"

"He's in the booth! Dressed as a priest."

Lucas rushed the confessional and tore open the door to a wide-eyed, startled young priest whose glasses fell off when he threw up his hands to fend off the attack. Lucas pulled him from the confessional as he pleaded for mercy.

His hands tightly fisted in the folds of the man's robes, Lucas demanded, "Who are you?"

"Sandy brown hair, glasses, but no mole on his cheek, Lucas."

"I-I'm Father . . . W-Will-yam," he choked out.

From behind them, Lucas heard Sister Audrey shout simultaneously, "It's Father Will! Don't hurt him!"

Mother Elizabeth rushed in next, shouting, "This is outrageous conduct, Detective. This isn't your reservation chapel. I will kindly ask that you two please leave Our Lady, now!"

Lucas, realizing the mistaken identity, desperately tried to smooth out the man's robes, and he reached into the booth to fetch his glasses, apology following apology. "Sorry, Father William."

"I apologize as well, but we had provocation," Meredyth defended. "Show them what was floating in their holy water, Lucas."

Lucas held up the severed index finger.

"My dear God," moaned Father William as he straightened his glasses and inched away from Lucas, shrinking away. "I just used the fount to cross myself, and I saw nothing in the water when I entered."

Mother Elizabeth and Sister Audrey collectively gasped at what they saw in Lucas's possession. "Is it . . ." began Mother Elizabeth.

Meredyth nodded. "Most likely from Mira Lourdes."

"Found in our holy water . . ." Elizabeth slumped to a pew seat.

"Defiling the holy water?" asked Audrey.

"Yes, afraid so. I saw someone in the uniform of your school race out the door, but I didn't get a clear look at her."

The old woman placed a hand across her heart. "Give me strength." Sister Audrey located a handheld cardboard fan. "Did you find the records you wanted?" Elizabeth asked.

"I'm afraid not, and Lauralie appears to have stolen her file, Mother Superior," Meredyth explained.

"Theft, defiled holy water," muttered William. "One would almost have to believe that Lauralie had come for a visit. What is your interest in her records? Why are you here?"

"We'll let Mother Superior fill you in. It's a long story."

"Apparently, William, she's become involved in a most unsavory affair with someone who has abducted and killed a woman."

"Our Lauralie? Involved with a murderer?"

"Do you have a photo of Lauralie anywhere, Mother Elizabeth?" asked Lucas.

Again Elizabeth had to defer to Sister Audrey, asking if she had any ideas on the subject. Sister Audrey instantly replied, "The yearbook, Mother Superior. She'll be in it. I'll bring one from the storage closet."

Elizabeth caught her breath and formally introduced Father William Stoughton to Lucas and Meredyth. "Father William comes twice a week to take confessions, to look in on us, make reports to the bishop, and to dine on our food, right, Father?"

"That's right, Mother Superior. Dr. Sanger, Detective, if

there is *anything* I can do to help"—Stoughton brought the hem of his robe up to meet the glasses in his hand and began cleaning the lenses, lifting them back to his eyes, testing, cleaning again, as he spoke—"*anything* whatever, don't hesitate to contact me at St. Pete's Cathedral downtown."

"Did you know Lauralie Blodgett well when she resided here?" asked Lucas, immediately taking him up on his offer.

"Not really. I help *those* who help themselves, so I hardly noticed Lauralie. She was sullen, moody, you know how she was, Mother Elizabeth. Extremely hard to reach."

"Yes, she was all those things," Elizabeth agreed.

Father William continued, seeming anxious to distance himself from Lauralie. "She refused any notion of confessing her sins, told me she *had* none. Imagine it. I tried to counsel her, of course, but she remained stone-hearted, insisting she had *nothing* whatever to confess. I explained the doctrine of Original Sin to her, of course, the blood of the lamb, all of it, but she remained adamant that *she* was without sin; that she was sinned *against*."

Meredyth took Lucas aside for a moment to confer. "Should we call in Chang, have the church vestibule and fount cordoned off as a crime scene?"

He shook his head. "They won't find anything useful, and we'll only disturb the rhythm of this place more than we already have. I say we keep it to ourselves for now. But how is this girl so closely shadowing us that we don't see her?"

"Hell, you're the Indian. You tell me. But I did see a girl. It could've been Lauralie, but it could as well have been Rachel, or one of the others. Actually, at first, I was *sure* it was Rachel, wanting to add to her testimony, you know, but I was stopped at the sight of the bloody holy water."

"Another defiled religious holy item," he muttered. "A pattern emerges."

Sister Audrey returned with the yearbook, two pages already marked for their perusal. Lucas and Meredyth studied the two photos of Lauralie Blodgett that had made the yearbook, her head-shot graduation photo and a photo taken with her entire class. She was a striking young woman who appeared far older than eighteen years of age. In the full body shot, it was evident that she had filled out her Catholic school uniform, and she exuded sex appeal even in the frumpy plaid skirt and suspenders over a white blouse.

"No way Father William didn't notice her," whispered Lucas to Meredyth. "Given his nervousness when asked about her, I wouldn't put it past him to have put a move on her."

"Or she on him for favors."

Lauralie stood almost a head taller than any of her classmates. In both photos, she wore an expressionless face, but her eyes rose up from the flat page and seemed to burn with a strange, penetrating radiance. Dark-skinned, exotic in appearance, she might pass for Mexican or Indian. When Lucas asked about her nationality, William said, "Mexican . . . she was Mexican and Caucasian."

"No, Father Will, she was Irish on her mother's side, Croombs, and a mix of Mexican and Native American on her father's side."

"Croombs?" asked Meredyth.

"She showed me her father's photo once, and a photo of the woman she had located, Katherine Croombs. Quite the Caucasian, looked like the Irish stereotype."

Lucas and Meredyth thanked the woman again for her time and hospitality as they prepared to leave. Mother Elizabeth, forgiving them their trespasses against Father William, suddenly insisted that they *must* remain for the dinner meal, "To see how well the children prepare the meal, wait the tables, and clean up afterwards."

Meredyth begged off, saying they hoped to get to the county clerk's office before the Children and Family Services Department shut down for the evening. "As it is, we may not make it."

"All the more reason to stay for the meal. Father William always stays for dinner."

The mother superior had earlier asked Father William to replace the holy water in the fount, and he'd seemed anxious to fulfill her wish and had eagerly gone to the front vestibule for the chore. Lucas went to Father William now and asked, "You have no idea of Lauralie' s current whereabouts? Where we might find her? We really need to ask her a few routine questions."

"Sorry . . . as Mother Elizabeth can tell you, none of us have seen or heard from Lauralie in months."

"She was a pretty girl, Father."

"All children are beautiful in the eyes of the Lord, Detective."

"I'm sure they are." Lucas put a mental note in the back of his head to talk to Rachel again someday about Father William. Instinct told Lucas that the man was not the saint he purported to be, and that perhaps Rachel and others here were not so demure as they were frightened.

Lucas and Meredyth left, to Mother Elizabeth's and Sister Audrey's smiles and waving of hands as Lucas pulled from the lot, Sister Audrey again electronically opening and closing the gate.

"Place is like a small castle missing a drawbridge and a moat," said Lucas. "There must be ways in and out the students alone know about."

"What're you suggesting? That we have the church staked out?"

"Maybe . . ."

"Whoever's playing games with us, she knows the lay of the grounds here, the ins and outs, and Rachel mans the kitchen door. Suppose Rachel is still being dominated by Lauralie. Suppose Rachel's suspicion that Mother Orleans's accident was no accident is true. Maybe the fire was no accident either, but a first attempt on the old mother nun's life? Rachel might make an excellent witness for the prosecution if Lauralie is as involved in the abduction and death of Mira Lourdes as she seems to be."

"Where is Lauralie?"

"I'd like to get Rachel out of that place and into a real interrogation room downtown."

"Rachel knows a lot, agreed. Like someone who has spent her entire life here should know."

"And I'm telling you now, Mere, there's something not kosher with that priest. He may deserve a great deal more thrashing than I gave him."

"He did seem odd, defensive, especially when you were strangling him with his own robes!" She laughed recalling the image.

Both Meredyth and Lucas felt great relief at passing from the church grounds and back into the world of the city of Houston. "Poor Rachel," Meredyth said. "I feel like we ought to've hidden her in the trunk of the car and rescued her from all those characters."

"I know . . . me too, but then that'd be *agin* the law."

"Mother Elizabeth is a strange mix of strength, intelligence, and naiveté, isn't she?"

"I think her heart's in the right place, but no one's playing by her rules, not really."

"Behind those bars, she's created a fanciful fantasy existence, a place apart for her separate peace, yet she's *convinced* herself that she's preparing those girls for the real world."

"Still, I liked her. Heart of gold. *I been searching for a heart of gold . . . and I'm growin' old,*" he sang out.

MEREDYTH INSISTED THEY try to make the downtown courthouse before closing time, but Lucas replied, "In this traffic, no way we can make it before the offices close. We may as well call it a day, Mere."

"Damn it, Lucas, I can't recall if there was an infant named Lauralie Blodgett or Lauralie Croombs as one of my first cases or not. But given the mounting coincidences, I'm assuming I did handle the case. It's got to be why I've been targeted by this maniac, and Lauralie has got to be at the center of it all. Maybe the Post-it Killer is her boyfriend; maybe he has made promises to her."

"Promises?"

"Promises to help her wreak revenge on me. She could be the brains behind the hand of this Frankenstein."

"Why target me then?"

"Because, Lucas, they've gone to school on me, so they know all about me and my surroundings, my likes and dislikes, and so they know I'm . . . that is, that we are close, and by hurting you, they *know* they hurt me."

"Is that an admission of love?" he asked.

"A great and abiding fondness with a capital F," she replied.

He laughed at this and drove on. After ten minutes of silence, he said, "You know me, Mere. I don't normally leap to assumptions and conclusions on a case, but it's increasingly clear that someone, most likely this Lauralie someone, has it in for you so badly that it borders on a kind of religious abhorrence she has against you."

"To've mailed those body parts to us, and to've placed that severed finger for me to find in the holy water . . . Indeed it is a furious hatred she's harboring for me."

"True whether she's done all of this herself, in person, or has had others following her orders. Kinda like you!" he joked.

"She certainly knows how to control people."

"Yeah, even men of the cloth like Father William."

"You really didn't like Father William, did you?"

"Call it an instant dislike."

"But how do you see him helping Lauralie—or whoever is behind Mira Lourdes's death and mutilation?"

"Small favors, I suspect, for sexual favors perhaps. I get a bird-of-prey kind of thing coming off that beak-nosed priest. He curries favors with all the girls, I suspect, but maybe Lauralie became too much for him to handle. I get the feeling he's damned glad he hasn't seen her in some time and doesn't know her whereabouts and wants to keep it that way."

"That's quite a leap, Lucas."

"Suspicious mind of mine has kept me alive this long."

"Well, one thing I believe we can agree on is that our female courier is not so innocent. The finger was not tucked away in a box. She knew what she was defiling the holy water with."

"Which means that our Post-it Ripper is not a *he* but a

they, a couple out to panic Houston, and bent on destroying you and me in the bargain, like . . . like a jealous lover."

"I know it'll only sound paranoid to anyone looking at the circumstances from the outside," Meredyth said. "Hell, as a shrink, I'd say the same thing of someone coming to me with a story as convoluted and crazed as this . . . but after all, it was a man-and-woman team who abducted Mira Lourdes, and why Lourdes, if not to make a point with the convent? And-and, Lucas, why'd they mark the return address on the first parcel to you as Our Lady of—" She stopped herself in mid-sentence, pondering something new.

"What is it, Mere?" he asked, stopping at a light.

"The other return address, the mortician's. They're a twenty-four-hour business, right?"

"Yeah, it's over on Lowe near Clinton, off the canal . . . a commercial district. What're you thinking?"

"I'm thinking a lot of people have tragically died around Lauralie Blodgett. A few years ago it was her mother superior, and this year her birth mother. So where do you suppose her mother's body went for burial if not that return address on Lowe?"

"I hope they have better record-keeping skills than the sisters of Our Lady of Miracles."

Lucas turned the car in the direction of the mortuary.

MORTE DE ARTHUR'S was the first and only mortuary Lucas had ever seen that sported a neon sign, but within they found a clean, well-lit, marble-floored, darkly paneled place of real mahogany walls, all polished and kept from the original mortuary on this spot, likely in business for most of the century before losing out to economic hard times and family illness and death. They also learned on the inside that the new proprietors, Giorgio and Carlotta Fellini, did keep better records than did the convent school. They were quickly able to locate a burial service for a Carmilla Blodgett, a Walter D. Blodgett, a Terrence K. Blodgett, and more recently a John D. Blodgett.

"No Katherine Croombs Blodgett?" Meredyth asked, shaking her head.

"Sorry. If it ain't there," said Carlotta, "then we didn't handle her."

Meredyth scanned the John Blodgett card and read aloud. *"John D. Blodgett, aged fifty-two. Amer. Indian/Mexican male. Height 6'2", weight 210 lbs. Generic service. Determination of death: heart attack. Survived by common law wife, Katherine Croombs, and daughter Lauralie. Services and burial at Greenhaven Meadows Cemetery held May 4, 1997."*

"Bingo! It's her!" shouted Lucas.

"Yes, she's on Blodgett's card as his wife and Lauralie's down as his daughter."

Lucas examined the card. The date of Blodgett's funeral and burial at Greenhaven Cemetery predated Giorgio and Carlotta's taking over the business. "Greenhaven . . . Blodgett. The vandalized gravesite Kelton learned about? It's got to be him, Lauralie's father."

"So where was Katherine's body taken?"

"Try the C's," suggested Lucas.

Meredyth then thumbed through the three-by-five cards under the Cs, and there she located a Katherine Anne Croombs who had been embalmed and prepared for burial here. "It's her, Lauralie's mother, Lucas. It's got to be Lauralie behind all this. She's leaving all these telltale signs."

"Bread-crumb trail. She wants to get caught."

"More likely, she wants us to know her motives."

"If it's not her, someone's going to a hell of a lot of trouble to make us believe it's her."

"Like wily Father William Stoughton, you mean?"

"It may sound far-fetched, but suppose she's got something on him. Suppose he needs to incriminate her in order to get out from under any charges she could now, or in the future, bring against him."

"Molestation charges? Maybe you've got something there."

"Lot of temptation for a man in that place, and a lot of

nooks and crannies to do something about it in, if you ask me."

"You do have a dirty mind, Lucas."

"No, a detective's mind is all."

"Take nothing at face value, huh?"

The mortuary record cards were arranged in alphabetical order and then by date of burial. John Blodgett and the other three Blodgetts, all of mixed Native American and Mexican descent, all predated the change in management. "All these Blodgetts were likely related. I wonder why someone in the family couldn't have taken Lauralie out of that convent to return to the family."

"Crack baby, remember? Mother without direction or goals. Father unavailable. All we know, John Blodgett never knew he had a daughter. If so, no one in his family would have known either."

"I'm sure Family Services didn't bother to find out."

Her face flushed red as if he'd slapped her. She turned to the bookkeeper, wife, co-owner, and asked, "Carlotta, were all these Blodgetts related?"

Carlotta shrugged. "No way to be sure. They were all serviced by Xavier and Sons, before we came."

"*Before* the advent of Morte de Arthur's—translated— the Death of Arthur's," replied Lucas, thinking, *Before the Xaviers sold out to a tastelessly run franchise.*

Lucas next took the card on Katherine Croombs from Meredyth and read the words. "*Katherine Anne Croombs, age thirty-seven, Caucasian female, 5'9", 180 lbs. Catholic service. Determination of death: alcoholic overdose w/ ambien pills. Ms. Croombs is survived by a daughter, Lauralie Blodgett. Services and burial held at Greenhaven Meadows Berwyn Cemetery, July 20th, 2004.*"

On the back of the card, the remaining information summed Katherine's life up to a last known address. An address for Lauralie was given as 1386 Ravenswood, Chicago, Illinois. The mother's address was on North Groiler.

"Alcoholic poisoning, just as Mother Elizabeth said," Meredyth almost whispered.

"She didn't say anything about sleeping pills. Man, the lady was only a couple of years older than us, Mere."

"Do you suppose Lauralie is living at Katherine's address?"

"It's certainly worth our while to find out."

"Stakeout?"

"I think we have enough for a warrant to search. I'll make the call." Lucas went for his car radio, leaving Meredyth in the mortuary office with Carlotta Fellini, the proprietor.

"Do you recall anything at all about the daughter?" Meredyth asked the flamboyantly dressed, heavyset, buxom Carlotta, who acted as secretary and gofer for her husband, Giorgio. When Lucas and Meredyth had first arrived, Mr. Fellini, according to the name tag on his lapel, had greeted them at the door. Giorgio—in black bow tie against a ruffled baby-blue shirt beneath a navy-blue blazer a size too small, his ruffled cuffs flitting about on nervous wings at seeing Lucas's gold shield—had sent them to the office to speak to his wife about records. Giorgio was in the middle of a wake just the other side of the door.

Carlotta stopped chewing her gum at Meredyth's question, as if doing so might help her think. "I remember her, sure. Flirtatious bitch . . . all over my *Giorgio*. And cheap, paid in cash, said little, no tears . . . showed no emotion *at all*!" The emphatic *at all* was condemnation and curse rolled into one in Carlotta jargon.

"Anything else you recall, anything at all?"

Carlotta's jaws worked the gum again. "Let me get Giorgio in here. He dealt with her more'n I did. I just took her money."

"Did she say she was staying at her mother's address on Ravenswood?" Meredyth held up the file card to her.

"Said she was at some Best Western, I think. Said she had come in from out of town to make arrangements is all. She left an out-of-town address, Chicago. It's on the card."

Meredyth had already jotted the two addresses down on a notepad she carried with her. She imagined the Chicago address a fake, a dead end. Certainly, Lauralie was closer than Chicago, and like Lucas, Meredyth wondered if sweet daughter Lauralie had perhaps taken up residence at Mom's old place.

Carlotta buzzed Giorgio on his pager, and Lucas reentered the office alongside Giorgio, who, smiling beneath his handlebar mustache, greeted them as if meeting them for the first time. "How much more can we help you?" he asked, his arms expansively opening to them, his smile a commercial habit.

Meredyth showed him the three-by-five card and asked, "Do you recall anything at all, sir, about the daughter?"

"Was she with anyone to lean on, a man?" asked Lucas.

"No, alone she was . . . all alone. I recall how sad that was, but she was stern, you know, like a rock"—he held out a fist to emphasize this point—"how do you say it, stoic . . . yes, stoic. Said her mother was a lifelong alcoholic, a victim of her chosen lifestyle, and as sad as it was, you know, a wasted life, that her overdosing came as no surprise to her, the daughter, I mean."

"That was her attitude? Matter-of-fact?" asked Lucas.

"She was under a lot of stress . . . depressed, you know," said Giorgio. "It is common under the circumstances of a death in the family. It is something I see every day."

Carlotta, who obviously did not work the wakes, wore a multicolored neck scarf, a halter top, and jeans. Hearing Giorgio's words, she leaped to her feet and came around from behind her desk like a charging bull, getting into Giorgio's face, shaking her head and waving a stern index finger. "She wasn't all that broke up, Giorgio! Don't confuse a stone-cold heart with honest depression!"

"You are too harsh, Carlotta!"

"She took you, Giorgio! We lost on that service, thanks to your thinking with your little head!" She said to Lucas, "That tramp was stone cold *and* cheap *and* flirting with my man the whole time. You . . . you men!"

Giorgio piped in. "Flirting? Come on! Yeah, all right, she was cool perhaps, and cheap, sure. I give you that, but she said the trip to get here on a moment's notice had emptied her bank account, and that she had only come in to bury her mother. I told her all about our memory-preservation and plot-maintenance programs, you know, how we send out anniversary cards with Mom or Dad's picture each year on the date of death, and how we keep up the grounds, place flowers on the grave every other week, but—"

"—but she wanted no frills, just the pine-box special," finished Carlotta. "She went all out for dear ol' Mom," Carlotta facetiously added. "She walked in here wanting to pay nothing, and short of that, as little as possible. And when I told her how easy it would be to take the maintenance plan out of her credit card each month, she said she didn't *do* credit cards. I had to pry a home address out of her."

"Did you see what kind of vehicle she arrived in?"

"'Fraid not," replied Giorgio.

"And at the funeral service?"

"Arrived in a cab."

"Alone or with a man?"

"Alone, always alone, she was."

Carlotta let out a low growl like an angry cat. "All I know, she kept coming onto you, Giorgio, to get the price down, and you *dummy,* you let her. She got a sweet deal on a plot out at Berwyn too, I can tell you."

"Is this her?" asked Meredyth, flashing the open yearbook before the pair.

"*Ahhh . . . hmmm . . .*" hedged the man. "She was older, sexier. No *kid* like this," he emphasized, as if to say he didn't chase kids.

His wife disagreed. "It's her in the picture, Giorgio, only not wearing that skintight dress she came in here with."

"Yeah, if Carlotta says it's her, it's her. She's got a thing for faces."

Carlotta laughed. "And you, you got a thing for asses."

"Hey, so I got a thing for bodies—ain't it my *business*? Look around you, Carlotta. Come on, I'm jokin' here. Don't you get it?" Giorgio's arms went up and out, the ruffled cuffs flitting like two downy birds as he spoke. In an aside to Lucas, he winked. "Get it, my business? Bods?"

Carlotta gave her man a cold glare, her arms folded.

Lucas thanked them for their time and escorted Meredyth, clutching the yearbook to herself, out and onto Lowe Street. A ship came into view at the end of the street as if cruising the neighborhood, and it gave a blast of its fog horn, startling Meredyth. "Houston Ship Canal," Lucas explained as she watched the giant dark side of the ship disappear behind warehouses lining the canal. "Doubt you've ever had occasion to visit this side of town."

"What next?" she asked. "Raid Momma Croombs's house?"

"May be impossible to get a warrant. I spoke to Jorganson. He thinks we've got flimsy cause, a string of coincidences, he calls it, but he's going to wake up Judge Diehl. She's our best hope for a warrant."

"Meanwhile?"

"I'd like to see the police report on Katherine Croombs's death. How 'bout you?"

"Well . . . we have the date of death and her address. Getting hold of the report should be a simple matter."

They drove back for the precinct house and made inquiries, soon getting hold of a computer-generated copy of the police report on the death of one Katherine Croombs, occurring July 17th in the 29th Precinct. The body was autopsied in Leonard Chang's crime lab by Dr. Lynn Nielsen.

The police report, on the surface, appeared a routine mop-up after an unintentional death by overdose of sleeping pills and drink. Lucas commented on how cut and dried the report read, and in fact he thought aloud, "Perhaps too cut and dried."

"Meaning?"

"Meaning when cops don't want to spend all night in the station filling out a report, they resort to *generalities* like the ones we're seeing here. A cliche-ridden report is like a good paint job—covers a multitude of sins in quick time."

"What're you saying, Lucas?"

"In all my time with the COMIT program, going through all those thousands of Cold Case files, I know when a pair of cops have made up their collective minds to go along with *surface* appearances, and once an assumption of suicide or accidental overdose is made, it's hard to buck."

"You think this might be the case here?"

"If Lauralie is as dangerous as we've been led to think, *yes*. I may be out on a limb here, but the reports're too pat, the woman dying of an overdose without any question being raised, especially since—look here at the autopsy report."

She followed his finger to the line on the report he wanted her to read.

"She didn't swallow a lot of pills."

"Although her bottle was found empty on her night-stand," Lucas pointed out. "Cops at the scene made the assumption she swallowed the bottle of pills along with the alchohol."

"She died in bed in a peaceful pose," Meredyth said, pointing to one of the crime-scene photos he'd brought up on screen.

"That's screwy too. Death brought on by alcoholic poisoning doesn't fit with the neat, orderly position on the bed, folded arms, body perpendicular to the edge this way. *Nahhh*, no way."

"She laid down on her back, folded her arms, readying herself for death," Meredyth said, shrugging, playing devil's advocate.

"When people drink too much—and she had over three fifths of straight bourbon with gin chasers—they don't wake up all neatly fixed and folded in bed. Someone posed her body after death. Now it may've been the neighbor who called it in . . . the one with the key . . . come in to check on her, but given testimony of the lady, it could've been her daughter, purportedly living with her and in Chicago at the same time."

Meredyth stared again at the digital computer images showing the deceased *posed* in death, as Lucas theorized— arms folded across her chest, ankles overlying one another. "Could still be an overdose, Lucas, and Lauralie, finding her mother in an unflattering position, poses her. Doesn't mean she killed her mother."

He nodded. "Could be . . . could be. Report does say *she* discovered the body and called it in." He paced the Cold Room floor now. "Could also be she did a lot more than pose Mommie Dearest."

"Could be she had to lift her off the floor, the sofa, the bathroom toilet," replied Meredyth, sitting cross-legged on the edge of his desk.

"That's where you find most falling-down drunks, and the investigators look the other way when a loved one moves the body out of a sense of . . . propriety."

"So you're not buying any of it."

"Lauralie is an effective actress, capable of lulling anyone into any belief she dangles before them. I believe she staged the body and the murder, just as she staged the death of the Mother Superior at age twelve."

"She does have a theatrical flare.

"Had Tebo's temperature rising, Father Will, and I'd bet a month's pay on Giorgio."

"How then did she do her mother in? Simply by providing her with the booze? Going out to a movie and returning?"

"There were unexplained marks on her wrists and ankles, Mere."

"Where does the report say that?"

"Coroner's protocol here." He brought it on screen. "Chalked up to clumsy handling of the body, men holding onto wrists and ankles when moving her from bed to body bag. Called a coroner's contusion. They can tell if it occurred after death from the discoloration of the skin. There's a reason you grab the deceased under the arms, and there's a proper way to hold the ankles tucked against your body."

"Sounds like you've hefted a few."

"I have. Look here too, the broken neck—chalked up to what they call a coroner's fracture. Likely from the same manhandling. Not easy properly elevating and hauling deadweight."

"So you're suggesting the M.E. wrote off restraint marks to coroner transport wagon bruises?"

"Possibly, yes."

"Are you saying that the cops lied so they could get off duty on time? And that the M.E. helped them out?"

"No, no, no. I'm saying they made a tacit blanket *assumption* and acted on it, and they justified that assumption with their language on the report. They didn't lie so much as they *convinced* themselves of what their eyes told them."

"So while the detectives on scene may have had misgivings, they all turned into smoke?"

"Look, I still have doubts about how Marilyn Monroe was supposed to've died. Why? The scene was too clean, too damned neat, and she lay posed in bed, her body recently washed clean and dressed for the coroner, dead of an overdose. But God forbid she be found *under* the bed. Gives a guy doubts."

"And I suppose you think Elvis still lives?"

"Only as an icon for his estate and his legions of fans. He lives in that he's still number one. But that's show biz. No, I can easily accept the prognosis of an overdose in Elvis's case."

"Why Elvis yes, but Marilyn no? Because the death scene was not doctored or candy-coated?"

"Exactly. Elvis, unlike the Queen of Hollywood, was found dead at the foot of his toilet. No posing of the body, no *gussying* it up. Now that's unquestionably an overdose no one had a hand in but Elvis—an honest-to-God unintentional suicide."

"You buy into Marilyn's having been murdered?"

"At least *assisted* into her overdose by someone. Most cops know the body would at least be half on, half off the bed, and not posed in a peaceful slumber against the pillows."

"Then you suspect Lauralie's desperate hunt for her birth mother all those years—"

"Desperate's not too far from determined, the word Mother Elizabeth used to describe her tenacity in the search for Mom and Dad."

"From the beginning, all that effort in order to kill Katherine?"

"*Some* reason, huh?"

Meredyth's mind filled with the thought. "To search for so long, only to learn that no one was searching for *her* . . ."

"Sounds like a motive for anger, and take anger up a notch to hatred, ratchet it up to acting on your hatred, and whataya got?" he asked.

"Imagine, though, seeking out one's own mother for the express purpose of killing her. It's almost too much to comprehend."

"Yeah, but it'd make a hell of a movie of the week."

"Perhaps there were extenuating circumstances, a falling-out, an argument that escalated to . . . to murder."

"Or *assisted* suicide?" asked Lucas.

"All we know for sure is that Lauralie *did* find her mother," she replied, clenching a fist.

"And within weeks of finding Mom, the daughter is having Mom prepped for burial at Greenhaven Cemetery by Giorgio and Carlotta. Or we could give little Lauralie, poor orphaned child, the benefit of doubt."

"Perhaps . . . perhaps she got caught up with—"

"*Crazy Joe Boyfriend?* Who not only planned and executed the abduction and murder of Mira Lourdes, but who also *offed* her mother, and maybe is the brain who devised the eerie mailings to you and me, Mere. No, it has to be they're *equally* involved—her with a motive for vengeance, him with a means to that end and a skill for dissection."

"If she selected Mira as a victim because of Mira's name—Lourdes—if she did that, then perhaps she is directing all the traffic, planting the clues she wants us to find, planning the abduction, the murder, the mutilation . . . which begs the question—"

"—did she plan her own mother's death?" he finished.

"—and did she have help even then from the mysterious boyfriend? Damn, a person could go crazy trying to decipher what floats here and what doesn't."

"Easy, Mere."

"And I hate it . . . I *hate* the thought of my contributing to all this *insanity,* however unwittingly."

He lifted her off his desk and into his arms, holding her

close. "I'd say let's talk to the investigators on Katherine Croombs's overdose case, *but* it'd likely be a waste of time. No one's going to admit to sleepwalking through a case."

"What about talking to the M.E. in charge of the death?"

"That'd be Dr. Lynn Nielsen, very sharp. No way she couldn't've had doubts, but she'd just come on—new woman on the totem pole. Perhaps she held back pursuing it as a result."

"Do you think she'd admit that?"

"No, not unless we can convince her of its relevance to what's going on now. Maybe then . . ."

"You mean it's worth a try?"

"Let's do it."

He made a call and Frank Patterson answered, telling Lucas that Nielsen had just put on her coat and disappeared into the elevator.

"Thanks, Doctor."

"Anything I can do for you, Detective?" But before Patterson could finish his sentence, Lucas had slammed down the phone, grabbed Meredyth by the hand, and rushed her out.

"Nielsen's on her way out of the building. Let's catch her."

When they found Dr. Lynn Nielsen, she'd already exited the elevator on the main floor, but she'd been held up by an intern from a lab who'd chased her down with a clipboard and a form she had to sign. Nielsen briskly signed, waved good night to the young intern, and made for the exit.

Lucas and Meredyth caught her on the stairs outside the precinct, one on each side, Lucas proposing they buy her dinner.

"What is it you two want from me?" she asked. "Come now. I know the American mind now. No such thing as a free lunch."

Lucas smiled and held up his hands as if caught. "Information on a case of yours that goes back to July 17th."

"That would be on file in the computer."

"A woman named Katherine Croombs."

"Croombs . . . Croombs . . ."

"Found in a state of alcoholic poisoning in which you noted two key elements that went *ignored* by your immediate supervisor, our Dr. Patterson, and the detectives on the case, who appeared in heat to sign off on it," Lucas explained.

She turned up her collar against the annoying drizzle, said nothing, and began skipping down the steps. Lucas and Meredyth followed.

"Do you recall the case?" asked Meredyth in her ear.

She stopped and looked into Meredyth's eyes. "Yes, I recall the one named Croombs. Acute liver damage, skin jaundiced to a tea-green color, other internal organs shriveled and saturated with the booze."

"Why do you recall her case so vividly, unless you have good reason to?" asked Lucas. "Say, because it haunts you?"

"I've said enough. Good night." She rushed for her car. They pursued.

"We suspect she was helped along that night toward her death, Dr. Nielsen," said Meredyth, catching her at her car.

Nielsen shakily worked to dig her key into the lock.

"We believe the woman's daughter not only killed her, Dr. Nielsen, but that she is involved in the mutilation murder of Mira Lourdes."

Nielsen had snatched her door open, about to leave, but this stopped her cold. She looked back at them. "The daughter? The two cases are somehow related? Everyone involved strongly encouraged me to believe the prevailing wisdom."

"Which was that the old woman died as she lived, *ODing* in a weekend war with her own worst enemy—her drunken self?" asked Lucas.

"Locked in a lifelong melee with alcohol, yes. Make no waves, I was told by Frank."

"Patterson. Figures. Feldman and Rowan investigate it, Patterson rubber-stamps it. But you saw the marks on her wrists and ankles," Lucas hammered now.

"Yes, true, but the case was—how you said—rubber-stamped, closed over my objections, so . . ."

"You also noted there was very little in the way of barbiturates in her system, while the police report said she had swallowed an entire *bottle* of pills," added Meredyth.

"They brought the empty pill bottle in a plastic bag along with six empty bottles of Jim Beam—six! She was killed by making excessive love to Jim Beam, they joked—right over her body, they joked! I never saw such a thing in my country."

Nielsen shivered with the recall. Lucas and Meredyth let her talk. "I knew it would come back to get me," she said.

"We're not interested in getting you, Dr. Nielsen, believe me."

"Dr. Chang will be disappointed to learn of it. He was out of the city then, on working vacation—Vancouver, giving a talk." Then speaking of Katherine Croombs, she said, "Poor woman looked like my grandmama, but hardly that age! She had two chipped teeth, and her lips were bruised too, a curious thing we see in abuse cases. It didn't make sense."

"And Frank didn't want to hear about this?"

She now climbed into her car, averting her eyes and face for the moment, fumbling with her seat belt. She turned the key, her Plymouth Voyager coming to life. "You must tell me why you think the Croombs autopsy is connected to the Post-it case we're now working. I must know if I am to bring all of this to Dr. Chang's attention and give in my resignation."

"What possible good can come of your resigning?" asked Meredyth through the car window.

"If anyone should be talking of resigning, it's Patterson. Trust Chang, yes. Confide the truth in him. You won't ever regret it," Lucas firmly told her.

"What is connecting the two cases?" she asked.

"It's a long story, and we'd truly like to tell you over dinner," Meredyth assured her.

She considered this. "All right, Michelangelo's, say in twenty minutes? I'll meet you there, and since it may be my last meal as Assistant M.E. here, be prepared to buy me the house specialty."

"It won't be your last meal, I promise," Meredyth replied. "We'll stand with you against Patterson. We know he put you in this position."

"I have been haunted by that Croombs woman."

She backed from her parking space and pulled out of the police lot, Lucas and Meredyth watching, hoping she'd show up at the restaurant.

They went for Lucas's car.

CHAPTER 12

Morning stars: to direct, guide

BEFORE ARRIVING AT Michelangelo's Italian Eatery, Lucas had called District Attorney Harry Jorganson, asking if they'd gotten the warrant on the address he wanted. Jorganson informed him that he couldn't sell it to the judge. "No dice. Judge says she fails to see that we've actually connected enough dots here, Lucas. Sorry, I know your instincts are right on, but the judge was adamant, got on her high horse about my coming to her to turn a blind eye to the Bill of Rights, the Constitution, the American Civil Liberties credo, you name it, every time Houston PD is feeling public pressure."

"Did you tell her we suspect it has to do with the Post-it Ripper?" he asked.

"I told her, told her more than once, but she was on a tear. I understand she got turned over on appeal in the Edmunds case, which sucks, and we just got her at really the wrong time."

Lucas invited Jorganson to sit down with him, Meredyth,

and Nielsen for dinner. "We can give you more of the details to go on."

"Sorry, Lucas, but ol' Jorganson's got two trials to prep witnesses on for a busy A.M. *mañana*. Again, sorry about the warrant. Get me a bigger hammer to wield, okay? Drive that sucker home for you with the right tools, you know that, you know you do. Well, gotta run. Enjoy dinner."

Lucas broke the bad news to Meredyth, who said, "Damn . . . damn fool judge, and what's wrong with Harry Jorganson?" She scorned and fumed the rest of way to Michelangelo's.

At the restaurant, they were well into their main course by the time Lucas and Meredyth explained all their reasons for suspecting the girl fresh out of the convent school. "It's possible that her boyfriend is doing the actual killing, but we suspect she's pointing out the targets," said Lucas.

"Then you suspect that the Post-it Ripper is two people," said Nielsen.

"Yes, we do."

Meredyth added, "There've been clues intentionally leading us to Lauralie Blodgett, and I'm afraid the sudden reappearance of Lauralie in Katherine's life was not the touching reunion scene we usually see on television programs and in the movies."

Lucas told Nielsen what they had learned at the mortician's.

"I think that Lauralie was and remains traumatized by her childhood experience of growing up without anyone, feeling like a prisoner inside the walls of Our Lady of Miracles," added Meredyth.

Nielsen nodded. "And now she's out to perform a miracle of her own, the perfect crime."

"With enlisted help, yes."

"This is good news then, that you two have narrowed your search from a nonentity, a boogeyman, to two specific individuals, one of whom you have a name for."

"It's all based on a great deal of speculation," cautioned Lucas. "Not solid enough for the DA or to get a warrant, it seems."

"Educated speculation," corrected Meredyth. "Due in large part because Lauralie couldn't resist leaving us bread crumbs to follow, as if—"

"Bread crumbs?" asked Nielsen.

"Clues, as if there beats inside her the heart of a person who wants to be caught and punished," explained Lucas.

"More likely she wants her *day-and-say* before the cameras and in court, as if she feels we *owe* it to her to catch her and make her a star," said Meredyth. "It's why she's selected Lucas and me to come after her, and perhaps because I was instrumental in placing her at that orphanage back in 1984."

"Damn twisted story," commented Nielsen. "Sounds too much like fiction not to be true, if you understand my meaning. *Beyond belief,* so it makes it credible by virtue of being beyond belief. Anything that bizarre . . . well, we have a saying for in Sweden. *It is the lunacy not yet dreamt of that will befall you.*"

"I like that," said Lucas. "Are you sure it wasn't stolen from the Cherokee?"

"Sad but true," Meredyth said of the aphorism, and then she added, "Now let me see if I have it right. The most incredible lunacy, not yet dreamt of, shall come to pass . . . and Jesus wept for all mankind." She toasted it with her wine glass.

They dined to the rattle of dishware and silverware, each nursing private thoughts for the moment. The waiter came, asked after their comfort, and left. The music was as authentically Italian as the cuisine, from an opera Meredyth recognized.

"What more can you tell us about the mother's death?" asked Meredyth of Lynn Nielsen.

"One of the first uniformed officers at the scene told me it may have been staged to look as if Katherine had killed herself, but he would never repeat it again afterwards. Detective Feldman, the lead investigator, seemed to have some personal interest in closing the case quickly. I think he needed to clear his homicide board for the month. Who knows?"

"Feldman's a jerk," Lucas muttered. "He's a nine-to-fiver, anxious to wrap up a case and go home."

"Always scratching himself in the crotch," she said. "Is this why they call him Itch?"

Lucas laughed, Nielsen and Meredyth joining in. Someone passing by jostled their table, an empty bottle of wine spilling out its last drop, telling Lucas to order a second.

Nielsen continued talking about the Croombs matter. "They took the statements of neighbors about the woman's on-again, off-again relationship with the bottle. Said she had it bad, her battle with booze. But one neighbor said she thought Katherine was doing better since she had rediscovered her daughter." Nielsen sipped her wine before continuing. "I read some of Feldman's remarks in the file. He cited a long police history with the address, numerous occasions of disorderly disturbances, fighting, you know. This was enough to sum it all up for the detectives. *Relapse.* And this time an overdose. Closed case. Death was *chalked down* to accidental overdose."

"Chalked up," Lucas corrected her.

"Yes, and I was strongly urged to get it off my desk and get onto the sixty-four or so other cases awaiting me."

"Dr. Chang never looked over the findings?" asked Lucas.

"No, he was away at the time, and Patterson was in charge. Not likely I would have gone over Frank's head in any case, being new on the job and not yet knowing how to tiptoe around him like I do now."

"If you had had full responsibility and freedom to pursue the case at the time, what would you have done differently, Dr. Nielsen?" asked Meredyth.

"I would have done more than simply express my condolences to the daughter as Feldman and the others did, releasing the body and ordering it sent to an undertaker of her choosing. They should have questioned the daughter far more extensively about her alibi; instead, they listened to her sob story of how she had just found and reunited with her mother. The men were falling all over her as I recall."

Meredyth displayed the photo of Lauralie. "Is this the daughter?"

Nielsen studied the photo. "Yes, that is her."

"We think she left us a *gift* at the convent," said Lucas. "Found this and a few ounces of blood in the baptismal at Our Lady." He showed her the index finger from what they suspected was Mira Lourdes's left hand.

"Like I said, no such thing as free lunch," Nielsen replied, wincing at the amputated digit.

"Sorry," said Lucas. "I thought all you coroner types were immune to such things as runaway body parts."

A waiter stood over them, gasped, and threw down the bill before Lucas realized he'd been traumatized by the thing nestled in the handkerchief. Meredyth grabbed the hanky, folding it away, but Lucas managed to grab it back. "Hey, that's still evidence."

"What're you going to do with that thing, Lucas? Take it to the witch doctor out at the Coushatta Reservation? See if we can get some voodoo input on the case?"

"Cherokee magic might surprise you, Mere."

"No amount of tobacco *twisting* and *burning* is going to help us here, Stone Man," Meredyth replied.

"Hey, I know you're frustrated, but you shouldn't knock what you haven't tried, Doctor," he fired back.

Meredyth dropped her gaze and wrung her hands together. "I'm sorry, Lucas. It's just this case is getting to me . . . *she's* getting to me."

"If you would care to leave the finger with me, Lieutenant," said Nielsen, "I can match the tissue against what we have, make a certain determination as to whether or not it is Lourdes's digit."

Lucas joked, "I thought I'd make a necklace of it, make it my Cherokee magical icon, but I am tiring of carrying it around." He handed it, wrapped in the handkerchief, to Dr. Nielsen. As he did so, Meredyth grabbed for the check. Lucas caught her hand and retrieved the check.

"I'm paying," she said.

"The hell you are."

Their waiter suddenly and noisily stormed out of the

restaurant, tossing his apron at the boss. "Look at that, Lucas. The guy quit his job. I hope you're proud of yourself. Now give me the check. You've caused enough trouble tonight." Meredyth held one end of the check between her fingers, and he held the other end in a tug of war that ripped it in two.

Lucas firmly said, "It's my treat. *You* can leave the tip."

"Leave the tip for whom?" asked Nielsen, amused at the two.

"You are such a . . . a man!" Meredyth sternly said.

Nielsen laughed and said, "Are you two sure you're not married?"

Lucas laughed at this, and tossed down several bills to cover the meal.

In the parking lot outside, they said good night to Dr. Nielsen and asked her to keep their discussion private for now, sharing it only with Leonard Chang. She agreed without reservation.

"Whatever you do, say nothing to Frank Patterson on the matter," Lucas said.

"I have no intention of doing that."

They parted company with Lynn Nielsen. As they went for the car, Meredyth said, "Wish we had some notion of Lauralie's whereabouts."

"We find her, we find the boyfriend, and we can shut them down."

"Wish I could be a hundred percent certain one way or the other of any part I played in helping shape this woman's obsession. Wish I could see those records at the courthouse."

"Tonight? Open the Harris County courthouse records? That'd also take a warrant signed by a judge. Tomorrow's another day, Mere."

"Another day and possibly another horrible mailing to you or me or both of us."

He pulled her into his arms and hugged her close. "It'll be all right. I promise you, it's going to be all right."

They drove from the restaurant down a series of meandering streets until Lucas pulled to the curb in a residential neighborhood. An Interstate overpass sliced the street in two, and cutting his engine, Lucas said, "I want you to stay right here, Mere. I'll be right back."

"Where the hell are we, Lucas? And where're you going?"

"Katherine Croombs's house. There're lights on inside. I'm going to have a look-see."

"But without a warrant, what'll happen?"

"I'm not going to break in, just determine if she's inside or not," he said, climbing from the driver's seat.

"And how're you going to do that?"

"Old Indian sleuth trick," he said, standing in the rain.

"What trick?"

"I'll knock." With that, he sprinted to the door.

Meredyth nervously watched him climb the stairs of the rundown tenement house. She listened to the whirring, whining, and roaring of cars, trucks, and buses whizzing by on the Interstate overhead. "Think I'd drink myself to death if I had to listen to this all day long," she muttered to the interior of the car. She glanced again at Lucas, now speaking to someone on the porch, an elderly lady who had probably caught him peeking in at Katherine's windows.

Then she saw Lucas coming back to the car. He opened the door, got in, turned on the ignition, and started away from the curb. "Dead end," he said.

"Whataya mean, dead end? What did you learn from the neighbor?"

"Says no one's been living below her. She's had an eye out for the daughter herself, wants to know who's going to pay the water and electric bills, neither of which were turned off. Says she's having it all turned off if she doesn't hear from Lauralie by morning."

"Then Lauralie *did* live there for a time after the mother's death?"

"Yes, for a month and a half. She says the girl went from saccharine sweetness when she first arrived to a bitch during and after the funeral."

"So the woman—"

"—Mrs. Crane—"

"—saw Lauralie at the funeral?"

"She was at the funeral, no thanks to Lauralie. She had to get the information from the police report in the *Chronicle*, and from there she called the funeral home for the details of when and where. Says Lauralie didn't invite her or any of Katherine's cronies, and when Mrs. Crane arrived with several others in tow, Lauralie hadn't a word for her or any of Katherine's few friends and neighbors. She also said that Katherine had been off the bottle and was making an effort to please Lauralie, allowing her to live with her, feeding her, buying her things, all that. But Mrs. Crane says Lauralie never showed the least gratitude or appreciation for Katherine's efforts. It's likely what drove her back to drinking that night, she says."

"So where is Lauralie now?"

"Got to be she's with the boyfriend, Mr. Mystery, his pad."

"Her personal butcher. You think he helped her in poisoning her mother?"

"According to Mrs. Crane, she never once saw Lauralie with a man. She came to think her a lesbian, and you recall Rachel's take on that back at the convent."

Meredyth mulled it over. "AC-DC as her needs required, depending on whom she felt a need to control or manipulate at any given time, be it Father William, Rachel, her mother, and perhaps the killer."

As they drove through the increasingly clinging fog—a fog doing battle with the orange glow of the city's lights— Meredyth's stress got the better of her. Lucas realized that she was sobbing beside him. He reached out and placed a hand around her neck, rubbing it tenderly.

"I can't believe we can't locate one convent girl recently released on her own from that place," lamented Meredyth, placing her head on his shoulder. "And that *place*. And the lessons of that place, what Lauralie took from there."

"And what would that be?"

"Just put yourself into her place. Imagine spending your entire life there, without a true home, without parents, without siblings . . . bullied by the older girls, possibly assaulted by them, possibly molested by a priest, learning only how to connive, lie, cheat, steal, destroy people and things, how to sexually manipulate others, until your behavior escalated into something far more sinister . . . escalating to fire-setting and causing accidents that result in death."

"It's not your fault or doing, Mere. Don't put all that on your head."

"No telling what kind of tyrant that Mother Orleans was. Do you think she drove Lauralie to kill her? First attempting to do it by fire, and later helping her down a flight of stairs?"

"We don't know any of this is true," Lucas objected.

"And—and as for Mother Elizabeth, I've never met anyone more in denial. She *knows* . . . down deep, Lucas, she knows Lauralie is a disturbed individual, and not another Rachel—not a child in need of *coddling,* but a child in need of a straitjacket."

"Exactly . . . got that right." He placed one arm around her as he drove on. "Time you got your mind off it tonight, sweetheart."

But she went on. "And us . . . look at *us* . . . two professionals going round in circles inside a *labyrinth* she has led us into . . . a maze created especially for us, and she's got to be laughing at us—Lucas, the big bad Texas Cherokee detective with an uncanny record for tracking down the monsters among us, and Meredyth Sanger, Ph.D, M.D., a forensic psychiatrist well respected in my field, and together we can't find a missing murderous child."

"Hey, Mere, damn now you've got to go easier on yourself—and me. After all, it's not as if we haven't gotten anywhere. We've come a long—"

"But we haven't. She's still out there somewhere free to do whatever her deranged mind—in cohort with Crazy Joe as you call him—can whip up! And we're no closer to stopping them."

"Oh, but we are! Thanks to your brilliant mind, we've put together a motive behind all this madness, Mere, not to mention we have put a name to one of the suspects in the abduction of Mira Lourdes. A name and a likeness, which will be placed on the all-points bulletin along with our Mr. X with the mole on his cheek. Tomorrow's papers will carry it, along with the news broadcast. It's on Captain Lincoln's desk."

"When did you do all this?"

"I used the graduation photo and made out a report while you were in the ladies' room, and left it with our fearless leader. Now, thanks to you, we're that much closer to ending this terror."

"No, no thanks to me, to her, Lauralie. She has consciously led us to her, Lucas; she wants us to put the puzzle together. Don't forget that. She not only wants to insult us, she wants to *control* us by controlling every step of the investigation against her. She's shrewd, calculating, and cruel—a terrible combination."

"All the same, we're a lot closer to closing this thing down than we were before going to the convent. You should take some comfort in that."

"Where're you taking me now, Lucas? I'm a nervous wreck, so worried about going home, finding another part of Mira Lourdes awaiting me."

"I don't blame you. I don't relish seeing another of Lauralie and Crazy Joe's gifts either."

"Then we have to dodge your place too."

"And the precinct," he half-joked. "We could always return to the desert, sleep beneath the stars again. Maybe this time, you'll include me on the cloud of your dreams. Whataya say, me-lady?"

"The desert sounds nice, but I have a better idea."

"Shoot."

"My family's country house. *She* can't know about that. Hey, let's do it. Let's go there. It's on a beautiful lake, and I don't receive mail there."

"Are you suggesting I meet your parents?" He half-smiled, staring into her eyes.

"No, they won't be there. They're in Paris."

"Paris, Texas?"

"France, on holiday. So, we'll be alone, and you won't

have any pressure whatsoever. We can pick up some groceries and bathing suits on the way."

"How far is it?"

"Between here and Huntsville. Not to worry. We can be back in the city in an hour and a half."

Lucas raised his hands as if arrested. "All right, you got me, Doctor. I am in your hands completely tonight."

"That sounds promising."

"Lead on, please."

"Interstate north," she said, "Derry Road exit, Madera Lake." She nestled into the crook of his arm, closing her eyes, persuaded she could get far enough away to escape any further thoughts of Lauralie Blodgett tonight.

ARTHUR BELKVIN'S GLOVED hands twitched ever so slightly where he gripped the freezer door over his head. The surgical gloves he wore made a stifled little barking rubber sound against the lid of the horizontal freezer. Arthur closed the lid over what little remained of Mira Lourdes where she lay inside her frozen coffin: *a pair of legs held together by lower torso and hips, two severed arms—one missing a hand, another a finger.*

Behind Arthur, her headless, armless upper torso lay on the stainless-steel operating table, where his rotary bone saw rested, silently dripping with blood. He stared at his reflection in the patent titanium blade, so efficient and clean was this blade. He defied any human eye to detect the microscopic tissue and bone fragments adhering to it. He'd have to give it a Muriatic acid bath to be certain the saw, like the ax, could not be DNA'd to Mira Lourdes, and so linked to him. He'd eventually wash down the table as well, whenever Lauralie finally resolved that they had come to the end of this dark journey she had set them on. At which time, he would take the table and all the tools far out to the desert, possibly as far as Mexico, dig an enormous hole, and bury it all.

He silently thanked God that the blood was at a minimum, most of Mira's blood having been lost when she was killed, and the remaining blood, pooling in the lungs and back, remaining thick and gelatinous from the corpse's having been so long in cold storage. The solid flesh made cutting easier, cleaner. The torso itself had been opened earlier to get at the organs that he had sliced up in thin leaves for the first box sent to Detective Stonecoat. Lauralie had tossed what was left of those organs into the brook that ran through the property, a backwater creek off the Navasota River. He recalled how she'd delighted in watching the creek ripple along on its path, taking its natural course. "On a mission, Arthur, like us," she'd said of the stream as she fed Mira's internal organs to the fish.

The only untouched and undefiled of Mira Lourdes's organs was the heart, now swimming in a formaldehyde-filled jar on a shelf over Arthur's shoulder. Arthur had closed up the huge Y-section cut he had made to the torso and abdomen to get at the organs for Lauralie. The crude autopsy scar on the torso looked like the stitching on a bloated football, Arthur thought. He'd done the procedure quickly and with a shaking hand.

"Lauralie, damn it now, you *promised* you'd tell me the whole story, and I think it's high time. I think I've earned your trust and the right to know everything."

"You are on a need-to-know basis, Arthur—you *need,* and I *know*." She laughed, while outside his dogs, locked in the run, whimpered and whined for the warmth and light inside.

"Lauralie, your reason for doing all this!" he demanded, pointing at the dissected, sewn-up torso lying between them. "You promised, remember?"

"You want rationalizations, Arthur? Will a good rationale help you get past your part in murder, Arthur, sweetie?"

"You promised. You said that you had a lifetime of reasons for what you've done, remember? And you promised to share them with me."

"I remember telling you I'd tell you, Arthur, when the time came . . . when conditions were right, when I was good and ready. Do you remember that, Arthur, do you?"

"I need to know why, Lauralie, now! Why am I doing

this?" *How could I have agreed to this?* Arthur wondered, but did not say. Arthur looked down over Mira Lourdes's armless torso and breasts, where he stood directly across the dissecting table from Lauralie. He imagined the eerie picture it must make, this meeting of the three of them, together again—Mira not *entirely* present physically, Lauralie not entirely present *mentally,* Arthur not entirely present *emotionally*—a strange bizarre twist on the eternal triangle, he thought.

Lauralie was angry with him, but she appeared to have calmed. Arthur had balked at her orders once again, balked at any further mutilation of the body. He dared voice his wish now. "We should end this thing now, bury what's left of Mira in the desert, and be done with it."

Lauralie only laughed, and between laughs, she said, "Mira, Mira on the slab, who's the prettiest of the hags? You talk about her as if you knew her, Arthur. Get over it. Look at what she is for what she is, an unfeeling and empty shell."

"She was a human being, Lauralie."

"*Was* being the operative word! Look at her now! We've excised her eyes, her teeth, a hand, and her head, not to mention the finger I left at the convent, and now you're going soft on me, Arthur? Don't be a wimp!"

Arthur again looked down at the upper torso of Mira Lourdes lying before them. Lauralie had operated the circular bone saw to sever torso from lower abdomen and legs. With Arthur's guidance, she had done all the cutting this time, and she'd done it with a kind of gusto. In fact, she took a kind of otherworldly delight in carving up the frozen corpse, while Arthur again questioned her reasoning and motivation.

Lifting a scalpel now, she asked Arthur how best to remove the breasts.

"Why do that?" he asked.

"To gross them out. The idea is to gross them out as much as I possibly can. Now tell me how to begin and where to go with the scalpel." Arthur did as instructed, swallowing his inner quaking and the sense of regret infiltrating his heart.

He forced one of the still-hard, cold breasts upward and using a red marker, made a line beneath and around the globe. He then did the same for the second breast. "Begin at the bottom and follow the line up from the center, here, on either side."

Holding the surgical scalpel against the marks he'd made, Lauralie carefully followed the ink path against Mira's flesh, soon removing the left breast. She smiled, her eyes delighted as it came away. "That was easy, Arthur. You're an excellent teacher. Like slicing off a ham."

Arthur was not surprised at the lack of blood, and the ease with which the breast came away. Seeing there was no stopping Lauralie's gleeful play, Arthur said, "Give me the scalpel and I'll finish for you."

"Call me Dr. Blodgett!" she teased, swinging the scalpel in the air like a Roman candle. "No, Dr. Belkvin, sir, young Dr. Blodgett needs the experience and will finish the procedure." And she did, severing the right breast with even more fanfare, and even less blood.

Lauralie had earlier prepared the box meant to receive the torso and breasts, but she hadn't planned well for the size of Mira's Joan Crawford shoulders and the girth of her torso. The fit was so snug and tight that Arthur had to help Lauralie force the torso into the Styrofoam-lined, colorful blue and green FedEx box. He then lifted the two breasts in his gloved hands, turning to take them back to the freezer.

"Now the severed breasts," Lauralie ordered.

"What?"

"In the box. Stuff them into the box too."

"But there's no room."

"Make room!"

He tested the possibility, shaking his head, saying, "How, where?"

"Squish them in, Arthur! You can do it."

"Why not send them *separately*?"

"Separately?"

"You know, to . . . to this Meredyth Sanger person instead of to Stonecoat?"

"It's a thought, would be freaky for the lady doctor,

wouldn't it? But no . . . no, I want her to get the heart next, and I want him to get all of this area at once," she replied, her hands going to her own breasts, the scalpel in one hand, her other hand caressing her breast area.

"Everything is about what you want, isn't it, Lauralie?" he asked even as he worked the severed breasts into the tight area left him. "Well, what about what I want?" he demanded.

"Oh, Arthur, you can be so commanding when you try. *What* you *want*? I know what you want, Arthur," she said in her most coquettish voice, her smile a flirtatious snake as she bared a shoulder with the tip of the scalpel.

"Damn it, I want to know *why* we're doing all this, Lauralie! I want to know *why* we're not on a plane for someplace safe!"

"Some island in the Pacific, Arthur? Tahiti's full of tourists this time of year. It may's well be another state in the goddamn union."

"You saw the newspaper!" He held up the late edition of the *Chronicle,* waving the image before her. "They've got my likeness on the front pages! It'll be flashed on the tube by now. My clients will all see it. They'll fucking have me on *America's Most Wanted.*"

"It's a lousy likeness, Arthur. Quit your worrying. It doesn't look *anything* like you."

"The mole, Lauralie. They've got the mole on my face. My black eyebrows, the thick glasses, my hair. It's close enough to nail me, I tell you. We've got to get out of the jurisdiction, to someplace where I'm not known."

"Christ, the mole's on the other side of your face," she said, slapping the newspaper into free flight and ripping through his likeness in a zipping Zorro strike of her scalpel. "Don't you go wimping out on me, Arthur! Don't do it."

"But we've got to be reasonable. What the hell're we going to do? What kind of escape route do we have? None. Can you imagine what will happen when I go back to the office, to the campus? I could be picked up, arrested at any moment for questioning."

"Fool, they don't arrest you for questioning . . . can't

arrest you until they have absolute, certain proof. You've got rights. They can only ask you to come in for questioning. It's called an interrogation . . . custody, question and answer, then arrest, if you fail their litmus test for telling the truth."

"A lie detector? I don't think I could pass, not after what—"

"Yes, you can, Arthur. It wasn't you who did all this. It was me, my plan, I drugged her . . . I killed her. What'd you do? You cut into a cadaver. What can they do to you for that? Suspend your license?"

Lauralie had laid aside the scalpel and stood squeezing a set of black rosary beads. "I took these off a dead nun at the convent . . . long time ago," she said, her eyes dreamy, as if reliving the moment. "She took an unfortunate spill down a nasty flight of stairs, and at her advanced age, I didn't think she'd miss the beads."

He stared at the black beads, picturing her leaning over the dying nun. As if reading his mind, she added, "She was our mother superior. Believed in the old saying 'Spare the rod, spoil the child.' I took a lot of crap from that old bat for a lotta years." Her eyes had roamed about the room as she spoke of Mother Orleans, but now they settled on him. "Look, Arthur, I understand your worries, but we can take steps, Arthur . . ."

"Such as?"

"We'll have the mole *surgically* removed."

"And who's going to do that?"

"How hard can it be? With just the right tools and your guidance, hell, I just removed two hot-air balloons from the cadaver." She replaced the beads in her hand with the scalpel. Its stainless-steel blade shone under the tensor lamp over the operating table.

"Me, operate on my *own* cheek by guiding you?"

"Why not? We've got the mirror." She swung a high-powered mirror on a swivel arm over the tabletop.

"I'd have to be alert, no anesthetic. It could be *painful.* I could pass out, botch the whole job."

"Damn *wuss,* Arthur. You tell me what to do, walk me through it, and I'll remove the bloody thing while you're under. We can use the chloroform, or we can just deaden the area around the mole, so you won't feel a thing." She appeared genuinely excited by the prospect of his being under her complete control. "You do trust me, don't you, Arthur?"

"A bandage over my cheek will only draw more attention."

"Then we bandage your whole damned head if need be. God, quit complaining."

"Forget about it. I'll take my chances with the mole."

"But if it'll help ease your worries, Arthur . . ."

Arthur grabbed the scalpel from her, cutting himself, cursing and tossing the instrument onto a tray behind him, where it clattered and where she couldn't reach it. "Enough with that. It's not happening."

"God, Artie, baby, take it easy. You hurt yourself. I was only *funning* you." She quickly wrapped his bleeding finger in a bandage.

"You changed the subject on me. I want to know why you're so *bent* on destroying this Dr. Sanger and this detective."

Outside, a long, rumbling thunderclap got the dogs braying again. Lauralie replied, "That bitch, Sanger . . . she destroyed me!"

"Sweetheart, love . . . you're not destroyed. You are beautiful and vibrant and alive and—and young, with—with your whole life ahead of you. We should be busy making a life together, a life for ourselves, a life with a future. I love you, Lauralie."

"When I'm done with Sanger and her man, then we'll talk about a life and a future, darling, but not before. Now stuff her breasts into the damned box. I knew I should have gotten the larger one!"

Arthur forced the severed second breast into the impossible space allotted. Lauralie closed the flaps and taped it shut. She placed the label over the top, patted the bulging box, and said, "It's done, all ready for overnight shipment."

"You're not going to be happy until you use up every part of the Lourdes woman, are you?"

"Arthur, you are beginning to get on my nerves. Now, what do you say to my removing that disgusting mole on your cheek?"

"Damn it, Lauralie, I thought we were off that subject for tonight."

"You think the cops and the news people are going to be off that subject tonight? We've got to do something about the damn mole. I never told you, but it has always bothered me, like . . . like the old man's dead eye in Edgar Allan Poe's *Tell-Tale Heart*."

"W-what's that supposed to mean?" He unconsciously touched the mole on his left cheek.

"I look at you, and it's all I see sometimes."

"Cutting the damn thing off may be the only way I can escape capture, but my students, my colleagues, my patients—that is my patients' owners—they know what I look like, Lauralie."

"No one'll ever believe you could possibly be the Post-it Ripper, Arthur. Everyone loves you. You make their animals well!"

"Mrs. Toohey's dog died in my care last month! Look, I know the police sketch isn't perfect, but it is *close,* and any one of the people that come into my practice, my receptionist even, could make the connection, and all it takes is a single telephone call, and I'm sitting behind bars being grilled by professionals who know how to make a man incriminate himself. They can even do it to an *innocent* man. Imagine what they can do to me!"

She allowed the thought to sink in. "All right, all right . . . so what you're saying is that even if you had the mole removed, some people who know you would become suspicious because you had the mole removed, and there's no getting away from this damnable mole either way, right? *Out, out damned spot,* like Lady Macbeth. So . . . Arthur, no small operation on that mole is going to help us now. Correct?"

"I suppose, yes, yes, that's what I'm saying, so it makes sense to maybe go overseas. I have some money saved up and-and-and I'm thinking of your safety too, sweetheart . . .

sweetheart. I would hate myself if . . . if, you know, if anything should happen to you, to us."

"Come here, sugar." Her hands and arms, empty now,
opened wide to him, inviting him in.

"What?"

"Come the hell over here, *lover,* now!"

He came around the table toward her.

"I think you need a good hug and a feel," she said.

Arthur dropped his head in a hangdog fashion, grinned,
and opened his arms to her. She wrapped him in her arms
where they stood against the stainless-steel table she had
backed him into. "Want to make love on the steel?" she
asked.

"Whataya mean? Now?" He looked over his shoulder at
the table, empty of any of Lauralie's parts, but alongside
the saw resting there, the surface was littered with bits and
pieces of chewed flesh and bodily fluids.

She pressed herself tighter against him. "Now, right
now," she whispered naughtily in his ear.

"But it's all filthy from the cutting and—"

"Just get naked. I'll spray it down with the hose while
you get naked for me, okay?"

"It's going to be cold as hell against the skin."

"Arthur, get undressed and lay down! You're going to
have the time of your life." She lifted the saw, putting it
aside, found the hose, and rinsed off the operating table
with warm soapy water. Water and human tissue and debris
swept down the built-in sewage drain along each side of
the table, taking the residue and blood to a tank that Arthur
had ingeniously attached to the underside of the table.

Arthur stripped as she worked to clean the table.
"We'll warm up this ol' steel right quickly, Arthur," she
was saying as he tested the cold steel, first with his hands,
then, climbing onto the flat surface, with elbows and
knees. He squinted with the chill of it, despite the warm
water she'd used. She turned the warm water hose on him
now, laughing.

Finally, he eased onto his back, the sensation creating a
trembling in him, the exact opposite of sliding down into a

steaming hot tub of water, this gradual getting used to a chilling surface.

His eyes closed against the cold pain to his backside, Arthur said, "Never imagined I'd ever be making love to a beautiful young woman on one of my operating tables."

"One of your dogs maybe!" she joked, snickering.

"Told my receptionist we had to sell the table to pay for the increase in rent on the office. She bought it, but when she sees the books again, she'll know I was lying. Guess I'll have to drop a hint that I've been gambling again. She knows about my habit with the horses."

"Arthur, please shut up, close your eyes, baby, and get your mind off all these worries."

He closed his eyes, comfortable now on his back, hardening at her gentle touch. "God, Lauralie, I wish we were in Paris or maybe London . . . at the race track even . . . you, me together without a care, just enjoying the breeze, the ponies, the excitement of the race, sex afterwards . . ."

"Dream on, Artie, baby," she said, bringing down the rotary saw against his chest, clicking the on switch, and plunging its biting, grinding titanium steel into his heart.

His startled brown eyes flew open at the sound of the saw long enough to catch the geyser of blood that blinded him, a spray that likewise discolored Lauralie's features, making a fiend of her—the last thing he saw before dying.

"No more goddamn questions out of you," she muttered over the still-twitching body. "And you needn't worry that the cops are going to put you away, Arthur. Nobody can hurt you now, and you never have to worry about hurting me or incriminating me in any way. Such a dear you've been and so patient throughout this long ordeal."

CHAPTER 13

Hogan: home, permanence

IT HAD BEEN a long time since Lucas had completely relaxed, but here at Meredyth Sanger's favorite hideaway, her familiy's country ranch retreat, a majestic log cabin and stables, proved dreamlike, convincing them both to call in the next morning to take the day off. Both of them had been physically and mentally exhausted by the pace of events, and *Doctor* Sanger had prescribed a full day of horseback riding, canoeing, swimming, and making love. The day became an idyllic Huckleberry Finn extravagance, a day without responsibilities or worries to plague them. Doctor and detective, for a time, freed their minds of the horrors Lauralie and her boyfriend had dealt them unrelentingly for days now. For the time being, the couple had gotten their lives back, while others back in Houston continued to work their more objective and scientific angles on the ongoing case of the Post-it Ripper, a name being used now in the press for the odd-looking, mole-faced killer gracing the tube and the front pages of the papers.

As was protocol, Captain Gordon Lincoln would have

to make the decision to release the photo of Lauralie Blodgett and her name as a person of interest, wanted for questioning in the case.

Lucas and Meredyth breakfasted and went out for a romantic mid-morning swim off the pier on Madera Lake, a loon somewhere in the reeds calling out, acting as a melodic backdrop to their water sport. They returned, had lunch, went to the stable and had a pair of horses saddled, and they rode about the property. She pointed out natural features, told him about neighbors around the lake, how they got together on occasion, barbecues and holidays. She said the Brodys directly across were especially friendly and nice. She pointed out a small home at the edge of her property where a lady and her two sons who maintained the stables and the machines on the ranch lived rent-free.

Nearing dusk, they went exploring by canoe among the reeds along the shore as they watched the sun calmly wink and drop from sight behind the juniper forest that tickled the underside of the darkening sky.

All day long they had visited Meredyth's childhood secret places, and she'd made love to him in each one of them. After dark, Lucas and Meredyth sat on the swing porch out front of the lavish log cabin home, listening to the insect and bird activity and staring out at the lake where loons continued gathering and playing their melodic tune. Here on Madera Lake, Houston and its problems, *especially* the Mira Lourdes case with its cruel dissonance, seemed a vague memory a world away. Still, as wonderful a day and evening as they had, thoughts of the case seeped into consciousness like water through rock, always winning out in the end.

"I'd better check in, see if anyone's thinking of firing me," Lucas told her as he stepped off the front porch, going for his car radio. Meredyth walked out to his car with him. There he got on the police-band radio and called in, asking for the duty roster desk. He got Kelton's night-owl replacement, Jim Bowker. Bowker calmly informed him, "So far, Lieutenant, there've been no new ripples in the P.O. murder case."

"The P.O. case? That's what its being called now down at the precinct?"

"That's right, sir."

"And everything's cool?"

"Copacetic, sir."

"Right, thanks, Sergeant Bowker."

"Enjoy what's left of your day off, Lieutenant, you've earned it, sir. I don't care what Captain Gordon thinks."

"Has Gordon been making noises?"

"Elephant stampedes through the department, sir. He's peeved you chose this time to disappear, you and Dr. Sanger at once, that is."

"Thanks." He looked across at Meredyth. Despite their attempt at being discreet, everybody at the Three-one knew about their romantic involvement. A precinct, like a reservation, was a breeding ground for rumors and gossip. Lucas had given thought to their hiding out on the res, but he was glad they'd found this place instead.

"What is it?" Meredyth asked him from outside the car, standing over him. "Everything okay?"

He reached a hand out to her. "Oh, yeah, just fine. Captain's happy we took some time off. Says it can only give us more objectivity when we come back at it fresh."

She accepted the lie because she wanted it to be true. Leaning into the car, she kissed his cheek and said, "The human mind can only take so much; the *emotions* can only absorb so much before a person shuts down. If I hadn't taken this step back, Lucas, I think I'd've lost it. Speaking for myself, I know I'll be more objective and sharper now that I've distanced myself both physically and mentally from the situation."

"I'm sure you're right."

"And none of the others on the task force have been personally assaulted as you and I have been. To have our homes invaded, our lives disrupted by these maniacs."

Lucas still sat in his car, and Meredyth, standing in the open doorway, climbed in, crowding him, putting her arms around him. "Been a long time since I made out in a car. Wanna climb into the rear?" As she spoke, she noticed the manila file folder on the rear seat. "What's this?" she asked.

"What's what?"

"This file." She reached into the backseat, retrieved the file, and attempted to pull free of his embrace, all the while struggling with Lucas, who said, "It's nothing. Leave it. Forget about it."

Tickling her and kissing her, he attempted to get her to drop the file, but she was determined. She pulled free of his grasp and straightened to a standing position outside the car, the file in hand. She couldn't make it out clearly in the dark. Lucas, alongside her now, grabbed for it, but she slipped around to the front of the car where Matchlight torches on the enclosed porch—meant to keep mosquitoes away—glowed round Meredyth's lovely ash-blond head and bathed her and the awful photos of the dead girl, Yolanda Sims, in light.

"Don't, Mere," Lucas pleaded, not wanting her evening spoiled.

She put up a hand to him, examining the manila folder further, realizing it to be a cold case file that Lucas had obviously been perusing.

"What's this all about?" she asked.

He put his arm around her and they walked back to the enclosed porch to escape the gnats and mosquitoes. "It's a long story."

"I've got all night."

"Are you sure you want to taint this beautiful place with the ugliness of my work?"

"It's all right, Lucas. You need to talk about it, and I'm supposed to understand that; it's my job, remember? If we're going to be together, romantically involved, then we share everything. So . . . tell me about Yolanda Sims."

Lucas began by saying, "Not much to tell, young girl abducted, tortured, raped, and killed, her body dumped 'home,' but the killer got the wrong doorstep."

"Wrong doorstep?"

Lucas explained the killer's mistake.

"One block over . . . same address," Meredyth considered the error. "Curious," she commented.

"Sloppy, clumsy fellow. Sounds on the surface like an unplanned attack from a person unfamiliar with the territory."

She nodded. "Certainly a disorganized killer as opposed to an organized planner. Someone who did it on the spur of the moment."

"Investigators keyed in on an uncle for a time only because he had a record for burglary. Then they interrogated the hell out of an old man, a neighbor with a record for child molestation. To this date most believe this Paul Mick Ryan, now deceased, did it. They also grilled two neighborhood teens."

"But if these people were familiar with the neighborhood, and they knew the girl—"

"—who disappeared from her backyard doorstep—"

"—then why go after the neighborhood's usual suspects? They wouldn't have dumped her at the right address one street over."

"Right, none of the people interrogated could've gotten her address so screwed up—including Ryan, who fried for other killings."

"Then they never caught the guy who did it? Of course not, that's what makes it a cold case file!" She plowed a palm into her forehead, in a gesture of realization. "How stupid am I?"

"You're relaxed! Come on, put that file away." He gathered up the paperwork and crime photos, tucking them back into the manila file and dropping it back into the large brown clasp envelope.

"*Whew* . . . 1956, Lucas . . . that's a hell of a long time ago."

"Remember that '48 case I solved?"

"Of course, but you had a great deal more to go on."

"Not much more. I'll keep at it."

"For Yolanda or for yourself?"

"Maybe for both of us."

"You're a good man, Lucas Stonecoat." She locked her arms around his neck and pulled his lips to hers. Under the torchlight, their shadows dancing, their passions flared once again. Lucas dropped the file folder on the porch swing, lifted her up into his arms, and carried her inside and to the bedroom.

"You can't be serious," she teased.

"Watch me."

"Living up to your Wolf Clan heritage, are you?"

"I'm passionate about you, Mere."

"Shut up and kiss me."

THE FOLLOWING DAY Lucas and Meredyth reluctantly returned to the world in which they had to honor their responsibilities, Precinct 31, each feeling the remorse of having to leave their secret retreat behind. It seemed the only place where the killer had not found them.

They split up at the precinct house front desk under Stan Kelton's watchful gaze, Lucas going for Captain Lincoln's office as Kelton advised, and she for her office, but not before Stan shared the morning *Chronicle* with them. Lauralie Blodgett's graduation picture stared back at them from its placement beside the unnamed assailant and murderer known only as the Post-it Ripper. Lauralie was wanted for *questioning* in relation to the case. A brief biography and the mention of Our Lady of Miracles as her last known address appeared below the photo, along with the phone number for CrimeLine.

Soon after checking in with her secretary, Meredyth announced she could be found at the county courthouse. She quickly located her car in the street lot where she had left it, and drove to the nearby courthouse in search of the records she felt she must review, the cases she oversaw during her year-long internship with Child and Family Protective Services in 1984.

As a forensic psychiatrist for the HPD, Dr. Sanger was well known at the Harris County courthouse, as her casework often involved testifying in various proceedings for the DA, and sometimes for the PD. Whether offense or defense, she, like any forensic investigator, had a duty to the truth, whatever it may bring, whomever it helped or harmed. She was called on to decide if a person under arrest or indictment was legally sane, whether the defendant proved capable of knowing right from wrong at the commission of a crime, whether the defendant proved capable of standing trial, whether he or she proved culpable in criminal premeditation, and to make any number of other determinations.

Of course, her most heart-wrenching determinations came in cases where the killers were children, largely unheard of when she began her practice, but now all too common. She blamed the culture of violence created since the advent of TV, films, and video games that exploited the basest, darkest reaches of the human psyche—*the thrill of the kill*. What child, unable to resist the slightest brainwashing over what brand-name shoes to wear, could possibly combat such exploitation of the worst instincts in mankind at the hands of computer-generated animation characters bent on mass destruction and murder? The lauding of serial killers by media and merchandisers? The lauding of killing for killing's sake in increasingly violent Hollywood films and video games, even in music videos born out of a generation fed on such bloodletting "classics" as *The Texas Chainsaw Massacre.* Cult followers had grown up with technology that now made *virtual* murder, sniping, knifing, mutilating, so *real* as to *be virtually* the real thing. Murder without consequence. Murder without concern for the life force, the soul of another human being. Children had learned this lesson over several generations now, and also that bloodletting for dollars was now a mega-business reaching into the billions each month.

She wondered, however, how Lauralie Blodgett, having an upbringing largely protected from the culture of violence, having limited access to computer games, Hollywood violence, and TV carnage, could become the demon she had become. Perhaps there was some truth to the argument that a genetic predisposition toward violence also existed. How a

Charles Manson or a Ted Bundy figured into such musings, perhaps only future science into the human genome system might tell. She wondered if at some future time a gene-zapping laser might be developed to eradicate the genetic predisposition to violence and murder, a kind of watchdog technology that could eliminate the ape-killer genes before such seeds could be firmly planted, and before the infant saw the light of this world.

It smacked of that Spielberg film *Minority Report,* only better, she thought as she entered the courthouse from the parking garage where her permit was good until December.

She was stopped short by Byron Priestly. "Meredyth! Where've you been? I've tried contacting you every which way I could. Went out to your parents' house in Clover Leaf. No one there and—"

"Byron, we—you and I—we are through, Byron, so you don't have to worry about me any longer, understood? And what're you doing going to my parents? Can't you take a hint?"

"Mere, can't we talk? Work things out?" Byron's blond hair lifted in the wind. His eyes pleaded, his brow creased in consternation. "You're hardly being fair."

"Fair? Byron, you wouldn't know fair if it swallowed you whole. Now, I'm busy. Out of my way."

He threw up his hands as if giving up, and he stood aside, bowing exaggeratedly to allow her to pass.

Realizing she was wearing down the enamel on her teeth, grinding so hard at having the run-in with Byron, she eased off her jaw. She wondered how he had learned she'd be here at the courthouse this morning. He must have weaseled it out of her secretary, whom she'd sworn to secrecy if and when Mr. Priestly should call. She hadn't the time or energy for Byron right now.

She pushed through a succession of doors in an area of the building that offered no access to the courtrooms, so she didn't have to go through a metal detector and give up her .38 Smith & Wesson. She quickly found her way down to the subterranean world where old files from the county clerk's office were stored.

She knew the way well, having often done research here over the years. Fortunately, once at the office, Meredyth encountered no obstacles from the staff or the machinery, and soon she had in her hands the paper-thin microfiche records she needed for 1984. She then settled into an uncomfortable plastic seat before a giant gray screen, searching through the records, which ran screaming through the microfiche scanner here in the semidarkened bowels of the old county courthouse. County officials remained cheap, so the old files and the old technology had not seen any change other than the layer of dust here.

Meredyth now listened to the whirring of the old microfiche tape as it continued to speed past 1982, 1983, and whirred down like the sound of a train slowly stopping at a station until she found 1984 under her fingertip.

"Gotcha." Her single word echoed in the Texas courthouse dungeon around her.

She had slowed the fiche to a crawl now, and then to a complete stop when she came to the fall of 1984. It was harder to control the film at a crawl than it ought to be, but she took pains and carefully surveyed each of the adoption files handled by the county in 1984 and '85 for her own name, for Katherine Croombs, for Blodgett, or the convent orphanage name.

Meredyth brought the film record to a standstill to briefly review any document that appeared relevant, then she moved on. As she did so, she tried to recall being of college age in '84. She could hardly believe she was ever that young. In 1984 she was in her late teens, working toward her undergraduate degree. She had to have two terms of practical, applied sociology and psychology under her belt to move through the program to advanced applied courses, and what better way to achieve it than working within the Child and Family Protective Services that fall of '84 and spring of '85.

She recalled how she had *excelled* at the work in Child and Family Protective Services, how much of it boiled down to detective work and psychiatry. She was good at it, so much so that Mrs. Hunter almost convinced her to go into social work instead of carrying on with her plans to become a psychiatrist. She recalled how arrogant and hard-working and well liked by those in charge young Meredyth Sanger was, and that as a result, she was given far more responsibility that year than she had ever dreamt possible under the auspices of the social worker she interned with, a Mrs. Viola Hunter, a matronly woman with a prim bun and spectacles. Mrs. Hunter had been delighted to unload some of her crushing casework on an eager-to-please workaholic.

The experience could not have been more educational, inside a system both flawed and overtaxed as well as upholding ideals so lofty as to be unreachable.

Meredyth finally came upon the one record she had come for, the Croombs-Blodgett case. Katherine Croombs had agreed to give up her then-nameless child if the child could go to a nice Catholic adoption agency. Katherine had been raised Catholic, and now Meredyth recalled promising her that they would find a good Catholic home to place the baby girl in. Katherine had put down the father's name on the birth certificate, and had wanted the child to have her father's name, Blodgett, her father's full name being John Dancing Blodgett.

Meredyth's hand was all over the case; she had indeed managed the logistics of getting the newborn from Mercy Hospital and into the hands of a *Sister* Orleans at Our Lady of Miracles in 1984. It had been *Sister* Orleans—not yet mother superior—who had signed the necessary documents for a child she had christened Lauralie.

"Lauralie's revenge . . . her sick motive . . . it's all here," Meredyth said to the silence around her.

Meredyth tried to pull all the loose ends together, to make *sense* of this *senseless* attack on her, one which involved the murder of Mira Lourdes simply because of her name, *Lourdes,* as a puzzle piece, a crumb to spread before Meredyth, to guide her to the understanding of why . . . why Lauralie had in essence hired or lured a killer to do her bidding, to abduct and murder Lourdes in order to have the human body parts to wrap up and forward to Meredyth, and to the man she most loved, Lucas. "Literally piece by bloody piece, she means to wreak her revenge," Meredyth muttered to the screen as she saw a strange birdlike shadow flit across the glassine surface. In an instant, she realized that it had been someone's reflected movement directly behind her. She swept around, banging her knee in the fixed plastic seat attached to the microfiche screen. "Damn!" she cursed in response to the painful injury, the bang reverberating around the room.

Looking about, she found no one in her view, despite the reflection that had been right behind her, uncomfortably close.

But whoever had been there was gone, moving down the stacks toward the rear of the room. One of the staff, Meredyth decided, just *flashing* by.

Meredyth turned her attention back to the adoption papers, studying her own naive signature on the form, wondering if it was even truly official since she did not technically work for the department in which she was interning as a student. After all, this was an official document, and she had been a college student, not a licensed social worker.

"Shit," she muttered, "why'd I ever get so involved at the time? Why didn't I argue with Mrs. Hunter about taking on such responsibilities? I didn't have the right . . . way in over my head." *Even so,* she thought, *how could anyone have predicted Lauralie's going on a rampage and becoming a multiple killer?* Meredyth checked herself. If the clues were correct, the girl had begun killing at a young age with the murder of Sara Orleans.

She heard the pitter-patter of the staff person who had gone by, this time returning with more noise in her wake, as if not wishing to startle Meredyth. At least her mind said it must be a staff person or someone else doing research.

Then she saw the image of a young feminine face leering out at her from the screen, reflected from over her shoulder. Meredyth wheeled around a second time, catching a glimpse of someone ducking from sight. The image was young enough and pretty enough to be Lauralie Blodgett, but Meredyth could not be certain. Could the disturbed woman have followed her here from the precinct?

She heard something like a footfall beyond the stacks in front of her, and she inched toward the sound. Turning a corner of the stacks, she found no one and not a sound.

Whoever it was, she had ducked behind the stacks, hidden now by the shelves filled from floor to ceiling with binders and file boxes. Meredyth then noticed a mirror perched in a corner of the ceiling above the door, and in it she saw the movement of light and shadow that followed this mystery person's wake, but even this slight hint was gone as quickly as it appeared.

"Who's there?"

No one answered.

"Is there someone there?" she said, louder this time, reminded of the convent church, the finger in the holy water. This felt like déjà vu!

Nothing, no answer.

"Damn you, *who* is there?"

A young black woman stepped from behind the stacks, asking, "Are you talking to me?"

"I'm being *stalked,*" Meredyth told the stranger. "Did you see anyone else in here?"

"Not by me, lady."

"Did you see anyone else in the stacks?"

She replied, "There was a woman bumped me going down the aisle, but no *guy,* no."

Meredyth pulled out the photo of Lauralie Blodgett that she had ripped from *The Lady* yearbook and kept in her purse. "Is this the woman you saw? The one who bumped you?"

The young black woman squinted and bit her upper lip. "You saying you're being stalked by another *woman*?"

"Was it her? Is it her?"

"It was . . . it is."

"Then she's here." Meredyth pulled her .38 Smith and Wesson from her purse, and the black woman put her hands out, backing off until she reached the door and backed through it. Ignoring the black woman's outcry from the other side of the door, Meredyth inched down the aisle of the stacks, going deeper into the archives, searching for Lauralie Blodgett, recalling her and Lucas's theory that this woman killed her own mother. She would have no compunction in killing Meredyth if given the opportunity.

Behind her, Meredyth heard the trampling of courthouse security guards tumbling over one another in an effort to get to the bottom steps and through the door and at Meredyth. She realized that she could be shot dead before any explanation of her identity or her brandishing a gun could be made. Perhaps Lauralie had even planned it this way, but how? How did she know she'd be here?

She heard the clickity-clack of a set of high heels just ahead of her. She wheeled and leaped into the next lane of stacks, coming eye-to-eye with a terrified file clerk who dropped her handful of files and fled. Beyond the clerk, she saw an emergency door exit slowly closing.

She raced for the door and was about to snatch it open when from behind her, she heard the order, "Freeze! Drop the gun and freeze, now!"

It was a male voice, one of the security guards.

A second guard came at her from another direction, his gun also pointed, saying, "You've got two guns pointed at you! Do as you're told, Dr. Sanger."

She knew the man by name. "Roy, you know who I am. You know I'm not some lunatic. She was *here*. She went through that door. Let me catch her before she gets away."

"Who was here?" asked Roy Purdue.

The other guard shouted, "Drop the gun, lady! Now!"

She did so, sighing heavily. Roy poked his head through the exit door and stared outside for a moment as his partner picked up Meredyth's weapon. "Nobody out there, Dr. Sanger," Roy informed her.

"The .38 is registered. I carry a weapon for self-defense and would only use it in self-defense."

"We'll just let the police handle it from here, lady," said the guard she didn't know. Reading his name tag, she replied, "Listen, Lewis, I'm a forensic police shrink, and I'm being stalked."

"Police are on their way, Dr. Sanger," replied Roy. "This is a matter you'll have to resolve with them. Maybe you should call your lawyer, Dr. Sanger."

"I'll do that." She plunged a hand into her purse for the cell phone, and Lewis crouched, aimed, and shouted, "Freeze!"

"Damn it, I'm going for my cell phone."

"Forget it!" shouted a red-faced Lewis, snatching her purse from her. He now had her gun tucked into his belt, and her purse dangling from one hand, his gun still trained on her. "Cuff her, Roy," Lewis said shakily.

"That won't be necessary, Lewis. We just escort her to the door. Put the gun down, Lewis."

"What?"

"She's unarmed now, Lewis, and cooperative, so back off!"

"Give me my phone back. I'll call my boss, Chief Lincoln," she pleaded.

"Let's all go upstairs, Dr. Sanger. Greet the officers when they arrive," suggested Roy. "We can turn your things over to them."

Meredyth pulled away and walked briskly ahead of Roy and his friend through the stacks and back to the microfiche machine she'd been working on when she saw something strange. Someone had ordered a hard copy of the record she'd come for. The paper copy lay in the tray, taunting her.

"She was here . . . *she* did this," said Meredyth, realizing how mad she must seem to these two courthouse guards. "I didn't order a copy of the record be made. She did. It's her way of telling me how close she can get any time she wants."

"Let's go upstairs, Dr. Sanger," replied Roy in his softest, kindest tone.

"It also means she's still in the building, still lurking in the shadows down here. We've got to do a search of this entire area, Roy!"

"No, Dr. Sanger, we're done here," declared Roy. "We're taking you upstairs, so please, come along."

She defiantly snatched the copy of the record of Lauralie's adoption as they led her through the door and to the stairwell. "She may have left fingerprints on the machine."

Neither security guard was listening now. They silently led her up to ground level.

The security guards turned Meredyth over to two uniformed policemen who had rushed through the courthouse security checkpoint, guns drawn. Meredyth's gun was turned over to the police, and one of them proceeded to handcuff her as she protested. "I'm a forensic psychiatrist! With the Three-one! I'm a shrink, a cop shrink. Check my ID."

Meredyth saw that people she had known for a decade, from the newsstand guy to lawyers and bailiffs and judges, all staring in disbelief. A crowd had gathered, mostly made up of civilians who populated the courtrooms in cases ranging from traffic tickets to murder trials. But among them, Meredyth caught a glimpse of Lauralie Blodgett stepping away, a smile on her face.

"It's her!" Meredyth shouted. "Stop that woman! It's her!"

But Meredyth was led out to a waiting police cruiser, its strobe lights flashing, and outside she had to face yet another crowd. The arrest was humiliating, and she was pleased when finally she could duck into the cruiser and be out of view behind the tinted windows. The handcuffs bit into her wrist, and when the officers climbed into the car, she pleaded with them to take off the cuffs, telling them to call Captain Gordon Lincoln at the 31st Precinct, again telling them who she was, adding, "What happened in the courthouse . . . it was all a big mis—"

"—misunderstanding," the two cops piped in in unison.

"Yes ma'am, ahhh, Doctor," said the driver. "Frank, you want to call the Three-one and bother Gordo Lincoln with this, or you want to book the lady?" They had driven off the courthouse sidewalk where the cruiser had parked, blocking the front stairs to the courthouse main entrance.

"I'm the forensic psychiatrist who's working closely with Lieutenant Lucas Stonecoat on the P.O. murder case, the one all over the news."

"The Post-it Ripper case, you?" The two officers stared at one another, and then the driver stared at her through his rearview mirror. "You really got Police ID on you, Doc?"

"Yeah, but my hands are in cuffs and I can't get at my purse."

The driver pulled over some blocks away.

"What the hell're we doing, Tony?" asked the cop in the passenger seat.

"Check her ID, Frank."

"I have a permit for the gun," she told them. "I'm the police shrink at the Three-one," she nervously repeated.

"Wait, whoa up, Doc. Are you saying that you're the one who's gotten all those body parts by mail—the eyeballs and the hand?" he asked as Frank pulled open the back door and rifled through her purse for identification.

"It's her all right, Tony. Dr. M. Sanger, Ph.D., M.D., Houston PD Forensic Psychiatry, Civilian Personnel. What now?"

"Call Lincoln." Tony adjusted his uniform tie.

"No . . . no, call Lieutenant Lucas Stonecoat, please. He'll verify I am who I say I am."

"*Hmmm* . . . think we've established that much. Tell you what, Doc. How would it be if we dropped you at the Three-one and we all call it a day? I'll talk to security at the courthouse; not likely to be any charges."

"Sounds like a sound plan," she agreed. "Thank you, thank you both."

"Don't mention it." said Frank, a half-kidding, nervous tension to his voice, "not to anyone!"

"Sounds to me like you've been under a great deal of stress here lately, Doc," replied Tony from the wheel as they pulled away, going now toward the 31st Precinct.

"Yeah, we've heard all about the eyes, the teeth, the head, and all the other stuff this nutcase has been mailing you," agreed Frank. "It's no wonder you're having a bad day."

Meredyth fell silent, deciding it was her only defense.

"No reason to involve a precinct captain in all this. . . ." Tony nudged Frank as he spoke.

"Huh? *Nah, nah,* no reason I can think of, no."

The two, Frank and Tony, began talking quietly to one another. "Stonecoat . . . isn't that the guy—"

"—yeah, the guy who broke the Mootry murder case."

"Broke that computer Internet assassination network?"

"Famous guy . . . Native Texan, right?"

"No, Native American . . . Cherokee, I think."

Meredyth shut them out, struggling now with puzzling questions alighting and seeping into her brain: *How did Lauralie know I'd be at the courthouse? When did she begin to follow me? From what location? The condo, the precinct? Or had she slyly gotten the information from Candice, my soon-to-be-"fired" secretary, as no doubt Byron had?*

Or worse still, had Lauralie somehow learned of Byron Priestly's connection to her, simply following him to the courthouse? And if she followed him to the courthouse, was Byron too in danger?

If so, Byron, needed a heads-up. She must notify him. "Can I get my cell phone back?" she asked Frank.

"What?"

"My purse, phone, and gun."

"Well, ma'am, ahhh, Doctor, sure . . . but since we're almost there—"

Tony finished for Frank. "Soon as we turn you over to this Detective Stonecoat."

"Heard a lot about *him*," said Frank. "Settle a bet for us. He's a Cherokee tracker, isn't he? Wasn't he a one-time Texas Ranger?"

"No, Lucas wasn't in the Rangers."

"But he was a vet, right? Nam?" asked Tony.

"And he's Choctaw or Chickasaw then, if he's not Cherokee."

"What's difference between a Chickasaw and a Cherokee?" asked Tony.

"Don't know," replied Frank. "Maybe the difference is their totems."

"Totems?"

"You know, spirit guides, all that. One tribe follows the fox, another the hawk, turtle, hare, squirrel." Frank pointed out a side street, and Tony turned down it.

"Squirrel?" Tony laughed. "No, no . . . it's all along family bloodlines who's in charge, who's the chief of one tribe, and who's the chief of another . . . family ties, so to speak. Not so different from tribes in Afghanistan or Africa or the mafia even."

"Sounds right, Frank, but totems are important too, I'll bet. What do you think, Dr. Sanger?"

"I think I want my phone."

CHAPTER 14

Arrowhead: watchful

LUCAS STONECOAT'S MORNING hadn't been near so eventful as Meredyth's. Before he got the call from the squad car transporting her to the precinct, he had met with a retired investigator who had worked the Yolanda Sims case. Detective Maurice Remo was haunted by the case, still angry at how it was handled by the original investigating team. Remo had taken it over when it had first come downstairs to him in the Cold Room. At the time, Remo was in charge of the Cold Case files. Disgusted by what he found in the file—or rather what he failed to find—he had, in 1957, launched his own investigation. A young detective at the time, he was now in his early seventies.

Lucas had telephoned Remo on a hunch after seeing his name on a routing sheet, expecting to be told by whoever answered the phone that Remo was long dead. All the other detectives on the case had long since passed away. But Maurice Remo answered his own phone and was very much alive.

Lucas told Remo, "Your notes on the Yolanda Sims

1956 murder case are not in the file. I only stumbled on your name when I was leafing through the routing sheet."

"I started my own murder book on the case," Remo explained over the phone.

"We don't have any record of a second volume."

"No way you could have, Detective Stone—what is it?"

"Stonecoat, sir."

"I worked the case on my own time. My captain and everyone else was convinced it was a guy caught for a string of murders, but Sims's killing was never proven to be connected. Even so, I was told to let it be. We had several higher-profile cases in-house at the time I could devote my time to, you understand?"

"Missing and dead white people, you mean?" Lucas rocked in his chair, certain that the old man would slam his phone down at the remark as soon as it slipped from Lucas.

"Yeah, something like that." He was still on the line.

"So . . . you did what?" Lucas rocked forward, planting his elbows on his desk.

"Took my report on the case with me when I left."

"You took it home on your retirement?"

"I would take it out from time to time. Try to convince myself her killer was a guy who fried for seven other child killings around the same time. They called him the Dumpster Killer. Can you guess why?"

"Yeah, I can. So you have all your notes on the case—"

"—here to home, my kitchen cupboard."

"Really?"

"Damn thing's a constant reminder. Points a finger at me every damn day I open that cupboard. My albatross."

"Would you care to share this cursed bird with someone?" Lucas asked.

"You mean *you*? I've read about you in the papers from time to time. I understand you're the man who got the HPD to join the computer revolution, that you got all the Cold Cases on-line, and now they're shared by every precinct and jurisdiction in the state."

"In the country now, sir, and with the FBI's VICAP program."

"Excellent."

"May I come over there and have a look at your murder book on Yolanda Sims?" Lucas waited out a long pause.

"Misdemeanor to take HPD property and not return it."

"I think we can say a statute of limitations is at work here. So, can I come have a look? If it's good enough, we'll include it on the database."

Another long moment of silence. "Tell you what, Stonecoat. I'll come down to the precinct house."

"I could save you the trip."

Remo nearly shouted into the phone, "I don't have reason enough to get out much, so let me!"

"All right, sir. Suit yourself."

"Not much for this retirement life."

Three quarters of an hour later, Maurice stood at Lucas's desk, introducing himself, a murder book clutched to his chest.

Maurice's take on the Sims case proved unique, an absolute eye-opening departure from the original investigators. Like Lucas, he believed that all four of the suspects interviewed, being familiar with the neighborhood, would *not* have left the body where it had been dumped.

"Dead wrong they were," Remo repeatedly said, somehow looking relaxed in a rolling office chair. "If the creep who killed her didn't know the lay of the land," he calmly said, finally breaking with his chant, "then it stands to reason he was no more acquainted with Yolanda than he was her house and her address."

"That's been my thinking," agreed Lucas.

"You go down there, you look at the houses on these two streets, and you find they are like clones all of 'em. All right then, you have to know the area well to be on the right street. All the streets in that area begin with the same letter, Denton, Denby, Densmore, Denlow. So the guy is nervous, turns down Denby instead of Denton, pulls up before 1214—the right address on the wrong street—at three or four in the morning. He then quickly carries the girl's body from his car or van and dumps it on the doorstep, not out of any grief or concern for the child's remains or the family's closure, Detective Stonecoat, but out of malice, to get even with her uncle, who inadvertently brought this horrible tragedy down on his niece, but the man is so broken up, he can't accept this truth."

"The uncle was dealing drugs? This was because he owed somebody? What?"

"The killer wants to shock and dismay someone at that address. He wants to rub it in the uncle's face. And he gives not one thought to the child's siblings or parents."

"What was it, drugs? Numbers? Gang-related turf war?"

"None of the above."

"What was the beef with the uncle then?"

"Love."

"Lovers? They were lovers?"

"Love kills . . . we see it all the time."

"A highly personal motive then."

Remo stood and paced. "The little girl was used to get back at her uncle by the man he abandoned."

"So the guy's boyfriend killed her with no remorse?"

"None, not this mole."

"Does he have a name?" asked Lucas.

Remo rubbed the white stubble at his chin, not answering Lucas, slowly allowing the thread of his thoughts to unravel, like a magician unfolding a trick handkerchief. Lucas patiently awaited the old detective's sleight-of-hand. Remo continued to pace to the eye-level window that looked out on the sidewalk here in the basement offices of the Cold Case file room. Finally, he said, "An outbreak of child abduction-murders occurred that year, and at first I suspected that Yolanda's murder was only the first in this string of killings."

"First because?"

"First because he was sloppy and careless in Yolanda's case, and because it seemed he had a conscience, that he tried to do one right thing."

"Bring the kid's body back home," said Lucas.

"But he failed miserably to do so, and possibly was seen in the act and frightened off. After this, the others, he didn't take such chances with; he never brought another kid back to where he had abducted her from. Instead, he discarded them in city Dumpsters."

"You mean this guy who they called the Dumpster Killer, Paul Mick Ryan, electrocuted in . . ."

"Sixty-three."

"But you never really believed Yolanda's killing was related, despite prevailing winds?"

"No. Fact is, I got over the notion fairly quickly."

"Why not Ryan?"

"The Dumpster victims were not beaten to death, burned, or tortured; not a bruise on them except the single deadly black-and-blue throat where the stranglehold was so intense they lifted whole thumb and finger images off the victims' throats, all a match to Ryan's prints. Yolanda was not strangled to death."

"And there was no sexual molestation in the Ryan killings."

"Neither before nor after, *none*. Shrinks questioned Ryan and learned he could only get off sexually by strangling his young victims, primarily little girls, but two boys as well. He masturbated over the bodies after death, but never penetrated any of them."

Lucas considered the disparity between the victims of Ryan and the Sims girl. "Autopsy showed that Yolanda died of internal bleeding from the beating her killer inflicted on her, and she *was* sexually molested using a blunt alien instrument."

"Yolanda had been tortured horribly . . . made to suffer the pain and fires of hell."

"Cigarette burns, yes." Lucas pictured the photos he'd seen of her battered body.

"Whoever did her, he was vicious, and while the DA wanted to make out that Paul Ryan was vicious, I made the M.E. explain to me every bruise on his victims. Most of the bruising other than at the throats came from their time in the Dumpsters, the jostling and falling debris while the body was in the Dumpster and emptied out into a dump truck. The M.E. was clear on this; the head and body bruises came long after death."

"And Ryan, did he ever confess to Yolanda's murder?"

"All his victims were white. He swore he never killed the Sims girl. No DNA typing then, so no way to know for certain, but he went to the chair claiming he only did the seven white children found in city Dumpsters."

"How was he captured?"

"Captured on a tip by a gray-haired woman with insomnia, taking out her trash. The old lady was smart enough to get a license-plate number. The ID happened when she saw him discarding his last body, a little boy. When detectives showed up at his house, Ryan lost it at the door, said something to the effect, 'Why didn't you guys form a task force sooner to stop me? Why'd it take you so long? Why didn't you stop me sooner? I ought to sue your asses.' "

"He didn't know the gay uncle and had never worked the area, right?"

"None of his victims were dumped anywhere near the Sims murder site. And try as they might to make correlations, they could not find any real connection, no."

"And you suspected someone connected to the uncle."

"Yeah, there was one guy stuck in my craw, the uncle's boyfriend."

"He got a name?"

"Gay Uncle Bobbie and his lover, Lyle Eaton, had a *nasty* breakup that same evening of the abduction. There'd been a scene, a car chase in which Eaton caught up to Uncle Bob where he was holed up."

"At Yolanda's house?"

"Using it for a hideout. Eaton got violent, breaking a window, beating on the door. A squad car was called out to the address to evict Eaton from the front porch."

"Any arrests?"

"Should have been, but no, and so no paper trail."

"How'd you learn about the fight? Interviews?"

"Yeah, the hard way. He was waving a crowbar when the cops cooled him down and sent him off. Had there been an arrest report, maybe so many years would not have gone by before anyone learned the truth, years during which Ryan appealed and awaited execution for the Dumpster deaths."

"And no subsequent confrontations at that address between the men?"

"I know. It sounds fishy, doesn't it?" Remo asked.

"I agree, doesn't sound like a typical breakup, either gay or straight. Most relationship breakups happen over a series of engagements, retreats, and further battles."

"Only *one* encounter after Uncle Bobbie moves out on a seven-year 'marriage' to Eaton, and it's without a word, according to Bobbie Sims. Then suddenly the man's niece disappears, is killed in horrific fashion, and suddenly *poof*— Eaton disappears from the city immediately after being cleared by virtue of a questionable alibi. Then a year goes by before I catch the case when the file sorta fell into my possession, and I confirm that Eaton laid carpets as well as tile, as well as doing odd jobs as a carpenter, and that he conveyed his own tools to the job sites in his cream-colored van. People spotted a white van sitting at the end of the street that night. You ever look at a beige van under orange street lamps? It's white!"

"Hoffman and Blake got none of these connections?"

"These were my leads, uncovered years later when no one wanted to hear the truth or be proven incompetent. I was a rookie in charge of filing down here in the dungeon. I prove I'm right, I also prove they're nincompoops, and they had seniority big-time in those days."

"You ever get the chance to interview Eaton?"

"Once. He choked on a weak alibi that ought to've been proven a lie. Eaton's grandparents also swore to Hoffman and Blake—and years later to me—that he was with them that night, all night, playing board games and watching *Gunsmoke* and *Ed Sullivan*. Soon after, Lyle and his van left the area, reportedly for a work site in Amarillo."

"That's bordering on leaving the state."

"Fact is, he didn't go to Amarillo. He went to Seattle, Washington. And valuable potential evidence, like the damned van, his carpet strips, likely under someone's carpet somewhere by then, his soldering iron, and other tools used to assault the girl, all gone. There's no statute of limitation on murder, but there sure can be on contaminated evidence."

Lucas squinted, thinking in pictures, trying to get a fix on what had happened, and how it had been allowed to play out as it did. Sure, it was 1956 and investigators had no fingerprint evidence in the case, and DNA was nonexistent, but they had the same findings from the coroner as Remo had. The difference seemed to be a sadly prevailing attitude taken toward the case, that other, higher-priority cases took precedence, and worse still, that Yolanda and her parents had somehow brought the tragedy down around themselves and so must accept it—almost as if it were an act of God. *An inexcusable excuse,* Lucas thought of the deceased detectives as his admiration for Remo increased.

"So you think Eaton found a nearby isolated place to park, never leaving the unfamiliar neighborhood, attacking her in the van and—"

"—and dumping her body on the wrong doorstep in his haste to get the hell out of the area, yes."

Lucas recalled the details of the puncture marks all over Yolanda's body. The words of the autopsy report flashed through his mind: *"sawdust in victim's hair and body; unusual puncture wounds over body, determined as marks consistent with beating from wood carpet stripping; cigar-sized, round burns on legs and arms consistent with cigar or possibly a soldering iron as wounds are clean of ash debris. Foreign object used in sexual battery consistent with marks made by a Phillips-head screwdriver . . ."*

"And this guy Eaton, you're convinced he doesn't know the neighborhood?"

"He'd only been in the Houston area for six months. Here's my take on it, if you'd care to hear it," replied Remo.

Lucas drew him a cup of coffee from the nearby urn. "Lay it out for me, Detective."

"All right. It's like this. A jilted Lyle Eaton drives down there in his white work van to Uncle Bobbie's neighborhood and is jilted *again* by his lover. He then goes away but not far. He cruises the alleyway and parks behind the house, hatching a scheme when he sees Yolanda playing on the back porch."

Lucas sipped at his coffee. "I follow you. Go on."

"Fact is, Lyle Eaton was lying in wait to have it out again with Bobbie, but Bobbie didn't come out that night, only Yolanda did—sent to the store to get Uncle Bobbie's smokes! Then *voila,* she returns safely home. Eaton watches her come and go but does nothing at this point. Then he sees her come out a second time, this time *rewarded* with an extra hour's playtime on the backyard grass, inside the fence. It's at this point that Eaton—having watched this trivial drama play out from the confines of his van—decides to make Bobbie pay through his niece. He exits the van and charms her right out of her backyard and into his van. Promises, I'm sure."

"This is unbelievable, that no one put this together at the time."

"By the time it got to me, leads were cold. Still, I went out and talked to the family, tracing the original steps Hoffman and Blake had taken, a pair of real Sherlocks. When I talked to Yolanda's father, out comes the story of Bobbie and Lyle on the doorstep, ready to kill one another. The old man claimed he told the investigating team all about it, but that they didn't think it *relevant.*"

"They accepted the alibi at face value?"

"Part of it, sure. Any rate, the catfight never got into their reports. Me, on the other hand, I became instantly curious, and I pursued it, but years later now both Bobbie and his boyfriend are long gone. Bobbie was overseas, had enlisted in the Army. I had to put out a call for information on Lyle Eaton, and word on the street was that he had moved to Seattle, but my contacts up there came up blank."

"And in the meantime the Dumpster Killer was an easy fill-in-the-blank for Hoffman and Blake."

"With the captain and the DA on their asses, you bet. The departmental push was on to clear the case by getting Ryan to cop to the killing. They tried to push it down his throat, but he wouldn't budge."

"Is Eaton in the system? Does he have a record?"

"Petty stuff, but yeah, prints, mug shot, all of it. But he seems to have disappeared in the great void out there. Likely somebody killed him or he died of an overdose or a dirty needle someplace and is buried in a potter's field God knows where. Like I said, his trail went dead in Seattle. A blind alley."

"Seattle's a big seaport. You ever think he may've joined the merchant marines? Shipped out for Singapore or Malaysia?"

"I considered it. Tough in those days to nail a man working a seaman's job. No cooperation, I can tell you. He could've gone that route, sure. But he never surfaced again."

"I'll put it in the system we're interested in talking to the guy. See what I can find out," said Lucas.

"Targeting Seattle?"

"The system is nationwide now, Detective. I can simultaneously request a cross-reference and a download on any information on a Lyle Eaton anywhere in the States, Europe with Interpol, Britain's Scotland Yard, Japan, New Zealand, Australia, Canada, even Russia nowadays."

"Imagine that. Russia and us cooperating on police matters."

"But of course."

"Just remarkable how far police science and communications have come. My hat's off to you."

"Let's see if we can get lucky." With a few key strokes, Lucas put the request into VICAP—the FBI's violent-criminal-apprehension program, and the WCW—the World Crime Watch program. "We'll let these requests percolate. See what comes of 'em."

"Amazing. Still, it's a hell of a long shot."

"Least we can do for Yolanda Sims after all these years is to take the shot."

"Right you are." Maurice Remo smiled at this, nodding. "Good show, Detective Stonecoat. Keep me posted on any results. Sure would like to go to my grave knowing what became of that scum. . . ."

They shook hands and were about to part when the old man looked around the newly refurbished Cold Room with a

calculating eye at its many computers and lack of hard files
and boxes. Walls had been knocked out, space utilization
improved along with the heating and cooling system; along
with newly installed lighting, a bathroom had been installed,
and the confining stacks of metal shelving once creating
tight dark aisles were all gone.

"Sure is a changed place, Stonecoat. Not the dust-bucket
I used to work in. Count yourself lucky."

"Trust me, I know. All the changes came after my
arrival. It was a damned dusty dungeon."

Remo turned to leave, but turned back and asked, "Why
does this girl's case interest you so much, Detective? She's
long in her grave, family has all died off for the most part
or moved away. Most likely her killer is dead, so what purpose does it serve you to spend time on her case?"

"I suppose for the same reason as you pursued her case
so many years ago. I suppose because of her eyes, the way
they look out at you, the way they speak to you."

He shook Lucas's hand again, his eyes holding Lucas in
place. Lucas said, "I want to thank you for coming down
here and helping me out, Detective."

"Been a long time since anyone's called me Detective,
son. I miss that."

The phone rang, and Lucas begged off, taking a call
from an unfamiliar cop named Frank who told him a gar-
bled story about Meredyth Sanger's being held in the back
of his squad car for brandishing a gun down at the courthouse.

"Is she all right? Is she there with you now, Officer?"
Lucas asked, shaken.

"Right here behind the cage, yes. We just took off the
cuffs, but we'll hold onto the gun until we can release her
into your custody, Detective, as a courtesy, cop to cop."

"Thanks. Frank is it?"

"Frank Lupo with the Two-five."

"Put her on, will you, Frank?"

"Tony, he wants to talk to her, okay?" Lucas heard the
cop ask his partner. After a bit of rattling to get the receiver
back to Meredyth, she came on.

"Lucas, it's me."

"Mere, what the hell's going on?"

"Shut up and listen to me. *She* was there, Lucas, at the courthouse, in the archives, *shadowing* me."

"Are you all right? Were you hurt?"

"I'm fine, just shaken up . . . emotionally."

"Are you sure it was Lauralie Blodgett?"

"Yes, I saw her in the crowd afterwards, when they arrested me. She was enjoying every second of my humiliation, Lucas, every second of it. I tell you, it was her. She must've been stalking me the whole time."

"Did she follow you there from here?"

"How should I know? But Lucas, Byron was there at the courthouse too. He'd run me down and—"

"Byron Priestly?"

"—and maybe she's been following him! If that's true, then we've got an obligation to warn Byron."

"Calm down. How far away are you?"

"What about Byron?"

"Fuck Byron! How far are you?"

"Five, six minutes."

"Have Lupo and Tony pull into the underground lot, and I'll meet you there."

Lucas hung up, and Maurice Remo still stood beside him, listening in. "I sure miss the action," the old man said. "Trust me, young man, never retire. Get yourself killed in the line of duty before you end up a sad old bastard like me with nothing to do all day but watch CNN, reruns, and soap operas. A hundred and thirty-two channels with nothing on . . . a channel devoted to flower arrangements, you believe that?"

"Maurice, Detective Remo, I'll keep you apprised of any new developments in the Sims case, I promise you, but I gotta rush right now."

"And what about this weird-ass case I read about in the papers, about this killer posting body parts in the mail to a detective and a shrink here at the Three-one? You know anything about that? Sounds like a case to sink your teeth into."

"It does indeed. Anything you want to know about it, I'd

be happy to share with you what little I know, but right now I have to meet someone. Thanks again for coming down, and please leave your murder book on Yolanda right there on my desk, okay?"

"Sure . . . sure."

Lucas rushed out for the parking garage. Behind him, he heard the old man shout, "If ever you need to confer on another case, if ever you want forty-six years experience on the job as a murder policeman, you don't hesitate to call, Stonecoat, you hear?"

"Will do!" he shouted back down the corridor before disappearing from the old man's sight. Something about Remo reminded Lucas of his grandfather. He liked Maurice, and he trusted the old man's experience and tried and true instincts.

He raced for the parking garage.

CHAPTER 15

Thunderbird track: bright prospect

I N   T H E   P A R K I N G garage the two officers, Tony and Frank, turned over the .38 Police Special along with a grateful 31st Precinct forensic psychiatrist. Both Meredyth and Lucas thanked them for their discretion and help. With the officers waved off, Meredyth threw her arms around Lucas. He held her, disregarding the comings and goings of other police personnel and HPD civilian support staff in the garage. "Come on down to my office," he told her, walking her to the Cold Room. "I've got coffee. We can talk."

"First, I hafta warn Byron." She got on her cell phone as they walked. Byron didn't pick up his cell. She left a cryptic message, saying, "Call me on my cell. It's a matter of life and death—possibly yours!"

Once in the Cold Room, he got her a cup of hot coffee and asked her to tell him every detail of what had happened at the courthouse.

Between sips of the steaming coffee, she imparted the entire story.

When she'd finished, she handed Lucas the document

she had gone after at the courthouse, the one Lauralie had cranked from the machine for her. Lucas took in a deep breath of air. "Had she wanted to, it sounds as if she could have killed you then and there, when you had your back to her."

"Don't you think I've thought of that?"

"So her purpose is not to kill you, Mere, merely to destroy your peace of mind, your emotional well-being."

"First she stalks us at the convent, leaving the finger there, and now the courthouse."

"But she didn't leave anything at the courthouse, did she?"

"No, but then I was hardly in a position to notice if she had. I was stopped from pursuing her by the security guards, and next thing I know, I'm handcuffed and pushed into the rear of a police cruiser."

"Did you see Priestly leave the lot?"

She hesitated, saying nothing.

"Did you see him drive off? Did he wave bye-bye?"

"No . . . no, I didn't. Byron . . ."

"She can't kill you." He stepped off from her, pacing about the office. "She has more tidbits and items she wants to show you . . . she wants us to discover."

"I don't like where this is going, Lucas."

"First the abduction and mutilation of Mira Lourdes, the planting of clues to lead us to the convent, the funeral home, the courthouse."

"What're you driving at? That we missed something at these locations?"

"We know she's sick, and we know she's got a sick sense of humor. She must have placed something at Morte de Arthur's and—"

"—and the courthouse?"

"With her twisted sister act, with her sick take on things, yes. Revelations yet in store, Mere. She has yet to show it all to us."

"What are we going to do?"

"Call in help." Lucas got on the phone and arranged for two police raids, one on the funeral home, the other on the

courthouse. Both required no warrants, as Lucas cagily
called each in to Stan Kelton as an *Imminent Threat
Response Team circumstance.* One push of a button sent
these search-and-seizure emergency-response units out to
a location. The teams responded to terrorist and biohazard
threats, bomb scares, and hostage situations. These teams
included armed men with tactical training, a CSI unit for
gathering evidence, and a public relations team to stave off
the press. The teams went into instant action when ordered
out, but the go-order must be based on hard evidence. On
his say-so, his responsibility, Lucas Stonecoat meant to
lock down a place of business and a county courthouse
annex building. He felt a flutter in his heart at the power of
it all, and the uncertainty of what would happen. It'd be
hell to pay with Captain Lincoln if they found nothing.

He made a second call, informing Jana North that he
needed her to coordinate the effort at Morte de Arthur's,
and she immediately agreed to oversee the raid there.

"Come on, let's get over to the courthouse," he said to
Meredyth when he got off the phone. "Maybe we'll find
the rest of Mira Lourdes."

They rushed for Lucas's car and the courthouse. Along
the way, over the sound of the siren, Meredyth bitterly
said, "A finger here, a finger there. This could go on
indefinitely—for as long as they have body parts to scatter."

"You perhaps should stay here in the car. Let me handle
this part myself."

"No . . . no, I'll stay with you, if you don't mind."

"Are you sure?"

"Lucas, this little bitch isn't going to get to me."

"That's the spirit." He'd placed his strobe light on top of
his unmarked car. The police-band radio was alive with the
activity of the simultaneous raids. Lucas imagined the
mortification and distress his order would create in Giorgio
and Carlotta's funeral parlor, and the curiosity and fear
they would soon arouse at the courthouse.

"This disturbed, distorted, screwed-up take *she* has on
her being abandoned, put up for adoption, pawned off to
foster homes as she sees it, Lucas, it all provides her a

sick motive to seek out a twisted revenge for all the wrongs she perceives people have done her. And me? I am the last of those women involved who placed her at the orphanage."

"You, Orleans, her mother, all three of you are on this record," Lucas said, holding up the document Lauralie had duplicated for them.

"And Lourdes? What was she to Lauralie?"

"A mere pawn in her game," mused Lucas.

"She wants to kill me slowly, slower than she did her mother or Sara Orleans. They died too easily and quickly for her liking. For me she has a different plan, an appalling purpose, as if she's mailing pieces of herself."

"The team's here, waiting for orders to move in," he said as they pulled around to the rear of the courthouse, the entrance to the low-lying wing housing the county clerk's department and Child and Family Services, and below these offices, the archival records.

A man in full body protection and an ITRT patch on his arm and back—head of the Imminent Threat Response Team—introduced himself as Elliot Andrews. "Lietuenant, these the two we're looking for? Armed and dangerous?" Andrews held up photos of Lauralie Blodgett and the man known only as the Ripper.

"That's right, but I want your team ready for anything, and I want every nook and cranny searched."

"You suspect a bomb?"

"Anything's possible."

"We've got a canine unit. They can sniff out just about anything."

"Trained on cadavers? We might find body parts left by the suspects."

"Oh, I see. This has some connection to the Post-it guy, right!" Andrews immediately responded, getting on his radio and ordering the dogs to be guided into the building ahead of the men. He repeated Lucas's search orders to his men. Lucas wondered how Jana North's team at the funeral parlor was managing. He trusted that she had a capable man like Andrews and a strong CSI team at her location.

Lucas and Andrews, with Meredyth tentatively following, paced themselves to remain behind the men leading the dogs into the courthouse annex.

THE DOGS, LARGE German shepherds, and their handlers, split off, one guided into the archives downstairs, the other taking the main floor. There were two floors overhead yet to secure. Andrews had the security guard named Roy on hand to point out all exits and entrances to the annex, including a service elevator only maintenance and security had access to, the one he'd escorted Meredyth onto earlier today. A second exit that opened on the main concourse of the courthouse itself. The lockdown meant no one could go in or out. Already people were clamoring to get past the exits, cell phones aflutter. Others jammed in hallways. People plastered to windows, looking out over the lot at the police activity. Loved ones had already begun showing up, jamming the courthouse parking lot, vehicles circling buzzard-fashion in search of parking, anxious to see their relatives unharmed. A police perimeter pushed them back, along with the news media.

Inside, the sound of the dog in the basement, sending up a barrage of agitated barks and howls, sent Lucas, Andrews, and Meredyth racing down toward the archives. The dog had alerted on something.

At the foot of the stairs, along this corridor to the archives, the dog stood, ears erect, agitatedly dancing about, yipping excitedly. His handler fed him a beef jerky cube from his hand as a reward, and they pulled back, allowing Elliot Andrews in. Lucas and Andrews, guns drawn, nodded at one another. Andrews so forcefully tore open the dark oak-wood door that it swung into the marbled wall, creating a reverberating blast down the corridor and up the stairs, and this, combined with the stench of blood let free, gave Lucas the feeling of a fleeting soul that'd been trapped inside where the body of an unrecognizable man lay in a pool of blood, his thrown-away tie, trousers, and half-torn-away white shirt stained with blood.

The walls—flecked with blood—told the story of multiple stab wounds.

"Dear God," muttered Andrews, turning his head away from the mutilated facial features after Lucas, crouching, lifted the chin and turned the eyes upward from the heap of clothing and flesh at their feet. "Who is he?"

Meredyth looked past Andrews now and screamed. "It's Byron! My God, it's Byron!"

Lucas made out the features and nodded to Andrews. He also held up Byron Priestly's wallet, his license and credit cards intact. He rifled for his keys and found them in the bloody pants.

A police woman alongside Meredyth had caught her from falling when her knees had buckled, and she'd led her to a nearby bench. Meredyth sobbed openly.

Lucas looked across at her, his heart feeling the pain of her anguish. She had broken it off with Priestly, but they had been friends for a long time. They had been talking marriage at one time. This shocking development could send her into a complete spiral, he feared.

Byron had been viciously torn apart in the confines of the small shoulder-width cubbyhole, and no one had heard his screams here just off the archives where Meredyth had been working that morning. Everything seemed now to move in slow motion as Andrews radioed for an at-ease and called Lynn Nielsen to bring in her CSI team, informing her over the secured channel that a body had been found at his location. Someone brought a thermos of hot coffee down to them, and Lucas sat quietly holding Meredyth's hands in his.

After doing an initial assessment of Priestly's body, Dr. Lynn Nielsen came to them. "Your friend Byron has been stabbed in the gut so many times that without cleaning the wounds thoroughly and viewing them under the lights at my lab, it is impossible to say how many times he was stabbed, but one thing is certain, whoever did this truly hated the man. It looks like a crime of passion, one of those estranged relationships in which one party snaps and can't seem to stop at inflicting only one wound or even three.

This is in the neighborhood of twenty-five, possibly more stab wounds, plus the afterwards mutilation to the eyes, nose, mouth . . . and we found something peculiar stuffed down his throat."

"What is it?" asked Lucas.

She held up a clear plastic bag. "Rosary beads."

Meredyth said nothing; she could only stare at the onyx string of beads.

To Lucas they looked like the symbol for the passage of days into night, nights into days in an old Cherokee pictograph—a string of beads. "Was Byron a practicing Catholic?" he asked Meredyth.

"About as much as I was, but no . . . he didn't carry a rosary with him, and no, I never gave him any as a present. I've never seen this rosary before, and I resent your implication, Dr. Nielsen, that I had anything to do with Byron's murder . . . except as . . . due to our proximity . . . anyone being close to me in the least, she's targeted. You're in danger too, Lucas, perhaps far more than I am."

"He had no advance warning, Mere, but I do. I know what those two maniacs look like, and I'm hunting them down."

Nielsen had begun to apologize, saying she hadn't meant to imply that Dr. Sanger had any part in Priestly's murder. Meredyth ignored her, continuing to speak to Lucas. "While Lauralie and Crazy Joe are hunting you."

"Whoever killed him, he, she, or *they* did it with a maniacal ferocity. I believe in the lab, we will find wounds in which the knife blade—a large one—will have exited the back. That's how much energy the Ripper—if this proves to be the work of the Post-it Ripper—put into the effort. It would have left the killer breathless, disarrayed, perspiring, and bloody but for the apron and the cleanup she did inside. There's a sink in there and lots of soap, and a stack of maintenance aprons, caps, hair nets, rubber gloves."

"She donned the maintenance uniform for him," said Meredyth. "Caught up to him, asked him for some help inside the closet—something on a shelf perhaps. She lured him inside, teased him as she put on the apron and gloves, the paper hat and hair net."

"Teased her way into his pants," added Lucas. "Explains the discarded tie and trousers."

"And when he most expected gratification, she stabbed him."

"No outcry alerting anyone."

Nielsen said, "He may well have gone into immediate shock, unable to call out—"

"—then came the ratcheted knife strokes, machine-gun fashion," said Lucas. "It all fits."

Nielsen said. "Killed by someone who had a personal connection, someone who had either hated him greatly or was driven to such an emotional pitch that after the first several stab wounds, he or she could not stop a wild violence against him. Like the killer of Yolanda Sims, whoever did it was emotionally involved, deeply so." She looked at Meredyth where she sat sobbing still. "Could this Lauralie have been sleeping with your friend?"

"Anything's possible. But I don't think so. He was just weak when it came to an overture by any female."

"I know a few men like that," Nielsen said sarcastically, trying to elicit a smile but failing.

"Don't you see? She'd like nothing better than to have me on trial for murdering Byron, to put me through that ordeal. To see me disgraced, my life in a shambles. Everyone I ever cared about either dead or scurrying to put as much distance between me and himself as possible. Putting my friends and family through a humiliating time. She wants you to indict me for Byron's murder—I was here at the time of his murder! I have the classic three necessities for a D.A. to put me away—motive, means, and opportunity. I knew the man, detested him, have complained of being stalked by him, been seen arguing with him right outside in the lot the morning of his death not twenty feet from where I sat behind those doors without an alibi."

Lucas added, "It's the work of that cunning bitch we've told you about, Dr. Nielsen. She wants it to look as if he were butchered by her in a fit of rage. But Meredyth doesn't do rage."

"If this is her work, she's done a good job pointing the finger at you, Dr. Sanger, if you can so incriminate *yourself*—with your own assessment. I urge you to say no more that someone might take as *self-incriminating*. Besides, liking you as I do, I would not wish to be called to the stand against you to say *yes* and nod to words taken out of context."

"In other words shut my mouth?"

Nielsen nodded, and then spoke to Lucas. "Now, Lieutenant, as to this sort of disfigurement to the face . . ."

"Yes?"

"Speaks to the kind of rage between estranged lovers as well, so my advice stands."

"Disfigurement is what this maniac does," said Lucas. "It's why we call him, her—*the two of them*—rippers—mutilation murderers."

"I understand, of course. I was just pointing out—"

"It looks on the surface very bad, we know," countered Meredyth. "And having been arrested on a weapons charge the same afternoon, well . . ."

"Technically speaking, you weren't arrested," he said. "You were detained and transported but not booked."

"All the same, multiple witnesses saw the incident."

"Your clever Lauralie was wise enough to have left no calling card or telltale signs of herself behind this time," Nielsen said. "A few toes, teeth, or fingers belonging to Mira Lourdes, left in or around the body here, that would insure it was she and her friend who hacked Mr. Priestly up."

"Only the damn rosary," lamented Lucas. "Only the damn rosary."

"That butchering bitch," muttered Meredyth. "Don't you see, the rosary is her calling card. She wants no mistaking this; she wants me to know she can hurt me at any time. That no one around me is safe either."

Elliot Andrews was standing nearby, picking up as much of what was being said as possible, when his radio crackled into life. He answered it and carried it to Lucas. "For you, your captain."

Lucas accepted the radio Andrews held out to him, Lincoln's ranting voice coming over even before he put it to his ear. His shouting focused on the chaos and phone calls caused by the raid on the courthouse. "I want to know if it's been worth it all. What've you netted there?"

Lucas relayed the gruesome find and informed Lincoln that it was connected to the Mira Lourdes murder, and that the CSI unit at the annex would be here well into the night collecting evidence. Lincoln was placated for the moment, but he wanted to be kept abreast of things, finishing with, "We'll red-ball this APB we have out on this Blodgett woman and her friend, Lucas. Shame what's happening. Give Meredyth my best, and we need to talk in full as soon as possible."

Lucas kept hold of the radio and returned to Meredyth on the bench. She was sipping at a cup of coffee now, a slight shiver escaping her.

"Lincoln's changing the APB on Lauralie Blodgett to a Code Red BOLO."

"Be on the lookout for a witch on a broom?" she muttered. "Then Gordon understands what's going on?"

"He's standing behind you one hundred percent. Mere, we'll get her, now that her likeness is plastered everywhere and she's a Code Red. Her wading pool is growing ever smaller. Only wish we knew what she and Crazy Joe are driving."

"A vehicle description, hell, a Texas driver's license . . . it would all be good. Meantime, we're being led around by the nose by a child mental case playing lethal games."

Lucas got back on the police radio and called Lieutenant Jana North at the funeral parlor raid. The sound of chaos came over the line before she finally came on. "What the hell's going on there? Sounds like a riot."

"We've cordoned off a wake here."

"A wake?"

"We didn't have any choice. It was in the open coffin."

"What was in the open coffin?"

"A pair of disembodied arms, one missing a right hand."

He listened attentively to the details of her report, replying with a series of yeses, and finally he said, "See to it no one disturbs the scene before your CSI unit can process it."

"You ever try that with a roomful of irate loved ones? Dr. Patterson's got his hands full, and he's on the run."

"Christ, they sent out Frank with an ITRT unit?"

"Told me he volunteered when he heard it had to do with the Ripper case, even said something about how you and he were close, Lucas. How he wanted to help in any way possible."

"Weasel knows I fingered him and some others for this nasty business when I thought it was all a tasteless joke."

"Bad blood between you guys, heh? You'll have to tell me about it some evening over drinks."

"He lost some vital evidence on a case of mine once. Cost me." He then said, "Jana, you may's well know that Meredyth and I . . . that we are seeing each other, and that for the time being at least, we're seriously . . . together."

"Then I take it drinks are out."

"Yeah, drinks are out."

"I'd better go. The natives are getting restless here. You're right about Frank. He's managed to antagonize the owners, the wake crowd, and I suspect the dead woman in the coffin."

"Sounds like Patterson."

"The crowd is made up of some pissed-off Mexicans. Talk to you later."

Lucas tossed the radio back to Andrews. He said to Meredyth, "They've found something at the funeral home."

"Do I want to know what it is?"

"A pair of arms, one severed at the wrist, missing a hand. Presumed by Frank Patterson as those of a young woman. I think we can presume Mira Lourdes."

"Where were the arms found?"

"In one of the caskets about to be wheeled out for public viewing with one of Giorgio's masterpieces of makeup inside—a regular *Ripley's Believe It or Not* event—a body within a casket freshly wrapped in yellow crime-scene tape. North is waiting for Frank Patterson to finish up the CSI work there. 'Fraid Nielsen and the team'll be here a great deal longer."

"And in the meantime, what do we do, Lucas?"

"Meanwhile, I'm taking you outta here. Come on."

"Byron was a jerk, Lucas, but he didn't deserve this. My God . . . what am I to tell his mother, Agnes? His sister? Hell, I dare not go near them. We've got to end this thing, Lucas. We must and soon. What can we do?"

"We go back to Lincoln with everything we know, everything we suspect, everything we suspect we know about Lauralie Blodgett, including your run-in with her here, and the near run-in at the convent school."

"She used *him,* Lucas, to locate me. Following his movements . . . perhaps seeing him leaving my apartment, she and her boyfriend must have tailed him in their search for me, and where was I? Hiding from it all out at the ranch, Lucas. She'd been watching his movements to locate me. Thank God my parents are out of town, out of harm's way."

"Lincoln's got to be updated. He's got to know all we know now."

"Yes, should anything *happen* to us, what little we've unearthed about her, the miniscule hard evidence dies with us, and should we follow the way of Byron, no one's going to weave this convoluted, tangled web of murder together ever again. . . . You saw Nielsen's face; you heard her words. She's not buying it." Meredyth looked in need of rest, and her eyes were bloodshot from tears.

"Come on. Let's go, Mere. Nothing more we can contribute here."

"She's watching it all, Lucas, from a safe distance, seeing us running about, all of us, SWAT people, CSI people, all of us back and forth, and her pulling the strings and getting high off the mix. Maybe . . . I don't know . . . maybe we, all of us, her mother, the church, the state . . . me . . . we all contributed to this day. We certainly created a stone-cold vampire."

"Byron's dead, Meredyth, but it's not your fault. Not any more than Mira Lourdes's death is your fault."

They'd made it to his car, newsmen shouting for a comment from Lucas. He instead urged Meredyth to get in, and he did likewise, shooting from the lot, successfully ducking reporters.

Driving for their downtown home, the 31st Precinct, Lucas got on the radio and was patched through to Gordon Lincoln's aide, who put him on with Lincoln.

"Yes, sir . . . reporters? A sea of 'em, Captain. They get the call same as the units, listening in on the band. Yes, sir. Meredyth's with me, sir. Count on it. We're on our way to your office now, sir."

Meredyth only half-heard his end of the conversation. When he got free, she said to him, "I hate her, Lucas . . . hate her. I no longer give a damn what a lousy hand she was dealt, the fact she wasn't even given a name by her mother. The nun, Mother Sara Orleans, christened her Lauralie, did you know? Think of it, imagine it. No one cares enough to give you a name."

"Don't waste any sympathy on her, Mere. This girl has mutilated two people, complete strangers to her, so she can play god-games to feel superior to us. Don't forget that."

"Lincoln might take some convincing." She wrapped her arms about herself and put her head back, exhausted.

Lucas felt a barren, dry wave of fatigue like a desert wind wash over him now. This case was draining them both. Frustration and a growing hatred for their prey threatened to make them less effective, less objective, less professional. He knew they must combat it. The alternative was a spiral from which Meredyth and he might not pull out.

She sensed his fears, reached over to him, and took his hand in hers. "We've got to stay strong, Lucas. In the face of all of it, stay strong to bring this *danse macabre* to an end."

CAPTAIN GORDON LINCOLN hung up the phone, having gotten word on the raids ordered by Stonecoat on a funeral parlor and the Harris County courthouse. The news from both locations was bad—but that coming out of the courthouse—an acquaintance of Meredyth Sanger's brutally, savagely knifed to death, his face slashed as an afterthought, his body stuffed in a maintenance closet—was truly disturbing. This news came on the heels of a call he'd gotten earlier from his friend Judge Wilfred Manning. Manning had conveyed a bizarre story of having witnessed an arrest in the hallway of the county courthouse. He'd relayed the shocking details of how, that very afternoon, not twenty-odd feet from Byron Priestly's murder, Dr. Meredyth Sanger had been "wrestled to the floor and a gun wrested from her" by security personnel who had then turned her over to city police officers. Lincoln's aide, Officer Jonah Kent, could not find any record of an arrest having been made.

Lincoln had assured Judge Manning that he would personally look into it, but that was when Kent had put through Sergeant Stan Kelton, who'd called to give his captain a heads-up regarding two ITRT raids authorized by Stonecoat—one on a funeral parlor, and the other on the Harris County courthouse annex building.

Now he had listened to reports filtering in from both locations, learning of the ghastly discoveries at each site. He could not imagine what had tipped Lucas off to a body awaiting police at the courthouse, and he tried to picture two security guards having to wrestle Dr. Sanger in her Ivanna wear to the marbled courthouse floor for a gun. Even harder to picture was the disruption of a Mexican wake down at that funeral home. He tried to imagine the mayhem there, the mix of horror surrounding the discovery of the disembodied arms coming on the heels of the natural outpouring of grief with the passing of a loved one.

But he had made his priority Meredyth Sanger's safety and well-being, and to this end, he'd been calling around trying to determine where she might be, fearing she was in some holding cell in another precinct, when he'd gotten the call from Lucas on site at the courthouse informing him that she was with him. *Those two're spending a hell of a lot of time together,* he'd paused to note.

He had been assured by Lucas that both scenes, courthouse annex and funeral parlor, had been secured and an ongoing investigation was in the works at both locations. The use of the ITRT units, while hell on his budget, had proven Stonecoat's instincts correct all the same. The "medicine man," some in the department called him, and he did seem to have some kind of magical powers of investigation at times. Certainly, his reputation as a hunter-tracker was well deserved.

Given Lucas's assurances, Lincoln had seen no need to rush to either of the scenes, at least not yet. Later, as the CSI units were winding down and could give him a full report, then perhaps he could stand before the microphones and cameras and give a guarded statement.

He started for the window and once there, examined the traffic going down Kensington, wondering if the trip home would be in gridlock. He stared at his gold watch. It was nearing four P.M., and he'd wanted to get out of the city for an engagement party at the Threepenny Oaks Country Club for his daughter and soon-to-be son-in-law, a nice young man in a safe occupation, textiles. He didn't want his daughter, Serena, to be a cop's wife, a fireman's wife, or a soldier's wife, to suffer the unrelenting stresses of being in her mother's shoes. Her mother had heartily agreed, telling Lincoln, who'd been in the service, and had once been a fireman, "I wouldn't wish some of my nights on a dog. Still, Gordon, I wouldn't have had it any other way. I love you."

Do I want to deal with this shit now or not? he wondered of the Sanger business at the courthouse. He had remained standing at his desk, calling for his car to be brought around as soon as he had finished with Lieutenant Stonecoat and Dr. Sanger.

No sooner had he given the order than Lucas and Meredyth arrived in the outer office. The aide, Officer Kent, informed Lincoln of their arrival.

"Well, send them in now!"

"Yes, sir, Captain, oh . . . and you wanted me to remind you, sir, of Serena's engagement party tonight."

"Yes, yes, I remember, I'm not a dolt."

"But, sir, you asked me to—"

"Just send those two in, Kent! Get 'em in here now!"

Kent escorted them through the door and sullenly closed it behind him. "Something big's happened on the Post-it case," Lucas said.

Meredyth simultaneously said, "We believe Lauralie Blodgett is not some poor kid brainwashed and frightened, but in fact the leader and dominant force behind the Ripper killings."

"That's quite a leap. You want to tell me what's changed?"

"We suspect she's manipulating the boyfriend. She's demonstrated a history of manipulating people. She's behind the choice of Mira Lourdes as victim, to create a clue out of her very body that would take me back to 1984."

"Whoa, slow down. What's 1984 got to do with this case?"

Lucas rattled the air with the court document she'd gotten from the archives. "Tell him about this, Mere. Tell Captain Lincoln the entire story from the moment we entered the convent school till we discovered Byron's body."

Lincoln sat down, an expectant look on his face, ready for the two of them to show him something. Meredyth leaned over the desk and said, "In the end, her fantasy is so off the wall, you have to *suspend* your natural tendency toward *disbelief* in order to believe it."

"Like any good fiction," Lincoln said, smiling.

"But this is not fiction. It's her game board."

"Game board?"

"She's a controlling, conniving woman, Captain, and she's laid all this out from the beginning," replied Meredyth.

"Really? From her photo, she *looks* like an innocent schoolgirl."

"We've known child killers before," countered Meredyth. "I'm staking my professional reputation on this, Captain."

"You may have already done so, given the theatrics at the courthouse, your having been pinned to the ground and reportedly transported off in a cruiser, and what, let off after being given a ride home? Meanwhile, your longtime friend is left behind murdered."

"I'll be proven right, when everything comes out . . . vindicated in time, I can prom—"

Lincoln put up a finger to gesture for her to hold on one minute. He made a call to his wife, explaining a break in the Ripper case had come and that he would not be making his daughter's engagement party on time if at all. After a bit of back and forth, he hung up with repeated apologies. He then turned back to Meredyth and said, "Now, start from the beginning, Dr. Sanger, and this better be good."

"I'll try to connect all the dots for you. Lucas can catch me if I forget anything. This case has more twists in it than a pretzel."

"Start at the beginning and please, get on with it," he ordered.

She did so. "As I said, it starts in 1984 when I was an eighteen-year-old intern at the courthouse. It starts with a six-month-old child I helped place in an orphanage for adoption, a girl named Lauralie Blodgett." She explained the significance of the victim's name, Lourdes, and how clues had been left for her and Lucas to connect the name to Our Lady of Miracles, to Mother Orleans and her questionable death, to Katherine Blodgett and her questionable death, coming full circle back to Meredyth's connection to Katherine and to her daughter in 1984. When finished, she held out the yearbook photo of Lauralie she had kept in her purse, so different from the head shot used in the press.

Lincoln studied the full body shot. "Voluptuous for an eighteen-year-old graduate, isn't she?"

"And she knows how to use it," remarked Lucas.

Meredyth continued, telling him about the record of how, as a young intern, she had signed off on Katherine Croombs giving up her daughter to the Catholic orphanage.

"I called Jack Tebo, my landlord, and asked him to look at the photo in the *Chronicle*," Lucas told Lincoln. "Jack ID'd her, saying she looked older than the girl in the photo, but that it was a dead ringer."

"So he positively identified her as the courier?" asked Lincoln.

"No hedging, sir."

"So we have her delivering a package, and you suspect her of multiple murder. But which of the two can you prove?"

"I believe if she's caught, she'll confess to all her crimes," began Meredyth, stepping to the window and looking out on the late afternoon traffic below. "In fact, I think that's precisely what she wants from us in the end."

"Whoa, I don't follow you, Doctor. She wants what in the end?"

"Wants us to give her a *forum,* a courtroom in which she can vocalize her pent-up rage and anger at all of us, Captain, at you, me, Lucas, the system."

"It's why she's playing the game, *peppering* the yellow brick road with clues for us to follow," said Lucas. "The Our Lady and Morte de Arthur's return addresses, the contempt shown for her father's grave site, the tackiness of how she buried her mother, the clues she left at the scene of her mother's murder, her selection of a victim named Lourdes *purposely* for us to make the connection, leading Meredyth to her own past association with Lauralie. And now these recent atrocities at the funeral home and the annex."

Meredyth turned from the window and added, "These aren't coincidences, but cries for help, pity, understanding— at least from Lauralie's perspective, she thinks she *deserves* our understanding, and perhaps, to some degree the monster was created by us."

"Lauralie Blodgett just graduated. Where do graduates go?" asked Lincoln.

"Most go on a field trip to D.C. or Disneyland," replied Lucas, "but I think Lauralie went to Greenhaven Cemetery to deface her father's gravestone instead."

"Many grads go on to college. Have you checked area colleges for a Lauralie Blodgett or Croombs registering for classes?"

"If not college, then an apprenticeship. Wait a moment." Meredyth got on the phone and called Mother Elizabeth

Portsmith. When she got her on the phone, Meredyth asked, "What did Lauralie want to become when she grew up? What profession did she wish to pursue?"

"She loved animals. Always kept a small pet. They'd always die on her. She wanted to be a vet."

"A vet. Did she have a school picked out?"

"She was looking at several in the area, but I don't know that she ever actually enrolled. Still, there's a chance she did."

"Thank you, Mother Superior."

"Will you please call me when and if you locate my girl?" she asked.

"Yes, surely."

"Dreadful seeing her picture on the TV screen alongside that killer. You must stop such nasty rumors."

"We'll see what we can do, Mother, and thanks again.

"Veterinary schools in the area. We need to check all of them," she told the men.

"Then let's find her, and when we do, we drag her and her boyfriend in here, and we put them in the pressure cooker and grill their asses until we get a confession from one or the other or both." Lincoln called Kent on the intercom to come in with a city directory.

Lucas now stood at the window with Meredyth, a protective hand on her shoulder. He said to Lincoln, "That lunatic was at the courthouse, shadowing Meredyth for a reason. She's plotting to harm her physically now, now that she's already torn away at her emotionally. It's the reason she's been shadowing us, first at the convent, leaving the finger in the fount, and then at the courthouse."

"All right," said Lincoln, "it's going to be a long night. Everyone on the team needs to be brought in on this. Let's pray she has a school transcript, and we work from the information there outward. We'll send cruisers to every damned veterinary school in the city and the suburbs if necessary, and we'll corner this young hellion."

"Someone in this city has to have some idea where these two are holed up and who they are," Lucas reassured Meredyth. "No one is invisible."

Kent entered with the Houston directory. Lincoln told him to go out and return with directories for the suburbs as well. "And order us in some food."

"What do you feel like, sir? Pizza, burgers, Chinese?"

"Anything, Kent, so long as it's hot. And close the door."

Lucas had quickly found the listings for veterinary schools in the city. "We'll start calling the task force together, Captain, bring them up to date, if you want to get out of here, attend that party for your girl."

Meredyth added, "We can get the word out on the vet schools just as well as you, Gordon. Go on. You can still make your daughter's day."

"Thanks, Doctor, Lucas. Are you two sure you can handle things without me?"

"Sure we can," replied Meredyth.

"All right then. Use my office as long as you need it. Food is on me." He passed Officer Kent, whose arms were full with directories, on the way out, giving one last instruction to his aide. "Get these two everything and anything they need, Kent, and call your wife, tell her you'll be pulling a double shift."

Kent frowned and dropped the additional directories on his boss's desk.

LATER THAT EVENING, the entire Post-it Ripper task force was brought together and brought up to date. Meredyth and Lucas again told their startling story of how Meredyth's friend Byron had died, and how she and anyone close to her had become targets of Lauralie Blodgett's obsession, and the twisted reasoning behind the postings of Mira Lourdes's body parts.

The late edition of the *Chronicle* carried both photos of Lauralie now alongside that of the mole-faced charcoal likeness of her accomplice. Along with this, the photo carried a cryptic history of how she was a recent graduate from Our Lady of Miracles School. Anyone with any information on Lauralie's whereabouts, or those of the mysterious Mr. X, was asked to call authorities immediately. Both suspects were considered armed and dangerous in this updated version forwarded to the press. On page three, the story of an unnamed body found in a closet in the court-room annex appeared with sketchy details. The story of the bizarre shutdown of a funeral parlor across the city in which police found severed arms inside the casket during an ongoing wake said the severed arms lay across the chest and were discovered by loved ones at the casket just as police arrived. The story went on to detail the name of the parlor and the deceased woman, hinting at some connection to the Post-it Ripper case. It quoted Dr. Frank Patterson as having said, "Mrs. Zoradia Ortiz's family members were questioned, but none of them are believed to have played any part in this unfortunate event. Crime-scene analysis both here and at the courthouse annex today points to the Post-it Ripper, who appears to have found another way to send his message, in a larger box, so to speak. A cryptic note left in the casket and tissue analysis is expected to confirm this."

A bank of phones had been secured along with men and women to man them, and calls were being made to every veterinary school in and around Houston in an attempt to locate one registered student by name. Meanwhile, the rest of the task force was introduced to the idea that an orphaned girl had been both the *motivating and driving force* behind the abduction and murder of Mira Lourdes. It required Meredyth's having to go through the details once again, and as the inexplicable tale began to unfold, all the others sat in rapt attention, curious over the next twist and the final turn.

"A story worthy of an Agatha Christie novel," said Leonard Chang, who had by now read both Nielsen's and Patterson's field reports. Chang, Nielsen, the others in the CSI unit, Detective North and her partners who had interrogated Dwayne Stokes, the young sketch artist, Anna Tewes, Sergeant Kelton, Dr. Catrina Purvis, and Dr. Tom Davies all now had a better understanding of why the killers, Lauralie Blodgett and her unnamed associate, had committed two hideous murder mutilations. They were also apprised of the suspicious deaths of Sara Orleans, Katherine Croombs, and the brutal details in the stabbing death of Byron Priestly.

Questions flew. Everyone wanted answers. Mistakes and oversights became apparent, especially in the handling of the presumed overdose death of Katherine Croombs. Frank Patterson had slipped in as they revisited the Croombs case. Frank quietly found a chair in a corner as there was no room left around the conference table. He sat silent in shadow, not contributing or objecting.

"All this is very intriguing and compelling," said Jana North, "and you two obviously believe in this pure and twisted revenge theory, but we're no closer to finding this woman, and we still have no idea who the accomplice is. No one seems to know the extent of his involvement, that is, what *his* motives or rewards are. Why has he done her bidding? Who is he to her? Are they related? What sort of a relationship do they share? What binds him to her? Is he merely following her orders, or is he an *encourager,* a cheerleader, possibly *the* leader, dominating her and pushing her over the edge? Or is it the other way around? Is *she* the driving force in their twisted relationship as Lucas and Meredyth have come to believe?"

"All questions impossible to answer with any certainty until the killing couple is captured and interrogated, and the truth wrenched from them," replied Lucas.

Meredyth said unequivocally, "He's her lapdog, pure and simple. She's in charge."

Jana North wasn't so sure. "Female murderers are rare. Only eight women have ever made the FBI's Most Wanted List."

"But don't you see, that's what drives her!" shouted Meredyth. "She wants to be *our* most wanted, maybe the *ninth* female on the FBI's Most Wanted. She wants to be on John Walsh's *America's Most Wanted,* on CNN. NBC, MSNBC, ABC, CBS, Fox, *20/20,* and *48 Hours.*"

"Take a breath, Mere," warned Lucas.

Meredyth didn't skip a beat. "This bitch wants the notoriety of the D.C. Sniper, and so she wins either way; whether we succeed in catching her or killing her, she wins. She gets to rise out of the obscurity of a life behind the gates of Our Lady's orphanage to world prominence as a serial killer with a new M.O., a new twist."

"She's not a proven serial killer, Dr. Sanger," said Nielsen. "Agreed, we suspect her in her mother's death, but that's a long way from proof, and we have even less evidence in the death of this nun, Orleans, and we can't be certain Lauralie actually swung the blade that killed Priestly, nor the ax that decapitated Mira Lourdes."

"She's intending to kill me next!" Meredyth exploded, her fist coming down on the table, silencing Nielsen and everyone else in the room.

For a long moment, no one said anything, all eyes on Meredyth, who finally broke the silence. "She's killed four times now, and she has intended from the beginning to make a statement. She is *becoming* a celebrity as we speak, a serial killer celeb to-to gain all the attention she can to-to shine a bright light on herself, her *heart-rending* personal story. She's obsessed with it."

Silence met Meredyth, all eyes staring at her, some of those eyes mutely asking if she were not obsessed with *it* and perhaps ought to be removed from the case as too emotionally involved. Breaking the awkward silence, Leonard Chang said, "Perhaps Dr. Sanger is correct in all she has said here tonight. After all, since Lauralie has *intentionally* left arrows in the sand for us to follow—*to the convent, to the funeral parlor, to the mother's home, to the courthouse*—all of it pointing to her being abandoned and *pawned off* as an infant in 1984, then she has masterminded the entire affair, so that despite whether Crazy Joe, as Lucas calls him, wielded the poison that killed her mother, the ax that killed Lourdes, and the knife that killed Priestly, she then emerges as the dominating force in the relationship."

Lucas picked up on this, adding, "We all know the history of killers who work in tandem. One is *always* submissive to the will of the other. While in most cases, the submissive one is younger, often female, we're looking at an older male submissive to a younger female."

Several people in the room spoke up.

"Information, how do we get more of it about Lauralie?"

"Her current whereabouts."

"Who she's associated with since leaving the school."

"Where she's been hanging, as they say," said Jana.

"We have people manning phones as we speak," Lucas assured them. "Trying to locate Lauralie through a possible lead—veterinary school transcripts."

"Vet schools?" asked Nielsen. "They learn how to use anesthetics, scalpels, sutures, and other medical instruments in vet schools."

"Mother Elizabeth says Lauralie had expressed an interest in pursuing a career as a vet," Lucas added. "By the way, our hot line on the case is racking up hundreds of tips, and these are being weighed and analyzed by our best people, led by Stan *the Man* Kelton. New wrinkle, Dr. Sanger here has put up a substantial reward of twenty-five thousand dollars for info leading to an arrest and conviction.

"Which has been matched by the Texas Department of Law Enforcement," added Lucas. "They're also lending support in following up on tips in the field."

"Fifty thousand, okay. That ought to bring out the rats, both those with and those without any idea of who Lauralie is or where she is," complained Frank Patterson. "We'll be lucky to ferret out the real tips from the goofballs."

Kelton added, "We've already had sixteen separate confessions to the crime, all of which have failed the litmus tests."

"Which revolves around the wording of the notes?" asked Davies.

"And the details of the packing material and what was in each box. So far, no winners." Kelton secured his nervously twitching left hand with his right, and then tucked both beneath the table in his lap.

"So now we're all on the same page, people," said Lucas to the assembled task force. "As new information becomes available, from whatever direction, please share it with the group."

The meeting broke up, and people were filing out when an officer in uniform pushed through, in his hands a brightly colored green, blue, and white parcel clearly marked *FedEx Ground*. "It's addressed to Detective Stonecoat," he announced. "Return address is odd—Greenhaven Meadows Cemetery on Berwyn at Ridge Avenue. We thought it peculiar and suspicious."

Lucas shouted for everyone to sit back down. The task force reluctantly returned to their conference room seats, the memory of the last box opened in this room fresh in their minds. "Has it been X-rayed?" Kelton asked the officer who had brought it.

"Our scanner is down, sir. But from the odor and the sheer weight, I'd say it isn't donuts or office supplies."

Chang slowed things, saying, "We have a sonar scanner upstairs that will do the trick, and we need to go for necessary tools and a cooler as well as a sheet to lay everything out on."

"I'll get what we need," Lynn Nielsen assured Chang.

"Dr. Patterson will help you out, Dr. Nielsen."

Nielsen darted a barbed but brief glance in Chang's direction, began to object, but decided to do as told instead. Patterson, in exaggerated politeness, stood holding the door for Nielsen.

Everyone else was told to take ten minutes but to not disappear. Most ran for rest rooms or the coffee and snack machines at a nearby lounge filled with plastic chairs, tables, and bulletin boards. When everyone had returned, remembering Anna Tewes losing it the last time they'd assembled, no one had food or coffee in hand.

After fifteen minutes had passed, Nielsen and Patterson returned, Lynn pushing a sleek steel cart, heavy with all the items Chang had called for, Patterson holding the door again. Nielsen wheeled the cart to where Chang motioned he wanted it. Atop it sat a compact sonar scanner attached to a computer accompanied by a monitor. From a shelf below the cart, Nielsen produced an ice-filled cooler, the sheet, and an array of metal instruments from a box cutter to a scalpel, and a large needle for drawing fluids. As Lynn Nielsen worked, Frank Patterson retreated back into his corner seat. He'd taken his cue from Chang to sit down and leave things to Dr. Nielsen. Frank's stiff body language spoke of a mix of hurt pride and anger. He'd have liked to take a more proactive role here in the presentation—as he had at the funeral parlor as lead CSI investigator. Instead, Chang had chosen to rely on Lynn Nielsen.

With the room darkened, using the sonar scan, Dr. Chang pointed to the computer monitor atop the cart and the image coming through. It was at first difficult to make out—the image flat, without depth or contrast, dreary gray, grainy, until some resolution was created by Nielsen, who handled the wand over the FedEx box. After a moment, Chang, using a light pointer, highlighted a flattened female areola, the nipple like an eye at the center. Around this there appeared a crush of flesh. "It appears to be the breast of a woman, but skewed, flattened as against a windowpane, and to the left, a half-hidden open flesh wound." The light pointer danced about the ugly image as he spoke. "Upper torso . . . here is clavicle area, you see, here in upper left-hand corner of this coffin is a shoulder ridge. Other shoulder blurred by what appears a tumor or bloody mass. My guess, the contents are a woman's upper torso and severed breasts."

To most in the room, the scanner image was one gray mass of unreadable flesh. Both Chang and Nielsen looked hard at the monitor image in a kind of professional fascination.

Leonard switched off his light pointer and asked for the lights to come up. Once they did, the image diffused into gray nothingness. Chang lifted the box cutter, carefully leaned in over the box itself, and began opening the bulging parcel—measured during the break as thirty-two inches in width by forty inches in height.

Everyone watched in silence as the tape split noisily under the blade, and Leonard's gloved hands trembled slightly as he pulled back the flaps and everyone held a collective breath. Leonard stared down into the box. Lucas had never seen Chang go white before, but he did now.

"Doctor, are you all right?" Lynn Nielsen asked him, placing a hand on his shoulder.

Chang shook it off. "As I said, it's her upper torso, jammed in tightly. The breasts have been severed and stuffed in as well. It will not *all* possibly fit into one cooler, Dr. Nielsen." Chang wiped his sweating brow with a handkerchief. "If any of you care to see it up close, it will be in my lab upstairs. I see no purpose in displaying it here as—"

"Thank God," moaned Anna Tewes.

"Yes, indeed," added Dr. Purvis.

Chang continued. "—as any further display here will *not* add to our knowledge of the killer or whereabouts of same." Chang lifted the box and hefted its contents onto the cart behind the monitor. The cart was balanced precariously, and the wheels, skidding as a result, almost caused the vile parcel to tilt over and spill out its contents. With lightning reflexes, Lucas shot out a foot and steadied the wheel, allowing Leonard to hold onto the box, right it, and steady it. Once all was safe again, Leonard, with Nielsen's help, exited with the cart and its strange cargo. Nielsen helped guide the cart to the elevators. They had left behind the forensic tools, the sheet, and the cooler. Using the sheet, Frank Patterson began to bundle these up.

Everyone else soon followed one another through the door, walking like pallbearers after having seen the latest pieces of Mira Lourdes come through the door. Hoskins quietly muttered to Perelli, "Lincoln's going to hit high-G when he hears about this."

Lucas and Meredyth remained behind, the sound of Frank's rattling instruments, as he rolled them up, like a sad litany accompanying the procession of the others. "All the coroner's horses, and all the coroner's men, could not put Mira Lourdes back together again," Frank said.

Lucas and Meredyth turned to stare at the man, who next said, "At the now-accelerated rate, we shall one day have all of Ms. Lourdes back . . . her *back,* front as well, side-to-side, up-and-down pieces, the over, under, above, and below of her."

"What is it you want, Frank?" asked Lucas.

"Just talk. Leonard at first held some notion he might miraculously stitch all the parts into one, but I suspect a judicious cremation of the parts is in order for the grieving family now. Otherwise, she's going to look like Frankenstein's bride in the casket."

Lucas pursed his lips and nodded at Chang's second in command in the M.E.'s office. "Sounds like a better plan indeed, Frank."

Lucas led Meredyth toward the door.

"Look here, you two, has it occurred to either of you that we need the full resources of the FBI on this case? And I mean right away, like yesterday?"

"We're told that Captain Lincoln is keeping them informed," said Meredyth.

"They're clamoring to come aboard, and he's keeping them *informed*?" asked Patterson, a slight man with pinched features. "We all know that the killer's use of the mail makes this a federal crime—screwing with the U.S. Postal Service. We also know that we can only keep control of the case if we invite their help and resources *now*, at our invitation," he repeated. "Otherwise, at any moment, they'll come swooping in and simply take charge entirely, waving us *all* good-bye."

"Technically speaking, Frank, the Ripper hasn't actually posted anything through the U.S. mails. Fact is, prior to the FedEx box, everything had been hand-delivered, save for the UPS delivery at the station house."

"What's your interest, Dr. Patterson?" asked Meredyth. "Do you think a high-profile case can raise your profile?"

"I have a well-established reputation in my field, Dr. Sanger, and I resent the implications of your question. As for my interest? It is the same as any citizen, any law-enforcement officer, the same as yours, Dr. Sanger."

"And that is?" pressed Meredyth.

"I want to see an *end* to this horror! To see the perpetrators apprehended and punished to the fullest extent of the law. Short of that"—he stepped up to the table and balanced his slight frame against it—"I'd like to see someone of Lucas's *ilk* here *kill* the perpetrators before they can take another inch off their victim. Think of it—treating her body like a frozen Popsicle, taking it from a freezer, slicing off this piece and that, returning it to deep freeze for another go at shocking you, Dr. Sanger."

"And you think the FBI can sooner end this thing than we can?" asked Lucas.

"Well, Lucas, you must admit, from all appearances, Dr. Sanger, and you by extension, have been led by the nose by a juvenile who, whether you care to admit it or not, has gotten you both where she wants you—on an emotional roller coaster. You've played right into the bitch's hands. You say she's manipulating her accomplice! What has she done to you, Dr. Sanger?"

"We're out ahead of her, Dr. Patterson. You can tell your pals in the federal building that," countered Meredyth.

"Out ahead of her? Everyone in this room tonight questions your objectivity, Doctor. As a forensic psychiatrist, knowing of such a personal stake in the outcome of any *other* criminal case, you would yourself recommend to Captain Lincoln that any officer or detective so closely *linked* to a suspect be *removed from duty* and certainly not placed in charge."

"Is that your opinion?" she asked. "Are you finished?"

"Yes, Frank is finished," said Lucas, taking her by the arm, escorting her out.

"Just one man's opinion," Frank shouted after them.

Lucas turned on him. "An opinion you've no doubt shared with the FBI?"

"I know my duty."

"And how much duty have you given the press?"

"I didn't go to the FBI. They *came* to *me*. I told them what I knew, what I gleaned from Chang and Nielsen, and today at the funeral parlor. The note left there—'*Arm in arm, we'll wrap ourselves in the warmth of childhood carousels, to dream round and round in flesh pound for bloody pound.'* This woman is in a competitive battle with you, Meredyth. You are a liability to this case unless handled properly by people who have had experience with such killers as this—the contrary murderer who will match you step for step."

Everyone on the task force had seen the note left in Zoradia Ortiz's coffin at the funeraral home, written in the same hand as the previous cryptic communiques. As with the others, they gave profilers and investigators few to no clues. Everyone would be analyzing the meaning of "childhood carousel" now. Meredyth already knew it referred to Lauralie's life in comparison to Meredyth's "dream" childhood. Lauralie was at one end of the spectrum of this carousel, Meredyth at the other.

"So long as we have Captain Lincoln's confidence, Dr. Patterson," Meredyth firmly said, "Lucas and I will pursue this case as lead investigators on the task force that we and Gordon Lincoln assembled."

"I wish you only success and a speedy one at that." Patterson, his bundle of instruments held close to his chest, pushed past them and was gone. But the odor of his cologne, thrown on heavily to mask the odors of the coroner's lab, lingered.

"I think we can expect a raking-over in the printed pages tonight or tomorrow, Mere," said Lucas.

"And a visit from the FBI soon after," she agreed.

"Creep Patterson. He's always chummed up to local FBI. I suspect he's shining their badges because he actually thinks it's his way through the back door. He's bucking for his own lab where he can call the shots—God help us! He knows he'll never be head of the HPD Crime Lab so long as Leonard continues to write up his annual evaluations."

"I felt the tension between them."

"Politics."

"Positioning."

They had started out the door and down the corridor when Stan Kelton met them in the hallway. "We may have a break in the case," he said.

"Whataya got, Stan?"

"Aside from some promising tips, we've located a school where Lauralie Blodgett registered for classes this year."

"Terrific! Where's the school located?"

"Harkness at Balboa, the Dean V. King School of Veterinary Medicine. I dispatched a radio car to the address she left with the registrar. They're watching the place, but won't move in until they hear from us regarding a warrant."

Lucas and Meredyth recognized the address as that of Katherine Croombs's place. "We've already canvased the place. She's not there, Stan."

"My, but she's been a busy girl," he replied.

Meredyth asked, "Stan, did they get a list of her classes and teachers?"

"It's on its way to us now. Let me check the fax."

They followed Stan to find the information waiting for them. Lucas and Meredyth closely studied Lauralie's registration form and signature. She'd signed up for three classes, two of which she was failing miserably. The third, Intro Surg Pro, she somehow had a B average in. The name of the instructor was A. Belkvin.

"What the hell is Intro Surg Pro?" asked Kelton.

"Introduction to Surgical Procedures. I know, makes your skin crawl in light of what we know about her," answered Meredyth. "And look at her signature, Lucas." Studying it, Meredyth added. "It may give us a glimpse into her personality. Notice the fanciful swirls, the looping Ls, the exaggerated crossing of the Ts, the G dipping so low, the capitals and the T's reaching so high."

"Sorry to sound like a broken record, but what does it mean?" asked Kelton.

"Means she's self-indulgent, a thrill-seeking exhibitionist freak, out for all the attention she can gather."

Lucas added, "She ought to've put all this negative energy into the theater. Could've been a hell of an actress, the next Vivian Leigh."

"She has her stage," countered Meredyth, "and her audience. All of us in the real world. The subject of an

APB, a BOLO. Certainly has our attention . . . subject of a nationwide hunt being played out on the front pages. She's created this lady of satanic divination who frightens us all; the bogeyman has become *bogeywoman*."

At the bottom of the faxed copy of Lauralie's registration form, in tiny, tight script, a hastily written note ran the length of the page. It'd been written, presumably by someone working in the registrar's office. It read: *"Ms. L. Blodgett is on verge of being dropped from classes due to failing grades and mounting attendance problems as she has failed to reply to repeated notices to see her counselor, Dr. Arthur Belkvin."*

"Belkvin, as in her instructor in Introductory Surgical Procedures? The one class she's passing?" asked Lucas.

"Kind of odd, I agree," said Meredyth.

"What? What's odd, the note scribbled on her registration form?" asked Kelton, trying to keep up.

"That the only class she's getting a passing grade in is taught by her *counselor*," replied Lucas.

Meredyth added, "And yet, according to the note, she has failed to report into him regarding problems with attendance. Looks and smells like a rat."

"Certainly incongruous." Lucas reread the registration form. "She's signed up for Zoolog Anat—"

"Zoological Anatomy," interjected Meredyth.

"—and Ca Teeth Extr."

"Canine Teeth Extraction." It made them both think of the teeth extracted from Mira Lourdes.

Lucas said, "We need to talk to this guy Belkvin, see what he can tell us about our girl."

"Are you kidding, Lucas? I want to meet this guy and see how he stacks up against our composite. He could well be our Crazy Joe Boyfriend."

"Older man, weak, easy prey for her . . . knows how to use a scalpel, a bone saw." Lucas ran a hand through his long hair.

"Belkvin . . . Belkvin," Stan Kelton began to chant. "Sounds damn familiar somehow."

"What's the number of the school, Stan?" asked

Meredyth. "I want to get this Professor Counselor Belkvin on the line."

Stan read the number off as Meredyth called from Stan's desk. The others listened to her side of the conversation. "I see . . . yes . . . agreed . . . absolutely. We can do that, uh-huh, yes, sir, Dr. Price. You have my word. We will look in on him. Can I get the address, phone number? That'd be good too, yes." She abruptly hung up, leaving Lucas and Stan to stare at her satisfied smile.

"What?" asked Lucas.

"Seems our Dr. Arthur Belkvin has been AWOL . . . classes canceled without notice twice over the past two mornings, and this A.M. he's again a no-show, but this time not even a notice given. The department chairman, Dr. Charles Price, said they've been unable to reach Dr. Belkvin at his home or his practice. Said it was becoming a concern for them."

"Belkvin," muttered Stan Kelton. "I tell you, that sounds familiar. Hold on a minute."

Stan returned to his desk, having to tell a growing number of people, both police officers and civilians, to hold their respective pants and requests while he conferred with his junior officer. Between the two men, they rifled though hundreds of phone-line tips as yet to be placed on the computer cross-referencing program. "Here's one of them, Sarge," said the junior officer.

"Here's the other," announced Kelton. He then handed the two reports to Lucas and Meredyth to review while he helped clear away the growing numbers confronting him.

"Two calls, both saying their *vet* fits the description of Mr. X in the *Chronicle*," said Lucas. "You'd think we'd have some similar tips from the guy's students at this King vet school."

"Students don't read anything but what's on the curriculum these days, and as for picking up a newspaper or watching CNN, they're too busy with role-playing video games and going to the movies to concern themselves with current events. I've taught, I know. When the D.C. Sniper shootings were going on, none of my students had an inkling until I put them onto it, and you know how saturated our lives had become with it."

"Scary."

"I got Dr. Arthur Belkvin's full name, SS number, street address for home and practice from Dr. Price," Meredyth told him. "And maybe now Jorganson can ram through search warrants for us?"

"If the bastards won't give us a go-ahead, we'll call in the ITRT again, but for the sake of building a case against this guy and Lauralie, who I suspect we will find living with him, let's go the warrant route first."

"So long as we put this investigation in motion."

Lucas grabbed the desk phone and called the D.A.'s office, telling Harry Jorganson what they'd uncovered. "Sounds like plenty of probable cause, and since the courthouse incident, I don't think I'm going to have trouble finding a sympathetic judge, Lucas. Meet you at the man's practice. The home warrant will come by way of my legal aide, Phil Merrick."

"We'll make the raids simultaneously. I think the noose is around the right neck, Harry."

No sooner had he hung up Stan's desk phone than his cell phone rang into life. He picked up to find Jana North speaking in an excited manner. "We got a an interesting development over here in Missing Persons, a report filed on a doctor of veterinary medicine gone missing for forty-eight hours, Lucas. The report was filed by his receptionist, a MariLouise Jones."

"Go on."

"Says her boss has missed appointments, surgeries, and such. Also says he looks a little like the artist sketch on our killer. This doggy doc's name is—"

"Arthur Belkvin," Lucas finished for her.

"Right, but how the hell'd you know?"

"We've got a warrant for his practice and home in the works. We have reason to believe he's the male half of the Post-it Ripper duo."

"I want in, Lucas."

"You've got it. Take a team of your best to this address."

He gave her the home address. "Phil Merrick from the D.A.'s will meet you there with a warrant. We'll cover the man's practice. Careful, these people are armed and dangerous."

"Imagine it, Lucas, our big bad boogeyman who cuts people into cubes turns out to be an animal lover . . . a doggy doctor."

Lucas hung up. "Let's get over to the clinic. Detective North's people're going to coordinate the raid on the house."

"I'll be damned," said Meredyth.

"What's that?" asked Lucas.

"Lauralie's little game takes on a new twist. She selects a man named Arthur at a vet school named King to do her bidding. King Arthur . . . Morte de Arthur's, the funeral home? Is it only coincidence?"

"A king with a set of surgical tools and hairy mole on his cheek."

"She's using him just as she's used people all her life."

Lucas said, "Says here his office is on JFK Drive, South, the seedier side of the Sixth Ward."

"Let's go."

"I want in," Kelton said.

"For sure, Stan. Get us a tactical team for backup, and put Chang on notice we may call for him or Dr. Nielsen at either or both scenes. Ahhh, tell him we'd prefer Frank Patterson be kept out of it. Will you do that, Stan?"

"Consider it done. And I'll bring Lincoln up to par as well."

"See you at the kennel and surgery then, Stan."

"Count on it."

Lucas and Meredyth located his car, a sense of hope, of impending closure wanting to rush into their hearts, but they warned one another against it, keeping it at bay, dammed up by a cop's normal caution in the face of optimism, a reining-in emotion called prudence, which spoke the language of care and vigilance. They had been wrong before; eyewitnesses had been proved wrong in case after case. The professor and veterinarian could well be missing for a thousand and one reasons, none having the remotest to do with Lauralie Blodgett or a murder spree. They could be entirely wrong about Belkvin.

Nevertheless, Lucas intended serving two warrants to open up his entire life to their scrutiny.

CHAPTER 16

Bear track: good omen

DETECTIVE JANA NORTH had the door knocked in by SWAT team operatives, and instantly Dr. Arthur Belkvin's private little world became public.

The men who stormed in and locked down each area, room by room, shouted out their findings. "Clear!"

"Clear in the kitchen!"

"Bedroom's secure."

"No one here!"

"Basement, all clear."

"Garage, all clear."

Jana began combing the rooms for any sign of Mira Lourdes ever having been here. She found instead a tidy, well-kept little apartment home with a garage out back, neighbors at each elbow, their windows close enough to spit into. She found plaques, certificates, licenses, awards, blue ribbons for first prize in area and state championship dog shows, and proud postings of the champions, a pair of greyhounds. In fact, animal photos adorned every wall and passageway. Whoever Arthur was, he proved a fanatical dog lover and a competitive one.

Evidence of several missing dogs, she mentally noted from food dishes with flies in them to photos of Belkvin with a large Dalmatian and two greyhounds, all caught in play, each photo pinned to the fridge by tiny dog-bone magnets. Turning the most prominent Dalmatian photo in her hand, she saw the block printing on the back read, *Pongo and me, 1997.* "Wonder where ol' Pongo must be now," she said, handing the photo over to Merrick.

Merrick's thin face pinched as he studied the photo. "Likely pounded someplace nearby. Maybe at Belkvin's practice. Looks like he loves the mutt, don't it. Guy looks as harmless as my brother-in-law."

She lifted another photo with Belkvin crouched between two greyhounds. The inscription on the back read, *Petie and Fritz, Fall 2001.*

Search as she might, she could find not a single item in the house that could be of the least importance to their case.

"All right, take this place apart!" she ordered her detectives. "I don't want a single unturned matchbook."

"Don't look to be a smoker to me," replied Phil Merrick, the warrant folded beneath the two dog pictures he'd laid over it now. "You guys got a bum steer. Look at this place. Guy has at least two, maybe three dogs, and it looks like the house that Mr. Clean built. My place, my kids have a hamster, but the house looks like a tornado ripped through."

"All the same, we're going to search thoroughly. I'm checking the back bedroom." She entered Belkvin's bedroom and angrily tore out bureau drawers, throwing clothing in the air. She came across sexually explicit magazines, X-rated videos, massaging vibrators, plugs, and assorted adult toys.

"Can't prosecute a guy for being horny, Detective," said Merrick from behind her.

She paid no heed to the junior D.A., going to the bed and tearing away the neat, tidy afghan and blanket to reveal soiled sheets.

Ahh-ha! Finally, evidence this jag-off actually ever spent time and bodily fluids here," taunted Merrick.

"Shut up or step outside, will you, Mr. Merrick. If Mira Lourdes was held here against her will, tied to this bed—"

"Was she sexually molested?"

"No way to know for certain with only her head to examine and none of her lower genitalia. Mouth was free of any discharges. That's all Chang could tell us."

"Yeah . . . forgot . . . sorry."

"Could possibly be some of her DNA on these sheets." She called out to one of her people, "Get a CSI unit to scour the place with blue lights for blood spatters and fingerprints, and bag the sheet." She'd already folded the sheet in on itself with gloved hands to preserve any fibers, hairs, and fluid stains. Setting the bundle aside now, she next upended the mattress, revealing more pornography beneath, this special cache displaying women in horrible submission and bondage, the pictures arousing some deep inner sexual feelings better left unaroused, she silently warned herself. But she was drawn to the photos of women roped and wrapped, their eyes covered, mouths gagged, and was mesmerized until Merrick startled her, yanking the bondage book from her hands, gazing at it liberally himself. "Still, like I said, can't put this guy away for porn and horn."

Jana ordered her men to box it all up. She then shouted for help, and with another detective, she upended the box springs. Below the bed, she finally found a place in need of vacuuming, dust bunnies flying.

"Damn it. He hasn't been using the place, not for some time," she told Merrick and the others. "We'll have to view the tapes he kept to determine if there's anything whatsoever bearing on the Ripper case."

"Who knows, you might get lucky," said Merrick. "Maybe he taped the abduction, murder, and mutilation of Mira Lourdes and left the video here for you guys to discover."

Exasperated and angry, Jana gave a fleeting moment's thought to the excitement and expectation that had catapulted her from headquarters to here. She had come with a

great hope, that they would find a mountain of evidence
here to tie Belkvin to Lauralie Blodgett, and signs pointing
a direct route to her whereabouts, and that this preponderance of evidentiary material would bury them both. Leaving with a box of videos, magazines, and dirty books, along
with a couple of photos of a guy who might, in a pinch,
pass for the man in the artist sketch, was a crushing blow.

She hated the thought of breaking the bad news to
Lucas and Meredyth. She hated what this awful woman
was doing to Meredyth, hurting Lucas in the bargain.
She'd come to realize, watching how Lucas behaved
around Meredyth, how very much he did love her, in a way
she herself hoped one day to be loved. For this reason, it
pained her greatly to see the two of them so victimized.
She, like many on the task force, had made a personal vow
to not sleep until the person responsible for the ungodly
packaging up of human remains to traumatize good and
caring people was caught and the assaults ended. And with
the murder of Byron Priestly, the resolve had become even
greater.

A little corner of her brain also told her she could be
misconstrued as being close to Meredyth Sanger—a girlfriend! She could be killed next because of a wrongful per-
ception, the victim of Lauralie Blodgett's semi-random,
somewhat predictable violence. But then so could Lucas;
in fact, Lucas presented a large and looming target. She
wondered if he'd given any thought to the threat hovering
over him, that he, more than anyone else in the Ripper's
viewfinder, represented Meredyth's present and future happiness and pleasure.

Jana secretly loved Lucas and would willingly die for
him; she wondered if he'd take her seriously if she offered
to stand bodyguard over him. Not likely. Not likely he
would allow it. The macho shit-head.

"What now?" asked one of her men as they were exiting
the house with the single box of confiscated pornography.

Neighbors on each side of the apartment and from
across the street had gathered, watching and wondering.
Jana North pointed to the small gathering of housewives

and retired folk and said to her man, "You and the others, fan out, and let's start interviewing. You know what to ask about. We got his vehicle info from papers found inside, and we've got his personal phone book. What we need are eyewitnesses to her comings and goings here."

Jana gave a fleeting thought to Lucas's tying her up like one of the women in Belkvin's bondage book. How she would enjoy being at the Cherokee's complete mercy.

"Damm it, North, get a grip," she muttered.

"What's that, Detective?" asked Merrick.

"Nothing . . . not a thing."

"I really am sorry nothing useful was found; despite my cynicism, I truly wanted this to go your way. From what I've read and seen of reports on this case, and what I've learned from my sources in police circles and forensics, this is one sick mothefucking little momma you guys are chasing."

"You know, Merrick, you aren't a half-bad-looking guy when you're not being so damn cynical."

"Really? Perhaps I ought to lighten up a bit, if it makes me more attractive to someone as attractive as you."

This got her attention, and she looked more closely at his eyes—good, strong, clear, moist icy-blue eyes. "Why, thank you, Merrick."

"Why don't you call me by my first name."

"I will if you will."

ACROSS TOWN, LUCAS and Meredyth took the warrant from Harry Jorganson's outstretched hand as if it were a baton in a footrace. Jorganson held back, wishing them good luck as they entered the Bright Day Animal Clinic. Dr. Arthur D. Belkvin's name was emblazoned on the sign below the clinic's name. Lucas and Meredyth held high but tempered expectations of finding evidence to prove this was the location of Mira Lourdes's murder.

Earlier, as they raced to the location, Lucas had confided, "Where else would he do her but at the site where the tools are readily available, his own cozy operating room in his own clinic? Where else would he feel safe to perform his deadly operations than in surroundings so familiar?"

"Perform is the right word, if he did it for Lauralie."

Inside, they found a blocky small building reminiscent of someone's basement, a small waiting room area scrunched against the reception desk, and a door leading to the rear, where two separate rooms for examinations and operations stood like barriers to the kennel in the rear.

"You hear that?" asked Lucas as they looked around, flashing their badges for Ms. Jones.

"What? I don't hear nothing," said MariLouise Jones.

"That's just it, a silent kennel."

"Oh, well . . . no, we haven't been operating so well since Dr. B's been gone."

A quick scan of the place revealed a storage room off the kennels, where the metal cages stood empty of occupants. It was a crowded little area, hardly worthy of the name kennel—a holding place for sick animals. The odors pinched Lucas's nerves.

However, the place was neat, tidy, and clean—too well cleaned, Lucas thought. If they were going to find evidence, it would be masked, he thought. Then he realized there was a gaping space in one of the examination rooms where once a steel table most assuredly had stood bolted to the concrete floor. "What's not in this room?" he asked Ms. Jones.

Ms. MariLouise Jones, a slender black woman with a pompadour hairdo and manicured nails painted red, stiffened at the question before answering. "Dr. Belkvin . . . he had to cut back on his practice sharply in the last few weeks, and he . . . he tol' me he *hadda* sell one of his operating tables."

"Anything else sold recently?" pressed Lucas.

"I noticed some of his older surgical tools gone one day."

"Recently?" asked Meredyth.

"Yeah, recently."

"Would those tools include a scalpel and a rotary bone saw?" asked Lucas.

"Am I in some *kinna* trouble here?" she asked where

she stood between the two strangers interrogating her. "Do I need a lawyer?"

Lucas bit his lower lip and instantly pulled out his cell phone, moving back toward the front of the clinic. Stepping just outside, out of earshot of Ms. Jones, he dialed. His call was to Leonard Chang's crime lab. Kelton, standing by here with a handful of other uniformed cops, had assured him that Chang was on standby alert.

In a moment, Chang came on. "Leonard, it's me. Get a team and a photographer over here pronto, preferably Steve Perelli. We may have something here."

"Terrific, then you *like* this guy for the mutilation murder, Lucas?"

"I like him *mightily* for it, yeah."

"The bastard chopped her up at his clinic, didn't he?"

"I'd bet my eyeteeth on it. Get this, not only has he wiped the place clean, he's ripped out one of two operating tables from the clinic and has stashed a lot of his tools, hopefully being unearthed at his house by now." Lucas gave a thought to Jana North's progress across town.

"Unreal. Don't worry, Lucas, my boys and girls, we'll find the nails to drive into these vampires' coffins. What a monster these two are together. We've got to get them off the streets."

"I have every confidence in us doing just that, Leonard."

"Wish everybody else did."

Lucas wondered how much flack Chang was being bombarded with. "FBI making a move on us, Leonard?"

"They're in Lincoln's office as we speak."

"Then you'd best be—"

"On our way."

Lucas returned to where Meredyth had continued to get a feel for Arthur Belkvin from his receptionist/secretary.

"Have you any pictures of Dr. Belkvin?" Meredyth was asking Jones when Lucas came alongside her.

"There's a lotta photos on the wall in here." Jones guided them to another operating room, one door littered with photos of Dr. Belkvin standing, crouching, leaning in various poses with dogs, cats, birds, ferrets, rabbits, even a monkey or two, sometimes with the owners, their arms thrown over Dr. Belkvin's shoulder.

"Doesn't look at all like your typical flip-out killer, Mere. All these people to interact with in positive ways. Holding down two good jobs—careers actually. No profiler would put this guy together with this crime."

"Agreed, but he's our man just the same, whether he fits or not." Meredyth found the best facial shot available and said, "We'll need this one, Ms. Jones, in our search for your boss."

"To find him or to shoot him down? I called Missing Persons 'cause he's *missing,* but you come in here turning him into some kind of bloodthirsty murderer—askin' don't I think he looks like the man on the news and on the front pages."

"Ms. Jones, we want to find him and question him, as much for his safety as that of others," Meredyth assured her.

Losing patience, Lucas bluntly asked, "Was he acting strangely, other than selling off his table and tools, that is?"

"He seemed agitated, yes . . . like he was in some *kinna* trouble. But, you see, he's a reformed gambler and, well . . ."

"Goes to the Gulf for the action there?" asked Lucas.

"*Used* to go to the Gulf casinos down below Galveston, *and* he played the horses a lot, but I was thinking he'd gotten past all that since he got into so much financial quicksand the last gambling binge. But now, however, now you mention it, I'm thinking maybe he fell back into his old ways . . . maybe."

"Meredyth had earlier held up the artist sketch of Mr. X, and while Jones had flinched, she'd denied it was him. "Dr. B, he can't be your Ripper man, no way."

"Why's that?" Meredyth had asked.

"He's got a mole, but it's not on his right cheek. It's on his left."

Meredyth now pointed this oversight in the sketch out to Lucas. "They've got the damn mole on the wrong side of the face."

"All the same, the general appearance, it's him, isn't it?" said Lucas.

When Jones simply glared at Lucas, refusing to answer, Meredyth softly asked, "MariLouise . . . can I call you MariLouise?"

"Ms. Jones will do just fine."

"Okay, Ms. Jones, what about the eyebrows? They look dark brown or black in the photo, and he has blond hair, right?"

"More like sandy brown than blond."

"And the eyebrows?"

"There's no way Dr. B's going to be a killer. He's just too gentle with the animals." She said this as if there could be no argument. "He couldn't've done no abduction and murdering. I know him too well. Nobody that knows the man will ever be convinced he coulda done what they— what you all're trying to tell me that Dr. B's done, never. And maybe you can send him to prison for it, or even to the death row, and the gas chamber, but I'll still know he's wrongfully accused."

"You don't think he'd kill, say, to pay off a bet, say thousands upon thousands lost to a mob loan shark?" asked Lucas somewhat facetiously.

"No . . . not even then could you convince me that this man kilt somebody. He's a gentle, caring man, Dr. B is."

"What about for his girlfriend, Ms. Jones? Do you think he would kill for her?"

She hesitated answering for a moment. "His girl-friend?" she asked. "He didn't *have* no girlfriend."

Meredyth flashed Lauralie's picture. "You ever see this young woman here at the office?"

"Yeah . . . yeah, but she wasn't his *girlfriend.*"

"What was she to him then, if not his girl?"

"His *student.*" Her tone and the bobbing and weaving head and rolling eyes left no doubt she thought Lucas and Meredyth a pair of simpleminded fools. "He said she had great promise . . . said he expected her to change the face of veterinary medicine someday. They laughed about it, but I swear I never saw anything going on between them, not like you're thinking. Course you being cops . . . but me, I don't own a nasty mind and don't particularly ever want to."

"How often did you see her here?"

"Twice, maybe three times."

"Ever leave at closing with the two of them still here?"

"Well . . . yes . . . once, maybe twice."

"But you never thought anything unusual was going on between Dr. Belkvin and Lauralie?"

"Never crossed my mind. He was old enough to be her father, and so far as I ever saw, Dr. B, he just never was interested in sex whatsoever."

"Let me get this straight if I can," Lucas said to her. "Lauralie shows up, hangs out here, does some interning with the doctor, no hanky-panky as you see it, but one morning after you leave them here together at night, you come in to find a whole damned operating table and a slew of cutting instruments gone—disappeared overnight—but you don't *think* anything unusual is going on between Belkvin and Blodgett, because you attribute his strange behavior to his old gambling habit. Is that right, about the gist of it?"

"That's how I see it still, and why not? Why would he lie to me?"

"He told you he had to sell the table and tools to pay old debts, Ms. Jones, and that was a lie."

"Please, Lucas." Meredyth backed him off, making a show of scolding him. She returned to MariLouise, apologizing for her partner's rudeness. "Tell me, Ms. Jones, how soon after meeting Lauralie did Dr. Belkvin begin to exhibit this stress level you mentioned?"

Ms. MariLouise Jones gave this time to sink in. "I see . . . I see what you're driving at. You're right. He started this . . . this crackup behavior soon after he introduced me to Lauralie."

She thanked the young receptionist and retuned to Lucas. "Why get rid of the operating table unless it's to get rid of incriminating evidence, but with his access to various chemical baths and acid cleaners, he could just as well have left the table and thoroughly cleaned it. Ripping it out of here . . . I don't get the logic, unless . . . unless . . ."

"Unless he transported the table elsewhere—possibly

her idea—to be used at another location, along with the tools."

"Like the house. We need to know what's happening there."

"This damned mystery screams for an answer."

Meredyth asked, "Ms. Jones, did you see who hauled off the operating table?"

"No, your partner's right 'bout that much. It disappeared overnight one night, 'bout two weeks ago."

"Two weeks ago? Are you sure, absolutely sure of the timing?" asked Lucas.

"Thursdays I get off early, every Thursday. I remember coming in on Friday and almost tripping out seeing that room all empty! The whole surgical table just gone! Dr. B swore he had to sell it off. Said he had plans of getting a new one with coaster wheels and an overhead hose and lights attached, you know."

A phone call came through for Lucas on his cell. He took it, responding to Jana North at the other end, his face showing his disappointment. "All right . . . all right, Jana. No, not a whole lot here either. Disappointing overall, but we'll find this guy. Only a matter of time now that we know both their names, and we know the type vehicle and a license plate thanks to your snooping there. Cars, plates, and people don't just disappear into thin air. Yes . . . yes, do that update on the APB-BOLO. I agree, go ahead and upgrade the search. No, already done . . . planes, trains, and buses. Dogs . . . three dogs? No, none this location, no."

Lucas hung up, exchanging a look with Meredyth, his shake of the head telling her nothing useful had come of the search of Belkvin's home. No tools, no table, no deadly workbench drenched in blood. "They're trying to locate his dogs at a nearby kennel, but no one there has seen the doctor or the dogs."

"Pongo?" asked Ms. Jones. "Pongo's with me. Dr. B asked me if I could take him for a while."

"When was this?"

"A couple weeks ago."

"That same Thursday night?"

"Right."

Lucas took a deep breath. Interrogating MariLouise might have been easier with a lawyer present, he thought, exasperated. "Other than his home and the school where he teaches, Ms. Jones, do you have any idea where he might have disappeared to and why he didn't take Pongo?"

"He took his other two dogs with him, Desperado Pete—Petie, and Lupe Fritz, his two old, retired greyhounds."

"Weird dog names," commented Meredyth.

"They were one-time racers, you know, on a track in Abilene, I think. They had names to bet on, you know, like racehorse names, Seabiscuit, Xtra Heet, What Up . . . all that."

"Two other dogs he took with him?" pressed Lucas.

"They were all three here at the kennel for a time. Said he was having his place fumigated. Next thing I know, he's asking if I could take Pongo for a week while he took the other two."

"But you have no idea where he was going?"

"I thought he was going home."

"But he disappeared instead . . . with two dogs in tow."

Meredyth asked, "Where do you think he is now, Ms. Jones? I mean if you wanted to find him, where would you start?"

She at first hesitated answering, considering, as if she thought it a trick question. Then MariLouise's eyes widened and she dropped her right shoulder, followed by her left. "I'd put in calls to the casinos in the Gulf . . . try the race tracks—horses and dogs."

Outside the clinic, they watched soon-to-be-disappointed dog and cat owners parking and coming toward the veterinary with pets in hand and on leashes. Lucas and Meredyth took a moment to speak with a few of Belkvin's customers and to pet their animals. They got the same reluctance as Jones had exhibited from the regulars when confronted with the likeness between Belkvin and the artist's sketch.

"Good God, man! He's a coach in the Pee-Wee League, damn good one," complained one man who voiced his fear that they could ruin Arthur's reputation with such lies and innuendo.

Another pet owner, a woman, said, "Dr. Arthur saved my Coochee's life! He's a saint."

"No way he's capable of what you're implying," screeched a blue-haired parakeet-toting matron. "This persecuting of Dr. Arthur ought to be against the law. Have you a permit to picket his clinic in this fashion?"

It was time to leave the clinic altogether. At the car, Harry Jorganson had stood watching and listening. "I take it you found nothing," he said to Lucas.

"But we will. I called in Chang's people. They'll find proof."

"And this Dr. Belkvin? Who's going to find him?"

"We'll get him, Harry, and we'll find the missing operating table too."

"Missing operating table?" Harry asked, his features pinched in confusion.

"Ask Chang about it," Lucas called out as he and Meredyth pulled out of the lot. As they did so, they waved to Chang's CSI unit van as it arrived, followed by Steve Perelli's car. In his rearview, Lucas saw the D.A. going for Chang as the Chinese M.E. leaped from the passenger side of the van. Lynn Nielsen climbed from the rear.

"If anyone can find evidence of Mira Lourdes ever having been here," said Lucas, allowing the thought to float on the air.

"Funny," replied Meredyth.

"What's that?"

"The depth of Mother Elizabeth's naïveté toward Lauralie has been matched!"

"By our Ms. Jones?"

"And her sheer gullibility toward her boss, yes."

DISAPPOINTED AT JANA North's news, and the fact the two raids had not revealed the whereabouts of either Belkvin or Lauralie Blodgett, Lucas and Meredyth wound up at a Greek restaurant called Plato's. They were enjoying a full-course meal and a bottle of Greek wine when Lucas's cell phone vibrated in his pocket. He asked Meredyth for her forbearance, taking the call that originated from the precinct house.

Lucas found himself talking to Stan Kelton, who wanted to know his whereabouts, adding that he had an antsy lady claiming to have rented a farmhouse out to a young couple fitting the description of Arthur Belkvin and Lauralie Blodgett.

"Hold onto her, Stan."

"Easier said than done. She's *hinky.*"

"If you have to sit on her, hold onto her. We're on our way." He hung up and slapped cash onto the table, sipped a final bit of wine, grabbed Meredyth by the wrist, and said, "Come on. We may have a break in the case. Jane Q. Public, claiming to have had dealings with Belkvin and Blodgett."

Lucas reestablished contact with Stan over the car radio as they drove for the 31st Precinct. "How reliable is this woman, Stan?"

"Lucas, her story sounds credible. She's a realtor and she freaked when she saw the images we posted of the fugitives. In the meantime, there's been a call for you from an inspector in the Mounted Police in Manitoba, Canada. Wants a call back, something to do with an APB you posted on the web for a Lyle Eaton, once of Houston and Seattle? They have good news for you. Seems he's doing time there as a sex offender of some sort, but his sentence is up in six months."

"That's damn good news, Stan! I want the prick on murder one."

"Closing down a Cold Case, are you, Lieutenant?" Stan asked. "Congrats. I ran into Remo when he was here, and he gave up some of the particulars. Bet you didn't know Muarice was my TO when I rookied here in '79."

Lucas imagined getting departmental funds to fly up to Manitoba with Maurice Remo, and the two of them laying out their case before this creep Eaton in his cell. The opportunity to sit across a table from the bastard who killed Yolanda Sims, to unnerve him and watch him come apart, to see him fold under the preponderance of evidence they *would* bring to bear . . . taking him through every step, every bruising blow, every soldering-iron burn, and finally the rape and murder *would* convince Eaton that he had no choice but to plead out in the case of a little girl whose ghost had pursued him all these fifty-odd years. Even if they could not get the death penalty for Eaton, they could nail him for a life sentence.

"You're likely to face extradition problems with Canada if you're bringing him back for execution," Meredyth said, hearing the news.

"No problem, so long as we promise Canadian officials we won't be seeking the death penalty against the creep. At his advanced age, life in prison'll suit Yolanda Sims, Remo, and me just fine. Eaton's got to be in his mid to upper sixties."

"A letter of assurance from Harry Jorganson that the State of Texas will not seek the death penalty, Lucas, would go a long way to assure your seeing him tuned over to Texas authorities."

"It'll culminate in a deal that'll please everyone except Eaton."

"Canada will rid herself of him," she added.

"We'll have closed a Cold Case, Remo will've been vindicated, and Yolanda Sims will finally rest in peace." Lucas smiled at the prospect.

Stan Kelton shouted over the radio, "Hey! Anyone there? Stonecoat?"

"Yeah, go ahead, Stan."

"It's the witness in your *current* case, Lieutenant."

"Did you tell her we're on our way?"

"Sure, I did, but somehow Frank Patterson got wind of her and then took her off."

"Off? Off where, damn him?"

"Interrogation room."

"Who the hell does he think he is?"

"He wasn't alone. Two FBI with him. They're questioning her now."

"Damn it all. What do we know about her, Stan?"

"She's with Lone Star Realtors, says she may have leased out a place to this vet guy, using an alias, only days before Mira Lourdes went missing."

"How shaky is our witness, Stan?"

"She's extremely sure, Lucas. I think we have to listen to her."

"Where's the rental at, Stan? Do we have an address?"

"It's in the sticks, north of the city, out some ways, Lucas."

"Remote?"

"Well . . . what's remote? It's all relative, isn't it?" Kelton's voice came over the radio loudly and evenly. "I suspect it's a drive, but I also suspect it may well be the kill site, Lucas."

Two great scores in a matter of minutes. It sounded too good to be true, but the fly in the ointment was Frank and his G-men friends. "Stan, is she cooperating with Frank and his FBI buddies so far?"

"Not going well from the look of it. She's asked for a lawyer."

"Assholes! They've frightened hell out of her, no doubt with unnecessary threats."

Lucas placed the siren atop his unmarked police car, and they raced to close the distance between themselves and the new credible witness now refusing to cooperate. What had Frank and his pals done to turn an ally into an enemy? "Call Jana on that thing," he said to Meredyth, pointing to the radio. "Get her and her team back to HQ. If there's anything to this, we're going to need to assemble a small army whether the FBI is involved or not."

Meredyth did as asked. Jana was already on her way back to the 31st. Meredyth had to suddenly grab onto her door handle as they took the final turn into the lot.

When they entered, Kelton directed them to the witness claiming to have rented a property out to a guy fitting the description in the artist sketch.

"Her name's Robeson. She's right here," Kelton said as they worked past busy people in the squad room and to a

glassed-in waiting room popularly called the Fish Bowl.
"Why've you got her in with the degenerates?" Lucas asked.

"It's where Frank left her. They're using it as a tactic to
get her to talk to them before her lawyer arrives. He's on
his way, someone she picked outta this." He tapped the
phone book on his desk. "Feds told Frank they think she's
just another one getting in line for the reward money. I
think they took a hike."

"Really? Then we have a shot at her, don't we. Bring
her down to the conference room. We'll hide her there for
now, and we'll talk to her."

A few moments later, Lucas and Meredyth greeted
Mrs. Robeson as Stan spirited her into the far more private
and secure area. They introduced themselves and apologized
for her ill treatment at the hands of the Feds and Frank.
"It's not even their case, Mrs. Robeson. You did the right
thing by not talking to them as you did, and when your
lawyer arrives, Officer Kelton will bring him or her here."

Officer Kelton assured her of it, and left to man the front
and to keep Frank at bay.

Mrs. Robeson, a Betty Crocker lookalike, sat demurely
in her comfortable swivel chair.

Lucas and Meredyth sat across from her, Meredyth
offering to get her a cup of coffee.

"Really, one more cup of coffee and I go floating away.
I came down here to make a statement in person, to be
taken seriously. I made several calls to your hot line and
got nowhere. No one is listening. Then what happens? I
come all this way only to be treated like my sole purpose is
to rob the city of that reward! So I played that stupid game
just to get back at them."

Lucas cocked his head to one side. "Stupid game,
ma'am? What stupid game is that?"

"In my shoe, right here. I pointed and took it off, and I
told them I was getting voices from inside telling me where
the Ripper is hiding out. About then they went beyond the
rudeness to a kind of dumbfounded ignorance, taking me literally. 'Bout then I told them I wanted a lawyer, and they
started arguing among themselves, the three of 'em."

"What a waste of your time," said Meredyth.

"It's worse than any waste of my time, Dr. Sanger. Lives may be at stake here."

Lucas asked, "Did they show you a photo array and ask you to pick out the man you rented your property to?"

"We never got that far."

"Would you do that for us?" he asked, spreading out six photos, five of which were lookalikes of Belkvin and one authentic. He did the same with six females, one being Lauralie Bloodgett. Sallie Robeson selected both accurately, which came as no surprise since she had seen their images in the media.

"Tell us what you know about this man," Lucas said, tapping his finger against Belkvin's photo.

She studied the photo, pulling it up close to her eyes. "Yes, well, he rented the property out on the creek under the name of John D. Croombs."

Meredyth exchanged a knowing look with Lucas. "Croombs. He used the alias Croombs?"

"Yes," she replied.

Meredyth smiled and breathed deeply. "We're definitely onto them."

"Then you don't think me some sort of thief interested in any old reward! How refreshing. Aside from your Sergeant Kelton, I have found no one here I can trust, until now."

Kelton arrived with her Yellow Pages lawyer, a young woman who looked fresh out of law school who introduced herself to her client as Karen Cahill, and she insisted on huddling in private with her client, but first she wanted to know the charges.

The situation explained, Lucas and the others allowed Robeson and Cahill to have the room. Outside, Lucas asked Kelton what had become of Frank and the Feds when they found Robeson gone.

"They came at me. I pleaded ignorance and suggested she walked out. They argued with one another and told Frank to call them when he had some credible information. Frank's busy filling out a complaint against me, regarding my carelessness in the matter."

"Excellent."

Attorney Cahill called them back inside. "My client wishes to cooperate with authorities in any way possible, but only if she can communicate through you two, Lieutenant, Doctor."

"Agreed."

"Quite acceptable."

Once all were again settled, Realtor Sallie Robeson began to relate her story in earnest. "I rented to him and the woman I took to be his young bride, and when I saw her likeness in the newspaper alongside his, I knew it was the same couple. Odd couple really."

"Odd being together, you mean, an odd fit as a couple?" asked Meredyth, anxious to understand every detail.

"She coulda been his daughter, and I worried for a moment what was going on, but she was giving all the orders, you know, making all the demands. She wanted *this* fixed, she wanted *that* redone, you know the type. For the price the old place was rented for, I told her to forget about a lot of upkeep on the part of the owners. I didn't think they'd take the place. Surprised me when they did. But him with those yelping dogs, and the big pens already on the premises, well, he was sold. But overriding all concerns, it seemed she had to be happy, or it was no good."

"She called the shots," agreed Meredyth, nodding.

"So you people already have a bead on 'em, don't you?"

"We do."

"What got me . . . what really struck me was when I saw his mole on the tube. I was glued to it on the screen just like I had been in life. Didn't know where to look when talking to the man. Whole time I was dealing with the man, I kept thinking to myself, 'Mr. Croombs, why not at very least clip the damn hair from your mole, so it's not so damned distracting?' You know?"

"When exactly did you rent the property to Mr. Croombs?" asked Lucas.

"Two and a half, maybe three weeks ago."

"Can you pinpoint on a county map exactly where the property is located, Mrs. Robeson?" asked Lucas, guiding her to a wall where a number of state and county maps stared down on them.

"It's in the North Country area, Bridger Falls—you know, that development that fell through when the owners went belly-up?"

"I know the general area, yes," replied Lucas. "Go on."

"Well . . . the old farmhouse on Hazard Creek Road belonged to the Kenyon estate. Whole thing's now in probate, but the house was placed with us to sell or rent."

She pointed it out on the map, smack in the Navasota River Canyon area. From there, they went to a computer, and typing in the search window, Lucas fed it the address and the owner's name, Kenyon. The computer quickly identified the exact location, and the fact it bordered on Waller County.

Kelton had arrived again, this time escorting Jana North to their cozy hideaway, introducing her to Cahill and Robeson. Getting Sallie Robeson's okay to remain, Jana—having been coached by Kelton—thanked the realtor for indulging her. Seeing the jurisdictional overlap on the computer screen, she said, "We'd best notify *and* involve Sheriff Dennis Laird over there. He can bring his dogs to the party. Always bragging he's got the best police dogs in the state."

"All right. We can rendezvous with Laird at County Line and Canyon Road, here," Lucas said, pointing to the screen.

The Dragnet program Lucas used also pinpointed the location of every state, county, and dirt road leading in and out of the property, displaying a flashing red O around the perimeter of their destination and several bleeping red Xs at each site where a roadblock made sense. Finally, the program bleeped a blue line from the address of Precinct 31 to the farmstead, the shortest route. As with Meredyth, Jana North stared at the computer image of their target and converging lines of approach.

"Are there any barns or other structures on the property?" Lucas asked Sallie Robeson.

She plucked at something jammed tight in her Lone

Star Realty purse. "Yes, a large barn and a toolshed, as well as a root cellar, used for hurricanes and tornadoes as much as for vegetables." She continued to struggle with the thing in her purse, finally tearing it free with a vial of lipstick, a half pack of Big Red gum, a wad of tissue, and a hair clip, all of which Stan Kelton rounded up from the floor.

She had pulled forth a folded Xerox map of overlapping pages held together by cellophane tape. A contented smile creasing her wrinkled face, she handed the map to Lucas. "I've got the locations of the shed and barn clearly marked, Lieutenant, case you asked, and you did."

Lucas smiled in return and asked, "Where's the root cellar?"

"Under the kitchen, a door going down from the kitchen."

Lucas nodded. "Did you ever see any improvements made to the house that Croombs or Mrs. Croombs made?"

"The pens the dogs're kept in were already there. Old chicken coops with high fencing, well maintained. Made a good run for the animals."

"I mean to the house . . . or perhaps to the barn? Any equipment brought in?"

"I'm not sure I follow you."

"We believe the couple meant to turn the property into a veterinary surgery," explained Meredyth, a bit of a lie to draw the woman out.

"Ahhh . . . explains a lot. I never knew that." Then Sallie sat biting her lip and staring off into space, her features a mask of uncertainty.

Lucas cautiously prompted her. "We're trying to locate a table, a stainless-steel table like you would see in a veterinary office. It's very important to our investigation."

"My, but I feel I'm inside a Nancy Drew mystery novel."

"Any medical materials or supplies at all that you saw?" pressed Lucas, a tinge of frustration filtering into his voice.

"'Fraid not, no. Saw their two dogs. Healthy, beautiful dogs. Greyhounds he said he saved from a gassing. He seemed a kind man."

Lucas keyed a few strokes and began printing a copy of the electronic map off the computer. "I've got them pinpointed," he said as the printer came to life.

"We'll need a SWAT team going in, hit the out-structures simultaneously, but first we have to brief everyone on the geography and layout while a warrant is being secured, unless Harry tells us the existing two warrants cover any rental property Belkvin entered into."

"Not likely," said Jana North, holding up the warrant she had used at the home. "This one's quite specific to the home, garage, any cars in his name *on the premises.* If you read the fine print on the one you used at his practice, it's likely also to be specific to that location only. They're just not interchangeable."

The realtor, Sallie, chimed in again. "The woman was in heat to get the electrical and the water up and running, but they never asked about the closest place to shop, which I thought odd."

Everyone strained to hear the words of the matronly realtor's tale as she had begun to whisper. "Said they had a lot more animals than those two dogs to care for, and that's why the need for plenty of space to run the animals, that sort of talk, but again, they didn't seem interested in knowing where the nearest *feed* store was, you know, for these phantom animals."

"Phantom animals?" asked Jana.

"They talked like they were going to fill the barn and the pastures with animals. Least he did. Talked on and on about it. Friendly in a nonstop talkative way," she said. "You think that's 'cause he might've been, you know, nervous?"

"Quite possibly," Meredyth said, nodding.

"You say you only saw the two dogs? Are these the two you saw?" asked Jana, holding up the photo of Belkvin and his greyhounds.

"That's them, the lovely things . . . so graceful and well behaved."

"They spoke of other animals on the way?" asked Meredyth.

"They . . . I mean he . . . Mr. Croombs, he made some

remark that the animals were in transport from Amarillo. When I asked if it was horses, *she* changed the subject, asked me to walk off the property lines with her."

"And did you?" asked Lucas.

"Oh, no! Heavens. It'd have taken a day to walk those boundary lines, so I showed her how she and Mr. Croombs could step off the lines themselves. Left them a map I'd brought out with me, just like the one I made up for you."

"How many acres is the property?" asked Lucas.

"Fifty-nine, and some odd shape it is; follows along a creek that's one of those ghost streams, you know . . . comes and goes depending on the time of year. Folks around Navasota call it Old Hazard Creek . . . runs smack through the property, and some parts of the section they rented cross the creek, and some don't."

"Creek is running flush now, I bet," said Lucas, "given last month's rains from those two passing hurricanes."

"It's full over its banks, yes."

"Jana, you know Judge Henry Lowell fairly well, right?" asked Lucas.

"I'll get you your warrant, Lucas."

"Tell Lowell what we have, plenty of probable cause on the photo and sketch IDs alone. Here's the location." He handed her a copy of the electronic map. "And we need the warrant to extend to any garages, outbuildings, and vehicles owned or rented by the suspects using the names Lauralie and John Croombs, Lauralie Blodgett, or a Dr. Arthur Belkvin."

"Just tell him it's to do with the Post-it Ripper case and he'll want in," said Kelton. "It's coming on election time."

"We'll need to call out another SWAT unit. Hope they don't think we're running on empty again," said Lucas to Stan.

"I'm on top of it, Lucas."

As Jana North and Stan Kelton rushed for the nearby telephones, Lucas stepped away from Mrs. Robeson and Cahill, allowing them to confer. Meredyth followed Lucas. He'd gone back to the large wall map, and now he jabbed a pin into each location on the city and county map where

Dr. Arthur Belkvin might be at this moment, including the old farmhouse. Lucas quietly said, "We've got multiple people now all claiming our sketch is of a man they encountered, one a John Croombs, the other a Dr. Arthur Belkvin."

"He's using her mother's name now?" asked Jana.

"Mere, I think you ought to hang back here . . . let the rest of us handle this out at Kenyon's."

"No way, Lucas. I've earned a right to be there. I want an end to this as much or more than anyone."

"It could be another dead end, you realize? For all we know, they've left the state, gone to Baja or Mexico City."

"No, not her. Him maybe, but not her."

"Okay, you can come along, but you're to hang back. I don't want to give this nutcase a shot at you," he told her.

"Me, what about you? She knows that I love you, and she knows that killing or maiming you would destroy me. You need to hang back as much as I do."

"You love me? That's something I thought I'd never hear after you let it slip that once." Their eyes met and they shared a smile. "All right, agreed. We let the SWAT team storm the place and take them down before we enter. We have Jana directing a separate team from relative safety against the barn, and Stan's earned a right to lead storm troopers against any additional outbuildings."

"We ought to bring Lincoln in on the raid too, Lucas."

"Yeah, Captain Lincoln's definitely going to want to be in on the capture. Election's coming up!" he quipped. "He's also going to want to know about Frank's blunderbuss attempt to make off with our witness and our case."

"I hear Gordon may be running for commissioner if Clarkson keeps his promise to the voters and bows out," Meredyth replied. "A collar like this could get Gordo elected."

"Call him at home," Lucas suggested.

Meredyth got on her cell phone and made the call, explaining to Lincoln the new developments. "Everything's on a snowball's course downhill now, Captain. We've got the bastards in our sights. We're seeing bear tracks."

"Bear tracks?"

"Lucas's word for good signs, good omen, sir."

"He teaching you Cherokee? Never mind. I just hope you two have better results from this information than you did with Belkvin's office and home."

"You've heard all about it then, I take it." She wondered how he had gotten the news, and from whom, and in what way it had been shaded. She also wondered if he had knowledge of Frank's bid to take over the interrogation of a witness with FBI in the room.

An awkward silence telegraphed his real message: *I hope you and Lucas know what you're doing this time.*

"We've got them, I tell you," she insisted.

"I certainly hope so. I don't care to continue to look the fool, Doctor. You might want to convey this to Lieutenant Stonecoat. So where is ground zero?"

She easily read the frustration in his voice. She gave him the coordinates from the map, saying they were getting warrants and involving Waller County authorities.

"I've got my radio car. Keep me informed at all times. And Doctor, tell that damned *Injun* detective of mine I'll meet him at the Interstate along County Line Road out there in Waller County."

He hung up, giving her no chance to respond.

CHAPTER 17

Lightning & lightning arrow: fast, swift

A LONG PARADE of police vehicles of every size and type rode the Interstate for the Canyon Park Road exit north of Houston. They had long since left the lights of the city for the deepening rural darkness of back country roads, sagebrush, jack pine, and Texas juniper when the order was given to cut the strobe lights, and next the headlights. Running silent, the motorcade looked like a nighttime funeral procession, but for the reflective glow in the dark HPD logos, the SWAT logos, and the Waller County Sheriff's logos. Bringing up the rear, a pair of Houston ambulance and rescue vehicles followed Chang's CSI van. News crews followed at a respectful distance like camp followers, having gotten word of the raid, their satellite vans like so many pachyderms shouldering their way forward as in an elephant walk. At least this is how it all appeared from overhead in the HPD chopper where Meredyth and Lucas had set up their communication and command post. A second police helicopter impatiently held off as well. While Lincoln insisted on leading the main force through the

front door of the farmstead, he had also insisted that Lucas
and Meredyth remain at a safe distance and altitude until
the suspect house and outbuildings were deemed all secure
by the captain of the SWAT team, Elliot Andrews. "I mean
to insure the successful conclusion of this horror personally," Lincoln had said, "and if that means locking you two
up, Stonecoat, I'll do it. It's for your own safety and the
safety of every officer going in. Detective North has told
me how this madwoman has targeted you for death. Well,
we're not going to bait her using you as a target, nor have
you rush in there and set off some sort of deadly booby
trap either. Understood?"

Lucas suggested they command the operation from the
safety of the helicopter, and Lincoln thought it a perfect
solution. Now hovering overhead and awaiting the SWAT
team deployment, the police helicopter impatiently hung
back, prepared to bathe the entire farmstead in light on
Elliot Andrews's cue. For now, the two choppers hovered
well out of sight, watching as Waller County units split off
from the motorcade, going for key roadblock positions.
The property was surrounded, locked down. The SWAT
unit with Andrews and Lincoln at the helm had turned onto
the tree-lined dirt road leading up to the farmhouse. A single light from inside the house seemed to wink up at them
through the trees in a mocking manner.

Andrews's voice came over the headphones Lucas
wore, using the code names they'd agreed upon. "Flying
Wolf, this is Badger One. My men are deployed, and we
are a go! Give us five minutes and light up the night."

Lucas replied, "That's affirmative, Badger One, Flying
Wolf out." He communicated with the second chopper.
They had clearly gotten Andrews's thumbs-up.

Just behind Lucas, watching from the bubble of the
chopper, Meredyth saw what looked like toy soldiers come
alive, having leaped from the two SWAT vans and run into
the tree cover, now on their stomachs, some crouching,
some moving left, others right as they encircled the farmhouse, the shed, and the barn. She watched them inch ever
closer to the clearing around the home. In the dark, their

forms looked like animated green brush, their camouflage making them living shadows. They were minutes away from an all-out assault on the farmhouse when one of the news vans shone a spotlight that revealed them and placed the men in danger.

"Damn those idiots!" cursed Lucas even as the light was doused. The element of surprise was compromised as the spotlight had flooded—*for the half second it was on*—directly into the living room window. Lucas ordered a move in, shouting to Andrews, "Go, Badger One! Now!" The two choppers flooded the entire area in huge circles of blinding light, and Elliot Andrews had not waited for Lucas's order, having already given the go order to his units at the moment of compromise. Andrews, along with Captain Lincoln, stormed in on the heels of the SWAT men who'd overwhelmed the place with forty-six AK-47 assault rifles pointed, men having spilled through every rammed door and shattered window. The shed and barn were simultaneously secured, Lucas and Meredyth hoping nothing untoward would happen to people on the ground, including the captain, Jana North, Andrews, and Stan Kelton.

No shots had rung out. Only the roar of the dueling rotor blades filled the air. Lucas and Meredyth saw some of Andrews's men already exiting the house, guns limp in their grasp, one or two on his knees as if in prayer, others bent over the porch rails, dejection on the heels of elation and adrenaline-pumping expectations now dashed. Others, their assault rifles shouldered, walked off in obvious defeat. The second chopper whirred low and over the scene.

"Damn it, Badger One, report back!" Lucas repeatedly sought information. "What've we got down there? What're we looking at?"

Through her headphones, Meredyth summed up her assessment of the body language on the ground. "If we have them, it's bad. A murder suicide or a suicide pact perhaps?"

"Andrews! Andrews!"

"There he is," said the pilot, pointing as Andrews, alongside Lincoln, emerged from the front door. Both men looked disheartened and overcome.

"Look for the car, Belkvin's BMW," Meredyth said, but no vehicle whatsoever came into their considerable view from overhead.

"Badger One, report back," Lucas asked again from the police whirlybird. "God, I shoulda been down there." Then he angrily tore off his headphones and ordered the pilot to set the chopper down in a nearby field.

They had checked with DMV for Belkvin's license plate, and the information matched that given by his secretary—he had only the one car. An exhaustive search by Jana North's people to locate Arthur Belkvin's relatives had turned up nothing. He seemed to be without any familial ties, another clue to his isolation and contributing, no doubt, to his being the perfect beau for Lauralie.

"Damn, I don't see his car out here anywhere," Meredyth said, cursing their luck. "Likely they've made off for Mexico as you feared. If so, at least it means an end to the killings, at least for the time being."

From the headphone in his lap, Lucas heard the helicopter cop in the second hovering craft shouting a response to Meredyth's request. "No vehicles at all in the open. Still, could be tucked away in the barn."

"Andrews! What've we got at ground zero?" pleaded Meredyth as their helicopter wobbled to an unsteady standstill in the boulder-strewn field, the rotors and engine still roaring as Andrews's voice came over the radio, saying, "Flying Wolf, come in . . . come in."

"We're here, Elliot, out," said Meredyth as Lucas replaced the headset.

"We got what appears to be left of Arthur Belkvin, a pair of dead greyhounds, and enough scattered evidence to put Lauralie Blodgett away forever, but we don't have Lauralie."

Moments before the chopper had bathed the farmstead in brilliant blue-white, Lucas and Meredyth had been watching the single light winking back at them—*on-off, on-off*—the result of their speeding past the foliage surrounding the dark little farmstead. This light had been left on for them, obliterated now by the radiance of the chopper's floodlights. Meredyth wondered what Lauralie had left under the light inside. She wondered if she really wanted to know.

Lucas didn't hesitate, leaping from his front seat out of the chopper, rushing ahead of her as if he meant to decide this for her. Meredyth climbed from the helicopter, seeing Lucas narrowing the gap between himself and the others now assembled before the broken-down farmhouse doorway—a shaken Captain Lincoln, a deflated Andrews, a businesslike Jana North, and Stanley Kelton in flack gear all huddling together, comparing notes on what was found at each structure. Leonard Chang's CSI van had been immediately called in, and it came right up to the front door, kicking up gravel and rock into a woodpile and pinging against a free-standing fuel oil drum.

Lucas stormed up to the group, anxious to know what they knew about the interior. The noise from the two choppers and the churned-up wind—*sweeping debris-filled dirt devils taunting on all sides of them*—added to the confusion. Lucas reached the others, and Meredyth saw Andrews throw up his hands as if to wash them of the operation. With Andrews stepping off and Captain Lincoln grabbing Lucas, keeping him from saying another word to Andrews, Meredyth gauged the level of emotions as being at the frayed final edge. Kelton took Lucas aside, trying to calm him as the SWAT team retreated to a respectful distance, and Chang began orchestrating his small army of evidence techs, Lynn Nielsen overseeing the preparation of field lighting going inside the house. Meredyth cornered Lincoln, asking, "What's in there? What'd you find?" She had to speak over the *whump-whump-whump* of two helicopters until the earthbound one finally cut its engines. "It's the rest of Mira Lourdes, isn't it?" She imagined what little remained of the woman dangling on a tether hook.

"No . . . no sign whatever of the woman, only the freezer they kept her body in," replied Lincoln.

"Then it's just Belkvin and his dogs inside?"

Lincoln gulped down large doses of the cool night air like a man splashing water into his face, trying desperately not to vomit or show any sign of weakness before the telescopic

cameras focusing in on him from some fifty-odd yards away
where the press was held in check. Then overhead, a 2News
helicopter began competing for space with the police chopper still lighting up the ground. Lincoln tore at the Velcro
snaps of his bullet-proof vest, the vest responding with a
rending sound, popping open like a loosed girdle, dropping
Lincoln's generous stomach out and over his belt-line. "The
man's heart, Meredyth, is literally on his sleeve."

Her mind immediately went to the old aphorism: *He
wore his heart on his sleeve.* "She's still making jokes,
taunting us."

"He must've had a real *heart-on* for her," Lincoln said,
attempting a dark joke. "The thing is positioned in the
crook of his well-posed arms. I think the message she means
to convey is that dear old Arthur wore out his welcome in
her demented world."

Lucas had stepped over the torn-away door and had
gone into the house, and he now returned to Meredyth.
"She opened up his chest, using a bone saw like a damned
can opener, blood everywhere . . . cut out his heart and
handed it to him, not to mention what she did to his John-
son. She cut off his whole package, including the balls."

"No sign of a car," commented Kelton, joining them.

"She's long gone," added Jana North. "You okay,
Lucas?"

"What'd she do with Mira Lourdes's remains?" asked
Meredyth. "Captain, we should have the area around the
house and outbuildings, and the interior of the barn, the
basement, root cellar all searched for Mira's remains. If we
accomplish nothing else here tonight, let's bring her home."

"I'll so order Andrews, and we'll leave the fine-tuning
sleuth work to Chang's CSI unit," replied Lincoln.

"I want a look inside," Meredyth said to Lucas.

"It's bad, Mere."

"I need to do this."

"Why? Why play her game?"

"Do I have any choice?"

Lincoln looked on, listening to their discussion, his features creased with concern. "I gotta go deal with the press."

"Arthur Belkvin's body is laid out on his own operating table, Mere, and—"

"We found the missing table."

"—and his two dogs, dead on either side of his feet, their bodies posed against the table struts like Egyptian statues, stiff as stone, intact, no violence done to their bodies. Poisoned, it seems. And there's a floor-model Freezer Queen taking up most of the room in the kitchen where a kitchen table ought to be."

"I gotta get inside, see what she wanted me to see," she firmly told Lucas.

Lincoln had stopped short, turned, and come back to them where they stood on the porch. "I want you two to know I've made up my mind. You're to stand down on this case after tonight. Too many eyes on us now, and you're both too emotionally inolved, and it's time others had a shot at this madwoman."

"What others are you talking about, Captain?" asked Lucas.

"All right, Lucas . . . FBI's coming in on the case now. We need their resources and experience, and we need national and international jurisdictional cooperation. This crazed Blodgett woman could be anywhere in the U.S. by now, or across the border."

"I'm sure that line will play well on the ten o'clock news, Captain."

The comment turned Lincoln's calm features into those of an angry gargoyle. "Hold on there, Lieutenant! That's uncalled for!"

"You gotta give us more time!"

"The hell I do! And what's wrong with getting more help, Lucas?"

"It'll take days to bring them up to date, for one. And we both know that caving into them now is only good for the cameras. That it's all PR *bullswallop*!"

"Christ, Stonecoat! You know damn well the FBI's coming in on the case whether I invite them or not!"

"You can stiff-arm 'em. You know they'll spend hours on disputing our findings, Meredyth's profile, all our hard-earned inches, every clue, and even after all that, if they are finally educated to what we have here, we've lost all those man hours away from—"

"Too late! At this point, it's out of my hands."

Lucas followed him down the steps and onto the gravel. "But Captain!"

"I held 'em off as long as I could. Tonight's raid was supposed to end in an arrest or a death—an end to this deviant bitch."

Lucas fell silent, staring at the earth, making a dust cloud of the dirt he displaced, his boot tip creating a lazy-eight configuration in the driveway, the symbol for infinity.

"Damn it all, Lucas, you have no idea the pressure I'm under. I don't always want to give into public pressure, pressure from the press, and certainly not from the damn Feds, but everybody's on this bandwagon, and I no longer have any choice."

"Sure . . . sure . . ." Lucas calmly replied, but the single word answer only added to Lincoln's distress.

"And what about you and her, Meredyth? You think you're Batman and Robin or something? You fucked up, the two of you. You both led me to believe we had the Blodgett girl and Belkvin cornered and outfoxed, dead to rights, finished! *Finito!* Not once but twice. But obviously she's made fools of you again, and now—and now!—the bitch is likely over the state line in California, Louisiana, New—*or goddamn old*—Mexico . . . for God's sake."

Lincoln stormed past the CSI van. Leonard Chang, with Nielsen's help, had just finished suiting up in full protective wear, including plastic laminate helmet. Nielsen too looked like a space man, covered from head to toe.

Lucas set his teeth and nervously studied the black woods off to their left. Anyone could be hiding there, just out of range of the helicopter's floodlights. Lincoln cornered Andrews, barking orders, and Elliot, in a show of bravado, led a contingent of SWAT members fanning out to search in all directions around the house for any sign of freshly turned earth. The men, women, and dogs of the

SWAT poured into the surrounding dark without complaint, disappearing from the artificial safety of the *camp-fire circle* created by the overhead floodlights.

"One pissed-off captain on our hands now," Jana North said to Lucas, at his side now.

"He's become quite the politician lately."

"Don't be too hard on him, Lucas. Like it or not, politics comes with the job, and his strategy for coping has always been to appease as many as possible without compromising a case. He's *not* the worst sort of brass I've ever worked with. How 'bout you?"

"No. Lawrence, now there was a prick." He turned to stare again at the single light in the front room when he realized that Meredyth was no longer on the outside. He saw her form through the shattered window, standing over Arthur Belkvin's remains. He rushed inside, leaving Jana standing alone under the glare of the chopper.

Chang and Nielsen entered on Lucas's heels, Jana North following them. Stan Kelton stopped in the doorway, tall enough to see over the others.

On entering the death house a second time, Lucas was again struck by how the eyes were immediately lassoed and pulled to the single light over the stainless-steel table at the center of the front room on which lay the nude, mutilated body of a sandy-blond-haired man. It had been this medical tensor lamp hanging over the table that had winked at Lucas and Meredyth through the foliage.

Below the light, Arthur Belkvin's blood-spattered and tortured features, eyes wide in a kind of amazed horror, easily matched the photo of the veterinary doctor. As Lincoln had warned, two stiff-bodied greyhounds sat on their haunches, propped against the table, positioned at Arthur's feet.

Chang had gone straight to the body, but Nielsen had found Belkvin's discarded pants, and she carefully wrenched a wallet from a pocket. Holding out the open billfold to the driver's license, she pronounced it belonging to Dr. Arthur D. Belkvin. Chang had switched on a tape recorder attached to his belt, taping her reading of Belkvin's name, age, color of hair, eyes, nationality, and address.

As Chang worked, he continued to record their findings, stating that the dead man on the slab matched the photo ID, eyewitness descriptions, and now the driver's license information. He next began to describe the condition of the body as he hovered over Belkvin, when suddenly he bumped one of the dead dogs and it fell over with a noisy thud. Startled, he swore and stopped the tape long enough to shout at a pair of evidence techs, "Get these stinking dogs outta the way! Put them on ice. We'll autopsy them back in Houston."

Meredyth had stood frozen by the sight of Belkvin's heart in his hands, his chest splayed open, a bloody, meandering, flapping, puckering snake of a wound some one and a half to two feet in length from clavicle to navel. A handheld rotary bone saw had split him open. Lying nastily where his genitals ought to have been, between his bloodied thighs in a pool of crimson, the saw rested skewed to one side.

"Heart lying in crook of Belkvin's right arm. Appears cut from its moorings below the rib cage, ribs having been cut, presumably using saw found between victim's legs. Each arm neatly folded across the mutilated chest. Missing altogether are the genitals. Am making request of all present to find Mr. Belkvin's genitalia."

Everyone got the message, glad to have a chore to perform in this nightmare room. But try as they did, they could not locate the man's missing parts. Jana, spotting a jar on a shelf with human tissue inside, rushed to it, saying, "I've got them!" But she quickly corrected herself. "Sorry . . . don't know what this is, but it's definitely not Arthur's nuts and bolts."

Lynn Nielsen took the big Mason jar in hand, studying its contents. Another human heart, this one floating in formaldehyde.

She cradled it and carefully walked it to Chang, who agreed. "Yes, most likely from the Lourdes woman. A final memento to Dr. Sanger, I suspect."

The remark felt like a dagger plunged in her own chest,

Meredyth thought, wondering if Chang, like others in the know, was beginning to consciously or subconsciously blame her for the string of deaths. She held a handkerchief over her nose, battling the odors, struggling to stabilize a sudden nausea and dizziness threatening to overtake her. Nielsen belatedly handed out scented surgical masks and gloves for them all.

"You all right, Dr. Sanger? You look a bit green. Want to go back out for air?" asked Jana. "We can try again later, after Chang finishes up."

"No . . . no, I want to see this through." She fought to compose herself as Steve Perelli appeared, chanting the single word *damn-damn-damn* over and over with each frame he shot.

Using a video camera, Perelli filmed every conceivable angle of Belkvin's body and the severed heart—lying in the crook of his folded arms. Then Lynn Nielsen pointed Perelli to the jar Chang had replaced on a nearby shelf, and she said, "Get a couple of shots of this, Steve."

"Should've filmed the dogs before you had them carted off, Dr. Chang," commented Lucas. "Juries respond nastily to dog killers."

Chang and Nielsen were again speculating on *where* they might find Arthur's genitals. "I bet you a day's wages, we'll find them in his mouth," Nielsen wagered, and using a tongue depressor, she began searching the throat. "*Hmmm* . . . damn, not here."

"I'll take the hole in the chest. They're stuffed in to replace his heart," guessed the evidence technician Ted Hoskins, who now carefully cradled the hefty little rotary saw in his gloved palms, cautious not to touch either the blade or the grip. "I'll take this out to the van . . . dust it for prints."

"My bet . . . the dogs," said Chang thoughtfully, removing his protective helmet, seeing it was useless to keep the crime scene from contamination with so many curious onlookers tramping through. He was a slightly built, slender man, and his protective suit, far too large for him, made him look the part of an escaped balloon from a Macy's parade.

"The dogs' what?" asked Nielsen.

"Whataya bet we find the genitalia in the dogs' stomach contents when we autopsy them?"

"Is that your final answer, Doc?" asked Hoskins. "She fed his penis and balls to the dogs."

"Won't know for a *sure thing* until we autopsy the grey-hounds, but with this woman, I would not put it past her to have done so—after liberally packing the flesh with rat poison." Chang held up an empty yellow and brown container of D-Con.

"One wicked bitch," Hoskins said with a moan.

Lucas said, "I'm going to have a look at the back rooms." He eased down the cavelike corridor to the back bedrooms to the sound of circling aircraft beating over-head. The police chopper had come in low again, assisting the men in the woods in their seaarch. Lucas's gloved hands found the dust in two smaller rooms undisturbed, but the master bedroom had been used by the deadly cou-ple. A duffel filled with men's clothing and a few toiletries lay at the foot of an unmade bed, and the bathroom showed signs of use—a bar of soap in the dish, a jar of Mennen Skin Bracer, a Bic razor, hairpins, a nail file, an eyeliner brush, wrappers in the trash can. Windows had been opened to air out this single bedroom alone, the sashes doing battle with the cobwebs. Someone had wiped clean the surfaces of the furniture, a faint whiff of lemon and Clorox in the air.

When he returned to the others, Lucas suggested Nielsen dust the right rear room for fibers and hairs in the bedding. "Maybe some DNA from the stains. Looks like another love nest for our happy couple. Other rooms are untouched." He held up his hands to display the dirt and grime clinging to his plastic fingertips. "No need wast-ing your time there."

"Thanks, Detective, that cuts out a lot of wasted effort," Nielsen replied.

Lucas watched only for a moment as Chang and Nielsen, using high-intensity flashlights, searched the enormous cavity in Arthur's chest and abdomen. "Thank God for small favors," Chang said. "She only removed the heart."

"She seems to have left in a hurry. Had to know someone would eventually recognize Arthur from the sketch, his students, people at the clinic, his neighborhood."

Lucas, hearing Jana North and Meredyth conversing in the kitchen, where they'd migrated, joined them. When he entered, Jana was in mid-sentence. ". . . doing that to a man she *presumably* had *some* use for!"

"In psychiatric terms, emasculating a man says as much about the woman as it does the man," replied Meredyth. "I'm sure it had great symbolic and cathartic meaning for her."

"Imagine what she'd do to a man she had *no* use for."

"It would appear his *usefulness* came to an abrupt end, unless his missing parts show up on my doorstep tomorrow."

"She's got balls, as they say . . . literally," Lucas said, following up on Meredyth's remark.

Jana laughed at the black humor and erupted with a cop joke of her own. "Like a bad blues song. We'll call it, 'What I *Lost* for Love.'"

Meredyth silenced the laughter, saying, "For God's sake, the man lost a lot more than his dick. He lost, Jesus, everything he had in this world, not just his life. He lost his reputation . . . his career . . . friends, family, colleagues, and finally, after all the emotional and psychological emasculation, she performs a physical emasculation on him. Poor deluded devil probably thought she loved him."

Chang, overhearing from the other room, called out, "Mercifully, he was dead *when* she emasculated him. Can't say the same for the blade going through his chest."

"That's gotta be some consolation to Arthur," Lucas dryly called back. Lucas had learned to take Leonard Chang at his word. He knew no one who made better forensic judgments with the naked eye. Chang had showed him on earlier occasions how he could determine which wound of several was first, second, and third in order of coloration and blood loss.

Lucas focused now on the large floor-model freezer unit, seeing that it not only dominated the kitchen area, but that it had been examined already—presumably searched immediately for any sign of Mira Lourdes's remaining parts. An overhead bare bulb lit the old kitchen. Looking down into the cavernous, ice-walled unit, they saw that the frosty bottom was littered with bits and pieces of what appeared to be flesh, blood, and fluid stains. One section looked like the spoilage of an upturned rainbow snow cone, save the colors were muted reds and browns.

The sound of Perelli's camera filled the kitchen now as he too had discovered the freezer unit. Steve did a pirouette about the freezer, creating his video record of the exterior and interior of the thing. "Chang damn sure has his work cut out for him," he said to Lucas.

"You got that right." Lucas then asked Meredyth, "Seen enough?"

"Where the hell is Lauralie, Lucas?"

"Not in Mexico."

"Agreed. Yeah . . . she's not finished in Texas yet, is she?"

The question made Jana North stare at Meredyth and then at Lucas.

Outside, the discordant barking and howling of search dogs fashioned a counterpoint to the whirring of the police chopper.

Jana asked, "Are you saying, Dr. Sanger, that she's taken what's left of Mira Lourdes with her? That she intends more surprises and packages?"

"Through Christmas if she can. That'd be my guess, Detective."

Lucas sensed some tension between the two women.

"We should hold judgment, give the dogs time to determine that," cautioned Jana.

"They won't find her, Jana," Lucas said.

Meredyth added, "Lauralie still has her . . . what's left of her, that is."

"We don't know that for sure, Meredyth." Jana had gone to her and placed a hand on her shoulder, squeezing, but Meredyth pulled away, stepping to the far side of the room.

Meredyth looked across the top of the now-closed freezer unit and into Jana's eyes. "Arthur Belkvin's posed body, his exposed heart, and his private parts notwithstanding, Lauralie is still on a mission."

"A mission?" asked Jana.

"A quest as obsessive as any crusade, as mad as any religious fixation," replied Meredyth, her voice calm. "The fixed, tightly packed, impenetrable idea to *end* what she has begun. And that adds up to my life—*or the destruction of my peace for the rest of my life*. And she meant for us to find two hearts here instead of one. It was no mistake, her leaving Mira's heart on a shelf, his on his sleeve. It's how the bitch views us, Lucas, me and you—my heart on a shelf and yours in your hand. Her cunning little assessment of our relationship."

"You really give her too much credit, Meredyth," Jana replied to this. "Tell her, Lucas. Go on, tell her."

"Perhaps you are overstating it, Mere."

"She took time enough to pose her boyfriend in that grotesque manner with his spirit guides—his animals."

"Okay, so what?" he asked.

"What is it you Cherokees believe in? *Anima*—the sacred spirit of animal guardians—the anima in man, the bear, the wolf, the fox, the turtle—all manifestations of the Great Spirit, all spirits put here to guide mankind."

"What does any of that have to do with—"

"Lauralie knows all about you, Lucas, and your heritage, the culture of the First People, and your penchant for blood vengeance on any who take the life of a family member. She knows you often make decisions based on passion, the heart."

"You're reaching, Mere."

"Am I? She also knows me, Lucas. All things Meredyth. For instance, she knows how long now I have put my heart on hold . . . like a heart in a jar on a shelf put safely up, out of harm's way. So for me, she left Mira's heart."

"I'm sorry, Dr. Sanger," said Jana, "but this all sounds just a little too far out there for me, and I've seen some strange shit in my eleven years on the force. Couldn't it just be that she rushed outta here just ahead of our coming and in her haste simply forgot Mira's preserved heart? I mean, it looks to me as if she'd prepped it for her next mailing to you."

"I thought you suspected that would be Arthur's balls," countered Meredyth.

They stood clearly sizing one another up now. "Did I say that, or was that Lucas's line?" asked Jana.

"Lauralie meant for us to have *two* silent non-beating hearts, Lucas," Meredyth said to him. "One male, one female . . . one for you, one for me."

Lucas went to her and put an arm around her, saying, "Enough. I'm taking you home." He pointed to the nearest exit, the kitchen door that looked out on the rear of the property where on the map the creek bottom ran. Standing open to the night, the door represented a welcome escape from this hell. "Come on. What do you say?"

She stared at the shattered creaking door that seemed to *breathe in and out,* swaying in response to the wind created by the hovering chopper—a breeze that eddied about the frame, marred by a torn screen door, partially ripped away, clinging to a single hinge. The black exterior of forest beyond the door made up a horizon that enveloped this horror house on all sides. The shadows created by men and dogs searching the grounds appeared in, and as quickly disappeared from, the rectangle of the door frame. The cloudless, onyx sky and the freedom of it beckoned Meredyth to step out, to dare the *at-hand* darkness of the Texas night, to abandon the safe walls of the brightly lit kitchen where, for days now, Mira Lourdes's remains had lain in cold storage. Meredyth had a quick sense of it, the need to act on her courage or to lose it entirely, here and now.

Under Lucas's guiding hand, she moved toward the door. All the *true* darkness in the world had come to visit this once-peaceful, uneventful farmstead, coloring it with the evil hues of dark spirits now haunting its deep corners, closed doors, cupboards, nooks, and crannies. While Lucas had been off examining the back rooms, Jana and Meredyth had braved with flashlights the grim darkness of the root cellar, a cubbyhole of a basement below the kitchen. Meredyth felt the cold fingers of the earth in the cellar close round her soul again now, the long fingers of tainted banshees saturated with the odor of mold and mildew that had washed the cellar's stone walls with a luminescent green.

Once a benevolent home, the farmstead was now forever stained by the violent *danse macabre* of Lauralie's insanity. The evidence of evil *promenading* in shadow-box fashion here would soon fill a murder book fleshed out with Perelli's film tape and Chang's observations, but the stains on the floors, the walls, the curtains, the very DNA of the two dead here, and the one who walked away would remain indelibly on this house no matter the amount of ammonia and bleach used to combat it. *The ugly dark dye of evil this way had spread,* Meredyth thought, and its palpable presence remained inside the farmhouse, as if on a phantom plane, yet here too on this quantifiable plane, reaching out to the living with ghostly fingertips that scratched the ethereal nerves of angels.

But worse than having turned this old farmstead into an eternally dark interior place, was the darkness let loose on the exterior world from here—as if spirited away on a black-hearted demon's back. She should have seen it while hovering over the chimney below, how the evil had swept up and out the chimney on a spectral beast. Worst of all was the darkness lurking *free now,* outside somewhere, and going by the name of Blodgett . . . Lauralie Blodgett.

Meredyth went ahead of Lucas, stepping through the doorway and out into the night air, breathing deeply of its clean purity, reclaiming it as her right, and daring the dark to descend upon her. *Courageous, defiant girl,* she told herself, remembering her father's words once when she had had to get stitches in her knee for a terrible gash.

"She's out there someplace, Lucas, with all that pent-up

hatred and rage toward us all," she quietly said, sensing him beside her as she searched the darkness.

Lucas, his hand on her shoulder, replied, "You can't see it for the helicopter light, but just beyond is a harvest moon . . . the stars. Light in the firmament."

"Lucas, I want to look beyond tonight, beyond this case, and I want to make a future with you. I want to share your heart, and for you to share mine."

"Who knows what irony Lauralie has wrought, that she has inadvertently brought us closer than we have ever been before. All stemming from her hatred and lunacy. Ironic."

"She hates everyone she perceives has let her down, and all men have failed her miserably, as did we all, *miserably*. As far as she's concerned, all men are interested in only one thing, gratifying what's between their legs. So her emasculating Arthur is classic behavior; it fits with her worldview of currying favor with men for sex. But this thing with the hearts, I tell you, that runs even deeper. Her own heart has been turned to stone."

"Yet she was a child born of passion,"

"At least we see her coming. We understand her somewhat. Arthur didn't have a snowball's chance in Hell." She began walking toward the front of the house, Lucas at her side. "This dark in her soul, Lucas, it's a real black place, an abyss like the one the Biblical monster Abbaddon crawled up from. She's filled with this inky blackness. And she's out there someplace in the world lying in wait for us."

Six hours and too many cups of coffee to count later, Chang and company shut down the crime scene, and everyone left the farmstead while it was still dark, leaving yellow police-line tape over the doors and windows.

Chang had the two dogs transported to his lab along with Belkvin's body. Still the man's genitals had yet to be found. The two hearts were placed in separate coolers, each labeled and numbered. Each was also initialed with the supposed name of the owner: ADB and ML.

Meredyth and Lucas had remained until the end, and

with the APB that had been placed on Arthur Belkvin's BMW and on Lauralie Blodgett, they felt relatively sure that someone somewhere soon must spot the vehicle and/or its occupant and call in for the reward.

Yawning, tired, headachy, Meredyth now lay her head on Lucas's shoulder as he drove for her ranch home. They had informed Captain Lincoln that since he intended on turning the case over to the FBI, they were taking some time away. Jana North could play host to the FBI, Lucas had told the captain, who, not wishing for any argument, had agreed. "You two have done a remarkable job of taking the case to *first and goal*, Lucas," Lincoln summed up in football terms. "Time others *carried* the ball into the end zone."

"Lauralie's the one who'll select the end zone, Captain. Watch out for her."

"She's eluded us, I'll give her that," Lincoln replied, "but not for long now. I think it's a good idea, you two stepping back, getting out of harm's way for the time being. Take a trip; get out of Texas altogether for a time. You are her primary target, Meredyth. Makes sense your not wanting to be a sitting duck here. When she learns she can't find you, she'll become frustrated, and she'll make a hasty, foolhardy move, and we'll be ready for the misstep."

The agreement was that any further packages arriving for either Lucas or Meredyth, either at their homes or at the precinct, would be handled by the FBI.

Lucas yawned again, needing oxygen to the brain. He feared he'd fall asleep and run off the road. He flicked on the car radio for music or a talk show to keep awake. It was miles yet to Meredyth's getaway. She'd fallen asleep on his shoulder altogether now.

A pair of headlights roared up behind him and around the car at a good twenty miles an hour over the limit, a sporty-looking expensive car, but he let it pass without thought. No way was he going to get involved with a speeder, and to get on the horn, he'd have to wake Meredyth off his shoulder. Besides, the sun would soon be up, and he wanted a bed and sleep, not a police station and paperwork to fill out.

Another pair of headlights came up on the rearview, but this driver remained at a safe, sensible distance, maintaining the limit.

CHAPTER 18

Fence: guarding good luck

LUCAS STONECOAT BREATHED in deeply, taking in the dawn air as it streamed in through the window of the moving vehicle. As they passed below a covered bridge, he smelled the aged, gray wood and the pleasant greenery that graced the banks of the little river below. He had memorized the way to Meredyth's home away from home. He could see the shimmering edges of the lake in the distance, the waning moon creating diamonds along the lake's placid surface. He made out the beginnings of acres of white rail fencing that seemed to move with the grass and the rolling hills. He soon made out the stand of trees around the main house, and beyond this the stables. He thought of Yesyado, the thoroughbred horse he'd ridden the last time he was here. He thought of their excursion in the canoe, and their lovemaking on the bank. He had grown so fond of Meredyth.

Fond, he thought, mulling over the euphemism they had now for so long substituted for the word love—the real feeling they held for one another. He kissed her head where it lay on his shoulder, taking in the smell of her perfumed hair. He kissed her a second time, realizing she was completely oblivious to him. "I love you, Meredyth Sanger. Do you hear me? I love you."

She squeezed his thigh, letting him know that she had indeed heard the endearing words. "I love you too, you dumb Cherokee. I've always loved you."

"You're awake?"

"Not really, but I will remember this in the morning. . . ."

"We're almost home," he informed her, changing the subject.

"I can't wait to hit the bed."

"I hear you."

"You don't happen to have any peyote on you, do you? Maybe some stashed in the car?"

"Are you nuts? This is a police car."

"*Hmmm* . . . just wishful thinking."

"How 'bout some of that stockpile of brandy or wine in your cellar?"

"Dad's cellar . . . but I'm sure we can find something to agree upon."

She lapsed into silence for a few moments, then spoke again. "Lucas."

"Yes, dear?"

"Tell me again why you pursued the fifty-year-old case of Yolanda Sims."

"Somebody had to do it."

"No, seriously . . . tell me why. What power on earth led you to it in the first place?"

"I don't know really . . . it's a mystery. I was so fixated on finishing the transfers, you know, from hard copy to disks. Had all my people working down in the CC room overtime, weekends, Sundays, and racing through, when Donovan lifts a box and tilts it coming down from the ladder, and this murder book slips out and hits me in the eye. The photos of the girl littered the floor. Later, when I could see better, I opened the file up, thumbed through it, was about to hand it back to Bill when I decided to just hold on to it for a while."

"But why did you pursue it?"

"Maybe it was just for me; maybe I'd sleep better at night knowing I at least tried after looking into that little girl's eyes. Her death photos didn't do it, but that one full head shot of her *alive,* smiling, her eyes intense . . . it just told me I had no choice."

"That's what I love about you wild Texas Cherokee tough-guy types, that streak of intense empathy, that big heart. It's a rare man who cares as much as you do. There's not enough like you in this world."

"I'll take that as a compliment."

She lifted her lips to his, kissing him as they turned onto the long, winding dirt road leading up to her family home. In the distance, the first rays of the sun blinked over the horizon.

"Parents still in France?"

"Right, but even if they weren't, they hardly ever come out to the old place anymore. They're kinda sorta down to the one house now over in Clover Leaf. Closer to the action, shopping, theaters, and my condo."

"We've made it. We're here."

"At last," she replied. "Home . . . safe . . . perchance to sleep."

"I think it was perchance to dream, Mere."

"I'll settle for sleep this time round. What about you? You must be as exhausted as I am."

It had been an emotionally and physically taxing twenty-four hours, and Lucas knew that he too, laying his head on a pillow, would be instantly out. "Brandy and bed and your embrace?" he suggested.

"Sounds good to me . . . sounds very good to me."

THE CHOKING ODOR of last night's French-fry grease permeated the all-night, all-you-can-eat, empty-of-customers M&M Cafe, the lone waitress and cook sleep-walking through a routine of gearing up for the coming rush of their usual crowd here on Route 4. The local morning crowd, Lauralie Blodgett imagined, would be trickling through the doors within the hour; what passed for a rush hour here, twenty-odd miles from any road that might take her to the Interstate and escape. Escape did not appear promising, not from here.

She thought of the effect the deaths of Dr. Sanger's lover and her parents would have on her, how the woman would suffer for the rest of her days. The thought sustained her.

Lauralie Blodgett sat in the booth that looked out on the parking lot and her BMW, trying to enjoy a quiet moment over a plate of home cooking—meat loaf, turnip greens, mash potatoes, and gravy—and sipping at a Coca Cola, when the brown police cruiser pulled into the spot alongside what had been Arthur's car. The two policemen were laughing over something, one shoving the other as they climbed from their cruiser. In the trunk of the BMW lay the plastic-wrapped half corpse of Mira Lourdes.

She pictured flirting with the two officers in their Smokey the Bear hats—state troopers. She imagined smiling, nodding, blinking, and pawing catlike at them the way men couldn't resist. She searched her brain for an explanation about the car, should they suspect it stolen or wanted in connection with the Ripper crimes. She imagined one officer captivated with her, while the other insisted she pop the trunk to display her cargo, and their subsequent shocked reactions. They'd be catapulted from their obscurity to national fame just by virtue of having stumbled upon her at their local watering hole, the heroes of Harris County.

"That'll be the day that I die," she muttered, and the heavily made up blonde-wigged waitress looked over in her direction, only to see the two state troopers beyond the window in the faded twilight.

"Maury! Troops've landed! Put on two double cheeseburgers and fries!"

"What?" Maury called back from the kitchen. "What you say, Mary?"

"Del and Nolan're here! Troops're here!" shouted the waitress, her manner telling Lauralie that the troopers were regulars who apparently came to the M&M diner routinely each dawn.

Lauralie's mind raced with concern about the police, watching them intently, while the answer to a puzzle played out in her head as well. Mary and Maury. She put it together with the M&M on the big neon sign outside; that waitress and cook must be the M and M who owned the place. Simultaneously Lauralie listened to the TV news anchors on the tube in an overhead corner. She reveled in having created so much chaos, fear, and wonder, and she was pleased with the coverage up till now. In fact, she had fed on the *power* of knowing she alone was in control of this situation the press had dubbed the Post-it Ripper killings. The TV news and talk shows were now talking about it virtually twenty-four hours a day. The talk show hosts and anchormen and women ghoulishly picking over Mira Lourdes's bones, trying desperately to put her death together with various police raids across the city of Houston and last night's raid on the farmhouse. Reports praised police work in raids that had netted information that connected the murdered Dr. Arthur Belkvin to the Ripper case and the fugitive, Lauralie Blodgett. They then flashed her school photos on the screen along with a hot-line number. The TV cut back to a roomful of commentators and armchair profilers, expectant and anxious, awaiting the next chapter in the story that Lauralie was writing. One even had a chart of which parts of the Lourdes body remained to be delivered to authorities, and which had already been severed. They didn't have her heart. Lauralie felt certain that Dr. Meredyth Sanger must understand the significance of the hearts she'd left on display at the farmhouse.

She only half-heard the TV now, her attention on the two cops coming through the door as one stopped and pointed back at the car beside their cruiser. *"Two News has learned that two high-ranking officials with the Houston PD to whom the Ripper has communicated . . ."* The two policemen made tentative steps back toward the lot and began inspecting her car, moving about it like a pair of flies, curious and growing more so.

"The killer in this case does not fit any of our normal typologies when it comes to serial-killer profiling," came

the voice of a so-called FBI expert on the TV over the counter.

From her booth, Lauralie pointed to the TV and said, "I know more about that shit than anyone on the planet."

The waitress looked more closely at Lauralie now, studying her features as if trying to place her. "Yeah? Really? You don't look old enough to know a lot about crime fighting."

"I know more than that idiot profiler, *more* than any newscaster, *more* than anyone in law enforcement, *more* than all the damned politicians and religious leaders! *More* than even God himself *if only there was a God,* which I have never particularly relied upon, Mary."

The waitress unconsciously touched her name tag and recalled giving the young woman her name when first waiting on her. "You shouldn't say such things about God, honey."

"Mary, Mary, quite contrary, Mary, Mother of God . . . no, I don't hold faith in the Exalted One, *despite* or *because of* the years I've spent behind the black gates of Hell."

Mary stared at the stranger, trembling now, giving herself away in the eyes and wavering lower lip. They both realized in the same instant that Mary had recognized Lauralie's likeness as the woman law enforcement wanted for questioning. *Considered armed and dangerous.* The waitress's eyes moved off Lauralie a moment too late, going to the big plate-glass window, determining where the two troopers had gotten off to.

The TV news anchor was again relaying the story, with video, of an isolated farmhouse on Old Hazard Creek Road in Waller County, not terribly far from here, where the mutilated body of one Dr. Arthur D. Belkvin, a veterinary doctor and instructor at the Dean King School of Veterinary Medicine, was found in a commando-style raid by police—in an *apparent failed attempt* to locate Belkvin and an accomplice alive. The raid was the culmination of a week-long missing persons investigation in which authorities knew the missing woman had already been killed since her *chopped-up remains* had been mailed *piece by severed piece* to *several* high-ranking police officials in Houston.

"Liars!" Lauralie shouted at the TV. "They were only sent to the famous forensic shrink Dr. Meredyth Sanger and to her lover boy Lieutenant Lucas Stonecoat, and that's all. So why don't they name that bitch, huh? She's the cause of all this."

Mary, frozen in place, said nothing and did not move. Again Lauralie stared up at the TV to see her yearbook photos displayed.

"I got what I wished for, Mary. Finally . . . *wanted.*" She laughed. "Wanted by everybody now . . . hell of a price on my head, you know that, Mary? Mary, Mother of God, you think you'd like to collect on that bounty, Mother dear?" Lauralie again laughed.

Maury called from the kitchen, saying, "'Nough yammering out there, Mary. Burgers'll be up in five!"

"If you want to stay safe, get down behind the counter, Mother Mary," Lauralie told her as she snapped open her purse, tilted it in Mary's direction, and flashed the muzzle of a gun lying within. The muzzle looked like the head of a snake to Mary, but she knew what it represented.

Lauralie had seen the activity of police vehicles going for the farmstead as she had filled the gas tank at a Mobil station on the main artery leading to her and Arthur's "sugar shack" as she'd called it. She had waited at a careful distance, watching as slowly the raiders came away, leaving the area. One car in particular, belonging to Lieutenant Lucas Stonecoat, she had followed to this vicinity, noting where the shrink and the cop had turned off, approving of the location.

"I can't stop them from knowing they've located Arthur's car," she told herself aloud, "but I can stop them from calling it in."

"What's that, honey?" asked the waitress, trying to bolster some courage in her heart and some feeling in her knees. Pretending ignorance and failing miserably. The heavyset blonde's makeup had melded with the grease here, her pores shining. "Didya want something else? Some coffee maybe?" She lifted the steaming pot and took a step, coming out from behind the counter, when Lauralie lifted the 9mm Glock from her purse, causing Mary to drop the coffee on the counter and duck. The explosion of the coffee urn sounded like a gunshot inside the empty diner. Outside, the two state troopers snatched out their weapons.

She wasn't yet ready for capture. She pulled the trigger of the 9mm she'd purchased from Clive's Gun Emporium, two blocks distant from the orphanage, the day she walked out of Our Lady. The first shot exploded the plate-glass window dropping the closest trooper, his body slamming into the pebbled drive, his feet twitching in his boots. The exploding shards of glass had dug into the second trooper's face and eyes while he pulled off a single shot, narrowly missing Lauralie's head, hissing by her ear. Her second shot created a bloody hole in the other trooper's chest as he fell back on the hood of the BMW, instantly lifeless, his body slumped down to the grille, where he appeared merely to be in a slumped repose.

Maury had come racing in from the kitchen, had grabbed Mary by the arm, and was guiding her out the door behind the counter, rushing for a rear exit. Lauralie calmly stood, shouldered her purse, and walked around the counter, almost slipping on spilled coffee, going for the couple, her weapon smoking in her hand.

As she made her way to the rear of the M&M, Lauralie imagined Meredyth Sanger lying in the crook of Lucas Stonecoat's arm right now, sleeping blissfully under the canopy of safety she enjoyed, while she, an orphaned child without home or family or loved ones, was engaged in killing people she did not even know in her effort to make Sanger feel fear and self-loathing for her part in all of this. Lauralie meant to shatter Dr. Sanger's every conscious and perhaps unconscious moment of well-being and comfort, whatever it took.

She'd narrowly escaped the farmhouse raid, thanks to a sixth sense that police had zeroed in on Arthur. She suspected it had unraveled because Arthur had babbled on too

long with the realtor lady when they'd rented the farmhouse. This, along with the likeness in the newspaper,
made Arthur a liability, and adding to her growing dislike
of Arthur and his touch, she'd had to listen to his increasingly constant nagging about her motive for hating
Meredyth Sanger, until finally she'd simply had enough.

Lauralie moved down the narrow passageway and
examined the kitchen, searching for where Maury had taken
his waitress bride. She yanked open the freezer door, her
gun pointed at the frozen, hanging carcasses of beef, East
Texas elk, and buffalo. She recalled seeing elk stew and
buffalo burgers on the menu. She rushed from the kitchen,
back into the shoulder-width corridor, going for the rest
rooms.

No one in the women's room.

No one cowering in the men's room.

Back to the grimy cave of the corridor, and she flashed
on a momentary thought that wily Maury had gotten past
her and rushed out the front. Not likely.

She looked past stacks of boxes—food and vegetable
crates—to a blue door in the rear. *Gone out the back, Jack,*
she thought, going for the door.

She heard a motor trying unsuccessfully to turn over
just the other side of the blue rear door. As she pushed past
boxes and cartons in her way, her sleep-deprived brain
struggled to keep on task—*on Mary and Maury*—part of
her saying, *To hell with them . . . let them go . . . let them
live to tell the tale of her great marksmanship . . .* while
another part of her mind drifted back to Arthur and the way
she had left him at the farmhouse. *At least I gave the dog
man an everlasting home, a fucking stomping ground he
can haunt unendingly, his very own personal eternal habi-
tat,* she thought, recalling how much she had liked the old
place, and how he had completely spoiled it for her. Aside
from killing Arthur—something she'd known she would
do from the beginning—Lauralie had had to abandon the
farmstead prematurely, *before* she was finished with her
original plans. There remained a lot to carve up and forward to Dr. Sanger. But as in all things, one opportunity

lost meant another found. Lourdes's entire bloated lower portions, like the racked carcasses in Maury's freezer, presented the largest and most shocking image Lauralie had imagined possible. Her next move against Sanger and Stonecoat necessitated that she wrap with care the rest of Mira Lourdes's body and transport it here.

She stood at the rear of the restaurant now, throwing up her arms and the gun to protect her eyes from stone and gravel spitting up at her from the barking tires of Maury's red Dodge pickup as it roared from the rear lot, ramming into a Dumpster and dragging it along with it. Lauralie leveled the gun, feeling a slight admiration for the M&M couple for making it this far.

Aiming for the back of Maury's head, his chef's hat still on, Lauralie steadied the gun with both hands and fired. The bullet zipped through the rear window, creating a little hole in both the window and the back of Maury's white hat, coloring it red, and opening up a gaping hole on the exit side, blood and brain matter all over the dash and dripping down the steering wheel as the truck plunged into a bank of public phones that now crumpled and jammed below the truck's demolished grille.

The red pickup held in place, its horn sent out a cry like a wounded, trapped animal. Only Mary, jammed in behind the passenger-side airbag, had any mobility left, should she leap from the disabled vehicle.

Lauralie looked around. Cars whizzed by on Highway 41 fronting the M&M Cafe. No one had pulled in, and no one had paid any heed to the scene at the diner.

Lauralie heard Mother Mary whimpering within the confines of the cab as she neared the disabled vehicle. *Let the woman live. Think of the horror she now has to live with, if you let her live,* Lauralie's head told her.

"No . . . not a time to take chances now . . ." she answered her doubts. *Not until I make Sanger's life not worth living . . . not until I kill her man and maim her for life.*

Again she leveled the gun, watching the stunned, blubbering Mary struggling against the duel problems of

Maury's weight and her imprisoning air bag, which had bloodied her face on impact. Her wig lay half on, half off her head. She tore with both hands at the ballooned air bag.

"Let me get that for you, honey," shouted Lauralie, firing into Mary's head, the bullet exiting and exploding Mary's brain and the air bag simultaneously.

Since the troopers had not acted quickly enough, no one would know that the random killings here had anything to do with Lauralie Blodgett, she reasoned.

She dropped the smoking gun back into her purse. "And they say there's no such thing as a free meal," she joked, stepping lively now for the front of the cafe and her car. Passing the dead trooper sitting upright against her grille, she suddenly felt a pair of icy hands wrap around her ankle. The dead trooper had reached out and latched on, but he hadn't the strength, and she flicked her ankle, freeing it, coming away with a bloodstained stocking.

She reached into her purse, fingering the gun again, but the trooper had again gone dead. She let it be, got into the car, turned the key, and pulled straight back from the parking space. One trooper lay in the painful pose of a swastika, his body going in four directions at once, while the other lay in repose where he had softly slid from her grille to the pebbled drive when she had backed out.

She turned and pulled out onto the highway, and drove north toward the Spring Brook area and Meredyth Sanger's secret getaway home on Lake Madera. From what she had been able to learn of Meredyth's parents, they seldom visited the Spring Brook home anymore, residing as they did in faraway Clover Leaf. She had learned that Mom and Dad would be arriving home from Europe tomorrow—information she had gleaned from a neighbor when Lauralie and Arthur had arrived at Mrs. Gaines's door, posing as realtors wishing to talk to the Sangers. Mrs. Gaines had been more than willing to help them, and she'd informed them that the Sangers were vacationing in France. Lauralie had gotten the Clover Leaf address when following Byron Priestly on his obsessive search for Meredyth the same day of his death. Now the ideal pair of wealthy parents would be blown up in their idyllic golf community, when they turned a key in the door to their picture-perfect, gas-heated retirement home. All it would take now, a single spark between lock and key. Lauralie had gained entrance by night, setting off the alarm, but she had charmed the bored, jaded young security guard who'd led a team of younger men to the location. She'd claimed to be the clumsiest daughter of Mr. and Mrs. Sanger, visiting from California, and promising the man a date while she was in town, and young Mike had bought it, waving off the other security guards.

After Mike had finally gone, Lauralie wandered the luxurious house, and she watched the fish in the aquarium self-feed from a dispenser, and then she opened a gas line and left. The deadly gas had now had a twenty-four-hour buildup, and it would be forty-eight hours when the cab from the airport pulled up tomorrow. "What a homecoming for Momma and Papa Sanger," she said to the empty car.

From Paris to paradise, she mused, locating the niche off Highway 41 that led into the Madera Lake Estates. She needed sleep badly and wondered who on the lake might accommodate her.

Tonight she would strike Sanger at her heart, "And just when the bitch thinks she can't possibly stand another blow, she'll learn about Mom and Dad dying in an inferno."

Sleep . . . rest now, her mind told her. She could not recall the last peaceful sleep she'd had. Her mind seemed always in turmoil, always racing, if not with what she must do, then what she had done, examining, questioning, shoring up, and tearing down.

Her eyes closed, the sound of traffic going by on the paved road just the other side of the stand of trees filtering into her consciousness. Somewhere in the distance, she heard the faint whine of sirens. A ghastly discovery at the local diner, no doubt. She saw a mailbox with the family name carved into the wood—The Brodys—and turning in, she followed a winding dirt road toward the lake, when the Brody house peeked from behind the forest wall. She stopped short, viewing the house in the wood. It loomed large and lovely, a beautiful wraparound porch, several tur-retlike pinnacles, a Cape Cod design. She also spied a row-boat this side of the lake at the pier.

She backed up a bit and pulled into a clearing among the trees, parked, shut down the engine, and considered her options. Somewhere on this same lake, Meredyth Sanger and Lucas Stonecoat were enjoying the warmth of their bed, wrapped in one another's embrace.

Sitting in the morning gloom, Lauralie thought of how she had posed Arthur's body, his heart on his sleeve, his dogs at his feet. She'd wanted Sanger and the others to find him in the mocking pose, and to find Mira's heart in the jar. After posing Arthur, she'd had to struggle with Mira's frozen half-corpse alone, wrapping her and transporting her to the car, breaking her nails and scarring her hands in the process. She had *intentionally* left her DNA in the freezer. Any idiot could put her together with the abduction and murder of Mira Lourdes by now. The investigation was a farce; any leads they enjoyed had, after all, been supplied by the Ripper herself.

"Catch me if you can, but not before I let you," she said to the empty woods around as she exited the car and began to walk the distance to the house, her purse slung over her shoulder, the weight of the gun pulling it down.

"Time for a neighborly visit . . ."

COGNAC. **LUCAS AND** Meredyth had, early that morning, settled on aged, expensive cognac, and after a playful con-test of who could hold the most liquor before falling into a much-needed, deep slumber, they had nestled into one another's arms and had melded into one another's cognac dreams. Now, at three in the afternoon, they awakened after eight hours of sleep to cognac hangovers.

Meredyth asked herself if she had keyed in the security code downstairs before they had gone to bed. The log cabin–style home was equipped with a state-of-the-art security system, and was built to be impenetrable from the outside—no exposed wires, no weak spots. She brought up the memory of punching in the code, and she also recalled having taken both her cell phone and Lucas's off ring to accept messages only, so as to get some uninterrupted sleep.

Now it was mid-afternoon and Lucas was administering more cognac to combat the hangover, and it worked. They showered together and made love under the warm spray until they took their lovemaking back to the bed. There they luxuriated in one another's embrace, passions, and playfulness.

Sated, lying in one another's arms again, they were moved by hunger to dress, go downstairs, and raid the kitchen for anything they could find in the fridge and on the shelves. As she prepared sandwiches for them, Lucas joked that a typical reservation house could fit into Meredyth's kitchen.

"Is that designed to make me feel guilty?" she asked, punctuating her words with the knife in her hand.

"No . . . just an observation."

"Well, I hear the Indian casinos are making a bundle," she countered. "So not everyone on the res is piss poor."

"Casinos pay a petty tribute to the tribe, not enough to make a difference to the common good. In effect, an Indian tribe on a modern reservation is a commune—everyone helping everyone, everyone doing his part, all that. But it doesn't ever work out that way, now does it?"

"No . . . it doesn't. Human nature being what it is."

"Most of the casinos are run by shrewd half-breeds who are as shameless as any CEO you have trading on Wall Street, NYC," he said.

"It can't be that bad."

"You haven't been out to the Coushatta."

"Well . . . perhaps we can get a little public awareness going, start a drive, have a marathon or something, generate some funds."

"You don't understand. It's not that simple."

"Why not?"

"Because of who we are—American Indians. We have been made charity cases by the state—the U.S. Government—for almost two hundred years now, since the 1820s."

"What's that got to do with what I'm proposing?"

"Damn, it's got everything to do with it. The Cherokee were robbed of their Eastern ancestral lands, an area covering most of Georgia, Alabama, Mississippi, Tennessee, and portions of Kentucky. They were given Oklahoma before the Okies arrived, and it became an Indian state. My ancestors migrated from the Tallaquah, Oklahoma, promised lands to here, East Texas, and we cohabited with the Alabama, Coushatta, and other western tribes. What I'm saying is that the Texas Cherokee in particular didn't want any handouts from the U.S. Government. My people left the ancestral lands *before* Andrew Jackson forced all the southern tribes out of the Southeast on the Trail of Tears. They saw the writing on the wall, so to speak. They next left Oklahoma before the white man's treaty there was made and broken again. In Texas, we found a third home so as to not accept the white man's charity along with his worthless, stinking treaties."

"Nice history lesson, but I still don't see what it has to do with raising awareness and funds for the reservation families and children."

"They don't want your charity, however heartfelt it may be, Mere. Don't you get it?"

"You don't have to shout!"

He raised his hands as if arrested. "Sorry . . . let's eat."

"I didn't know it was such a touchy subject with you."

"Not me . . . I'm no reservation Indian, remember? I got off the res a long time ago."

"I'm sorry White America has treated your people so wrongly, Lucas. I wish there was something I could do, that's all."

"Meredyth, no one, least of all this clansman, holds you responsible for the thefts and rapes and lies committed in the past by the U.S. Government and military in the name of Manifest Destiny and assimilation of the aboriginals. So let's leave it at that . . . and while we're at it, you've got no business feeling guilty in the least for Lauralie Blodgett's becoming a twisted and cold-blooded killer either."

"You saying that maybe I take on too much responsibility on my shoulders?"

"Precisely, yes."

They fell silent for a time, listening to the robins and sparrows circling and darting through the trees outside the kitchen window in what seemed an eternal dance, but was in fact a series of short-lived bursts of energy in a chase of give-and-take, back-and-forth. A Texas raven cried off in the distance, while hummingbirds, tasting of the nectar of oleander bushes, silently hovered about the windows. A mild scent of oleander wafted into them. Meredyth smiled and pointed at the hummingbirds, telling Lucas they had once had a family of hawks visit the cabin and take up residence for two months before they'd disappeared.

Together, they made their way out on the wide screened porch, taking their sandwiches and drinks with them. Here they looked out over the lake to one side, the horse stables to the other. "What shall we do now?" she asked. "Water play or horse play?"

A phone rang somewhere deep in the house. "That sounds like my cell phone," he said. "And I left it upstairs in the bedroom."

"It's most likely mine. I switched it back on when we woke. My secretary at the practice is likely wanting to know when she can begin scheduling patients again."

"So where's your cell?"

"Upstairs alongside yours. But I didn't activate yours again," she lied.

"So not even Sophia knows the phone number to the cabin?"

"Not even Sophia, no, since there is no phone in the house. It's my one sinful indulgence, this place, and I vow it will never be spoiled by TVs, telephones, radios, computers, E-mail, or any other gadgets of labor. If I have to make a call out from here, it's done on my cell."

"You mean to tell me you don't have one TV or radio in the entire house?"

"I thought you knew that from your last visit."

He blew out a lungful of air. "Guess I was having too much fun to notice."

"The only radio is the one in your car, Lucas."

"*Hmmm* . . . I see. And you're not curious about what's going on downtown?" he asked. "I mean with the case, any results on the APB on the girl or the car?"

"Not in the least, not today."

"I can't help but wonder if there've been any sightings of her . . . what her whereabouts might be . . . any new developments we should be paying attention to . . . that sort of thing, you know."

"Lucas, listen to yourself. No wonder you're so tightly wound."

"Whataya mean?"

"You left the scene of a grisly murder maybe ten, eleven hours ago, one in which you were *relieved* of command by your superior—remember that?"

"Yeah, yeah, but—"

"But nothing! You as much as told Lincoln to cram it."

"I did? I don't remember telling him to—"

"You told him he could rely on Jana North to assist the FBI, implying you wouldn't be available for such duty, and he took you up on it, Lucas."

"All right . . . I remember . . . but you know as well as I do that we're both too much a part of this case to simply step off."

"Lauralie has seen to that, and up to this point, she's been pulling all the strings, pal, but not anymore . . . at least not *my* strings. I'm more highly invested in this case than anyone, Lucas, but I'm not playing her game any longer. I am *stepping off* this lunatic's merry-go-round."

"Bravo! I think that's excellent advice you're giving yourself, Mere. Go for it."

"I intend to. Maybe Patterson and Lincoln are right, Lucas. Maybe you and I should have turned over the investigation from the moment we realized the killer's mania was focused on me and you."

"Well, now you've got your wish. Removed from the

case, way out here in a place where she can't get at you . . . it's the right thing to do, Mere, absolutely."

"You make it sound as if I'm washing my hands of any responsibility."

"No, not at all. I don't mean to suggest anything of the sort."

"What's the alternative? Go on the offensive? Attack this crazy young woman where she lives? I might like the plan except for the fact we don't know where the fuck she is or where the fuck she will be in an hour, a day, a week. And you, Lucas 'Wolf Clansman' Stonecoat, what do *you* do given an opportunity to wash *your* hands of it? You fight it tooth and nail!"

"All I'm suggesting is we answer the cell phone, Mere."

The ringing from upstairs stopped.

"Bullshit. At least be honest with *me,* Lucas."

"What?"

"My restless Cherokee detective. You want to *leap* back into the chase with both feet. You're chomping at the bit like Sayswho and Yesyado when Jeff jingles their reins. You are that anxious to get back to tracking that bitch."

"All right, I admit that I'm a little eager to know what, if anything, has come to light since we put out the APB on the car."

"Do you *have* to be a cop twenty-four-seven?"

"What about you, Doctor? Heal thyself. Do *you* have to be a *shrink* twenty-four-seven?" he countered.

"*Touché, mon amour.* I guess we both know each other better than most couples, hey, Lucas?"

"That's usually a good thing, isn't it?"

"Dr. Phil would say so, but sometimes there's such a thing as too much honesty."

"Really? And when is that?"

"When the truth is clearly that two people are *incompatible.*"

"You think that's the case with us?" he asked.

"Do you?"

"What kind of word games are we playing here, Mere?

What's more important than the truth that . . . that I love you?"

This silenced her for a moment. She raised her lips to his, kissing him. "I love you too, Lucas, truly."

The noise of birds skimming over the lake at the bottom of the lawn rose up to them. "Then we have no problem we can't overcome."

"You buy into that? That love can overcome any problem, any obstacle?" she asked.

"In my culture, aside from God, it is the most powerful force in the cosmos."

"Once you loved Tsali, and once she loved you, but what happened to your powerful force then?"

He dropped his gaze and sipped at his lukewarm coffee. She saw that she had hurt him, her words stinging. "That was young love. *Our love,* Meredyth, makes us *feel* young, but it's more solid, grounded. We have much more in common than you had with Byron and I had with Tsali, and we learn from each other each day."

She wrapped her arms around him. "So much evil is done in the name of love, like this love-starved, love-seeking Blodgett girl, searching for the attention of the world because she couldn't get it from her own mother."

"Every beat cop and detective on the force knows that love kills," he replied, holding her tight. "If it's not a prostitute murder, it's a stalking-ex murder, and if not that, the father who kills his family, why? Because 'I loved them too much.' "

"So many deaths all balled up with love and its many permutations. And yet so many beautiful and wondrous outcomes have resulted from pure, genuine love."

"Let's don't ever take our love for granted, Mere."

"Agreed. Let's celebrate it often."

"Right you are. All the same, sweetheart, I am curious to know if anything's come of our APB."

"Christ, Lucas, it's not *our* APB anymore. Ahhh," she mock-screamed. "I give up. Make the call. No! Wait a minute. Hold on!" She had pushed him away from her and stepped back. "If you love me, you'll get it off your mind for a while."

"Celebration time, you mean?" he asked, holding his arms out for her to return to him.

She fell into his arms. "I'm not referring to sex. I'm talking about having some fun—F-U-N!"

He held her at arm's length, staring into her sea-green eyes. "Hell, you're right. I've forgotten how to spell it. As for the Ripper business, it's not even my case anymore. Let *them* deal with it."

She pulled away and went to the porch swing, pulling herself into a ball there. "I really don't want to hear another word about the fucking case, Lucas." She pulled her feet up and under her. The swing swayed only slightly, unhappily.

"Isn't that what I just said? Am I missing something here?" Lucas watched her sulk, and then he stared down at the movement around the stables. Men who worked the horses and saw to their needs had already begun to exercise some of the animals. "Let's go for a ride, shall we?" he suggested.

She remained balled up, but her eyes found his. After regarding him for a moment, she smiled. "Now your're talking."

"Walk you to the stables?"

"You're on." Meredyth's smile broadened, lighting up her features.

"Is this how you intend to *always* get your way with me?" he asked.

"Whatever are you talking about?" She pushed open the porch screen door and skipped down the stairs. "I have no *modus operandi* that you don't know about."

He followed her down the steps and along the gravel drive to the path leading to the stables. "I meant the way you had me come to the deduction you wanted."

"Are you suggesting that I would stoop to some sort of *Aristotelian third degree* to bring you around to the conclusion you'd already logically deduced, Detective, in the subterranean depths of that big head of yours?"

"Aristotelian . . . is that a shot?" He grabbed her and began tickling. She ran ahead of him with Lucas giving chase. Their laughter joined with the robins and the sparrows nipping at one another, flitting in and out of the trees. Their laughter echoed in the quiet and rumbled down to the workmen at the stables, who looked in their direction, and the laughter traveled across the lake.

Now, arms entwined, they sauntered the rest of the way down the path toward the stables, hibiscus bushes and a thicket of trees lining their way. "Kind of like Oz for grown-ups here," Lucas confided. "I really like this place, Mere."

"Good . . . I'm glad you do. Strange thing is, Lucas, it's always been special for me and my parents, but now, having you here to share it . . . well . . . it's positively dreamlike."

"I know what you mean . . . the sharing of it, like we shared the desert that night—that's what makes it doubly special."

A tractor down at the stables roared into animation. Behind them, just out of earshot, Lucas's police-band radio crackled into life as well, and Stan Kelton's voice came over, asking, "Lucas? Lieutenant Stonecoat? If you can hear me, please respond."

After a pause, Kelton cursed and broke off.

In the house, on Lucas's cell phone, Jana North was leaving a message at the same time. "Lucas . . . I tried Dr. Sanger's cell and now I'm trying you. There's been an *unusual* shooting at a cafe in the Spring Brook area, not far from the Waller County line and the farm we raided. Four dead, two civilians, two state troopers. Looks like a hell of a firefight, but the troopers only got off one round. And, Lucas, a silver-gray BMW was seen leaving the scene."

A groundskeeper who came in and did the landscaping once a month arrived, pulling in alongside Lucas's unmarked squad car. He regarded the car as something unusual, and seeing the house had been opened, he guessed one or more of the family had come up from Houston for the weekend. Surveying the stables, he saw Dr. Sanger and a guest waiting for a pair of fine-looking, eager horses to be saddled up. Howard Kemper wondered at the injustice in the world, that some people had all this freaking free time and lavishness in their lives, while he had played the Texas and Louisiana lotteries religiously for the past ten years, to win the occasional fifty or a hundred bucks.

He shook his head, climbed up on the back of his truck, sat on the lawn mower, and turned the ignition key. He drove it down the ramp and out onto the thick grass, where he began the chore he would normally have completed by now if circumstances in his life hadn't gotten so hectic this morning. Riding high on the mower, Kemper thought he saw something shiny and reflective off in the trees down by the lake. When he looked again, it was gone, whatever it was. Likely just the way the sun had spanked the surface of the lake right now, he guessed. Damn beautiful lake, and unless you were native to the area, you'd never guess it a man-made lake.

After a moment of feeling odd, as if someone were watching him, Howard began cutting grass in earnest, and whenever he did so, his complete attention went to the job. He and his machine became one; for Howard, it was a kind of Zen thing, cutting grass.

In what other profession could a potbellied, middle-aged man with no education or desire for one, with a pickup and the right tools, make a living riding around on his rump, enjoying the sun, the fresh air, the view, the squirrels, and the birds in the trees? *The Zen of Lawn Maintenance.* He thought it'd make a great book title and a bundle of money, a book like that, but he wondered how he could get it written. Mr. Brody, across the lake, was rumored to have made his money writing paperback Westerns and suspense novels centering around a turn-of-the-century Sherlock Holmes type. He reportedly wrote two books a year—living off advances and royalties. Perhaps Brody'd be interested in cowriting the lawn maintenance book if Howard proposed dictating it to him, but then Brody seemed pretty disinterested in his own damn lawn, leaving all decisions regarding that green nuisance, as he called it, to Howard's judgment. Brody claimed to hate grass and anything smacking of lawn work. *How does any man ever cultivate such an attitude toward his own lawn?* Kemper wondered.

CHAPTER 19

Peace

THE HORSEBACK RIDING at an end, Lucas and Meredyth found themselves invited by the horse wranglers, brothers Jeff and Tommy Farnsworth, to dine on steaming-hot tamales, burritos, and Texas chili cooked up by the boys' mother. Lucas learned that they lived in a small house at the end of the property. They ate off the back of their pickup, the gun rack in the cab displaying a bolt-action Remington rifle that fired a .223-caliber bullet at high velocity. Lucas began talking guns with the young men, telling them of his handgun collection, and bragging that he owned a U.S. 7th Cavalry eight-shooter hanging on his wall at home, one which had been authenticated to have been taken off one of George Armstrong Custer's men by a Sioux warrior at the Battle of the Little Big Horn. He left one brother fascinated, the other squinting and skeptical.

"Damn!" responded the younger brother, Tommy. "Could it be Custer's gun?"

"No, but it definitely belonged to one of his men."

Jeff skeptically said, "Custer fought the Sioux. How'd it get into your family?"

"Came down to my family in a horse trade. My grandfather recognized the value of the thing. He was a shrewd man."

The boys were duly impressed. "Sure would like to see it sometime," said Tommy. "Think next time you're out this way that you could bring it along?"

"Sounds like it ought to be housed in a museum," said Meredyth, "and not carted about like a baseball trading card."

"I keep it in a gun case, and I transport it in a gun box, not a cereal box, Mere."

Lucas wound up handling the Remington bolt action .223-caliber rifle, looking down its sight, testing its scope. "Do you know this thing is loaded?" he asked the brothers.

"Keep it handy for runnin' off the occasional coyote," said Jeff matter-of-factly.

"And sometimes, real, real early in the morning," added Tommy, "you get a fox messin' round the henhouse. Lost some good layin' hens to foxes. Really got Ma pissed off."

Lucas's large red hands caressed the length of the Remington, his eyes taking in its every line and feature. "Damned pretty weapon."

"It's good for two hundred and fifty freakin' yards," boasted Jeff.

"Bagged a lot of deer with her," added Tommy.

Meredyth had begun humming the tune to "Pretty Woman," and then began singing, "Pretty weapon . . . firing down the street . . . pretty weapon . . . the kind I'd like to meet . . . to clean one day . . . come what may. . . ."

The men ignored her. "What do you carry when you're on duty, Lieutenant?" asked Jeff.

"A Police Special .38, Smith & Wesson on the ankle, but in my shoulder holster I carry a German-made Glock nine-millimeter semiautomatic."

"You got it on you now?"

"No, no. Left 'em up at the house, otherwise we'd get in some target shooting."

"Enough with the gunplay already," announced Meredyth, who then whispered, "Anyone would think you love your gun more than me."

"I hate to imagine what a good shrink might do with that," he replied, causing a snicker to erupt from Jeff. Tommy asked his big brother what was so funny.

Meredyth ignored Lucas's remark and said, "Are we or aren't we going fishing on the lake, Lucas?"

"Yeah, sure."

Jeff Farnsworth replaced the Remington on the gun rack dangling across his rear window. Meredyth, looking off in the distance toward the lake, saw Howard Kemper puttering about on his lawn mower still. "Howard's working late," she muttered.

"Got a late start, 'bout an hour ago," said Jeff.

"What time is it?" she asked.

A glance at his watch told Lucas it was nearing six P.M. He showed her the watch face.

"We should see a beautiful sunset over the lake," she said.

Lucas offered her his arm, and they started in the direction of the boathouse. The closest neighbors were also on Lake Madera, but they were across the mile-wide water on the opposite shore. As Lucas and Meredyth walked off, behind them Jeff and Tommy shouted their good-byes.

Approaching the boathouse from a winding path leading away from the stables, they lost sight of Howard and his mower, but they could hear the motor growing fainter and fainter as it moved back up the hill toward the house and driveway.

Coming on a clearing, they saw that the gardener had done an uneven job of it, whole areas still thick and in need of cutting. "Got to be something wrong with Howard's mower," she said.

"Or Howard. Does he drink on the job?"

She playfully punched him in the shoulder. "No, not that I know of, that is."

Lucas watched the lawn man puttering about the back

of his truck now, having climbed off the mower. Lucas had expected Howard to drive the mower back up the ramp and onto the flatbed of his large truck, but he simply shut it off and left it sitting alongside the rear tire in the drive. From this vantage point, looking up the steep knoll to the house, the spindly upturned rakes, hoes, and other garden tools looked like dead tree limbs reaching skyward, creating a bizarre mosaic against the darkening eastern sky.

Meredyth stared to where Lucas watched Howard grab some hedge clippers from the well of the truck, and slowly the middle-aged gardener began snipping away at the oleander bushes surrounding the house.

"Looks like he's fine, Mere. Just missed a section of grass is all."

"Damn, he's really hacking my oleander bushes all to hell. Maybe I'd better put a stop to that before we go out on the lake."

"Must know what he's doing, Mere. Isn't it true that the *more* you cut flowering bushes back, the *more* they flower?"

"I don't know. You're probably right." Her body language told him she opted for the lake over a confrontation with Howard Kemper. She now pulled Lucas onward toward the docks, and soon their shoes were making a pitter-patter against the weathered boards winding about the boathouse. On one side bobbed a canoe and a rowboat, and on the other, beneath the canopy of the boathouse, Lucas made out a motorboat hovering on davits just above the water.

She placed a hand over the switch that would send the motorboat down and into the water. "Your choice," she said. "I just want to enjoy the sunset from the lake."

"Rowboat. It's more romantic, and I can use the exercise."

She pointed out to where the fishing poles hung in the boathouse, adding, "And there's live bait in the cooler. We keep it stocked at all times. By the time we get out on the lake, the worms will've thawed, and you can count on their wiggling their behinds coming off hibernation. We'll have lake perch for dinner. You clean 'em, I'll cook 'em."

"Nothing better than lake perch," he replied, opening the cooler and staring at its empty contents. "No worms here. No ice either."

She looked over his shoulder, perplexed. "Must be those damn Farnsworth boys. They've emptied us of fresh bait and not replaced it."

"Forget about it. Let's just go boating," he suggested, replacing the fishing poles he'd lifted from their hooks.

As they boarded the rowboat, Meredyth continued berating the Farnsworth brothers. "Gotta talk to those two. I don't begrudge them enjoying the lake and using what's here while we're gone, but the least they could do is show a little respect for the property of—"

"It's only worms, Mere. Let's just enjoy the lake and the evening."

"You're right." She nodded, smiling. They went out on the water as the final rays of daylight began to wane in the west. Meredyth sat in rapt attention to the display of light, color, and brushwork across the sky created by the mix of sunset, cloud, and haze.

"Oh, Lucas, look at it!"

"Beautiful," he agreed.

"It's like a light show, like I imagine the aurora borealis to be."

"I've seen the northern lights in Alaska."

"Alaska, really?"

"Now there's a show," he said. "Looks like God's version of a Navajo sand painting, only in the sky."

"When were you there?"

"On a trip last year, one of those adventure travel packages that followed the 1890s Gold Rush from Skagway to Dawson. Want to do it sometime? It's a rough trip but great fun. We can see the lights together."

"I'd like that. I really would."

"Alaska's incredible, Mere, a religious experience."

Lucas had rowed them out to the center of the lake, had

rested the oars, and had allowed the boat to drift and glide, going about in a lazy circle with the wind and the eddies. Meredyth had gotten comfortable, her shoes kicked off, and she now lay nestled into him, her back to Lucas, and he leaned into her and wrapped his arms about her. They watched the changing, lavender sky, considering each unique, evolving reflection that changed with each drifting cloud in the western horizon.

The wind had grown cold and biting, lifting Meredyth's hair into his face, and Lucas laughed as he struggled with it. The rowboat twirled now in the wind like a Disneyland Tea Cup ride. They laughed at the joy of it, Meredyth shouting, "Horray! Whoa!" as if on a roller coaster.

"Wind's really gusting. I'd better get control of this thing," he finally said.

"Why? Let it be. I love seeing the sky and clouds go round and round."

Something hit them a hard, teeth-jarring thud that shook Lucas's oars off their gunwale rests, noisily jangling the oarlocks.

"What the hell was that?" she asked.

They were rammed by something large and threatening, and Lucas wondered aloud, "Some big-assed Texas alligator maybe?"

In order to look around, Lucas hefted her up to a sitting position and they both gasped, simultaneously seeing a loose rowboat on the now-dark waters. The moon had disappeared beneath scudding clouds, and the lake had become a black mirror image of the night sky.

"What the hell . . . a loose boat."

"Happens out here on occasion," she calmly replied. "Looks like it tore loose from the Brody pier."

The boat had ricocheted off and was drifting away from them. Flies hovered above the little ghost boat, and Lucas began swatting a few that had jumped ship and come aboard with them. Getting to his knees and using an oar, he began pulling the errant boat toward them. "We'll run it back across the lake to your neighbors," he said.

"Forget it. They'll find it in the morning."

But as the wayward little green boat approached under Lucas's control, they both saw the flesh of a dead man under returning moonbeams, the dead man lying stripped and cold against the bottom, covered in squirming, feeding worms.

"Your missing worms . . . thawed out hours ago."

The worms covered the man's features, and his blood-soaked throat, where they slithered like miniature snakes in and out of a gaping knife wound zigzagging from ear to ear below the rugged beard, creating a second mouth that crawled with life.

"My God, it's Howard Kemper!"

"The gardener? That's impossible."

"Yes, it is!"

"Then who the hell was up at the house on the mower in his clothes?"

"It's her, Lucas! Lauralie! She's somehow found us!"

"I need you calm, Meredyth! Calm down. Get a grip." He held her shoulders firm in his hands, shaking her.

"And here we sit, *literally* sitting ducks, in the middle of the fucking lake, defenseless!"

"We can row for the other shore, get to your neighbors, call for help!" He lifted one of the oars and pushed off the boat that had carried Howard Kemper's worm-eaten body to them. He then lifted the second oar and began rowing desperately for the opposite shore.

"There're no lights on at the Brody place," she shouted, shaking the boat. "There's always a light."

"Maybe they're away!"

"No . . . they'd use a timer. Something's terribly wrong. She's been there . . . used their place to watch us . . . used their boat to come across to my house, killed Kemper, and masqueraded as him." She recalled the ferocity with which Kemper had attacked her oleander hedges.

"Then we'll break in at the Brodys, sound an alarm, get people out here one way or the other, and snare her in her own trap."

"She's up there in my house. God knows where . . .

doing what? Making a special delivery of some sort. God, what I'd give for my cell phone right now."

"And my guns."

A muffled thunderclap came tumbling down to the lake from the house, followed by a second identical clap. "What the hell was that?" asked Meredyth.

"Sounds like rifle fire crackling in the distance." *Like gunfire heard in Civil War reenactments,* Lucas thought, except these shots were live rounds.

In the gloom of darkness, it was difficult to see what was happening on land at the house, and at the stables, but Lucas and Meredyth could make out the faint silhouette of the Farnsworth pickup truck up at the house, in the driveway alongside Kemper's truck. Following their eyes down the slope of the lawn, they saw the two bodies downed by gunfire, and in a moment, a glimmer of hope welled up, as each boy, Tommy and then Jeff, showed signs of life.

"The bitch somehow got hold of the Remington," Lucas said, "and shot them with their own gun. Damn her!"

"She sent them running toward the lake, toward us."

"Then opened fire."

Tommy and Jeff, both shot and bleeding, had begun to crawl for the cover of trees. Lucas and Meredyth watched, helpless to do anything as another shot rang out, killing Tommy. "Nooo!" Meredyth cried out.

Another shot hammered into Jeff's back. Both young men were dead. No one could survive two such rounds. Lucas had seen Jeff's body respond to the fourth shot, absorbing the powerful impact. "God damn the bitch!" he shouted.

"What're we going to do, Lucas? We're next!"

A fifth shot rang out, and Tommy Farnsworth's head exploded. She was now using the bodies for target practice, telling Lucas and Meredyth that she could hit any target she wished from the upstairs window of the house, and given that it was hunting season, no one would think the shots unusual.

Lucas had already pulled Meredyth down below the

gunwale of the rowboat, hoping to leave Lauralie with as small a target as possible. But bullets began to ping into the metal hull. "We've got to take our chances in the water!"

Lucas rocked the boat, calling for Meredyth to do the same. Another bullet whistled past, spitting up water. Suddenly, the boat gained momentum and flipped, sending them into the lake. Holding onto the upturned boat, Meredyth came up fearing that he had been hit, but he assured her otherwise. "Keep hold of the boat and kick like hell for shore!" he shouted as more rounds pinged into the water around them.

They guided their cover toward the opposite shore. "We've got to get out of range of the gun," Lucas told her.

Bullets continued to ping off the rowboat.

"She's stringing this out," gasped Lucas, spitting water. "She could have hit either one of us with that scope and range. Likely had both of us in her crosshairs."

"Else she's a lousy shot." Meredyth gulped lake water, continuing to kick for shore.

"A weapon like that . . . with the scope, a child could pick us off out here. No, she deliberately chose to wound those two Farnsworth boys, and she also chose to finish them off when they posed no threat at a moment when she could have put one through my head or yours, Mere."

"But she didn't, and we both know why."

"She wants to watch us sweat . . . doesn't want to end the game between us, not yet."

"She wants me to think about life without you, Lucas, before she takes you away from me."

CONTINUING TO USE the rowboat as cover, they paddled farther and farther from the sniper's scope, kicking for the Brody pier. Panting, Meredyth said, "Lauralie means to make me suffer for the rest of my life, Lucas. which means—"

"She never intended to kill you."

"Exactly. It's you, Lucas, she's after. She intends to

destroy my life by killing you and anyone I love. She wants me to mourn all the people I love that she's taking from me. Thank God Mom and Dad aren't here."

They reached the Brody pier, but remained in the water, pulling themselves along beneath it as cover until they reached shore.

"She wants me to suffer the guilt of all these people dying around me, Lucas. Now those poor boys out there on my lawn brutally killed, my innocent gardener, for God's sake, Mira Lourdes, the old nun, Katherine Croombs, even Arthur Belkvin and his dogs . . . she wants *me* to feel responsible for it all. That I somehow caused all their deaths—and the culmination of it all? The death of the one I love most, you."

The gunfire had ceased as darkness had enveloped Lake Madera.

"The moon's gone under again," he said. "Now's the time! Make for the house. Gotta get to a phone."

As they ran, dripping wet and cold, toward the darkened house, the upturned rowboat floated off and into a weedy backwash. No shots came as they made it to the stairs, Meredyth slipping and falling. No shots came as they made it to the front door left ominously ajar. In the driveway, they'd seen the family RV, waiting like a patient dog for its master. They burst into the Brody home, Meredyth calling out each of the Brodys by name. "Myron! Lorene! Candice! It's Meredyth Sanger! Where are you?"

Meredyth called out over and over for them as Lucas tore open doors in search of the family. No answers, no finds.

"No lights," he ordered her as they searched the downstairs den for a phone. Grabbing it, Lucas heard the dead air of a disconnected line. "Bitch has cut the lines. No big surprise." He looked around for a weapon, but the man's glassed-in gun rack was smashed and all his weapons were missing. Lucas instantly realized on seeing this that they might well find a triple murder here, quite possibly mutilations on the same scale as they'd found with Byron Priestly and Arthur Belkvin. Lauralie seemed to take glee in slashing people open. "Stick close by me," he solemnly ordered Meredyth.

She took a tentative step up a flight of carpeted stairs, but he stopped her, pointing to a trickling trail of blood on the kitchen tiles. The blood looked burgundy in the absence of light. "She's left us another intentional trail to follow."

It led them through the expansive kitchen and to a basement door off the kitchen. Meredyth buried her head in his chest, and he held her. "My God, Lucas, she's killed them all."

Lucas had no words that might comfort her. He reached a hand out to the basement door, cautiously opening it, and staring into the black hole of the stairwell. "Stay here, Mere."

"Don't you dare leave me alone."

"I have to step inside and close the door before flicking on the light switch. I don't want that madwoman to know where we are. Understood?"

"I go with you."

He saw the adamant fire in her eyes that said no use arguing. "All right, but it could be a shock. Brace for it."

Once on the stairwell, he flicked on the light, and it instantly revealed blood on the interior door and on the panels of drywall on both sides of the stairwell. They were, in effect, surrounded by a red rain that looked like paintbrush flecks and spurts, the kind of high-velocity blood residue that comes of gunshot wounds at close range, creating a crazy mosaic only a blood-spatter evidence expert could read. It said to Lucas, *They were shot here at the top of the stairwell and the killer used their own weight to her benefit, simply allowing the bodies to fall atop one another*. The flood of light revealed the heap of three bodies lying in a pool of blood at the bottom of the stairs.

"That bitch knows we're here looking at what she's done," said Meredyth, trembling under his embrace. "Directed us across the lake and to the kitchen and here,

Lucas. She's orchestrated the whole damn thing . . . watching us tip over in the water, climb out at the pier, all of it."

"She can watch our every move through that scope," he agreed. "But she can't see through walls."

Lucas held Meredyth's head close to him, not wishing her to look down the stairwell again at the carnage that lay there, mother, father, and teen daughter. He ordered her to stay on the top stair as he went below. At the foot of the stairs, Lucas got to know the Brodys up close and personal.

Myron, Lorene, and their child, Candice, all with gags, blindfolds, and hands tied at their backs. They'd been summarily shot in the head on the top step. Lauralie had guided each to the basement stairs one at a time, fired into each cranium, and had simply let gravity do the rest.

Myron Brody was at the bottom of the heap, and it recalled Lucas's time in Viet Nam below such a death heap. He truly hated this Lauralie Blodgett now, and he wanted in the worst way to see her dead before this night was over.

Lucas now worked to separate the dead from one another in an effort to find keys for the RV and possibly a cell phone. He pried Myron Brody from the weight of his wife and child and fished into the pants pockets for keys. There were none. He tried Mrs. Brody's pockets. No keys. Finally, he tried the young girl's jeans. Nothing. Finally giving up, he located a tarp and covered the Brodys.

He hurried back upstairs to Meredyth where she sat quietly sobbing. He helped her to her feet, turned out the light, and guided her back into the kitchen. "No doubt she's emptied the place of any keys and cell phones along with any weapons." He indicated the empty chopping block.

"Not entirely," said Meredyth, upending the dining table.

"What're we doing?"

"Arming ourselves." She began unscrewing one of the table legs. In a moment, she had a baseball-bat-sized weapon with a two-inch screw protruding from the end.

Lucas removed a second table leg. "Makes a damn nice war club."

"Lucas, you see what I see?" Meredyth pointed to a clear cookie jar on the countertop, and inside were keys.

Lucas grabbed the jar and emptied out the set of Chevy keys. "I think it's the RV. Come on! We're out the back door and to the car."

Outside, they strapped in before Lucas learned that neither the correct key nor hot-wiring would do, as he could not get a spark from the ignition. Exiting the RV, he rounded to the front and lifted the hood, flashing a light found in the glove compartment now over the dead motor. She had gotten out, clutching her table leg and asking, "What is it?"

He pointed. "She's made off with the distributor cap. *Biiiitch!*" He ground out the word.

"She's got us right where she wants us, doesn't she?"

"How could she've known we were without our phones, my gun?" he lamented. "Hell . . . I even left my Texas toothpick in your bedroom, Mere."

"A bowie knife's hardly going to help us now."

"I think it'd beat *nothing*."

"We have our war clubs, remember?" She hefted her chair leg. His lay on the seat inside the RV. "Lucas, she's thought every detail through. She's been in this house for hours and hours, all damn day. And she's been watching us."

"From where? Exactly where to watch our every move, Mere?"

"Upstairs . . . Candice's room in the front. It overlooks the lake and she . . . she is a stargazer, owns a super telescope."

"How damn fortunate for Lauralie."

"She knew when we got up, when we ate, when we left for the stables and left on horseback. All of it."

"She saw the rifle when we passed it back and forth at the stable," he thoughtfully said. "Saw everything that happened across the lake."

"She saw when Howard arrived to do the lawn, and

gauged how much time she had to row across and take his identity before we'd be back."

"But how'd she arrange for Kemper's body in the boat to bump into us out there on the lake?"

"She didn't, but she arranged it as a horrid, heinous crime designed for maximum effect *whenever* I should discover it," Meredyth said. "Didn't matter whether it was tonight, tomorrow, or the next day, because—"

"—because you'd be left alive to savor all the terror she wants to rub your face in."

"Exactly." Meredyth's knuckles had gone white with the grip she held on her table leg club.

"So . . . here we stand in the dark, and she could be anywhere out there, taking a bead on you at this moment, Lucas. She'd like nothing better than to leave me entirely alone, holding your bloodied body in my arms throughout this night of terror she has planned for me. So, if you please, can we take cover and decide what we do next?"

"What are our options?"

"We go back inside the house, huddle up in the dark in a center room without windows, and wait for daylight."

"Can we walk out of here?"

"Not another house or a road for several miles this side of the lake, and if she is watching, she'll stalk us and either kill us or turn us back."

"What about Jeff and Tommy's place, their mother's home?" he asked.

"God, I pray she hasn't been killed, and oh, God, if she is alive, how are we to tell her about her sons, Lucas? How do we explain their deaths?"

"As the senseless act of a madwoman, Mere. Their deaths are not your fault. You give into such guilt, and Lauralie wins. She puts you precisely where she wants you."

"Oh, you mean like now?" She threw up her hands, the flashlight in them sending up crazy circles of light into the leaves of overhanging trees. "Look where she has us! Dripping wet, freezing, trapped, and at her mercy!"

"Then we don't lay down for the bitch."

"What do you mean? Go after her?"

"Go after her, yes."

"Tonight?"

"Now."

"In the dark?"

"In the dark."

"With a lake between us and her?"

"Guide me to Candice' s room and that telescope."

Meredyth took a deep breath and nodded. "Follow me."

"Douse the light first, will you?"

"Yeah, good idea." Meredyth's mind again filled with the image of Jeff and Tommy lying dead on her front lawn. This followed by the image of the dead in the Brody basement. This followed by the awful image of the worm-covered gardener at the bottom of the waterlogged rowboat.

She led Lucas back into the house through the rear door, both carrying their war clubs. He followed her inside, up the stairs, and to Candice's pitch-black room. Meredyth switched on the flash, but he grabbed it, covering it with his hand and shutting it off. "No lights! It'll tip Lauralie off to our plans!"

"Sorry . . . I knew that." The little light that guided him to the telescope came in the form of stars reflecting off its metal veneer where it poked through the open window. Balancing the table leg in his crotch, Lucas settled in at a chair before the telescope, realizing that he was in the exact position that Lauralie Blodgett had been in for most of the day. Had she planned this too? For them to be here in the dead girl's room eyeballing Meredyth's cabin on Lake Madera through the very telescope Lauralie had used?

How devious is this sick mind we've locked horns with, he wondered, *in this life-and-death competition?*

From the condition of the Brody family bodies downstairs, he guessed the murders here had taken place as early as nine A.M., possibly earlier. He imagined that somewhere hidden in the surrounding woods they might find Arthur Belkvin's BMW, but stumbling about in the dark in search of the car would likely prove as futile as an attempt to walk out of here or around the enormous lake to Mrs. Farnsworth's for a phone. The nearest contact opportunity remained the one he now stared at across the lake, his radio car, if she had not destroyed it.

He searched the grounds for any sign of Lauralie, imagining that by now she had shed the gardener's clothes for something out of Meredyth's closet. Behind him, he sensed Meredyth's growing trepidation.

"What do you see? Anyone on the water? Any movement up at the house?"

"No . . . nothing. She could be anywhere, like you said."

"Damn it, Lucas. What're we going to do?"

"The horses. If we could get to the horses, we could ride out of here."

"No, it's too risky."

"It'd be a piece of cake. We could upend the rowboat. It's still down by the pier, and we float quietly over to the boathouse. From there, we take that back path to the stables."

"Don't you see, Lucas? She's planned it this way, every step of the way. She knows we'll go for the horses, because she's cut off every other alternative means of escape or communication with the outside."

"All right, say she is lying in wait at the stables. We at least know to expect it, and so we're tuned in."

"And she's tuned in at two hundred yards from the house with that damned gun of Jeff's. You don't stand a chance."

Frustrated, he swore and stood up, pushing the chair over and making her start and back up. When she did so, her back hit something solid in the dark—Lauralie Blodgett, her mind screamed even as she called out the name! And the dark figure swayed and *returned* to hit Meredyth a second blow, and she slipped and fell, her bare feet skidding as if still wet. On hands and knees, she was stung by an unmistakable odor of blood, bile, and decaying flesh as it filled her nostrils. She screamed again as Lucas pushed himself between her and the shadow in the darkness—the thing attacking her. He grunted with the power behind the blow he dealt Lauralie—defending Meredyth with the table leg, slamming it into the dark terror.

Meredyth, from the floor, flashed the beam on the assailant, hoping to help Lucas, expecting to blind Lauralie Blodgett, but instead, the light illuminated the dripping half-torso of Mira Lourdes, her legs and lower abdomen dangling in the blackness, each heel lashed to Candice Brody's white ceiling fan.

"Christ, my heart!" shouted Lucas.

"It's our final ration of fun with the Antichrist and her twisted miracles," Meredyth bitterly said. "Behold the beast cometh. Damn that ugly bitch child of evil wherever she is."

Lucas slipped now on the dank gruel below the half-corpse, and he instantly grabbed Meredyth up in his powerful arms, giving up any effort to regain his feet so he could lift her at the same time from the wet floor soiling their clothes.

"I'm going after her, Mere. You stay here, and I will track her in the night, corner her, and bring her pain and ours to an end."

"No, you can't leave me here alone, and you can't go after her alone, Lucas, no!"

"I can move faster and stealthier alone, Mere. Having you to worry about is more apt to get me killed, trust me. You remain here. I can revert to the old ways and blend in with the night. I can get close enough to break her neck before she sees me coming."

"She's got a high-powered rifle with a scope. I can at least help create a diversion."

"Doing so could get you killed."

"No, don't you see? She gets me in her scope, she won't pull the trigger. She wants me to survive and suffer your loss."

He took a deep breath and then began peeling off his clothing down to his black BVDs. "Try to keep up," he told her, taking his table leg with him.

Even as she kept pace down the stairs, Meredyth peeled off her own clothes, beginning with her soiled pants, down to her Navy blue bra and panties. She'd not forgotten her war club, which thudded down the carpeted stairs with her. "Lake's going to be cold," she said, shivering at the thought.

"Cold is a state of mind. Hold on to that thought and you'll be all right."

Lucas turned on the flashlight and placed it on the chopping block so it would flash to the ceiling. It decoyed their whereabouts, as it would be seen clearly in the window in Lauralie's telescopic lens. They exited out the back, and belly-crawled to the water's edge down from the pier among the reeds where the capsized boat had hung up. There they inched into the water and took hold of the waiting, upturned boat. They began to make their way across the lake, back toward Meredyth's home.

Once on the other side, they were masked by the boathouse, where they tied the roaming overturned boat to a mooring. They went into the boathouse by swimming under. Once inside, they caught a moment's rest. Meredyth was trembling and exhausted. He found a blanket and wrapped her in it. "My squaw," he said, smiling. Then, holding his table leg high, he asked, "Where is your war club?"

"At the bottom of the lake by now. I couldn't hold onto it and the boat any longer."

"I want you to remain here until I get back with the horses," he ordered her. "No arguments."

"Just because I dropped my . . . my war club?"

"Come on, Mere, we both know your ethics alone prevent you from drawing blood. And like I said, I can move faster and safer on my own."

"Lucas, it's too dangerous. She's up there in one of those windows just waiting for one glimpse of you and—"

He put his finger to her lips. "It's not so easy hitting a moving target, especially a painted Cherokee with a war club."

"Tell that to Jeff and Tommy."

"Jeff and Tommy were forced to run ahead of her down a slope, their backs to the bitch. She won't know when I'm coming. She won't see me coming. When and if she fires, she'll miss. If you hear multiple shots, you'll know she missed. Just have faith and wait here for me, understood?"

"No, Lucas! No!"

But he'd already dived into the blue fluid floor, swimming underwater to the outside, going for the boggy, swampy area on the north side of the structure. "Damnit, Lucas!" she whispered, then dropped the blanket and dove in after him.

CHAPTER 20

Snake: wise, defying

MEREDYTH HAD WATCHED Lucas disappear below the water and swim out of the boathouse to the hidden side where trees and bush covered his movements. She followed, bobbing in the water, watching him now as he caked himself with mud until he became a living shadow. Hearing her in the water and seeing that she'd disobeyed him and followed, he shot her a disapproving look. He waved for her to go back into the shelter. Then he disappeared into the cover of the path they had so leisurely taken down to the boathouse that afternoon. Lucas seemed to become part of the weave of the green-black cloth of the world around him, and once more she was reminded of just how wild and predatory he could be when circumstances warranted. In the past, she had been both excited by this side of him and afraid of it, but tonight Meredyth thanked God for Lucas's wild side; tonight, she realized she would always be safe in his care. She knew that Lucas was risking his life for her, and that he *wanted* this opportunity at *blood vengeance*—payback usually reserved for the death of a loved one. This situation, she decided, was close enough to satisfy his Cherokee blood.

But if she were to lose Lucas tonight as Lauralie planned, if there were no more tomorrows with Lucas, Meredyth decided that she would not want to go on. This conclusion spurred her to climb from the water and coat her body with the war paint of the muddy bottom. Lauralie had brought her to this, a state of being calling for her to smear her scantily clad body with muddy, pungent earth. And to a state of consciousness never before experienced, one of *pure hatred* for another human being, for Lauralie's unfixable, poisoned soul. And what of the classically mad Lauralie? For all the research and study and analysis and scrutiny of Meredyth's life that the younger woman had done, Lauralie actually had learned *nothing* of Meredyth's core traits. Now her raw personality, stripped of any pretense and faced with a monster relentlessly stalking her, stepped forward. Not even Meredyth was familiar with the Meredyth now smearing the lather of sludge over her face and the remaining white corners of her skin.

As a scudding army of dark clouds continued to hold captive the moon, Meredyth made her move, doing a slow, even belly crawl along the tree line leading up to the knoll her house sat upon. Lauralie occupied the high ground in this private war. As Meredyth crawled past Tommy's body, his white oversized cowboy shirt lifting in the wind, the bloodstain long dry by now, made a gentle slapping sound rivaling the insect hum. The sight made her think of all the innocent people who had been caught in the vortex. Closer to her as she passed his body lay Jeff, his eyes staring wide, his hair matted with blood. At any time, their mother might drive over in that little coupe of hers in search of her boys, and if she did, Lauralie would likely take her down with a sniper shot as well.

"Where is the bitch?" she muttered to herself. Might she be at the barn, say in the loft? Or was she in the house at the bedroom windows, one overlooking the lawn, the other the stables? Was she alternating between the two views?

She inched onward, gaining confidence with each foot, each yard gained. She could read Howard Kemper's logo— *LAWn ORDER*—on his truck from here, and she made out Lucas's car just the other side of the gardener's truck. If she could make it to the driveway undetected, get to Lucas's radio, she could call out for help, if only—*big if*—Lauralie had overlooked the radio in the unmarked vehicle.

She moved on, praying Lucas was being as cautious as she. At any moment, she expected a gunshot to ring out. She feared how she might react when it came. A single gunshot without any follow-up shots must mean Lucas had been hit and brought down like Jeff and Tommy. She prayed it would not come before she could get to the squad car.

Then she froze, seeing the sash at the second-story window overlooking the lawn and lake move with the glint of steel revealed by returning moonlight, but that same blue moon meant danger for her and for Lucas. She dared not move a muscle, her painted face turned up, her eyes watching the dark figure at the window. It was Lauralie.

She wished to God she could get a message to Lucas; he was free for the moment to rush the stable door and gain the safety of the interior, but he had no way of knowing Lauralie was surveying this side of the house. "Go, Lucas, go now!" she whispered, willing him to somehow psychically hear her plea. But suddenly Lauralie was gone from the window.

"My time to go!" she told herself, lifting from her belly and racing for the safety of the Farnsworth truck, hiding behind it. Glancing inside, she saw there were no keys in the ignition. She slipped around the rear, and glancing up at the bedroom window, she dashed to the gardener's truck, skirted round it, and found herself kneeling outside Lucas's car.

She was winded from the effort, breathing so heavily, she feared anyone within fifty feet must hear her. She inched along the length of the car to the front door, quietly, cautiously squeezed the handle, and opened the door just as a blast from the hunting rifle thundered, startling Meredyth into action. She leaped into the car and grabbed for the radio receiver, but it was not there. It'd been ripped out, gone.

She sat for a moment, paralyzed, hearing only the single shot and fearing that Lucas was down, bleeding, lying halfway between the trees and the stables in the sawdust road. She then heard a second shot and did not know whether to be relieved or not; she recalled what the second shot had meant for young Tommy and for Jeff.

"Lucas!" she called out, and leaped from the car, returning to Kemper's truck and grabbing at his tools, finally selecting a long-handled, three-pronged earth turner, a kind of clawing pitchfork. With it clutched in her hands, disregarding any obstacle in her way, she raced up the steps and through the front door as a third shot rang out. A good sign, she prayed. Perhaps Lucas, while spotted, and perhaps even wounded, had found a hiding place, and Lauralie was attempting to ferret him out with additional shots. *A lot of good a damned table leg was now,* Meredyth thought bitterly as she inched her way quietly to the second floor.

Making the second-floor landing, Meredyth now inchwormed her way toward the expansive second-story bedroom. Glancing in, she saw that Lauralie Blodgett's complete attention was on Lucas, trapped somewhere below and under her gaze through the scope. Was she about to squeeze off another shot to pump an additional bullet into him where he lay helpless? Or was she patiently awaiting his next move, anticipating where he would next dart? Meredyth could feel the woman's unadulterated hatred culminating in the finger curled about the trigger of the big gun held snug against her shoulder here in the dark.

Slowly, cautiously, the barefoot Meredyth tiptoed over the carpet, moving within striking distance, raising the neat little earth turner with its three razor-sharp prongs overhead. She could stab the woman in the back of the neck and end it now and shed no tears, but a small voice held her in place. Can you do this? Is it murder? How will it play in the cold light of day to the outside world, to the police, to a D.A. . . . , a grand jury, a judge? Was she justified morally and legally to murder the murderer? Lucas would not hesitate. *It's either her or Lucas,* her mind screamed at the instant one of the cell phones in the room went off, causing Lauralie to start and turn just as Meredyth let the mini-pitchfork fall. The fork bit into Lauralie's neck just as she had turned. Lauralie tried to bring the big gun around to bear, the pitchfork swinging wildly around with her, Meredyth having let go of the handle. The trio of teeth at the end of the spear had bitten deep into Lauralie's jugular vein, spraying the air with her blood, causing her grip on the rifle to steal away. The deadly weapon hit the windowsill and thudded against the garden tool, which had already released its stinging bite on her, leaving her fatally punctured. Lauralie's eyes had gone wide, her nostrils flaring, bleeding, and her gaping mouth swallowed repeatedly, desperate for air, choking on her own blood, struggling against the pain in a pirouette of horror about the room that painted Meredyth's white bedclothes red. Even dying so, Lauralie fought to speak.

"Mommie? Is it . . . you? 'Ave you . . . come back . . . for . . . for me?"

She fell forward into Meredyth in a paroxysm of cold trembling, and Meredyth, overwhelmed, took Lauralie's hand as she lay dying in Meredyth's ams. Meredyth's muddy feet had left a trail from the doorway to here, and Lauralie's blood commingled with the muddy tracks in a starburst of purple spreading over the carpet.

Meredyth eased the now-silent girl from her embrace, and she rushed to her bathroom, finding and tearing into her state-of-the-art first-aid kit to the sound of a gurgling death rattle beginning a slow roll that welled up from Lauralie's depths. She tore into the case, tossing aside creams and syringes, bottles and pills to get at the Fresh Flesh textured bandage wrap, an item developed in aerospace technology for stopping blood loss in a battlefield wound. She rushed back to Lauralic Blodgett and worked the bandage into the wound, allowing the blood to coagulate around the porous synthetic weave of the bandage to eventually stem the blood flow.

Lauralie spat up blood as Meredyth worked to save the

life of the multiple murderer. On her knees over the woman, Meredyth caught a glimpse of herself in a full-length mirror. Her features and body caked in dried mud, she realized that the lunatic Lauralie had driven her to become an assassin herself. "Christ, what am I doing? Saving you for what? To give you just what you've wanted all along? A media-circus arrest and incarceration, a jury trial, a forum for your twisted mind? A lifetime in a federal facility for the criminally insane?"

Meredyth's action to stop Lauralie's bleeding to death here and now had simply been an automatic response to help the wounded animal at her feet. But now she slowed for a moment in her ministrations over the weakened, wounded Ripper, allowing the ramifications of saving Lauralie to sink in. "I should fucking let you die. Damn you . . . damn child of Satan."

A moment's hesitation more, and then Meredyth's instinct to save the young woman took root, as she yanked tightly at the bandages and tied off the porous, textured spider's web of nylon threads that acted as an effective seal, a dike and a tourniquet at once. The blood flow at the wound site ended.

Blinking, her brain getting more oxygen now, Lauralie looked up into Meredyth's mud-caked features. She painfully choked out a handful of broken words. "Hooow'd you . . . clim' owt . . . hell?"

Meredyth realized for the first time that the girl, in her pain-induced hallucination, mistook her muddy appearance here in the dark for that of her mother's cemetery ghost, returned to drag her into eternity with her, finally a family. Lauralie then fell unconscious.

"Go ahead, die, Lauralie Blodgett. Go with your mother," Meredyth said, and thought: *Justice it isn't, your going out so peacefully, but maybe now Mira Lourdes and the rest of your victims can rest in peace.*

MEREDYTH LIFTED THE bloodied rifle and went to the window with it in her hands. She called out to Lucas down below, unable to actually see him. "I've ended it, Lucas! You can come out now! She's dead! The wicked bitch is dead! Here's the rifle!" She hurled the Remington as far as she could. It responded with a thunderous clatter down the tin roof of a shed situated below the window, and then it slid to the earth into a clump of bushes to do no more harm. Atop the shed, the night breeze twisted a black, wrought-iron windmill in the shape of a greyhound, reminding her of the two hounds Lauralie had poisoned and posed at Arthur Belkvin's feet.

Lucas emerged from the barn, riding bareback and guiding a second horse, saddled, by the reins. He lifted his war club table leg overhead in the melancholy, soft sapphire moonlight, looking like an ancient warrior, but then his club slipped from his grasp and he slowly, painfully, slid down the side of Yesyado. Meredyth screamed, seeing the blood smear down the side of his horse, the one she had gifted him with that afternoon. Somehow Lucas got back to his feet, and limping, he started toward the house, but only a handful of steps and he fell, rolled onto his back, and loosed an audible grown to the heavens.

"Oh, my God! Lucas! Hold on, Lucas! I'm calling nine-one-one now! Hold on! I'm coming!"

In the same instant, Meredyth felt three sharp blunt punctures strike her nude back at the bra line, but the blow proved weak and failed to puncture her deeply.

"Turn roun', Ma-me dear'st," came Lauralie's chilling voice. "Wanna see y'r eyes."

The sharp pain in Meredyth's back did not slow her from wheeling to protect herself, throwing up her hands to block the next blow from the dead woman who'd somehow slipped back from death's hand. *Short attention span,* Meredyth thought, finding the prongs of the long-handled pitchfork inches from her eyes. "Damn hellion! I should've let you blccd to death."

Lauralie jabbed and Meredyth feinted left, grabbing the handle and wresting the garden tool from the wounded woman's faint grasp, the weeding fork falling once more to the floor between them. Gathering all remaining anemic strength, screaming, Lauralie lunged now with Lucas's bowie knife, using her weight and catapulting her body at *her mother,* to put her once and for all in her grave.

Meredyth dodged, stepping aside, and Lauralie's tripping over the pitchfork combining with her momentum sent her careening out the window and onto the shed below, a howling banshee scream rising back up to Meredyth, echoing off the house and into the heavens.

Meredyth looked down once again at the shed. Lauralie—still alive, her legs, arms, and extremities twitching—looked like a beetle stabbed through with a needle. She lay faceup; the wrought-iron greyhound windmill had caught her weight and had spiked her through the back. She lifted a defiant fist to Meredyth and muttered, "See . . . in Hell . . . mow-ther . . ."

"I'll make that call now, bitch!" Meredyth swore, and rushed for the phones lying on the bed, finding hers and dialing 911. "I have an emergency . . . need help immediately at—"

"What is the nature of your emergency?"

"Christ . . . *ahhh, ahhh.* . . . Six, no, seven dead, an eighth dying—in desperate need of paramedics immediately."

"Gun wound, head trauma?"

"Officer down! Gunshot to . . . to the body, I believe."

"Is the shooter still a threat, ma'am? Are you in any immediate danger?"

"No, no! Damn it, she's dead. Hurry, please!"

"You're on a cell phone, ma'am. I'm Larry. Remain calm and give me your address, and stay on the line, please."

After giving the dispatcher the address and the Brody address, Meredyth snatched up the space-aged bandaging that now must save Lucas's life. She grabbed a blanket and a robe as well, and she then raced down to where Lucas had gotten to his knees and had slumped against a tractor, his eyes glazed, in trauma, unable to coherently answer her.

As she neared him, she saw the horrible exit wound in the middle of his back, between the shoulder blades, just below the neck. She feared she didn't have enough bandages left, and cursed herself now for having wasted them on Lauralie.

She then saw that Lucas had also been hit in the right side, lower abdomen, and there was no exit wound there. She imagined the bullet having careened about inside him, exploding into various deadly shards that had likely ripped at his organs. She feared the internal blood flow would kill him, that the NASA-developed super bandage could not save him if she'd had a mile of it. He needed emergency medical attention; a team of surgeons and experts might have a chance to save his life. She shouted into the phone at the dispatcher, "He's in shock! He's dying! Hurry!"

"Tell me your name, ma'am. Calm down and tell me your name."

"What?"

"Your name."

"Meredyth . . . Meredyth Sanger. We need an airlift for Lucas! Officer Stonecoat. He's been shot twice! He's suffering internal wounds, and he's hemorrhaging and in shock."

"I'll relay that, Meredyth."

"Doctor! I'm a doctor. I know what I'm talking about! Get a chopper out here, a medevac chopper! Stat!"

She looked into Lucas's eyes, rolled back in his head. He looked ready to faint, in need of medical assistance fast. He'd made it to the barn and the horses, but at what price? "Lucas! Stay with me! Hold on!" She'd thrown the blanket over his legs, and she worked the Fresh Flesh into his back to staunch the blood flow there. She talked as she worked, telling him he was going to be okay. She didn't have enough of the bandage to reach around his wide chest, so she held it in place until the blood was absorbed into it, the absorption creating enough glue to hold the bandage. She got up, raced to the stable, and located the sports-wrap bandages used for binding the legs of horses, and returning, she dressed the back wound with the sports wrap.

"Grandfather . . . calls me," muttered Lucas.

"I've called for a medevac chopper, Lucas! Hold on! Don't you go anywhere! Don't you listen to that old man either!"

He tried to get up.

She forced him to remain sitting, taking him now into the folds of the robe she had thrown on herself. She kept talking to him. "We must look like a couple of aliens in all this mud and dirt. No telling how long our hideaway is going to be a crime scene. They'll have to process the house, the stable, the grounds, the damn rowboats, not to mention the Brody house." She kept talking to him, trying to keep him conscious.

She heard a car drive up behind them. "Oh, dear God . . . it's Janie Farnsworth . . . come looking for her boys. How am I going to deal with all this, Lucas, without you . . . without your help? You can't leave me, Lucas! I won't let you, damn it! Not now . . . now that we've finally discovered we can't live without one another. What the futz! It's not fair. Tell your grandfather to go back to the Great Spirit or wherever he came from! *Doya-hear-me, doya?* I need you in *this* life; I need you *here*!"

Lucas's glazed look signaled his slipping into some invisible place ahead of him. Again he tried to get to his feet. She struggled to keep him down as a concerned Yesyado sniffed and whinnied at the pair of them. "Damn it, Lucas, stay down! Don't fight me! Stop it! Don't move! You'll only cause more blood loss!"

He's dying. Get used to the idea. Nothing you can do about it, a nagging ugly voice said at the back of her head, sounding like Lauralie, and then she heard Janie Farnsworth standing over them and saying, "My God, Meredyth, what in the name of heaven and hell's happened? Where's my Tommy? Where's Jeff?"

She looked up at the middle-aged single mother of two, unable to tell her what had happened, but her eyes spoke clearly enough. Mrs. Farnsworth gasped and raced for the barn to locate her boys, calling out their names and getting no answer. "Where's their truck?" she finally asked, and looking up at the house, she got her answer.

"Those boys didn't do anything wrong, did they? Who shot your man, Meredyth? Talk to me, damn it!"

"Jeff and Tommy're . . ."

"Spit it out!"

". . . are dead, Janie. I'm sorry. A maniac got hold of their rifle and used it on them. She shot Lucas too."

"My boys . . . are they badly hurt?" She didn't want to hear the word *dead*. "Where are they? Where are my boys?" Tears flowed freely now.

"Out on the lawn, halfway down to the lake."

She climbed back into her car and raced up the path to the house, plowing over the lawn in her car to get to where her boys lay. Meredyth's heart, once more, was ripped apart.

She heard the dispatcher on the phone calling to her. "Meredyth . . . Doctor . . . are you still there?"

"Where the hell's the help we need?"

"You're in a remote location. They're on their way!"

"I need blood plasma, maybe a transfusion; he needs stabilizing now!"

She saw that Lucas's normal red pallor had a skein of ashen white painted on now. His usual vigor and bravado had been replaced by a limp body and a lethargic malaise. He no longer fought her, allowing himself to be enveloped in her arms. She feared he would die here in her arms at any moment. "Don't do it, Lucas. Don't leave me! Please, don't."

She got no response from him. Lucas Stonecoat lay in her arms in a hemorrhagic coma.

In the distance, she heard the sirens that could not get here soon enough to suit her. In another three minutes, her tree-lined drive around the lake was lit by a parade of fire engines and paramedic vans followed by police cruisers.

"Where's the damned chopper!" she called out through the phone. "He's gone into coma!"

"The chopper's on its way, Meredyth. It's on its way," replied the calm voice of the 911 emergency dispatcher. "It's in the air and on its way."

She heard the faint sound of chopper blades—*chomp-chomp-chomp-chomp*—competing now with the ambulances and fire trucks that'd pulled down to the stables, encircling them. Over the blackened horizon, she saw the helicopter come into view. On its side, she read the luminescent logo—2NEWS. It was a damned news crew chopper!

It's too late . . . too late, came the evil voice in her head. *And it's all your fault for wasting time on that lunatic bitch.*

Paramedics flooded round them, and someone tugged her away, freeing the medics to attend to Lucas's wounds. They'd come from nearby rural Harris County Memorial Hospital, their emergency response unit. They immediately put Lucas on a plasma-and-glucose hookup, attempting to stabilize him for transportation. They examined the bandages Meredyth had wrapped him in, and these were replaced with sterile wraps. In what seemed a lifetime for Meredyth, they finally had him on a stretcher and into the waiting ambulance. Meredyth jumped into the rear with him, and they drove out into a field, and from overhead, a medevac chopper appeared, setting down, ready to take Lucas aboard.

Meredyth insisted on taking flight with him, certain it might be the last opportunity to see him alive. He remained in a coma.

CHAPTER 21

Medicine man's eye: vigilant, wise

DR. LEONARD CHANG shakily balanced himself atop the tin-roofed shed, having left the safety of the ladder he'd ascended, and now he cautiously made his way to the impaled body. The sight stopped him, so chillingly ironic, the proud head of the metal greyhound protruding out of the woman's abdomen.

Fearful of falling, Steve Perelli followed and stopped short alongside Chang, crouching to keep his balance, his video camera in one hand. He too stared down at the curious wrought-iron spike and made out the greyhound's arrogant grin and alert ears painted in blood, poking through the young woman's abdomen. "Looks like something out of a B horror movie," the police photographer said.

"Get the shots, and let's get her off this thing. You'll lend me a hand?"

Perelli gaped at the M.E. "That's not my job. I never handle the bodies. I place rulers beside them to indicate scale, and I get in close, to within a hairsbreadth of a puncture wound with my camera lens, but I don't touch dead people."

"Union rules?"

Perelli replied, "My rules." He'd photographed the worst kind of bloating, discoloration, bruises, slashes, even a screwdriver though a guy's skull once. He'd filmed the results of nail guns, staple guns, ordinary bullet wounds. He'd filmed brutalized, raped, and murdered women, and people run down by cars, tire marks so clearly and indelibly imprinted on their clothing and flesh that people had been put away on the evidence. He'd photographed jumpers, floaters, burn victims, and he'd busted his ass getting shots as detailed as the broken front teeth of a murdered prostitute beaten to death. In fact, he'd photographed areas of the human body that anyone else would be arrested for. But he had never been asked to handle one of them. "It's one thing to film the dead, another to touch, roll, or move the bodies. That's not my job, Dr. Chang," he repeated.

"I need you, Steve. We're stretched thin here." Chang held up a pair of surgical gloves for Perelli to don.

"You got a small army out here. Where's Ted? Nielsen? Detective North's in the house with four Feds, doing nothing so far as I can see. Call her for help."

Chang gnashed his teeth. "Take your video. I'll get someone."

Under the first light of a cloudy dawn, from his elevated position on the shed roof, Chang could see all around the property. He watched the activity down at the stables, Ted Hoskins leading an investigation into the blood trail left by Lucas Stonecoat only hours before. He could also see the Harris County coroner and his crew finishing up with the two gunshot victims on the lawn. Through the open window, Chang heard North arguing with one of the Feds and stomping around in Meredyth Sanger's upstairs bedroom, from which Lauralie Blodgett had obviously fallen—or had she taken a leap? And if so, had it been her intent to die or simply to take flight? The hunting rifle used to shoot Lucas and the two dead boys on the lawn appeared to have flown down with her, coming to a rest alongside the shed in some brush there. Curious too was the neck, wrapped in bandages spotty with bloodstains. Chang bent over and began unraveling the bandage, that incredible new stuff he'd invested in years ago, Fresh Flesh. When the bandages came away, Chang mentally gauged the wound to the throat—three puncture marks equally spaced. It would fit with the garden tool found in Meredyth's room upstairs.

"Another puzzle piece," he muttered.

Through the tops of trees sloping away from the house, Chang made out the pier and the man-made lake, his gaze finally finding Dr. Lynn Nielsen, tall and slim in a wet suit. Assisted by divers in the water, she was dealing with the dead man in the rowboat, and confiscating the other boat riddled with bullet holes and floating upended.

Further on, across the lake, Dr. Frank Patterson had been diverted immediately to the Brody family crime scene. Via a linkup with Meredyth Sanger from the mede-vac chopper, Chang, en route to the multiple crime scenes, had been given details of where the bodies lay. Once at the Sanger cabin, Chang had set up a command post with Detective Jana North's invaluable help. Everyone was told to also be on the lookout for any sign of body parts and remains of Mira Lourdes.

Meredyth, distraught, had not remained long on the phone. She told Leonard she feared the worst, that Lucas might not make it. The thought had cast a pall over the gloomy work, and the weather reflected the grim inner turmoil Leonard felt for his badly wounded friend listed in critical condition and lying on an operating table.

DETECTIVE JANA NORTH leaned again out the window from which Lauralie Blodgett had gone to her death. She needed the air. She was exasperated with the Feds, her body language told anyone caring to read it, like Chang down below on the "hot tin roof" where he motioned for her to join him. The local ASAC—assistant special agent in charge—and his followers had insisted on being brought in on the case, kidnapping being their angle. But Fuller and his boys remained woefully behind and hadn't done their homework. "They have no idea how vested our Missing Persons Bureau is on this case," she had bemoaned to Captain Lincoln over her cell in a private moment, pleading with him to hurry out to the scene.

Lincoln was on his way still. He'd stopped off at the hospital to look in on Meredyth and learn what he could of Lucas's condition. Jana caught herself blaming Meredyth, telling herself that if Lucas died, she'd hate Sanger for the rest of her life. At the moment, no one at ground zero here knew if Lucas was dead or alive.

She stared down at the remains of the deadly Post-it Ripper. Lauralie didn't look like much in death, but Jana had seen what the petite vixen had done at the cafe not far from here, as well as what she'd wrought here on Lake Madera. From her safe vantage point, she watched Chang carefully unwrap Lauralie's throat, freeing it of the bandage-tourniquette. A hell of a lot of loss of blood in the bedroom told the story of Lauralie's bleeding out here, and no doubt Chang's eyes would verify that a struggle for life and death between Meredyth and Lauralie had occurred, and Meredyth had not only won the battle, but had staunched the wounds of her defeated enemy while Lucas lay somewhere bleeding out.

She turned and surveyed the brightly lit crime scene again. From the appearance of things in the bedroom, including several spent shell casings, along with the location of the Remington breech-loader, Jana had a good sense of what had happened here. While Meredyth had been treated for superficial wounds caused by a three-pronged forked garden tool, the trail of mud and dirt leading up to the room suggested that someone most assuredly attacked Lauralie, bringing the garden fork down and into Lauralie's throat.

Jana paced to the door and started down the stairs and out of the house, responding to Chang's gesture to join him atop the shed. She got on her cell phone and dialed. Chang came on instantly.

"Dr. Chang . . . Leonard!"

"Detective North? Why're you calling? I can hear you

from where I'm standing." He looked up again only to find her gone from the window. "Wait . . . where are you?"

"I don't want anyone else to hear this."

"Go on." The sun had slipped through the cloud cover, and a wide swath of blinding rays sent Chang's arm up to shade his eyes as he looked up at the window again, not ten feet overhead, still searching for the detective. "What is it? Where'd you go?"

"Got a call from the Brody house, one of the evidence techs named Tory."

"Yes, Tory. She is a promising intern."

"She's gotten ill over there. Has a strange story to tell about 'something' hanging from a ceiling fan in the teenager's room."

"And you think it is the rest of your missing person, Mira Lourdes?"

"Sounds extremely likely. The ET, Tory?"

"Yes?"

"She says Dr. Patterson has known about the remains in the second-story room for two hours."

"My God, no!"

"This is the first you've heard?"

"I just discovered my cell phone was switched off accidentally."

"All the same, Frank Patterson knows damn well how important finding the rest of Mira Lourdes is to me—ahhh, the family—you, all of us, and he's so damn strange that he's failed to share the discovery with the rest of us. Why?"

"You tell me, Detective North, why? Why is Frank doing this?"

"Because he's waiting for those bozos with Fuller to CSI the place before any of the rest of us, even before you, Dr. Chang."

"Still currying favor with Fuller's team. Damn Frank . . . never knew what side to butter his bread on."

"Tory came to me with it because she'd been unable to reach you, and she knows how Nielsen and Frank have been feuding, so she didn't want to go to Lynn out on the lake without first running it by you."

"What shall we do . . . what shall we do . . ." Chang muttered as if to himself.

"I have no idea, but the young intern, she's been dismissed by Dr. Patterson because she dared push him on the issue. Meanwhile, Patterson's focus has been on the downstairs kitchen and basement areas. She called him an ass."

"Yes, that'd be Frank all right. What do you propose we do? We have our hands full here."

"I'm going over there, but I don't want this intern getting into any trouble over this."

"I see Captain Lincoln's car coming in. Why don't you take him over there with you. Let Frank explain things to him?"

"Great, good idea. Just wanted you to know what's going on across the lake."

"You got someone up there can help me pull Blodgett off this doggie windmill? I need someone strong."

"Sure. I'll send down a couple of big, strapping FBI boys."

She hung up. Chang cursed Patterson's inept people skills. He could well imagine how Frank had treated young Tory, who no doubt felt traumatized at finding parts of Mira Lourdes's corpse dangling from a ceiling fan.

Perhaps a silver lining, he thought, in that Mira's final remains might be located and reunited with the rest of her body—all the parts still in frozen limbo at Chang's morgue, downtown Houston, where her body was treated with the decorum, dignity, and humanity that all his guests received. If it were Lourdes's remains up in that second-story room, and Frank had let it hang there beyond the time it took to make a video record, he was breaking Chang's rules of conduct with respect to the dead.

Leonard had hoped to have a full and detailed map of precisely what had "gone down" here, as Gordon put it, by the time Captain Lincoln had arrived, but obviously a lot of the puzzle still needed fitting into place. Sending off the captain now with Detective North was a stroke of luck he realized, watching North intercept Lincoln at the driveway as he exited his car, seeing her point to the Brody house,

and smiling to see Lincoln and North climb into the rear
seat of his squad car and turn back for the cutoff to the
Brody house across the lake.

Earlier, while en route to Madera Lake, Lincoln had
called Chang, and had bellowed into the phone, "Leonard,
I want to know what went down exactly when, and in what
order. I need a time line. Every bloody detail, Leonard. I
want to know what happened to Lucas Stonecoat. Shit, you
know how many cop-killing wakes I've gone to this year,
and it's only September."

Lincoln would be back soon for all the *answers*. His
going to the Brody house with Jana meant only a temporary reprieve. Chang did not know all the answers, not
yet. Hell, he had just learned of the Lourdes remains at
the Brody house. It seemed only God and Frank Patterson
knew all that had gone on there. And what about the
weird shit that had "gone down" out there on the lake
itself? The naked dead guy covered in worms? One for
the table conversation at the American Forensic Society's
annual next month, *if* Nielsen could figure the mystery
out.

Chang had made cursory rounds, setting up the individual teams, going from house to stable to lawn to lake, and
now the top of the shed. Somebody had to be in charge,
and he had been nominated, but Lincoln demanded an
impossible magical time frame. A typical crime scene took
time, lots of it, but this, seven bodies spread over six—*now
seven*—crime scenes (shed top, second-story bedroom,
stable front, the lawn, the rowboat, the Brody basement,
and add the Brody second-floor bedroom). On top of that,
they had an officer down, quite possibly the eighth
body . . . awaiting Leonard back at Houston General—and
what of the sheer number of vehicles involved?

Leonard finally saw the young Feds coming out of the
house, one of them approaching him. Belkvin's BMW had
been found and was being impounded by the Feds. Three
vehicles littered the driveway, and another sat at the Brody
house, all in need of at least a cursory going-over.

Leonard gave another moment to Lucas back in Houston,

still fighting for his life, he hoped, but the stories filtering to Leonard made his friend's condition sound a great deal worse than merely uncertain. Last word had him in a perilous fight for his life on the operating table.

ATF and FBI personnel and forensic crews continued to scour the entire yard for additional shell casings, their leaders drawing diagrams based on findings, attempting to clearly identify Lauralie Blodgett's position and movements at the time of each shot fired, and how she had overpowered the husky 269-pound Kempcr.

No agent came to help Chang. The one he'd thought approaching continued on down the path to the barn. "I need help here!" he shouted up to the second-story window on hearing Fuller's voice still there.

"Hold on down there!" shouted one of the FBI agents from Meredyth's window.

"I asked for a couple of men here!" Chang shouted back. "We need to get her off this roof and into the van for transport."

The FBI agent shouted back, "I got a local guy with a cherry picker on his way. It'll help in getting her down from there."

"A cherry picker? We don't need no stinking cherry picker!" But the agent had ducked back inside already. Chang shouted louder, "Agent Fuller! I just need two men. She's getting ripe up here."

Perelli breathed a sigh of relief on hearing of the cherry picker, and he quickly found his way back to the ladder ahead of Chang, balancing his camera as he made his way down.

Chang returned to Lauralie's body and thought how shapely she was, and that she had a beautiful face for a maniac. He mused about the men in her life, all those she had used with such ease. "You could have been anything you chose to be, if only you had put your genius to a good cause. Why did you choose evil?"

"Talking to the dead, Dr. Chang?" Fuller called down to him.

Chang saw that he'd sent his team racing off toward the

Brody house with their own evidence technicians and cameraman.

"So this is jurisdictional cooperation," he called up to Fuller. "We must do it more often."

WHILE AWAITING THE FBI-ordered cherry picker, Leonard Chang had climbed down from the shed roof and had returned to the second-floor bedroom crime scene for another look. From there he got on his cell phone and rang Frank Patterson at the Brody house for an update there. Patterson picked up his cell and replied to Chang's question. "Maybe another hour, maybe two. Depends."

"You don't have two hours, Frank. Lincoln's on his way up the steps now, and Fuller's team is behind him."

"That's just great, Leonard. Now I've got to stop everything and play nursemaid to King Gordo?"

"Just walk him through the crime scene as you can best piece it together, Frank. Use the phrases *I think, perhaps,* and *quite possibly* a lot. That way no one can hold you to anything you've said, like being a politician, Frank . . . like running for office. Now tell me, what the fuck are you hiding over there in the upstairs bedroom? Something dangling from a ceiling fan?"

"Leonard, you of all people've got to understand. I've got my team concentrated on the three—count 'em, Leonard—*three whole and undivided corpses* as opposed to dealing with the slaughterhouse remains of Mira Lourdes upstairs. Three gunshot victims in the—"

"Then it's true, you've known about the Lourdes remains there and you've kept it to yourself? Why wasn't I informed, Frank?"

"As I said, my first duty, as I see it, is to determine how the Brodys died here, not how a half a decayed woman's body found its way through the door."

"I suggest you do precisely as Detective North and Captain Lincoln wish, Frank."

"North?"

"She's coming through the door with Lincoln as we

speak. I have them in my sight. They'll want you to drop everything, Frank, to sort out the Lourdes woman's remains, as I do, Frank. Tell me, Frank, is it the entire rest of the woman or not?"

"It's all the rest of her."

"Thank God for that."

"Leonard, had you been here, you'd've done the same as I did. You'd've focused on the larger problem first—three bodies in the basement to process and bag, not to mention the walls we've had to cut through."

"Walls?"

"Blood-spatter evidence."

"Frank, photos would just as well suffice. The killer's not going on trial in her condition."

"Just being thorough, Leonard."

"You need me to look in, run interference with Lincoln?"

"No, everything's under control here."

Ten minutes later and Chang, looking through binoculars, saw Jana North pacing the Brody porch, waving her hands, and exchanging words with Captain Lincoln, who kept pace with her. Leonard thought it like watching a silent film without benefit of titles—frustrating. Still, the overall message was made clear when Lincoln suddenly took her by the arm, led her to his car, and they drove off, disappearing from view.

Chang sensed that neither Captain Lincoln nor the female lieutenant were happy with Frank Patterson or his decisions after actually viewing the final piece of *divvied-up* remains belonging to Mira Lourdes, and they'd likely had just as bad a reaction to dealing with Frank.

Leonard imagined the partial corpse in its indignant pose, dangling there in an airy, pastel-colored room, surrounded by teddy bears and other stuffed animals the teen had held onto, the ruffled curtains and bedspread, the walls no doubt graced with posters of Britney Spears, the Back Street Boys, and perhaps a poignant remnant of her younger years—say a painted wall sporting a character like Winnie the Poo and his thousand-acre wood. Candice

Brody, unknown to Lauralie Blodgett, dead at thirteen, her room turned into a horror chamber.

Chang imagined the impact the scene must have had on Jana North, who by now had become so personally involved and familiar with Mira Lourdes's history, her nature, her life and loves, hobbies and preferences in music, eyeliner, clothing, and favorite TV stars and cartoon characters.

"All right, Frank," Chang said into his cell. "I'll be over soon. When I get there, I'd like whatever there is left of Mira Lourdes bagged and put away. That poor woman has told us all she's going to tell us, Frank."

"I'll do what I can when I can, Leonard. I'm only one person."

"Then use your people. Delegate. Get what's left of Mira Lourdes downtown now, and let's assemble her as best we can for burial or cremation . . . whatever the family wants. Let the family have some closure, Frank. Can you imagine the hell they've been put through?"

"Sure thing . . . absolutely."

Chang hung up, on the verge of losing his temper. The moment he hung up, his phone rang again.

It was Lincoln. "Thought I'd let you know, Chang, that business we discussed about Frank Patterson?"

"Yes?"

"I'm with you. The guy's a first-rate prick."

"Then you saw this morning's papers?"

"Yeah, I saw the papers, and I saw what was left of Mira Lourdes hanging from her decayed ankles in the little girl's bdroom. All this could be twisted to put Lucas and Meredyth in a bad light. Not only has the *Chronicle* identified them, but it makes my forensic psychiatrist and one of my best detectives appear *somehow* the cause of this nutcase's obsession—like as if their high profiles mean they asked for it or some such bullshit."

"And you think Patterson is—"

"Frank's sabotaged this investigation once too often, and the jerk upset Detective North to no end, so I pulled her outta the Brody place. Nothing more she and I can do here. We've decided to get back to Houston and zip over to the hospital. Get a firsthand look at Lucas, assess the situation there, give Meredyth our support, all that, you know."

"Sounds like a good move. Let's take care of the living."

"Yeah . . . yeah . . ." The unspoken words floated between them over the phone connection: *If Lucas is still among the living.* "So, Leonard, I leave the decision about Frank up to you. Me . . . the board, we're behind *any* decision you make regarding Frank Patterson."

"Thanks, Captain, but you know I don't need board approval or your okay to fire Frank."

"Technically, I know that, Leonard, but you'll want all the support you can muster *when-if* comes a time Frank should file a lawsuit for reinstatement or loss of pay and defamation of character—as if he had one."

"I appreciate your confidence and advice, Captain. I'm going over to the Brody home as soon as I can. Expect to close down all the crime scenes within one, one and a half hours."

"I'll need you at the five P.M. news conference, One Police Plaza downtown, since obviously, Leonard, you know more about what went down out at the lake than anyone else."

"Thanks, Gordon. I'll be there."

"With the answers?"

"Absolutely."

Lincoln waxed nostalgic for a moment. "Remember a time when crime was on the downswing, a time when we were young and optimistic, Leonard? A time when we thought we could win this war?"

Chang didn't know what to say. He let Lincoln continue. "Now so many crazies out there you gotta wonder if it's not something in the water or the preservatives in our food. So many people affected by this single madwoman."

Chang didn't know how to respond to this either, but he didn't have to. The next sound he heard was a dial tone.

Chang had left the upstairs bedroom and had stepped outside, where he now stood on the front porch, all doors standing open, technicians entering and exiting. He dialed Dr. Nielsen, and in a tired voice asked, "How is everything going down there? You able to finish up soon?"

"You see me in hip-deep water here, Dr. Chang? I'm working as fast as I can here."

Why was she so curt and annoyed, he wondered, guessing that the nature of the crime scene she was asked to handle would get to anyone. "I'll get back to you."

Chang hung up as Hoskins joined him. Ted Hoskins had drawn up a thumbnail map to help in his synopsis of precisely where Lucas had taken the first hit, falling into a stack of uncut six-foot logs and crawling below a big green John Deere tractor. A few feet farther off to the right, he took a second hit as he appeared to have left the ground, diving for cover below the stable canopy. "The blood trail and his barefoot prints tell the story. Picked up a female track as well, presumably Dr. Sanger's. She was with him at the end," said Hoskins.

"What end? He's not dead yet."

Hoskins apologized. "I meant the end of the ordeal."

"Sorry. What else do you have, Ted?"

Inside the stable, the blood told the story of his preparing the horses. Hoskins then showed where Lucas had finally fallen, where Meredyth had held him wrapped in the blanket. "Preliminary reports from the paramedics said that Lucas would have bled to death had she not jammed that super-gauze bandage into the exit wound at his back. There would not have been any use for the medevac chopper."

Chang and Nielsen had been nearby at the Longhorn Inn after having spent hours at the M&M Cafe in an attempt to link four murders there to Lauralie Blodgett. No one aside from Lauralie Blodgett had known that just down the road Lucas and Meredyth vacationed in relative calm. For this reason—and the fact that Nielsen always slept to the monotone of a police radio, they'd arrived at Madera in time to see Lucas airlifted by the medevac helicopter. He'd seen Meredyth leap into the chopper alongside him, shouting at the medics to do something. That had been the last time he'd seen Lucas Stonecoat, and it pained Leonard Chang to have seen so virile a man carted off like an inert and deflated gunnysack. The man Leonard Chang most admired for strength, stature, courage, and sheer instinctive ability. It was like seeing the unarmed John Wayne gun downed by Bruce Dern in *The Cowboys,* a feeling of stark surprise and horror. If a guy the size and breadth of Lucas Stonecoat could be brought down . . .

Chang's stomach lurched and began to growl, reminding him he hadn't eaten anything other than a donut and a cup of coffee all day. It was nearing noon, and the closest diner, down the road, was useless—closed down as a crime scene by the State Patrol and County Sheriff's Office, both of which were represented here as well now. They had called Leonard Chang to the murders at the M&M Cafe, and when time ran late, he'd been convinced to get adjoining rooms at the Longhorn.

Little physical evidence pointing to the multiple killer at the diner had emerged aside from spent shell casings from a Walther 9mm, nothing to connect the kill spree with Lauralie except that the only eyewitness saw a BMW racing away from the scene with an olive-skinned blond woman at the wheel. When a photo of Lauralie had been shown, the ID had proven inconclusive. All the same, he and Lynn had remained to help out the locals in the worst crime ever committed in the typically peaceful region.

Chang had tried desperately to get the word out that it might well be Lauralie Blodgett who had done the terrible deed at the diner, but he'd been unsuccessful in locating either Lucas or Meredyth, having to settle for Detective North and Captain Lincoln. No one seemed to know Lucas's whereabouts, and he wasn't answering his cell phone or his car radio. Meredyth had remained silent as well, despite a number of messages left on both their cell phones. Lincoln ordered any information relative to the Blodgett investigation, however tentative, be shared by Leonard with Fuller's regional FBI office.

Now Chang knew the reason why neither Lucas nor Meredyth had been reachable.

While Chang looked extremely young for his age, he felt old today. He had organized the largest death scene investigation of his career here on Lake Madera. It would beg to be written up for the journals some day, once he could step back and view it in its entirety with an objective eye, but for now the thought of wanting to share the story with other professionals in his field and in law enforcement in general was a long way off. For now, uppermost in his mind must be to gather all the various threads together and weave them into a mosaic that made sense, and to create a time line of events, and at the same time preserve crucial evidence—not to prosecute in this case but to vindicate actions taken by Meredyth and Lucas, and to explain exactly how the Farnsworth boys, Kemper, the Brodys, the people at the diner, and others had become targets of an audacious madness.

At least Lauralie Blodgett was dead and could harm no more. Precisely how she'd died along with each of her unfortunate victims, this was the mosaic he was now after. It would take more than the hour or so he'd promised Lincoln; even Lincoln had to know that an hour or so in forensic jargon meant four or five. "I work on a Chinese clock," he often joked with an impatient Detective Stonecoat.

He fought back a tear. He only hoped that when he next saw Lucas, he could tell him all about the complexities and problems of this enormous case.

"Dr. Chang, we got the way it went down with the two Farnsworth boys," said Agent Ron Meserve of the ATF, an assistant alongside him looking young, bright, and excited to be a part of the investigation.

They explained it in graphs they'd made that followed minute details of spent shell casings where the Blodgett woman had stood at the Farnsworth pickup firing off rounds at the backs of Jeff and Tommy Farnsworth as they ran, unprotected and unarmed, down from the house toward the pier, as if ordered to.

"She was dressed as the gardener, pruning those oleander bushes," said the younger ATF agent. "The two male victims drove up, unsuspecting, got out, and moved toward her. We surmise that she trained a weapon on them, this one." He held up a Walther 9mm. "Clip was emptied already at the M&M, and the Brody house, but the boys had *no-way-a-knowin'-it.*"

The older agent, Meserve, summed it up with, "Had they called her bluff . . . had they jumped her, it might've been a whole different story."

And Lucas and Meredyth would've been spared, thought Chang, *along with the two young horse wranglers, along with their pitifully grieving mother.* Mrs. Farnsworth had been going between Jeff's and Tommy's body, holding first one and then the other, here on the lawn when Chang and the others had first arrived. Lynn Nielsen, a great help at the M&M Cafe, had somehow managed to talk the grieving mother away from the crime scene, sending her home with a female deputy from the County Sheriff's office.

A picture of what had happened at the stables and the direction of the gunshots from the upstairs window emerged, and now an equally clear picture of Lauralie Blodgett firing from the front porch on the Farnsworth boys had come into focus. The boys were killed hours before Lucas had been wounded, their bodies and the insect activity over them telling the tale.

So now Chang had a partial time line, and he knew that with Lauralie wearing the gardener's clothes and hat, discarded at the steps, the missing Howard Kemper was dispatched sometime *before* the two boys were gunned down. Prior to this, across the lake, Lauralie had apparently killed the Brodys sometime during the early morning, after which she'd exchanged her viper's nest at the Brody home for her sniper's nest at Meredyth's bedroom window.

From bullet holes peppered into an upturned rowboat found on the lake, it had been surmised that Lucas and Meredyth had been fired on while out on the lake, unprotected, unarmed, helpless. Firearms experts had assured Chang that a child using the Remington and its scope could not miss a target as large as Lucas Stonecoat out on the lake, but neither he nor Meredyth were hit while in the bullet-riddled boat.

A broken table leg was found very near where Lucas had been gunned down, and early reports from the Brody kitchen spoke of a table that had been upended and scavenged for its legs.

How had Lucas and Meredyth gotten to the Brody home alive under the crosshairs of that bolt-action, high-powered Remington? And once in the Brody house, why had they chosen to return here, crossing the lake and painting themselves with muck in a vain attempt at getting the horses from the stable? All questions he wanted to put to Meredyth, but she was, for the time being, unavailable to him.

Why didn't Stonecoat simply wait it out across the river? Why didn't he walk out? Why come back in the face of overwhelming firepower when he was unarmed? *Macho shit-head fool,* Chang summed up, *what did his Cherokee bravura get him?*

FROM WHERE SHE stood in hip-deep lake water, Dr. Lynn Nielsen watched the skittish unmanned rowboat and its contents as it was guided to her by the divers. They'd had to swim out to the center of the lake to fetch it; there it had bobbed in their wake, eluding touch, acting like a shy cat, not wishing to be cornered. Finally, the two swimmers took hold of the gunwales and guided it into the shallows and an increasingly anxious Dr. Nielsen.

A third wet-suited diver stood alongside Nielsen in the shallows, and he now lifted his water-proof camera and began taking shots of the unholy sight at the bottom of the floating coffin, gagging at what his lens and his eye reported to his brain.

From the safe distance of thirty or so feet, a news camera in a helicopter overhead focused in on the activity at the lake. A dead man lay in the flat pool of water in the bottom of the boat, covered in worms, his throat a jagged mass of blood where his jugular had been severed, his lips moving with worm activity, and the soft tissue of his eyes, already eaten away, had sunk into their sockets, the worms finding a home in the collapsed orbs. Nielsen imagined these news camera pictures would *not* be finding their way into American living rooms, at least not until some money-crazed TV producer somehow created a reality show forum for crime-scene and autopsy photos. Newsroom vaults were crammed full with video deemed unfit for public consumption and viewing. Still, pretty soon nothing would be unfit, she told herself, if these Americans continued on their present course.

The diver with the camera, Bert Quinn, continued to snap shots in such a way as to *not again* look into the dead man's missing eyes.

"Jesus, damn most *horrible thing* I've ever seen," said Bert's partner, going for shore, anxious to distance himself from the floating coffin.

The third diver kept one hand on the gunwale, steadying the boat for Dr. Nielsen, his attention on her. "How'd you ever decide-ta become a coroner, Dr. Nielsen?" he asked, staring across the boat and into her eyes. "I mean, didya just wake up one morning and say to yourself I wanna work with stiffs, or what?"

"I went to med school to become a physician, and I somehow wound up working under an extraordinary man in forensic pathology who gave me great respect and from whom I could learn. . . . A too good chance to pass up."

"Everybody over in Norway talk so cute?"

She felt uncomfortable now at his attention. "I am from Sweden, not Norway, and I do not have the time to teach you the difference."

"Maybe over dinner sometime?"

The cameraman looked over his lens to see her reaction to the other man's pass.

"I don't think this is the right place to talk of such matters."

"That's why I'm saying we ought to continue this over dinner, maybe some wine?"

"No, no, thank you. I don't date men outside my profession," she lied. "Still, your offer is a . . . a compliment. Thank you, but no, thank you."

Nielsen had begun to work as she spoke, pushing aside worm colonies from the nude body of the middle-aged gardener, searching with her gloved fingers and her sharp eye for any obvious wounds other than the enormous one at the throat. She immediately isolated a smaller curious puncture wound also in the throat, one masked by the larger wound. She ran her gloved hands down the torso, her eyes following, searching for any contusions, bruises, anomalies, or irregularities.

"This guy was hung like a thumb tack, like the size of an earplug, that thing," said the police diver who'd propositioned her over the body.

"Agent, if you're trying to embarrass me, you *can't,* and if you're simply being rude because I said no to you, then I have to suspect you are hung like an earplug as well. Now please, allow me to do my job."

Both Bert the cameraman and his friend on the FBI dive team laughed at their colleague, Bert saying, "She got you good, Al."

She continued to survey the nude corpse, her gloved hand and eye now down to his scarred knees—recent bruising—and next she noticed the deep brown, tobacco-like stains under all his toenails. She took scrapings and efficiently put these into a vial, safely tucking them into a valise on a strap she'd placed around her neck. Finally, she said, "All right . . . we're needing to come at this in a fresh venue."

"Whataya make of what happened to this guy, Doc?" asked the third diver from shore now.

"Obviously, someone's cut his throat. Presumably Blodgett."

"That little woman?" erupted one of the divers, and this started a cacophony of disagreement.

"I saw her pictures! You're right. Skinny as a coyote."

"No bigger than a hen."

"The guy had almost two hundred pounds on her."

"Okay, gentlemen. I want the boat upended like the one we dragged into shore already, one with all the bullet holes." This boat had already been examined and photographed.

"Why're we turning the boat over with him in it?" asked the one named Al.

"I don't need or want the worms in the body bag, gentlemen, so let's upend the boat and feed the fish, shall we? We'll then float the man to the pier and lift him out there. I can better examine him once he's been . . . ahhh, baptized."

They reluctantly did as instructed, flipping the rowboat after some effort and spilling its contents out into the lake. The divers gently guided Kemper's floating body, facedown, to the pier. His plunge and short swim to the pier had dispersed the worms, and it had the added virtue of cleansing the wound that had killed him.

They lifted Kemper's body from the water, as the news chopper did another flyby, further grating on Nielsen's nerves. Kemper lay now faceup on the weathered dock, but the body bag, so patiently awaiting his arrival till now, suddenly flew off and into the lake on the other side of the berth, caught up in the whirlwind of the chopper as Nielsen climbed the ladder from water to platform.

"Kee-rist!" she shouted up at the chopper pilot, waving him off. "In Sweden we'd have shot those fools from the sky by now."

The body bag was retrieved, and the 2NEWS bird backed off while Lynn Nielsen leaned in over Kemper's throat for a closer look. She was unaware that the newsman overhead was shooting close-up footage of her lanky, curvaceous body now, and the divers too sat back and appreciated her statuesque beauty kneeling in over the corpse, the wet suit stretched to its limit. Nielsen's own attention was on the remaining, clinging worms that had stubbornly come along for the ride, burrowed as they were in the eye sockets and the gaping neck wound.

She again identified a small but deep gouge at the center of the throat other than the critical wound that had emptied the man's blood. There'd been no blood in the bottom of the boat, curiously enough, only cold, clear water, and of course the feasting worms. He'd been killed elsewhere and dumped in the green boat crudely carved with the Brody names— Myron, Lorene, Candice. The worms remained a mystery.

From the angle of the deadly jugular slash, Nielsen surmised that the killer was perhaps two and a half to three feet taller than Kemper—*impossible,* she could hear Chang saying—unless Kemper was kneeling at the time he was caught from behind and his throat cut right to left. Was he made to grovel on his knees perhaps?

There were other questions as well. For the slight Lauralie to have attacked so large a man and gotten his inert body down to the lake, she'd have had to have some sort of help, but Belkvin was out of the picture, long since dead. Had she lured a new boyfriend into her web, some local dupe she'd met at the M&M Cafe perhaps, to do her bidding? Had one of the *Farnsworth boys* fallen under her charms, only then to be murdered along with his brother? Perhaps she had even tempted both young men. She seemed to have an uncanny, near-supernormal power over men.

"Bag 'im, gentlemen." Nielsen stood and turned to face the lawn and the driveway, the house on the knoll. She saw Chang directing some guy in a cherry picker from his standing position atop the shed. She lifted a perfunctory wave in his direction, seeing that he was staring back at her now. Her eyes then went to the lawn, where the unevenly cut grass had been trampled by officers from the county, ATF, and FBI. She saw men smoking cigarettes, leaning against trees, cowboy boots resting on black valises, men and women in ball caps and Stetsons, some in uniform, others in jackets pulled over white shirts and ties. The overall effect was of a bizarre Norman Rockwell painting: a crowd of picnickers stepping over a pair of corpses, the bodies acting as focal point in the composition. Other than gabbing and biting on pipes, cigars, and cigarettes, these people on the lawn and standing around the vehicles in the drive looked as if they were doing nothing. She guessed most were standing about discussing the weekend college ball games. These thoughts wafted through her head, when suddenly it struck her. She knew how Lauralie had killed Kemper.

The lay of the grass coming toward her, creating a near-imperceptible path, screamed in her head; the lawnmower had made this errant path down to the docks. The more she stared at it, the clearer the picture came into edgy focus. She now recognized the faint little dirt and mud trail along the pier boardwalk, a trail they'd managed to trample over—the evidence that the mower had been *guided* with Kemper still sitting astride the cushion, with *her* knife at *his* throat while she straddled the back.

She heard the unmistakable sound of the body bag zipper closing on Kemper, plunging the body into darkness. "Hold on a minute." She returned to the body and slipped the zipper down far enough to investigate the neck wounds once again, zeroing in on the more tentative jab that had aroused her curiosity; seeing it again, almost lost in the puckering folds of the larger tear, she *knew* what it meant.

She closed Kemper from her sight again. "Okay, thanks. You can get that waiting van down here and put him aboard for the trip back to Houston."

She walked out to the end of the pier and back, giving her theories time to percolate in her head. Once Lauralie had forced Kemper down to the pier, she had him flank the boat she'd come across the lake in. Once the mower was aligned alongside the boat, she slit his throat, and he bled out over the wheel of the mower. The pool of blood would be found on the floorboard of the same big red Toro that everyone had treated as an obstacle, stepping around it all morning long up at the house where Lauralie had left it beside the lawn truck.

Nielsen pictured the events in her mind. Lauralie didn't want to shoot the gardener, knowing she'd never be able to drag his body from sight, and she didn't have to leap from the bushes to take him by surprise. With the noise of the mower, she might easily have stalked up from behind and stabbed him in the back, but as it was, she had to completely reach around him to cut his throat from left to right, and besides, she wanted him to strip, she wanted his clothes. Of course, it was an easy matter to cut the hefty man's throat after *charming* him out of his pants and into giving her a ride on his great big red mower. She had simply presented herself to him in those same tight-fitting jeans and that low-cut blouse she'd died in, the same outfit that had perhaps charmed the Farnsworth boys into dropping their guard as well . . . maybe . . .

Lauralie had stepped up to Kemper as he was mowing the grass, introduced herself as someone visiting from across the lake, and seductively talked him into a ride into the trees, where she convinced him to make love to her. Once she'd gotten him to drop his uniform, she showed her true colors, likely pulling a gun on him, the one used at the cafe. She ordered him back onto his mower in the buff. Once at his rear, Kemper no longer enjoying his *luck,* she suddenly put the knife to his throat and dug it in deeply—the initial wound—making certain he knew she meant business. She then ordered him to drive down to the pier. When he hesitated, she pierced his skin even deeper with the first cut, drawing blood.

After this, Kemper played along, doing as instructed, pleading for his life perhaps, wondering what she wanted perhaps. On stopping the mower halfway down the pier as ordered, he had no idea what she wanted. She stood up on the back of the mower guard, and keeping the razor-sharp knife at his throat, with the extra strength that standing over him provided, Lauralie thrust the knife into his jugular and dragged it across his throat.

Kemper immediately slumped forward over the wheel, his blood flowing down into the mower well at his feet, much of it soaking into his toenails. It was no simple matter, but from there, she managed to push his body from its sitting position on the mower to roll onto the dock and into the boat—surely almost toppling it over given his size and girth. He landed faceup to the heavens, his surprised eyes open along with his mouth and the gaping wound in his throat.

Nielsen began peeling off the wet suit, garnering stares from the men again. As she did so, she watched the body of the hapless, unlucky gardener, who had succumbed to Lauralie's lies and wiles, being carried unceremoniously to the waiting coroner's van.

Lillian Weist, an evidence tech intern, had come bounding down from the house. "I got some info on the guy in the boat."

"Kemper, yeah," replied Nielsen.

"How'd you know his name?" Lillian asked, clutching the form in her hand, all the blanks filled in. "It took me all morning to get all these facts."

"His truck. It's on his truck, Lil."

She scrunched up her nose and face in the universal facial expression that asked others to agree with the idiocy of its owner. "Duhhh," she said. "I got most of this from papers in his glove compartment, but didn't think to read the truck logo. Anyway . . . talk about being in the wrong place at the wrong time. Kemper normally arrived and did his work in the A.M., but yesterday he came in the P.M. He'd visited a family friend in hospital and had lunch with his wife at the hospital cafeteria before arriving here. Had he been on his *usual* schedule, he'd've been long gone before this lunatic's arrival."

Nielsen began verbalizing her theory of precisely how Howard Kemper met his end, telling Lillian, but also gathering the interest of Bert and Al. Young Lillian and the two men listened to her story with skeptical silence, Lillian nodding and struggling to stay with her, while the nodding of the men implied a condescending unwillingness to believe she could possibly know such details.

Nielsen stared up the lawn toward the mower. She could prove her theory at the mower. There she would find the evidence of the man's blood in the well of the mower bed. Evidence only *inches* from one FBI man who this moment stood leaning up against the Toro, blissfully unaware of its importance.

"What about his clothes?" asked Bert.

"Yeah, what became of his clothes, Dr. Nielsen?" asked Al.

Lillian provided the answer, pointing to the form in her hand. "Clothes were found beside the front exterior steps leading up to the Sanger home, discarded and bloody— particularly the lap area and the pants legs."

Dr. Nielsen had their rapt attention as she detailed her theory, anxious to air it, to test its validity in her own ear. When she finished, Bert, busy putting his camera and lenses away, replied, "All right, say you're right about the clothes, the mower ride onto the pier, dumping his body from mower direct to boat *without* tipping the damn thing over . . ." Al and the others leaned in to hear this. "It still doesn't explain how the damn worms got into the freaking boat with him, does it?"

Al jumped in, still smarting from having been burned by her. "Yeah, how do you explain the worms?"

She breathed deeply, shaking her head. "I don't know *yet*."

"They didn't just *jump* in on their own," added Bert, snapping his camera case closed. "Must've been hundreds of them," he told Lillian.

"A thousand or more," said Al to the intern. "You had to see it to believe it. Feeding on his eyes and inside his wounds."

"The worms were night crawlers, big reds," said Bert. "Good for fishing."

Al agreed. "Kind you buy at the bait and tackle."

"That's it, bait," said Dr. Nielsen. "Explains the water at the bottom of the canoe too."

"I don't follow you," replied Lillian.

"Someone's cooler full of *frozed* worms," she said, her accent showing doubly on the misspoken word for "frozen."

"Frozed? Frozed?" asked Al, poking Bert, and together they laughed.

Ignoring the men, Nielsen stepped to the boathouse door and scanned the interior. Lillian trailed curiously after. The two women had stepped inside just as the van carrying Kemper's body backed over the mower trail Nielsen had earlier photographed. She pointed out the wall of rods and reels hanging in the boathouse, and below it an empty Styrofoam cooler lying on its side, the lid inches away. A discarded blanket lay half in the water off the little boardwalk. The motorboat that filled most of the space was up out of the water on davits.

"No expense spared here," said Lillian, lifting the lid of an electrically powered metal icebox, the wall unit. A handful of dead, dried-up earthworms lay at their feet.

The men poked their heads into the boathouse just in time to see Lillian drop the Styrofoam cooler down into the wall unit, a perfect fit. "This is a storage cooler for bait—worms," she said.

"Now we know where the night crawlers came from," said Nielsen.

"Yeah, they were frozed in here and thawed out in the boat," joked Al badly. "So, you saying she threw in the worms for sport?"

"Explains how they got there."

Nielsen now glanced across the lake at the activity of men and women going in and out of the Brody house. She wondered how Dr. Frank Patterson was doing there. It had irked her that Patterson should get the plum assignment, the house with three bodies to grid, while she was put on a dead gardener in the boat. After all, she had been on the Post-it Ripper case with Leonard from the "get-go," as the Americans liked to say, but when push came to shove, seniority had won out. Still, even though Frank was the *Ass*-sociate M.E., and she was a mere Assistant M.E., Patterson, unlike her, had *not* been involved on the case from the "get-go." No matter how she turned it in her mind, Lynn felt cheated.

Bide your time, she kept telling herself. *Your time will come.*

She then chided herself for daring to think *she* had problems; her problems were *small potatoes* compared to what Meredyth Sanger must be going through right now. She allowed a silent prayer to escape her for Meredyth, and for Lucas, one that would also suffice for his departed soul, should that be the case. Aside from being colleagues in a sense, the pair had become her new friends as well. How was Meredyth to cope? Lynn knew how desperately the woman loved Lucas. It must be so hard on her.

She started up the incline toward the house, working her way toward Leonard Chang even as she put her cell phone to her ear, having dialed him, but her eyes remained fixed on the mower. The Blodgett body apparently had been successfully plucked from the windmill by the cherry picker, and Chang was escorting the body, now on a stretcher, toward an ambulance. Nielsen didn't want to be distracted, but Lillian, trailing after her, still waved the form she'd come with originally. "You'll need this for your final report, Dr. Nielsen."

Nielsen had already filled a spiral book with observations, comments, notes, measured distances, maps, thumbnail sketches of the pier in relation to the boat, and an explanation on how it was *impossible* to get a true triangulation of where the body was discovered since there was no fixed position, the boat having wandered about on the lake. What had alerted authorities in the first place were the birds coming and going from the boat, their beaks full with what Bert called *red beauties*. Still, she knew about the thousand and one trivial little details needed to fill in all the blanks on all the damn forms waiting back at the office, and even inconsequential items—say a victim's Social Security number or his mother's maiden name—would be called for, delaying the proceedings unless the information was accessible.

At such a time she'd be thanking God for Lil's standard form. She thanked Lillian and took her report, laying it into her notebook just as Chang came on the line.

"Lynn, good! You've finished up with the Kemper body, have you?"

"And you with the Blodgett body?"

"Some truly curious details forming up here at the house. Meredyth tried to save Blodgett's life even after all this."

She countered, "I am dying to hear all about it, but it doesn't compare to the bizarre story I have for you, Leonard."

"Then you have answers, good!"

"Answers, yes. Meet me at the lawn mower."

"The lawn mower? All right . . . on my way down."

Reaching the driveway and the mower, she saw Chang

rounding the back of the ambulance where he'd left Blodgett's body in its black bag. After the niceties, and questions about where they might find a bite to eat, she laid out
how the gardener had died, and she walked him over to the
mower, and pointing, showed him the coagulated blood at
the bottom of the well beneath the wheel. It was there, and
so were some distinctive shoe prints—small, feminine
ones. "She drove the mower back to here, her feet wading
in Kemper's blood. By time he was bleeding out, he was
barefoot. The first giveaway was the dried blood I found
under his toenails but nowhere else."

"Impressive," he replied. "Perelli! Got any film left in
that camera?" Chang pointed to the blood pool imprinted
by a pair of unique shoe prints, while Nielsen went to the
ambulance and tore away one of Lauralie's shoes from her
feet. She returned with it, and the match was clearly visible.
"A matched pair," she said.

"A match made in blood," Chang replied.

Lil stood staring, learning, soaking up things, and realizing she wanted very much to work more closely with
Dr. Nielsen.

Chang suggested they retire to the Brody house. They
took the road that meandered around the lake, disappearing
amid the tall sentinels of the pine forest. Along their way,
they passed the spot where men in FBI and ATF wind-
breakers dealt with the BMW found nestled in the trees
just beyond the Brody house.

DR. FRANK PATTERSON, in white shirt and tie, stood
now over the bodies at the foot of the basement stairs in the
Brody home, his gloved hands going to his aching back.
He'd been bending over the dead family for forty minutes
now, assessing how each had died, their relative positions,
relative ages, and searching for any additional bruises or
obvious marks. Hands tied, the three bodies had been
dumped here in the basement as if hurled down the stairs,
but the gunshots had all occurred at the top of the stairwell.
There the blood spatters, along with brain matter, along

with gunshot residue, painted the unfinished wall with enough crazy art to call it a Jackson Pollock painting.

His assistant revved up a small rotary saw and went to work removing the section of wall in question. He'd take it back to the lab with him, study it in detail. Under the right light, and with the help of blood-spatter specialists, he would be able to tell in which order each of the Brodys were killed—father-mother-daughter, mother-father-daughter, or some other variation. The crime would be re-created down to its last detail. If it proved interesting enough, he could write it up in the prestigious *Journal of the American Medical Examiner*. They paid well in both cash and cachet.

The sound of the saw ended, and Patterson looked up to the top of the stairs, thinking Jennings an efficient man to finish with the wall so quickly, but Jennings hadn't finished. He'd merely stopped to allow Dr. Chang and Dr. Nielsen the right-of-way. They came down the stairwell now for a look at the cruel massacre here. "Anything I ought to know here, Frank?" asked Chang.

"Dunno . . . little soon to tell, but it's pretty clear the victims were forced to tie one 'nother up. Probably with assurances nothing would happen if they cooperated. Looks like a page out of Truman Capote's *In Cold Blood*. They cooperate and he—*ahhh,* she, if it proves to've been Blodgett, she blows their brains out anyway, all in the same manner, right here." He put an index finger behind Lynn Nielsen's ear to demonstrate the location of each entry wound, and said, "Pow! Just like a professional or someone familiar with the *Godfather* films."

Nielsen pulled away, annoyed he'd chosen her head to demonstrate on, his finger jabbing into her head. "It does appear to be *her* work," she said.

"And how would you know that from what little we have?" challenged Patterson, as had been his habit with her.

"She wasn't a big woman, only one hundred ten pounds at most. She wisely used her victims' weight against them here, as with getting Kemper off the mower and into the boat."

"What mower?"

"It's why they were shot at the top of the stairs and allowed to tumble down. She didn't have to drag, carry, or push them here."

"Good point," said Chang.

"Of course it is," said Patterson. "It's why I'm having the wall removed. They were shot at the top of the stairs and their bodies came tumbling down."

"What about the upstairs, the girl's room?" asked Chang. "Your guys finished there?"

"Finishing, yes."

"The other half of Mira Lourdes is on ice?" he asked.

"Well, no, not that far along yet, but it'll get done."

Chang gave a little nod to Nielsen. "Get up there and see to it Miss Lourdes's parts are bagged and put in the refrigeration van, Dr. Nielsen."

"I can handle it, Leonard," said Patterson.

"You've got your hands full here, Frank. Trust me, we've got enough autopsies to go around."

With Nielsen gone and the saw renewing its work at the top of the stairs, Chang stepped over the bodies and surveyed the basement—a lovely rec room with a Ping Pong table, a bar with a neon Coor's sign over it, lit and blinking, and on the bar a family photo of the Brodys on holiday in a snowy Christmas scene with skis—Aspen, Colorado, Chang guessed.

He continued examining the basement area. A washer-and-dryer unit at one end, little windows high overhead looking out on the earth. One corner sported a lounging area and a reading nook, with a bookshelf filled with dog-eared paperbacks, assorted magazines, and a hardcover crime novel entitled *Unnatural Instinct* lying on one chair, a marker indicating the reader was halfway through the book. When Chang slipped it open, he saw the expensive bookmark was engraved with the name of Candice, the daughter.

Patterson had shadowed Chang. "Frank, life is too short. I came down here from upstairs, from Candice's room. I saw what's been hanging there all this time."

"What's the big deal, Leonard? I made the call. Priority *one,* the basement, *two,* the sweep of the kitchen—lotta things disturbed in the kitchen. Didya see that overturned, broken dining room table? And *three,* the upstairs rooms—not just Candice's but the master bedroom too. One that looks out on the forest out back."

"You lied to me, Frank, and you didn't follow my orders either. Look, we both know you're unhappy working under someone you feel superior to, Frank—a slant-eyed Chink."

"I never said anything of the kind. Who told you that?"

"You tell me that, Frank, every day."

The silence between them was rocklike. Chang broke it. "Look, I don't want to argue this here, not now. When this case settles, once all the reports are in, all the dots dotted and Ts crossed, you can defend your actions involving this case in a full rebuttal, okay? But Frank, I say it's time you started floating your resume."

"What? Whataya mean, Leonard? Are you *firing* me? You can't *fire* me, not without the approval of the board."

"I have their okay, Frank."

"You son of a—"

"My mother is descended from a royal Chinese princess, Frank. You never knew that, did you? So I'll forgive your calling her a bitch."

"You think this is the last word on this, Leonard? You couldn't be more wrong."

"See if ATF or FBI is interested in your talents, Frank."

"I'm a good M.E., Leonard."

"That's the shame of it, Frank. That's the shame of it. You are a kick-ass clinician. No one can touch you in the lab, but there's more to this job than slides, test tubes, and microscopes, and I've got to be a pragmatist. You're never going to be the people person you need to be, to deal with the public, the families, the detectives, your own peers in the lab."

"You want me out so you can put Nielsen in my spot. Whataya doing, Leonard—a good family man like you? You two sleeping together? Have a fucking good time at the Longhorn Inn down the road?"

"I've got a friend at County General lying in a coma, Frank, a man who may or may not live through the day. I've got another friend sitting at his side, holding his hand, talking him through. I'm finished here for the day, and I suggest you quit making graphs and measuring the distance from the top of the stairs to the bottom, and close this scene down."

"Fuck you, Chang. I'll say when it's time to close *my* crime scene down and not before. How many times've I listened to you, shut down a scene, only to wish I had taken more time at the scene? Too many to count, so it's when *I* say it's time."

"This place has given up all the clues it has to give, Frank, and as for the table, the legs were ripped off by Lucas and Meredyth to use as weapons. We found one at the stable where Lucas was shot."

"I still have say-so on how long we hold this place for forensic analysis. That much is still my call. That much you can't take away from me."

Chang looked over his notes, trying to collect his thoughts, how best to say what he must to Dr. Patterson to get it through to him that his career in the HPD Crime Lab was over. "Frank, you didn't just go over my head this time around; this time you went behind my back."

"What?" His look of exaggerated shock Chang thought laughable.

"You leaked sensitive information from my crime lab to the press, including Meredyth's and Lucas's names as the ones targeted by the Post-it Ripper, and—"

"That's a lie. Who's feeding you all these lies about me?"

"—and in the bargain, you told the city the name of the victim whose parts have been scattered all over this county by Blodgett. Christ, did you give one damn thought to Mira Lourdes's family, their wishes, Frank?"

"Captain Lincoln might have something to say about all this bullshit, *Doctor.*" Patterson contemptuously spat his final word.

"Captain Lincoln *has* had something to say about this, Frank, and he agrees with my decision."

"We'll just see about this." Patterson lifted his cell phone and speed-dialed Lincoln.

Chang stormed up the stairs, where the blood-spattered wall had been completely removed and lay now on the kitchen island block. Two men worked at spraying a clear plastic preservative and adhesive over its surface.

Frank always had a problem working with women. He would handpick those working under him, but Tory had been foisted on him at the last by Chang, who wanted her, like Lil, to gain some experience in the field.

Chang watched the two men spending so much time over the section of wall. He thought it an awful lot of effort to go through, preserving the blood- and brain-spatter evidence in such an old-fashioned form. The space it would take up alone threw it into question since a single state-of-the-art series of high-resolution photos could tell them the same thing in the hands of the right man, though in this case, it was Jeannie Wyatt, the right woman. But this *was* Frank's scene and so Frank's call.

Leonard found Nielsen had dealt with the remains of Mira Lourdes—bagged and in the caravan now. Chang ordered the van to take what they had directly back to the lab in Houston, calling for another larger vehicle to accept the Brodys when and if Frank ever finished inside.

"Best you not be here when Frank emerges from the basement," Chang told Nielsen. "I just fired his ass. Fool had the gall to suggest you and me were having an affair, and that I wanted to give you his job in return for sexual favors."

"That's so like him, Leonard. I can't tell you how I relish the idea of one day walking into the lab and finding him gone."

Together, they climbed back into Chang's car, preparing to leave the Brody home. "I'm placing you in charge of all the evidence collected on Meredyth's side of the lake, Lynn."

"What? Really?"

Chang drove back for the Sanger house. "See to it all the bodies and anything that's been bagged from all the various grids, the photos, the vehicles—that it all gets back to the crime lab and the morgue, and whatever you do—"

"Do not break the chain of command, I know."

"That goes without saying, but *also* do not turn *anything* over to Frank if he should have the impudence to try taking command."

She smiled widely at this. "You won't be disappointed, Leonard, I promise you. Count on me. But where're you going to be?"

"Hospital. Check up on my friends."

He dropped her at the Sanger house and heard her commands carrying all the way down the drive, and likely across the lake, as he made his way back toward the Interstate and Houston. As he drove, he punched on his radio, searching for music to get the images of this day out of his mind. Ads filled the airways, and the search button stopped on a news report: *An army of FBI, ATF, Houston, and Harris County law-enforcement personnel descended on Madera Lake in the early hours of this morning to investigate multiple murders at two crime scenes there. Too early to tell, but the buzz is that somehow the Post-it Ripper case has invaded this sleepy, peaceful area near the Navasota River reservoir. . . .*

Chang popped on a Mozart CD, struggling to escape the news and the stress. He got on the phone and called home to his wife for the second time today. The first time was to inform her of Lucas's having been shot twice and about his being in hospital in serious condition. This time he began by asking how she was doing, asking after the kids, apologizing about the forty-eight-odd hours or so he had seen none of them, ending with a retinue of complaints about the job, the system, Lincoln's pomposity, of having had to fire Frank *because of* Frank, and the general callousness of the world.

Finally, his wife Kim stopped him, saying, "Len-len, he is going to be all right. I just *know* Lucas is going to be all right."

"How do you know? Have you heard from Meredyth?"

"No, I just have one of those intuitions. I just know."

"Kim, the man is listed in critical, unstable condition. He's in a coma, and he lost so much blood." The strings of Mozart filled the cab and traveled through the phone connection to her ear.

"You once told me that coma is nature's way of dealing with shock."

"Yes, but—"

"And you once told me he's a fighter. He'll pull through."

"Are you *clairvoyant?*"

"I have *faith,* as so you must."

"How? How do you have faith, Kim, in the face of all . . . all I have seen on this day? All that this single crazed individual did to so many innocent people, the ripple effect to their families, to the collective fabric . . . to the soul of humankind?"

"Faith, Leonard. It's all we have left in the end, faith and one another."

He said nothing.

"My hand is covering yours, my lips cover yours, my arms are folding around you, Len."

He glanced at her photo, kept always overhead in his car, and he mentally embraced her. "I am holding you too. I love you, dear one."

She replied, "I know . . . you are a thoroughly married man with three children who love you too. My thoroughly caring husband."

"True, I love you thoroughly, my wife."

"Yes, and it makes me happy. When will you come home to us?"

"In two hours."

"Then you really mean four?"

"All right, four."

"You sound so tired. How can you work with such necessary precision if they don't let you get rest?"

"I've got to learn to delegate more now that I have someone capable of taking over for me . . . thoroughly."

"Dr. Nielsen?"

"I turned over a multiple-murder scene to her, Kim. You have to be proud of me for that. Isn't that what you want for me? Patterson could never be trusted to do things right."

"I am glad for you, Len-len, so why will it take you four hours then?"

"I'm on my way back to Houston now, but I want to stop over to see how Meredyth is doing, and to see Lucas for myself. Go over his charts. Give Dr. Sanger any slight hope I might find in them."

"Do you wish me to meet you there?"

"Yes . . . yes, I do."

East Houston, the Colony in the Glade home of Paul and Caroline Sanger

WEARING A CLEANED and pressed new Colony Security uniform and hat, Mike Wilson pulled up to the Sanger home in his official Colony vehicle with but one thing on his mind—*impress, caress,* and *best* Miss Lauralie Sanger from out of town. She hadn't called him back, and his repeated phone calls to the house had gone strangely unanswered. He went so far as to leave messages on the answering machine. The Sangers were due back today, but when he arrived, he saw no sign of their being home. Perhaps they'd been delayed at some point on their long journey home from Paris.

He skipped up the stone steps to the huge Colony in the Glade home on Will-o'-the-Wisp Court. It was the largest of the models, called the Palatial in the brochures. The Sangers hadn't owned it long. They had reportedly moved off a large estate in North Houston to the Clover Leaf area, the home there having become too much for them to care for since retirement, especially since they had become world travelers. "Can't imagine the size of the house that got away from them," he'd told Jake Everly, his friend and superior on dispatch duty today. Mike had boasted that he'd met the young daughter, and he'd wagered they'd be dancing at Cimarron Kate's Cow Barn tonight. If he had to, he'd teach Lauralie how to square-dance.

He rang the doorbell, humming an old tune he now tried to recall the lyrics to. "If you could read my mind, love . . . what a tale . . . what a story . . . what a . . . To hell with it. Come on, Lauralie . . . baby . . . answer the fucking door. Getting cold out here."

He rang the bell, rocking on his heels. He watched his breath escape him like cigarette smoke. The thermometer had plummeted overnight, calling for a high of only forty-two. It felt like winter, but it was only late September. Weird for East Texas.

He again rang the bell.

He wondered if he ought to let it slip that he'd been an All-American at Tyler High in Tyler, Texas, and would've gone on to play for the University of Texas if not for an injury that sidelined him from the game for life. He wondered if he played it just right, if she wouldn't find that special spot of sympathy in her heart that inevitably led to necking. *I can take it from there,* he told himself.

Still no answer at the damn door.

An odd faint odor reached his nostrils, but Mike couldn't quite place it. Still no answer. Had she gone back to . . . where was it? Someplace in California, San Bernardino someplace, she'd said, by way of Phoenix.

She said she'd come in to surprise the folks, so where the hell was she? Maybe she's in the shower. Maybe she can't hear the bell.

He rapped his knuckles loudly against the door and slammed down the brass knocker several times for good measure. Enough to wake the dead, he thought. But still no one came to the door.

He was getting antsy . . . downright edgy.

Mike yanked at his sagging gun belt and tucked his shirt in better. He took in a deep breath and went to the window to peer into the interior through the sheer drapes. He squinted hard, trying to make out any movement inside. Seeing no one and no movement, but catching his reflection in the glass, he fixed his hair and admired his wide shoulders and thick neck bursting at the collar. Again came the odor he couldn't quite place. He'd been doing battle with a ragweed allergy, and lately could smell nothing, but this pungent on-off odor ran ahead of him. Still admiring his reflection in the window, he now noticed something odd about the complete stillness within. Something looked wrong, and even though he couldn't quite put his finger on it, he felt compelled to stare through at the living room until it hit him, and it did. Through the gauzy haze of the sheer cloth drape, he saw that the big fish tank along the living room wall was as devoid of life and movement as the surrounding room.

Squinting harder, he studied the tank, realizing some kind of strange layer of scum floated across the surface. Staring harder, he realized it was not scum but the residents of the tank—all the fish were lying belly-up at the top of the tank.

"Weird. Something's wrong inside. Lauralie could be in trouble inside." He imagined saving the damsel in distress and being lauded a hero in the papers—a not-uncommon fantasy since childhood.

He got a whiff of the strange odor again. The cold air seemed to heighten the odor one moment, mask it the next, but there it came again, teasing his nostrils. Then it came to him. Gas! Natural gas!

"There's a gas leak inside!"

He snatched his key chain and his radio off his hip, calling it in. As he hailed help, he found the key he needed, a master for every house in the Colony for emergency use only. This qualified.

Jake Everly came on the radio as he inserted the key.

"Jake! That you?"

"Mikeeee! Wha's up, kid? Wha's your lo—"

"I'm at 1638 Willow . . . I mean, Will-o'-the-Wisp, and we've got a-a-a gas leak here, Jake."

"Possible leak?"

"A leak, Jake—the real thing!"

"A gas leak? In the Colony? No way!"

"I'm telling you, I can smell it through the g'damn door! I'm going in!"

"No, Mike! If you can smell it through the fuckin' door,

then it's too dangerous to go burstin' in 'cause if you do—"

Jake, at command headquarters for Colony Security, heard the massive explosion occurring at Mike's end. "Stupid kid! Stupid, stupid damned kid! Oh, fuckin' jeeze! Man-oh-freakin'-man!"

Jake could not hold back his tears. He stopped the tape that had recorded the conversation, and immediately got on the phone with 911, giving the address and the nature of the emergency.

Jake next called his boss to inform him of the explosion. "Christ," said his boss, "someone's got to get over there to rep us, Jake. You do it, Jake. Get your deputies in to cover the phones and the radio, and get yourself over there. I'm on my way! How the hell'd this happen? How the hell'd a gas explosion occur in the Colony in the Glade, Jake? Whose fuckin' house blew up?"

"The Sangers', a Mr. and Mrs. with a daughter visiting. Mike met the girl, sir, and—"

"They called Mike to the location?"

"Mike Wilson's dead, sir. That's all I know."

"Was he answering a call?"

"Awful, just awful!"

"What'd he go to the location for, Jake?"

"He was screwin' around, Dave!"

"Screwin' around?"

"Flirting with the girl there, the daughter. He went over to ask her out, and next thing I know he's shouting something about a gas leak, that he could smell it through the door, and he disregarded my orders and burst in, and-and-and—"

"Get hold of yourself, Jake! Don't have a coronary on me. Do we know if the family was inside? Do you know if the blast affected any surrounding structures?"

"No . . . don't know, but I felt the vibrations from here."

"Mike rushed in to help people inside. He died trying to save life, doing his duty, Jake, you got that? Get over to the site and be a rep for Colony Security. I'm on my way!"

When Jake arrived at the Sanger home, fire trucks were battling the blaze, and a Houston Natural Gas truck pulled up, followed by a taxicab from which emerged Mr. and Mrs. Paul Sanger, the look of shock and horror unmistakable.

Jake, knowing the couple by sight, stepped up to them and told them what he knew of how Mike Wilson tried to save their daughter, dying in the effort.

"Meredyth! Oh, my God! Meredyth's in there!" screamed Caroline Sanger.

"Mike said her name was Lauralie," Jake said to Paul Sanger, who was busy now holding onto his wife, pinning her to the cab to keep her from running into the inferno.

The cab driver leaned across his hood, staring at the activity of the firemen and watching the blaze. Scar-faced, scratching a three-day-old beard, the cabbie snatched his unlit cigar from his lips and said, "Looks like a g'damn Texas tornado went through here."

"Who the hell is Lauralie?" Paul Sanger asked Jake Everly.

"The girl staying at your place . . . said she was your daughter! Mike opened the . . . Maybe I ought not to say any more."

Paul Sanger got on his cell phone and dialed for Meredyth. When she picked up, he breathed again. "Thank God, Mere, it's you! I've got your mother here. She needs to hear your voice, Mere. Talk to her . . . ask about her trip." Paul pushed the phone on his wife, Caroline. "It's Mere! She's safe, honey! She's all right."

Caroline took the phone, relief the size of a tidal wave washing over her, yet she could not control her tears as she repeatedly called out Meredyth's name and said, "Sweetheart, we love you so much, Mere. How much you'll never know."

"You're safely home from Paris," Meredyth replied from Lucas Stonecoat's bedside in the hospital. "I've got one hell of a story to tell you guys, Mother."

"And we've got one hell of a story to tell you. It's the house . . . all gone." She continued to cry.

"Mom, are you all right? What's happened? Are those sirens I hear?"

Her father got back on. "We'll be staying out at the

ranch house, sweetheart. Your can reach us there. Think you could come out tonight, Mere? We really need to see you in the flesh and catch up. And by the way, do you know anyone by the name of—"

"Why aren't you going to the Colony home? What's happened there, Dad?"

"It's been reduced to rubble, apparently an explosion. . . . Don't tell her I told you so, but"—he whispered now—"Mom appears to have left the gas on the entire time we were gone, and some poor *schlep* with Colony Security did a piss-poor job of checking it out. Opened the door and died of the blast. Whole damn house is in flames, pieces of it on our neighbor's roof."

"Oh, my dear God, Dad! Are you and Mom—"

"We're fine! It blew, they're telling us, about twenty minutes ago. Had we not been delayed at baggage . . ."

Meredyth felt a creeping finger trace the nape of her neck and run along her spine—*Lauralie's icy touch extending from the grave.* Her fingerprints were all over this attempt to murder Paul and Caroline Sanger, to leave Meredyth without her parents. It was to have been Lauralie's final blow, and it nearly came to fruition.

"Before you go out to the ranch, Dad, you need to meet me at County General where—"

"We don't need medical attention, dear! We're shaken up, of course. Who wouldn't be. It's a shock, but we really don't need medical—"

"You don't understand, Dad. I'm stuck here at the hospital, but I need to talk to you guys before you go out to the ranch. So much to catch you up on, Dad."

"You're *in* the hospital?"

"Hospital?" Again her mother's crying erupted, commingling with the sound of fire trucks coming over the line.

"No, not me, Dad. It's Lucas! He's—"

"That detective you used to date?"

"He's in a coma, fighting for his life, Dad, and it's all my fault, and he may die, and I-I can't leave him, Dad. I love him."

"We're on our way, baby. Stay on the line."

". . . saved my life, Dad, and he's in a coma. I can't leave him. I need you guys."

She heard him shouting for the cabbie to get them to County General. In a moment, her father was on the line again. "We're coming straight there, Mere, honey. Don't you worry."

Meredyth was crying into the phone now. "I'm afraid he's going to die. All because of a sick woman who stalked us to the ranch . . . and because I couldn't get to him in time."

"Stalked you?"

"Yes."

"An old girlfriend of Stonecoat's?"

"No, it wasn't like that."

"That one from the reservation? Her name wouldn't be Lauralie, would it?"

"Well . . . yes, I mean no . . . but how'd *you* get her name?"

"Seems she got into the house saying she was our daughter!"

"No wonder Mom was in tears."

"They told us our daughter might be in the rubble of the house! The way it's shaping up, a Colony Security fellow named Mike was interested in our daughter—Lauralie from out of towns—and came *sniffing* around. No pun intended."

"An unintended result," she muttered, pacing Lucas's small corner of the critical care unit. People checking on his vital signs every fifteen minutes. No windows, no light save for the artificial dim glow of soft blue that made the place look the perdition it was.

"The security fellow was just a kid, a year outta high school. Got more than he bargained for. Sounds like this Lauralie came onto him, and he went looking to close the deal on a date or some such thing."

I don't want to know his name or any more details about anyone she harmed in her mad obsession to harm me, she thought. "No more about it now, Dad. I can't take any more."

"Sure, baby . . . sure. Good news is they think she's dead in the rubble out here at the house."

"She is dead, but her body's in the HPD morgue, Dad. I killed her, Dad, out at the ranch house . . . I killed her. Now, please, come to me."

"My God, baby. We're on our way, Mere. Hold on there."

EPILOGUE

Running water: continual life

Dawson, Alaska, five months later

LUCAS SAT STIFFLY against the Aurora Nights Inn bed, his bandaged body still making the occasional complaint—a sudden lightning attack of pain about his ribs, like a knife jab. The painkillers hardly touched it, and so he had begun to self-medicate with the old herbal solution—peyote. The room had filled with the smoke and tangy odor.

Meredyth breezed in from outside, a rattling ice bucket in her hands. She poured him wine to go with sliced cheese. After chilling the wine and handing it to him, she toasted with her own plastic cup. "To roughing it. From Skagway to Dawson at last."

"To this trip's not finishing me off," he grumpily responded.

"You're getting stronger every day, Lucas. Come on!" She yanked at him, and he gasped at the jolt of pain it caused in his upper torso. "Sorry, but the lights are running wild again tonight. You were right about them getting better as the week goes by. You've got to come out and see, Lucas. They're beautiful. Alaska is beautiful."

"You're beautiful, especially when you're happy."

She pulled at him, and he froze up a moment, fighting down the pain. "All right, but let me get up under my own steam and in my own good time."

"But you're missing the show." She rushed to the window and tried to see all that was possible from there. "There're chairs on the roof tonight for the viewing. Come on! You promised, remember?"

"I promised to bring you to Alaska to—"

"And you have!"

"—to see the northern lights a-runnin' wild. I didn't say I'd be sitting on the roof of a hotel with a moon pie in one hand and a plastic cup filled with wine in another."

She kissed and held him. "God, when I think how close I came to losing you, I could just . . . just . . ."

"Don't, don't!" he warned. "No more tears. You promised, remember?"

Lucas recalled nothing of his time in a coma or in critical care, but he recalled hearing her voice. "Gotta live. Gotta make plans . . . go to Alaska, remember? We've got a lotta living to do. Stay with me. Draw on your inner wolf, damn you! Come back to me."

He recalled seeing his grandfather before he had gone into the coma, the kind and gentle medicine man holding his palms open to Lucas in the universal gesture of welcoming. It had been while Meredyth had held him in her arms there at the cabin home on Lake Madera.

When he came out of the coma, Meredyth was there, her head lying over him where she sat alongside his bed, having fallen asleep, her hand around his. He ran his fingers through her hair, and dry-throated, he muttered her name and added, "Wanna see . . . the lights . . . with you."

She came awake, her eyes filling with happiness and tears. She grabbed him about the neck and hugged, and she called for the doctors. He'd had a full recovery, but he had a lot of healing yet to do. She had argued it was too soon for him to travel, but he'd stubbornly refused to listen, telling her it was their reward for surviving.

During his two-month-long stay in the hospital, she came daily, and each day she told him more and more about the final moments leading up to Lauralie Blodgett's death, and the details that Chang and Nielsen had learned from the crime scenes and how Lauralie had dispatched her various final victims. She told him about the near murder of her parents, and the death of the young security guard whose worst crime had been gullibility and a too affable nature that led him to suspect nothing untoward about the vampire girl he had literally opened the door to. Lauralie had booby-trapped the house, somehow learning of the day Paul and Caroline Sanger were due home. Regardless of her fate, death or arrest, execution or incarceration, Lauralie Blodgett had meant to leave Meredyth Sanger with no one.

Once Lucas had been brought up to date, and after a parade of visitors had come and gone (the Tebos, Jana North, Captain Lincoln, Chang, Nielsen, Stan Kelton, and others), Stonecoat told Meredyth, "I gotta go to Manitoba with Maurice Remo, and from there we, that is you and I, we *could* zip over to Alaska to see the northern lights together."

"Forget about Manitoba. Jana North's going to Manitoba with Remo. It's all been taken care of. Lincoln's footing the bill. They'll get that creep Lyle Eaton for you."

"There're some things a man's got to do himself, Mere."

"You're in no shape, Lucas, to go anywhere right now, and Lyle Eaton's time is up in a week. You have no choice."

"Remo's not even a cop anymore. I mean, he's not on the force."

"Lincoln's made him a special deputy of some sort. It's all worked out with the Canadian government."

Maurice Remo had been standing just outside and had overheard the exchange. He had then stepped in and assured Lucas that he and the lovely Detective North could handle the Eaton matter just fine. "Been a long time since I've been on a trip with a beautiful cop," Remo had finished.

Now here they were in Alaska and Lucas meant to enjoy himself, despite the fact the pain felt like ripping stitches. "Throw me my shirt, baby."

Meredyth did so. "Can I help?"

"Sure."

She buttoned him up, hefted his coat to him, and put her own over her shoulders. Holding onto one another, they made their way out and down the hallway to the stairs going up to the roof. In the crisp night air, couples all around them stared up at the purple, blue, green, and snow-white swirling mix of glittering colors against the black night sky.

The northern lights looked like the work of God at play. Lucas settled into a chair with Meredyth holding his arm, delighting in the carefree, gentle, and nimble dancing lights. The fairy lights created an array of emotions in Meredyth and Lucas, who again felt the power of nature in these shooting excursions of feathery, weightless, buoyant beams. The iridescent glow of interstellar particles pirouetted and changed into a life form of tint, shade, blush, color, and effect. The aurora borealis was a living thing.

"Sight like this gives you faith in God and nature," he whispered, his tone signaling his reverence for the lights.

"It's like some force has captured the light and shadow that plays at all hours over the Grand Canyon," she replied.

He paused to kiss her. She pulled away. "Hey, I wanna see the show."

"Be my guest."

"I am, remember? You're paying."

He held tight to her hand and enjoyed the child in her as the enchanted little girl came out, delighting in the ballet of the heavens overhead. A kind of mystic swirl of lunar wind and particles swept down and around them, a kind of sparkling fog. For a time, it enveloped them.

"Ever give any thought to retiring from the force, Lucas?"

"And do what? Sit on my thumbs?"

"You love the horses and the ranch. You could run the place."

"What as? Your hired hand? Besides, your parents are staying there now."

"Their house'll be ready soon."

"I don't know, babe."

"What about turning the place into a real stud farm. You know a lot about raising horses, and there's money to be made."

"You talking about putting me out to pasture?"

"It hadn't occurred to me, but maybe it's worth a thought."

"Not likely. I'm a tracker, Mere, a detective."

She gnashed her teeth. "Stubborn Cherokee wolf. You'd be in charge, running the place as my husband!"

He pulled his eyes from the light show and stared into her eyes, seeing the Auroras reflected there. He pulled her into his lap. "I thought you'd never ask."

"Is that a *yes*?"

He laughed. "Was that a *proposal*?"

"Call it what you will."

"I'll let you know when we get back from Alaska."

She punched him. "Damn you!"

He shrugged. "Come on, we both know it's a test, this trip. If we can survive one another roughing it from Skagway to Dawson . . . then perhaps we can survive marriage to one another."

"You're awful."

"Awful good."

Meredyth returned her gaze to the concert of lights overhead, the firmament's toast to cheer and merriment and future bliss. She wanted to reach up and capture it, bottle it, take it home to Texas, where she might take it out whenever she wanted to look at it, like a snow scene in a bubble.

"Why can't life always be this giddy and carefree?" she asked, while thinking, *Will living with Lucas be like trying to grab onto the ethereal northern lights? It can't be done, not even if I could bottle the energy and hold tightly onto him.*

But what if I lightened up? she asked herself. What if I stopped trying to psychoanalyze Lucas, accept him with respect and love, as I did when I feared his leaving me forever? Then I could hold onto him in a sense. He was after all Lucas Stonecoat, a brethren to the Cherokee Wolf Clan, a hunter by nature and spirit with a long and proud tradition, going back to the ancestor who wore the first stone coat, a warrior who had killed a conquistador in battle for the *stone-hard* metal jacket he wore.

There would be no taming Lucas, but there could be loving Lucas.

"I can do that now without fear," she said aloud.

"Do what?" he asked.

"Be Mrs. Lucas Stonecoat."

"Are you sure you have no greater ambition?" he jokingly asked.

"No, none greater."

"If I'd known the light show would win your heart, Mere, I would have brought you here years and years ago."

The activity of the auroras had calmed; other couples, growing cold, began disappearing, and soon Lucas and Meredyth found themselves alone and enveloped in an eerie but fantastical whirlwind of stardust fog, within which they embraced and kissed.